Other *Leisure* books by Richard Laymon:

DARKNESS, TELL US
NIGHT IN THE LONESOME OCTOBER
ISLAND
THE MUSEUM OF HORRORS
IN THE DARK
THE TRAVELING VAMPIRE SHOW
AMONG THE MISSING
ONE RAINY NIGHT
BITE

RICHARD
LAYMON

NO SANCTUARY

LEISURE BOOKS NEW YORK CITY

A LEISURE BOOK®

July 2003

Published by

Dorchester Publishing Co., Inc.
276 Fifth Avenue
New York, NY 10001

ISBN 0-8439-5103-6

Printed in the United States of America.

Visit us on the web at www.dorchesterpub.com.

NO SANCTUARY

Chapter One

The sound of breaking glass shocked Rhonda Bain awake. She went rigid on the bed and stared at the dark ceiling.

She told herself it *wasn't* someone breaking into the house; a framed picture or a mirror had fallen off one of the walls.

She didn't believe it.

Someone had smashed a window. She'd heard glass hitting a floor, so it was the kitchen window; the other rooms had carpet.

Rhonda imagined herself bolting from the bedroom, racing for the front door. But as she rushed past the kitchen, a dark shape would lurch out and grab her.

I can't just lie here and wait for him!

She flung the sheet aside, sat up, snapped her head toward the bedroom window. The curtains were open, stirring slightly in the breeze. She shivered and clenched her teeth, but not because of the mild night air on her bare skin.

I've gotta get out of here!

The window was no good. The damn thing was louvered. There wouldn't be time to pull out enough slats, remove the screen and climb through. If she barricaded the bedroom door and smashed an opening with a chair . . .

She flinched at the sound of a footstep—a shoe crunching broken glass.

He's still in the kitchen.

If I try smashing the slats, he'll know I'm here, and what if he gets to me before I can—

He doesn't know I'm here!

Rhonda swung her legs off the bed. She rose slowly. The boxsprings squeaked a bit, but then she was standing. She turned to the queen-sized bed. With trembling hands, she smoothed her pillow, drew up the top sheet, then the electric blanket, then the quilt. A few tugs and the bed looked as if it hadn't been slept in.

She crouched. She sat on the carpet. She lay back and squirmed sideways, the hanging quilt brushing across her body. It passed over her face. She kept moving. It slid over her left breast, then her shoulder. She scooted in farther. Stopping, she fingered the hem of the quilt. It was five or six inches beyond her left hip and about two inches short of touching the floor.

Good enough.

She lay still, hands pressed to the sides of her thighs. She was trembling badly. She heard her quick thudding heartbeat. She heard herself panting. But she didn't hear footsteps.

He's probably out of the kitchen, walking on carpet. Where?

Turning her head, Rhonda could see out with one eye. She watched the bottom of the doorway.

Calm down, she told herself.

Oh, sure thing.

Want him to hear your damn heart drumming?

She let go of her legs, rested her hands on the carpet, and concentrated on letting her muscles relax. She filled her lungs slowly and let the air out.

No Sanctuary

Calm, she thought. You're not even here. You're lying on a beach. You're at the lake, stretched out on a towel. You can hear the waves lapping in, kids squealing and laughing. You can feel the sun and the breeze on your skin. You're wearing your white bikini.

You're naked.

Her stomach twisted.

You're naked and hiding under a bed and somebody's in the goddamn house.

She suddenly felt trapped. Though the bed didn't touch her, it seemed to be pressing down, smothering her. She struggled for breath. She wanted out. She ached to squirm free, scurry to her feet and make a dash for safety.

Calm down. He doesn't know you're here.

Maybe he does.

The pale beam of a flashlight danced through the darkness beyond the bedroom door. Rhonda glimpsed it. Then it was gone. She held her breath and stared through the gap, waiting. The beam scrawled a quick curlicue, darted high and vanished again.

He'll come in soon, Rhonda thought. He'll find me. God, why didn't I make a run for it when the window broke?

Why didn't I go with Mom and Dad to Aunt Betty's?

She forced herself to take a breath.

The beam of the flashlight slanted through the doorway, swept toward Rhonda and up.

He's checking the bed, she thought.

See, nobody's here. So get on with it. Rob the place. Take whatever you want, you bastard, just don't look under the bed.

With the snap of a switch, the lights came on.

Rhonda's fingernails dug into her thighs.

Her one eye saw a pair of old jogging shoes in the doorway. The ragged cuffs of blue jeans draped their tops and swayed slightly as the man walked forward.

The shoes stopped, turned, moved toward the closet. Rhonda watched the closet door swing open. She heard some

3

empty hangers clink together. A loop of threads hung from the back of the jeans' frayed left cuff, dangling almost to the floor.

The shoes turned again. They came toward her, veered away, and passed out of sight as the man walked toward the end of the bed. She heard quiet steps crossing the room.

A sudden clatter and skid of metal made Rhonda flinch.

He must've yanked the curtains shut.

What for? The backyard is fenced. Nobody can see in. Maybe he doesn't know that. Or he knows it, but isn't taking any chances. Not with the light on.

The bed shuddered. It kept shaking above Rhonda. The edge of the bedspread trembled. She turned her face up. There was only darkness above her, but she pictured the man crawling over the mattress.

What's he *doing*?

He's right on top of me!

The bed squawked as if he'd suddenly flopped down hard. Something wispy—the fabric under the boxsprings?—fluttered briefly against Rhonda's nose.

She heard a click.

What was that?

Rhonda suddenly knew. The stem on the back of the alarm clock. She'd pulled it after getting into bed, wanting to wake up early for *Jurassic Park Marathon* on a cable channel.

He knows I'm here.

Rhonda squeezed her eyes shut. This isn't happening, she thought. Please.

The bed shook a little. Turning her head, Rhonda watched fingers curl under the edge of the quilt near her shoulder. The quilt lifted. There was more rustling above her. The quilt stayed up. Hands lowered and pressed flat against the carpet. Then an upside-down head filled the space between the bed and the floor.

A man, perhaps twenty-five or thirty years old, stared in at her. His light brown hair was cut short. Even though his face was upside-down, he looked handsome. In other circumstances, Rhonda might have found herself attracted to him. But she felt only revulsion.

She squirmed sideways, moving toward the center of the bed.

"Go away!" she gasped.

The man did a quick somersault off the bed, landed lightly on his back, rolled over and peered in at her. One hand darted out like a paw. The hooked fingers missed her upper arm by inches and raked back along the carpet.

Pushing himself up, he crawled on hands and knees toward the end of the bed.

Heading for the other side?

Rhonda heard nothing. She turned her head to watch the quilt along the right side of the bed. It was lower there, touching the floor.

She shrieked as cold hands grabbed her ankles.

They pulled. Rhonda skidded, the carpet burning her back. She swept her arms away from her sides, reached up and clung to the metal bedframe. The pulling hands stretched her. She kicked, barking a shin on the end of the frame. The hands tugged. Her body jerked, leaving the floor and pressing the underside of the boxsprings for an instant before she lost her hold and dropped.

The carpet seared her buttocks and back. She clawed at the bed, ripped the flimsy cloth, tried to grab springs, curled fingertips over the edge of a wooden cross-slat. But the man was dragging her too hard and fast. Nothing could stop her rough slide.

The quilt flapped her face.

Clear of the bed, she squirmed and tried to kick her feet free of the man's grip. He clamped her ankles against his hips. He smiled as if he enjoyed watching her struggle.

Finally, exhausted, she lay still and panted for breath.

The man kept smiling. He kept her feet pinned to his sides. His head moved as he inspected her with wide, glassy eyes.

Rhonda pressed a hand between her legs. She crossed an arm over her breasts.

The man laughed softly.

He said, "No need of modesty, Rhonda."

He knows my name!

"Who are you?" she gasped.

"I've been watching you. You're very beautiful."

"Leave me alone." Her voice sounded whiny, scared. She didn't care. "Please," she said.

"Don't worry. I won't hurt you. Just don't cause any trouble and do exactly what I say, and you'll be fine."

Rhonda started to cry.

The man kept smiling.

"Okay," she finally said through her sobs. "I'll . . . just don't . . . hurt me. Promise?"

"Cross my heart and hope to die."

Rhonda's body was found three days later and far from home.

Chapter Two

The jangle of the telephone forced its way into Rick's dream and woke him up. Moaning, he rolled onto his side. The lighted dial of the alarm clock on the nightstand showed five o'clock.

Braced up on an elbow, he reached over the clock and lifted the phone's handset. As he brought it to his face, the uncoiling cord nudged the clock off the stand.

"This is obscene," he muttered.

"How did you guess?" Bert started breathing heavily on the other end of the line.

"It's still night," Rick interrupted. "That's the obscenity. Human beings weren't meant to get up before dawn."

"There are human beings who do it every day."

"Not when they're on vacation."

"Speaking of which . . ."

"Must we?" Rick asked.

"Don't be so negative. You're going to love it. The fresh

mountain air, the grand vistas, not to mention the peace and quiet . . ."

"I've been camping before. It's not my idea of—"

"Never with me."

"Right. Bertha Crockett, Queen of the Wild Frontier."

The sound of her husky laugh reminded Rick of just why he had allowed Bert to talk him into a week of backpacking. "Are you still in bed?" he asked.

"I've been up for an hour. I'm all packed and showered."

"Dressed yet?"

That laugh again. "Wouldn't *you* like to know."

"Matter of fact . . ."

"Come on over and find out."

"Bye."

"Hey!"

"Huh?"

"I called for a reason."

"I thought it was just to interrupt my sleep."

"You'll be passing some doughnut shops on the way over. Why not pick up a dozen? We can eat them in the car. I'll fill a Thermos with coffee."

"Okay, fine."

"See you later."

"Half an hour. So long." He hung up, swung the sheet away, and sat on the edge of his bed.

We're actually going to do it, he thought. The realization made him tight and shaky inside. Leaning forward, he propped his elbows on his knees and stared at the floor.

It's today. Christ.

When they'd decided to make the trip, when they'd outfitted him, even last night while he was packing, the journey seemed somehow distant and vague, as if it were a concept, not an event that would actually occur.

Like having a will drawn up, he thought. You do it, but you don't quite figure on having any real need for it.

Then one fine morning . . .

You can still back out.

No Sanctuary

Hell I can.

Should've just refused when it first came up.

He had suggested alternatives: the MGM Grand in Las Vegas, the Hyatt on Mauii, a tour of Ireland, a cruise on a luxury liner to Acapulco, even a steamboat trip down the Mississippi. But Bert had her heart set on backpacking in the Sierras. Somehow, she'd let two years slip by without roughing it, and she *needed* time in the wilderness. She *had* to go, with or without Rick.

And who would she go with, if not with Rick?

Myself, she'd answered. I find myself excellent company, but you're pretty excellent, too.

That had settled it. The thought of Bert going alone was intolerable.

And what was true three weeks ago was still true. Rick was sure of that. If he backed out, Bert would make the trip alone.

He flinched at the sudden blare of his alarm clock. Reaching down, he picked up the clock and silenced it. He placed it on the nightstand. Hard.

Okay. You're going. So relax and enjoy it.

He put on a robe, walked down the hall to the room he thought of as his "entertainment center," and stepped behind the wet bar. There, he made himself a Bloody Mary with a double shot of vodka, light on the tomato juice, heavy on Worcestershire and tabasco. He twisted a wedge of lemon over the drink, added ground pepper, and stirred.

It tasted tangy and good. He carried the glass into the bathroom. After using the toilet, he took a shower. He wanted to linger under the soothing hot spray. After all, there would be no showers for the next week.

No soft bed.

No safety of walls and locked doors.

No Bloody Marys.

At least you've packed a fifth of bourbon and a revolver, he thought. Those'll help.

Bert'll crap when she finds out.

Tough. Not going into the wilderness without my peace-makers.

Rick turned off the water and climbed out of the tub. He quickly dried himself. He took a long drink of his Bloody Mary, then rolled deodorant under his arms. The shower hadn't lasted long enough to steam up the mirror. He lathered his face and shaved. Though his hand trembled, he managed not to cut himself.

Back in the bedroom, he tossed his robe aside and stood in front of the full-length mirror on his closet door to comb his hair. At least you're in good shape, he consoled himself. You were a wimpy teenager last time around.

Last time around . . .

His scrotum shriveled tight. In the mirror, he saw his hanging penis shrink.

Turning away from his reflection, he stepped into his underpants and pulled them up. The hugging fabric took away some of the vulnerable feeling. He took another drink, then finished dressing.

Bert had selected the outfit: a camouflage shirt with epaulets and pocket flaps, and baggy olive green trousers with pockets that reached down almost to his knees. He fastened the web belt, put on his socks and boots, and stepped in front of the mirror again.

All you need is an ascot and a red beret, he thought, and you'll look like a paratrooper.

Appropriate. You sure as hell feel like one—like a paratrooper about to take the big step without benefit of a 'chute.

Rick made his bed. He checked the bedroom windows to be sure they were shut and locked.

He finished his Bloody Mary on the way into the kitchen. There, he rinsed out the glass and put it into the dishwasher.

Then he went into the living room.

His backpack was propped upright against the front of the sofa. On the nearby table were his sunglasses, handkerchief, wallet and keys, Swiss Army knife, matches and a pack of thin cigars. He loaded them into his pockets. Then he mashed a battered old cowboy hat onto his head. He stepped over to his pack.

Forgetting anything? he wondered.

He had double-checked Bert's instructions while packing last night. He knew he was missing nothing on her list.

What else?

Curtains all shut. Lights off. The timer set for the living room lamp so that it would come on at eight each night and go off at eleven. Doors and windows locked. Newspaper delivery stopped. Mail put on vacation hold.

That seemed to be everything.

Rick hoisted the backpack and slipped his arms through its straps. It felt heavy, but had a comfortable fit.

He turned around once.

What are you forgetting?

Rick entered the courtyard of Bert's apartment building. On his way up the outside stairs, he paused and stepped aside while a man in a sport coat and necktie came down.

Lucky guy, Rick thought. *He's* on his way to work. Wish I was.

But that feeling changed when Bert opened her door. Rick stepped inside and into her arms, felt the moist warmth of her mouth, her tight hug, her breasts and pelvis pressing against him. He slipped his hands beneath her loose shirt-tails and caressed her back. It was smooth and bare. He moved his hands all the way up to the sides of her neck and slid them out along her shoulders. He was always amazed by her shoulders; they were slender but wide, giving her body a tapered look and feel. As he stroked them, Bert squirmed against him and moaned.

"How about one for the road?" she whispered.

"You're kidding," Rick said.

"Well, if you're in a big hurry to get going . . ."

"I think we can spare a few minutes. Or a few hours. Or a few days."

"However long it takes."

11

* * *

Straddling Rick on her hands and knees, Bert stared down into his eyes. Her mouth was open. She was still breathing heavily. "Well," she said.

"Well."

"Guess we'd better get a move on."

"Yeah."

She lowered herself and kissed his mouth. He felt her nipples brush against his chest. Then she pushed herself up. "I guess that'll hold us till tonight," she said.

"Isn't it customary to sleep after all this exertion?"

"If you want me to drive, you can sleep in the car."

"How about a shower first?"

"Already had one this morning."

"So did I. But this was a messy job, and—"

"I'll keep my mess, thank you. Something to remember you by," she added, smiling down at him. "You may feel free to take a shower, however, if you make it quick."

"Without you?"

Nodding, Bert climbed off him.

"I'll pass," Rick said.

He got out of bed and followed her. The air stirred against his damp body, cooling him. He watched Bert. Her short blond hair looked brown in the dim light, her skin dusky. She walked with easy strides. Rick's gaze slid down her wide shoulders, her back, her slim waist, and lingered on the smooth moving mounds of her buttocks.

When we're on the trails, he thought, I'll let her take the lead.

He tightened inside. He wished he hadn't thought about being on trails.

We're not there yet, he told himself.

He stopped in the entryway to the living room and leaned against the cool wood.

Bert continued into the room. Her head lowered as she looked at the discarded clothing. She was in profile when she bent at the waist, and Rick stared at the side of her breast.

She picked up her panties. Her breast swayed slightly as she shifted from one foot to the other and stepped into them. The panties were little more than a white elastic waistband. When they were on, she turned toward Rick.

"Am I the only one getting dressed around here?" she asked.

"Yep."

"Anything to stall."

"Magnificent view. Mount Bertha."

"That's twice." She raised an eyebrow. "Once more and you've had it."

"Bert's a boy's name. You quite obviously are no—"

"Bertha's a cow's name. My parents were mad." After a glance at the floor, she ducked down and picked up a white sock. She bent over, raised a foot, and started to put the sock on.

"What name would you have liked?" Rick asked.

"Maybe Kim, Tracy, Ann. But they didn't ask. How about you?" She stretched the sock almost to her knee and picked up its mate.

"Ernie," Rick said.

"Ernie's a trucker's name."

"We'd be Bert and Ernie. We could move to Sesame Street."

Bert shook her head. She lost her balance and hopped on one foot to steady herself. Rick watched her breasts shake. She finished with the second sock and straightened up. She looked at Rick's penis, then at his face.

"You missed your calling," she said. "You should've been a peeping Tom."

"Doesn't pay as well as ophthalmology."

"Taking care of other people's peepers."

"So they won't miss out on the glories of observing the human form."

"You're a humanitarian." She picked up her tan shorts and stepped into them. They were loose-fitting, with deep pock-ets and button-down flaps like the trousers she had picked

13

for Rick. After belting them, she sat on the floor and began to put on her boots.

She was deliberately leaving her shirt for last.

"What I like about you," Rick said, "you're so considerate."

"Maybe I enjoy being looked at as much as you enjoy the looking."

"Impossible."

"Then just consider it a perk. I know you're not thrilled about spending your vacation in the boonies. Anything I can do to make it more bearable . . ."

"So far, it's just great."

When Bert finished tying her boots, she reached around, picked up Rick's socks, and tossed them to him.

"I usually start with my shorts," he said.

She grinned. "Not this time." She leaned back, braced up on straight arms, and watched. Rick couldn't take his eyes of her. After his socks were on, she threw the shirt to him. Then his shorts, and finally his trousers. While he fastened the belt, Bert slipped into her faded, blue chambray shirt. Leaving it open, she rolled the sleeves up her forearms. Then she buttoned the front.

Show's over, Rick thought.

A sudden rush of panic squeezed him.

Bert frowned. "What's wrong?"

He shook his head.

"What is it?"

"Just butterflies."

"You look like you got kicked in the nuts."

Feel that way, he thought. "I'm fine," he said.

Bert got up. She put her arms around him. "What kind of butterflies?"

"Mallards."

"Mallards are ducks."

"I'll be all right."

"It's about camping?"

Rick nodded.

"I thought you just didn't want to go without the comforts. It's more than that."

"I had some trouble the last time."

Bert stroked the hair on the back of his head.

"I was fourteen. I was packing with my father out of Mineral Springs. We were in deep. Nobody else was around. I stumbled going across some rocks and stepped into a crevice. It was so dumb. I should've looked where I was going. Anyway, I sustained fractures of my left tibia and fibula. Dad left me alone to go for help. It was three days before I got airlifted out. Not such a big deal, I guess, but I was fourteen and it was a pretty desolate area like some kind of Dali nightmare landscape, and I felt . . . vulnerable. There were coyotes around. I'd see them slinking over the rocks near the camp and I figured I was probably on the menu. Hell, I was scared shitless the whole time. The end."

Bert held him tightly.

"No major deal in the scheme of things," Rick said. "But enough to dampen my enthusiasm for roughing it."

"You must've been terrified," Bert said.

"It was a long time ago."

"I shouldn't have pushed you into this. I mean, I knew you weren't eager to go, but I never suspected . . ."

He patted her rump. "We'd better get a move on."

"Maybe we should change our plans."

"Call it off?" Rick asked.

"Sure. It's okay with me."

Go for it, Rick thought. This is just what you've been waiting to hear.

"What about the call of the wild?" he asked.

"I'll answer it some other time."

"Without me?"

He felt her shrug.

"I'll go. You know what they say about falling off a horse. And about lightning striking the same place twice."

"Are you sure?" Bert asked.

"Absolutely."

She squeezed him. "I'll make you a promise. If you break a leg this time out, I'll stay with you. We'll stick it out together until somebody comes along, and send *them* for help. I'll stay and take care of you. If we run out of food, I'll fish and set traps. And I'll shoo the coyotes away."

It was the last thing Rick wanted to hear. "A deal," he said.

Chapter Three

Gillian O'Neill stared at the ringing telephone. She didn't want to pick it up.

This time, she thought, I won't.

If I don't pick it up, they'll be all right.

But as she watched, the handset rose into the air.

No!

She had a pair of scissors in her hand. She rushed forward, ready to cut the cord, but she wasn't in time. A voice boomed out of the phone as if from a loudspeaker: "Guess what happened to your parents!"

The mouthpiece sprayed blood. The red shower splashed Gillian's face, blinding her. She shrieked, lurched backward, tripped and began a long fall, and jerked awake.

Gasping, she rolled onto her back.

The bell rang again.

Not the telephone; the front door.

Trembling, Gillian used the top sheet like a towel to wipe her sweaty face. Then she scurried off her bed. At the closet, she grabbed her robe. She put it on as she rushed from the

17

room. It clung to her skin. She got the belt tied on her way down the hall.

"I'm coming," she called when she reached the living room.

"Okey-doke." It was the voice of Odie Taylor.

She slowed down. Just Odie. Good.

She opened the door.

Odie smiled nervously. His head bobbed and swayed, as usual, like the heads of the toy dogs Gillian sometimes saw in the rear windows of cars. As usual, he didn't look her in the eyes. His gaze stayed level with her neck.

"Wake you?" he asked her neck.

"I'm glad of it. I was having a bad dream."

"Gee, I'm sorry." He hitched up his sagging jeans. "You been gone."

"I took a little vacation. Want a Pepsi?"

"Thank you."

He stayed on the balcony outside the door while Gillian hurried into the kitchen and took a can of soda from the refrigerator. She knew better than to ask Odie in. The only time she had invited him into the apartment, he had gone wild-eyed and started stuttering, scared as a trapped animal until he was outside again.

She handed the can to him.

"Thank you very much," he said. He held it and stared at her neck. His head weaved and nodded.

"Is there a problem? My rent late?"

"Heyuh." It was Odie's way of laughing. "You're trying to joke me, Miss O'Neill." Odie seemed as nervous about calling her Gillian as he was about entering her apartment. "You don't pay no rent, you own the place."

"Oh, that's right. I forgot."

"You didn't forget, you're trying to joke me."

"*Is* there a problem, or . . ."

"Gee." He bit down on his lower lip.

"What is it?"

18

"I'm gonna have to go on back home. Pa took a spill off the barn roof."

"God, I'm sorry."

"Well, he ain't dead or nothing but he got busted up some. Me and Grace, we're gonna have to go on back home. I'm sure sorry."

"Will you be coming back?"

"I jist don't know. I jist might stay. I been thinking maybe with the baby coming we oughta stay at the farm. City's not a good place for a kid."

"Or for anyone else," Gillian said. "I'm really sorry to have you and Grace leave, you've done a great job managing the place."

"I'm sure sorry. You've sure been nice to us. I don't know what we'd of done . . ."

"You're good people, Odie. I'll miss you and Grace. But I bet you'll be glad to get back home."

"Well . . ."

"When will you be leaving?"

"Friday, I guess. The rents're all paid up for last month and everything's tip-top around here. Want me to bring the stuff over?"

"No, that's fine. Just leave it all in your apartment so it'll be there for the new people."

"Okey-doke."

"I might not be around for the next few days, so hang on a second and I'll get you your pay."

Odie stayed in the doorway while Gillian returned to her bedroom. Her handbag was on top of the dresser. She took out the checkbook and wrote a check.

Odie was drinking his Pepsi when she reached the door. She handed the check to him.

"Thank you very much," he said. Then he glanced at it. He raised it close to his face and peered at it. His head stopped moving. He looked at Gillian, looked into her eyes. "You made a mistake here, Miss O'Neill. You got a zero too many."

"It's no mistake, Odie."

"This says five thousand dollars. We get five hundred, not five thousand."

"It's a bonus for you and Grace being such good managers."

"Holy cow."

"If I don't get a chance to see you again before you leave, have a good trip." She held out her hand. Odie gripped the check in his teeth and pumped her hand. "Drop me a line sometimes, let me know how things are going."

His head started bobbing again. He took the check out of his teeth. "Sure will, Miss O'Neill. Gillian." His voice was high-pitched. He grimaced as if he were in pain. He fluttered the check under his face. "Grace, she's gonna lay a brick when she sees this." He shrugged.

"Take it easy, Odie."

"Yeah. Holy cow." Rubbing the back of his hand under his nose, he turned away and started along the balcony toward the stairs.

Gillian shut her door. She went into the kitchen to make a pot of coffee.

She would miss Odie and Grace. She had managed the twenty-unit apartment complex herself for almost a year before they showed up in their lopsided pickup truck. Odie was unemployed, but Grace had already lined up a book-keeping job that would bring in enough money to cover the rent and little else.

Gillian not only liked the two at once, she trusted them. She gave them an apartment rent-free and hired Odie, overjoyed to be released from the burden of running the place.

Now they were leaving.

I'll have to get someone else, she thought as she poured a mug of coffee. No way am I going to start managing again.

Sliding open the kitchen door, she stepped onto the sundeck and sat down on a padded chair. She stretched her legs out, propping her feet on a plastic table. She took a drink of coffee.

Damn.

Her stomach hurt. It wasn't just losing her managers, it was liking them and knowing she would never see them again after they left.

They weren't exactly *friends*. But she had cared about them, and now they'd be out of her life forever.

That's life, she told herself. That's why you shouldn't start caring.

She drank some more coffee. She rested the mug on the arm of the chair, closed her eyes and tilted her head back to feel the sun on her face.

How's about bugging out? she thought.

I don't know.

She'd only come back yesterday. The need wouldn't start getting strong for a week or two.

Right.

But with Odie and Grace taking off, she might be stuck here after Friday—at least until she could find someone to replace them.

If you wait, you might have to go without for a whole month. Maybe even longer.

You'll be climbing the goddamn walls.

Better go for it while you've got the chance.

Her decision made, Gillian felt a familiar stir of excitement.

Get a move on, she thought. If you don't have any luck today, you'll have to wait for Monday.

She finished her coffee and went inside.

Gillian drove to an area in Studio City where the homes were nice but not elaborate. Rarely did she venture into truly exclusive neighborhoods—except on occasions when she wanted a special treat. Not this time. She had no taste today for the luxuries of a million-dollar home. Nor for dallying with such frills as elaborate alarm systems and private security patrols. A nice home in a middle-income neighborhood was all she desired. This area was just right.

Gillian had spent a terrific week in a house not far from here. The Jenson place. Murray and Ethel, away on vacation to Boston, had been good enough to leave their calendar clearly marked with their departure and return dates. Gillian had simply cleared out the day before they were scheduled to return. That had been back in February. This was June, so plenty of time had passed. She never liked to return to the same general area unless at least three months had gone by.

After cruising the streets for a while, she spotted one of the white Jeeps with red and blue stripes used by mail carriers. It was parked near a corner.

Gillian left her car on the next block, then began to wander the streets in search of the mailman.

Within ten minutes, she found him.

She walked slowly toward him. With his detours to front doors, she soon overtook him. She left him behind. At the end of the block, she crossed to the opposite side of the street and watched him from there.

When he made no delivery to a house, Gillian wrote the address on a note pad.

She spent nearly two hours observing the mailman. By then, she had five addresses on her list.

She returned to each house.

At one, she heard voices through the front door. She walked away and scratched that address off her list.

At another, a surly old man came to the door when she rang the bell. He glared at her. "I ain't buying. I ain't donating, I ain't signing shit. Get outa here'n stop annoying me." Gillian smiled at him. "Are you saved?" she asked. "Get fucked," he said, and slammed the door.

Gillian scratched that address off her list. Her hand shook when she did it.

At the other three homes, nobody answered the doorbell.

One of these had an alarm system, two didn't. She scratched off the one that had the alarm.

In an alley behind one of the remaining homes, she peered through a narrow gap between the fence and gate. There was no swimming pool, but the back yard had a nice patio area and a hot tub.

She walked two blocks to the other house. On close inspection, she found that it had a swimming pool. A definite plus.

Gillian returned to her car.

On the way back to her apartment, she weighed the choices. A pool was preferable to a hot tub. However, the place with the hot tub had a vacant house next door with a For Sale sign in front. That would mean one less next-door neighbor who might get suspicious of her sudden presence.

Gillian decided on the hot tub house.

Chapter Four

They had set off with Bert driving. After the coffee and doughnuts, Rick nodded off and dozed for an hour. When he awoke, they were on the Grapevine, heading down through the Tehachapis. The valley below them looked flat and endless.

In Bakersfield, they stopped at a filling station. The gas tank was only half empty, but their bladders were full. Bert used a restroom while Rick pumped gas at the self-service island. When she returned, he hurried to the men's room.

He came back and offered to take over the driving, but Bert said that she wasn't tired yet. "Why don't I drive till Fresno?" she suggested. "That's when we start east. I'll let *you* experience the joys of the mountain driving."

"Fine. And you can navigate, since you're the one who allegedly knows where we're going."

When they reached Fresno, they were ready for lunch. Bert took an off-ramp. Along the sideroad were several restaurants. Bert said that a Burger King would do nicely, but Rick talked her into Howard Johnson's. "I've really got a craving for fried clams," he told her, "and that's a specialty at Howard Johnson's."

"You interested in the clams or the bar?" Bert asked.

"Both," he admitted.

"Just remember you'll be driving."

Inside, they each drank a Bloody Mary while they waited for the meal to be served. Then Bert had iced tea with her clams and French fries, and Rick had a beer. He nursed the beer along, wanting another but holding back so Bert wouldn't start to worry.

The car was stifling when they returned to it. Rick put on the air conditioner, and soon cool air was blowing against them.

Though the alcohol made him groggy for a while, it blunted his apprehension as the valley was left behind.

The land changed quickly. For a while, the road rose and dipped through brown foothills where cattle grazed. There were few trees, and only a scattering of rock. Then the rolling fields became littered with rock, and clumps jutted up like broken knobs of bone that had split the flesh of the earth. The road curved upward, a granite wall on their right, a ravine on the left. Then trees on both sides cast their deep shadows onto the pavement.

Bert asked Rick to turn off the car's air conditioner. They both rolled their windows down. Warm air that smelled of pine rushed into the car. "Delicious," Bert said.

She rested her elbow on the window sill, and Rick stole glances at her as he steered around the curves. Her forearm was sleek and tanned. Her face was tilted toward the window. The one eye he could see was half shut and her mouth was open slightly, smiling. The wind ruffled her hair and fluttered the open neck of her shirt.

God, she was beautiful.

In Rick's imagination, she opened more buttons and the wind flapped her shirt open.

Then his mind strayed away from her beauty. He found himself wishing he *were* Bert, face to the wind, relishing the scented mountain air. She seemed untarnished, pure and free, enjoying herself like a child. Rick longed to be inside her and feel the way she must feel. There would be no worries, no knot in his stomach, only the thrill of being in the mountains at the very start of a vacation.

He could remember the way it felt to be that way. The memories made him hurt for what had been lost.

Maybe I can get some of it back, he thought. Maybe some of Bert will rub off on me.

Just don't let me rub off on Bert. Don't, for godsake, ruin it for her.

Bert turned her head. "I once hiked three days," she said, "and never saw anyone. Can you imagine that? Nobody else on the trails. We camped by lakes and had them all to ourselves."

"That does sound nice," Rick said. "I hope we get a lake to ourselves."

"Yeah, I bet I know what you've got in mind."

"You can freeze your nuts off in those glacial lakes."

"Not me."

Rick laughed.

"It's not so bad," Bert said, "once you get used to it."

"I was never in that long."

"One does tend to take on a lovely shade of blue."

"I guess we'll find out," Rick said. "You swim, I'll watch you turn colors."

"Chicken."

"I'll be your towel holder."

"One doesn't use a towel. One lies out in the sun on a flat rock."

"That's how it's done, huh? Does one wear a swimming suit?"

"Not if one can help it."

"This is sounding better and better."

"But you've got to be somewhere isolated for that, so I wouldn't count on it."

"You mean we won't be isolated? I thought that was the whole idea."

"It'll be in an area that's pretty out of the way. I know the popular places that'll be swarming with campers, and we've steered clear of those. But we won't be in deep. Even if you do go in deep, that's no guarantee. Just means you meet a hardier breed of hiker. We'll probably have some company, but not much."

"Be great if it was just you and me."

"That, of course, is what we'll be shooting for." She ran a hand down his thigh, gave him a pat, then reached to the glove compartment. She took out a map. As she unfolded it, the wind snapped it taut. She lowered it against her legs.

"We almost there yet?"

"Not by a long shot. The fun hasn't even started."

"Which fun is that?"

"About thirty miles on an unpaved road."

"I can hardly wait."

"That's the part that keeps out the riff-raff." She spent a while studying the map. "It's not even on here," she said.

"Maybe it doesn't exist."

"Jean at the office was there last summer with her husband. They stumbled onto the road by accident and thought the area was great. I've got her directions." Bert patted her breast pocket. "We'll find it."

A while later, dwellings began to appear among the trees on both sides of the road. Some of them looked like summer cottages Rick had known as a boy. There were a few log cabins and several A-frames. He heard the sputter of a distant chainsaw.

A sign read: Bridger Creek, Population 63, Elevation 7,300.

"We're getting up there," Bert said.

Bridger Creek had a crossroads. On two of the corners stood A-frame real estate offices. On another corner was the B.C. Bar with a few pickup trucks and motorcycles and off-road vehicles parked in its lot. The fourth corner was occupied by a general store with gas pumps in front.

Rick stopped beside one of the pumps. A skinny teenaged boy in bib overalls trotted down from the porch. He wore a cap with its bill at the rear. He smiled through the window at Rick. Two of his upper front teeth were missing. "Help ya?" he asked.

"Fill it up with unleaded," Rick said.

The kid went over to the pumps.

" 'Duelling Banjos,' anyone?" Rick asked.

Bert gave the side of his leg a gentle punch.

After paying for the gas, Rick moved the car to the end of the lot. They went inside the store and used the restrooms. Before leaving, they bought a bag of potato chips and two bottles of cream soda.

He drove with the bottle of soda clamped between his legs. It was cold through his trousers. The open sack of chips rested on the seat. He took turns with Bert reaching into it. Sometimes, when he was concentrating on the road, his hand collided with hers.

Soon after the chips and sodas were gone, the road narrowed. It curved along the side of a mountain. Beyond the other lane was a sheer drop to a wooded valley. Rick's hands tightened on the steering wheel and he slowed down and edged to the right each time he met a descending vehicle. There were pickup trucks, Jeeps and vans, a few R.V.s. The big campers barely had room to squeeze by. Rick began pulling onto the gravel shoulder and stopping each time one of them appeared around a bend.

After the fourth time he did that, he slid a thin cigar out of the pack in his shirt pocket.

"Uh-oh," Bert said. "The man's getting serious."

"They help calm me down." He held the cigar out to Bert. "Want one?" he asked.

"Why not?"

Though she had never complained of his cigars, she had never smoked one, either. "You are in a festive mood," Rick said. He took one out for himself. His hands shook badly as he unwrapped it.

Cigar jutting from her pursed lips, Bert leaned toward Rick for a light and wiggled her eyebrows like Groucho.

Rick lit it for her. "You're a regular guy," he said.

"If I'm a guy, I'm irregular."

He grinned and fired up his own cigar. He checked the road. Then he eased off the rough shoulder and picked up speed.

Smoking the cigar helped his nerves. So did watching Bert with hers. She didn't smoke it so much as fool with it: she held it out daintily between two fingers; she stretched out her lips and sucked it like a monkey; she talked with the cigar clamped in her side teeth; she tapped off ashes with her pinky; looking at Rick with half-shut eyes, she licked its blunt wet end and slid the shaft deep into her mouth and out and in again.

"You're going to make me crash," he said.

"You're doing fine."

Long after the cigars were snuffed out in the ashtray, Bert unbuttoned the flap of her breast pocket and took out a folded yellow sheet from a legal pad.

"Does this mean we're almost there?"

"Time to start thinking about it," she said.

She spread the paper open across her thighs. There was no map, just handwritten directions. She looked at it briefly, then put it away and patted it. "There'll be a road on the right with a sign for Jacktooth Mountain."

"And we take it?"

"Nope. We check the odometer and go about twelve miles more. There'll be a big rock on the left."

"A rock? That's a great landmark."

"Some lovebirds painted 'Bill & Marie, 69' on it surrounded by a heart."

"Romantic. Do you think that's a year or their favorite pastime?"

"If it's a year, it's been around a long time."

"Maybe they make annual pilgrimages to touch it up."

"At any rate, after the rock we go about two hundred yards and there'll be an unmarked road on the right. We take that and follow it to the end. Then we'll be there."

Rick looked at his wristwatch. "Almost three," he said.

"Jean said it's about two hours from the Jacktooth Mountain sign."

"Lordy. I hope we spot it soon."

They passed it forty-five minutes later. Rick checked the odometer, added twelve to the mileage, and kept an eye on the slowly turning numbers.

Eighteen miles later, they spotted the rock. Bill and Marie had not been the only artists to leave their mark on it, but they'd been the most ambitious. Their heart, names and number were faded but twice the size of the surrounding graffiti.

"Two hundred yards," Bert said.

"Want to get out and pace it off?"

"Thanks anyway. It might be a mile the way Jean gives directions."

Rick slowed the car. The area to the right was thickly wooded, the spruce and pines brilliant green in the sunlight but dark in the shadows beyond the edge of the road. It looked foreboding.

Rick flinched at the blare of a honking horn. He checked the rearview. A van bore down on them. Without slowing, it veered into the other lane and rushed by. It had a mountain landscape, red in the sunset, painted on its side panel. Rick watched it speed around a bend.

"There!" Bert stuck an arm out of the window and pointed.

Rick eased off the road and stopped. He peered through Bert's window. "You think that's it?" he asked.

"Must be."

All he saw were tire tracks like parallel walking paths leading into the woods. Between the tracks was a hump with foliage growing on it.

"Fondly referred to as 'the fun part,'" Rick said, and steered onto the twin paths.

Only a few dusty shafts of sunlight slanted down and mottled the forest floor, not enough to dispel the gloom of the heavy shadows. The car rocked and bounced along. Sometimes, the springy limbs of nearby saplings brushed the sides of the car or scraped along with squealing sounds like fingernails on a chalkboard.

Rick wondered vaguely if they were scraping the paint.

The least of my worries, he thought.

"What happens if we meet another car?" he asked.

"It'll get interesting," Bert said.

"Or have a breakdown?"

"We'll call the Auto Club."

"Yuk, yuk."

"You worry too much."

A rock on the center hump scraped and clattered against the undercarriage.

Rick took one hand at a time off the steering wheel and wiped each dry on his trousers.

The tracks rose up a gentle grade and dipped on its other side. At the bottom, the tire ruts were puddles. The water whooshed as Rick drove through.

"Thirty miles of this?" he asked.

"Maybe it gets better," Bert said.

Around the next curve, the way was blocked by a fallen branch. Bert shrugged.

"You don't suppose," Rick said, "someone put that there to discourage us?"

"Could be an ambush."

Rick smiled, but he scanned the nearby trees before climbing out. Quickly, he walked in front of the car and stopped at the broken end of the limb. He crouched over it. The branch had neither been sawed off nor hacked with an axe.

Of course not. Rick felt a little silly for even suspecting such a thing. There was a long split up one side. The limb

31

had simply been torn from a tree by its own weight or a strong wind or a burden of winter snow.

He lifted it with both hands and stepped across the tracks, swinging it out of the way. He gave it a shove and let go. The limb dropped with a soft thud onto the brown mat of pine needles. There was sap on the index finger of his left hand. He bent the finger and felt the skin stick. He sniffed the brown stain. It smelled like a Christmas tree.

Turning back toward the car, he saw Bert behind the steering wheel. He went to the passenger door and climbed in.

"Mind if I drive?" she asked.

Bert seemed to enjoy it. Rick enjoyed watching her. She sat forward, away from the seat back, and peered intently out of the windshield. She held the steering wheel with both hands. Sometimes the tip of her tongue appeared at the corner of her mouth.

As time passed, however, Rick found himself watching the woods more often than he watched Bert. He gazed out the windows, half expecting to spot someone in the deep shadows sneaking around among the trees. He saw no one. But the farther they traveled along the dirt tracks, the more certain he became that they were not alone. Once, a sudden moving shape deep in the woods made his heart jump before his mind registered that the shape was merely a deer.

This is going to be a long week, he told himself, if you don't settle down. Nobody's out there. Nobody's stalking you.

But he wished his revolver were close at hand, not in the car's trunk at the bottom of his backpack.

He kept watching the trees. Sometimes, he looked over his shoulder and gazed out the rear window. If they were being followed, the man or vehicle was not in sight. Could someone looking closely at the tracks tell that their car had recently made the passage? He remembered the limb that he had lifted out of the way and wished he'd had the sense to place it back across the tracks after they'd gone by.

"What are you doing?" Bert finally asked.

"Just enjoying the scenery."

"You look like a cemetery guard keeping an eye out for spooks."

"Just a little edgy," he admitted, and made a weak smile.

"Hey, if there was anything to worry about, do you think *I'd* come out to a place like this? I'm the world's greatest chicken. I get the willies all the time. You should see me when I get back to my apartment at night. Especially after I've been with you and it's late. I check behind the furniture, look in closets. I've even been known to look under the bed. And I've usually got a great case of the shivers till I've made sure nobody's lurking around."

"Really?"

"Absolutely. I always figure some drooling maniac has gotten in, somehow, and is just waiting for a chance to rape or murder me. Or both."

"You're kidding. You?"

"Had me figured for a fearless Amazon?"

"Something like that."

"Disappointed?"

"Well, I knew you were no Amazon. You've got two boobs."

Bert grinned. "But really, the way I see it, a certain percentage of people are criminals or dangerous nut cases. Therefore, the smaller the population, the less danger of running into one. When you get out in a place like this, there's almost nobody so your chances of meeting a creep diminish to almost nothing."

"On the other hand," Rick said, "the larger population works to your advantage in that the nut has a larger pool of victims to choose from. Start decreasing the population, you might have fewer nuts but it also knocks down the odds that someone *else* will be the victim."

Bert nodded. "So if there *is* a nut out here, we win by default." In a teasing voice she added, "Better keep a sharp eye out."

Though Bert was making light of it, Rick wished he hadn't

pointed out the less comforting side of her argument. Getting her worried would serve no purpose. He should've kept his mouth shut.

"I've spent a lot of time in wilderness areas," Bert said after a while. "I've never run into trouble so far."

"Well . . ."

"That probably hurts the odds on this time out, huh?"

"Don't be such a pessimist," Rick said.

She laughed.

In the silence that followed, Rick's uneasiness came back. He felt a strong urge to resume his watch of the surrounding forest, but he fought it. He watched Bert instead. Then he lay down on the seat and rested his head on her lap. Drawing up his knees, he propped his feet on the window sill.

Bert smiled down at him. "Comfy?"

"Very nice."

Rick felt her warmth through the fabric of her shorts. Her flat belly eased against his cheek sometimes when she inhaled. The front of her loose shirt, jutting out like smooth hills just above his eyes, stirred slightly as the bouncing, rocking motions of the car shook her breasts.

"Down there," she said, "you can't keep a look-out."

"The view's fine."

She let go of the wheel for a moment and brushed a hand through his hair.

"If you're nervous about going back to your apartment at night," Rick said, "how come you won't stay over at my place?"

"I believe we've been over that ground."

"Well, you could do it sometimes. Maybe just on weekends."

"It might start with just weekends, but pretty soon that wouldn't be enough. I know men, and I know myself. Before long, you'd be pointing out with infallible logic that keeping my apartment is a wasteful expense, that I should move in with you and get rid of it."

"And you," Rick continued for her, "value your independence too highly—"

Bert stopped the car.

"What's wrong?"

"We're there."

Rick's stomach did a small flip, but he managed a smile. "And I was just getting comfortable." He sat up slowly, keeping the side of his face against Bert. His cheek nuzzled her breast. He turned his head and kissed it. Her nipple was stiff under her shirt. He opened his mouth wide and ran his tongue over the fabric.

Bert slapped his stomach gently. "Stop it," she said. "People are watching."

Rick stopped. He bolted upright and looked out the windows. Perhaps he'd *sensed* rather than seen somebody back there in the trees. He stared. Hard. Nothing moved.

"Just kidding," she said. She pinched the cloth away from her breast. "Look what you did."

His mouth had left a dark wet patch on the blue pocket. "But it felt good, right?" he asked.

"Feels damp."

"Better get into a dry shirt."

She gave him a smirk, then took the key from the ignition and rolled up her window. She punched the lock button down. Rick watched her climb out. The back of her shirt was wet and clinging, though not as wet as he'd made the pocket. She swung her door shut.

The car had stopped in a clearing. Rick saw no tire tracks ahead. There was a heavily wooded slope, dim with shadows. Looking out of his window as he cranked it up, he saw that the clearing provided enough room to allow the car to be turned around. He elbowed down his lock button, then checked the rear doors. They were secure.

He joined Bert behind the car as she opened the trunk. She gave the key case to him. "Don't lose it," she said.

Her comment triggered new worries. What if he lost the keys? What if they came back here, ready to depart, and the battery was dead? What if the car had two flat tires? What if it was vandalized or stolen while it sat here unguarded for a week?

So many things could go wrong. They might get through all the camping unscathed only to find themselves stranded when they were ready to leave. By that time, their food supplies would be depleted . . .

Bert reached into the trunk.

"I'll get it." Rick lifted out her pack. He held it while she slipped her arms through the straps. Then he propped his own pack on the edge of the trunk. Bert held it steady. He crouched and found the straps. Standing, he felt the solid weight pressing his shoulders and back.

Bert took their hats from the trunk and shut the lid. She plopped Rick's hat onto his head and put on her own. It was a tan, Aussie hat with one side of the brim turned up. It might look silly on some people, Rick thought. On her, it looked great.

"Now what?" he asked.

"Now we find the trail and start walking."

"Maybe we should spend the first night here."

"Sleep in the car?"

"There's a thought."

"Jean said there's a nice area near a stream about half a mile from here."

"The way she gives directions, it's probably two miles."

"We'd better get moving, then. Need to get there before dark." Bert dug deep in a pocket of her shorts. She came up with a compass, held it flat in her open hand and studied it. "Trail should be thata-way," she said, and pointed to the left.

Rick followed her past the front of the car.

"Ah-ha!" she said.

At the edge of the clearing, nailed to a short brown post, were two slats of wood with carved messages. She pointed to the left and indicated that Mosquito Pasture was two miles distant. The other pointed straight ahead. Dead Mule Pass was eight miles in that direction.

"Encouraging names," Rick muttered.

Bert smiled back at him. "You'll be glad to know we're not heading for Mosquito Pasture."

"Dead Mule Pass doesn't sound like the Garden of Eden."

Bert tucked a thumb under each of her shoulder straps. She flexed her knees and pulled the straps as if to adjust the fit of the pack.

The wet patch on her pocket was still dark.

She turned away and started walking down the trail.

Rick looked back at the car. Then peered into the deep shadows among the trees. Get a grip, Rick. There are no boogey men out there. Believe me

Hurrying to catch up with Bert, he began to sing. "Please Mr. Custer, I don't wanna go."

Chapter Five

The parking area under Gillian's apartment building was deserted. She slid her suitcase onto the floor of the car in front of the passenger seat, set down her purse, then went around to the rear and opened the trunk. Reaching inside a nylon satchel, she took out a pair of license plates. It was one of six sets she had removed, late one night last month, from cars parked along a secluded lane in Brentwood. She had used WonderGlu to fix strong magnets onto the back of each plate.

She covered her own plates with the stolen ones, and drove out.

She shivered as she drove. The tremors seemed stronger, less pleasant than usual.

Maybe this is too soon, Gillian thought. Maybe I'm pressing my luck.

Nothing to worry about, she told herself. You've never been caught, and there was only that one close call.

That, and the house on Silverston.

The "close call" had happened nearly a year ago. She'd

been swimming in the pool at the Farnsworth house in Rancho Park when car doors thudded shut nearby. Thrusting herself out of the water, she ran dripping to the corner of the house. From there, she saw the roof of a van beyond the top of the gate. She heard quiet voices. The Farnsworths weren't due home for two more days, but they must have cut their trip short. In seconds, they would find themselves prevented from entering the front door because of the burglar bar. When that happened, they were bound to come through the gate to try a back door. Gillian, choked with panic, raced around the end of the pool. At the rear of the yard, she sprang at the redwood fence, boosted herself up and squirmed over the top, scraping her thigh in the process. She dropped into the alley on the other side.

Fortunately, she'd left her car parked around a corner from the Farnsworth house, with an ignition key in a magnetized compartment under the rear bumper.

That wasn't good fortune, she thought, that was good planning.

The good planning also paid off in that Gillian had taken nothing into the house that could be used to identify her. She lost her suitcase, clothes, security bars, purse and camera (along with a roll of film in the camera that must've given the Farnsworths food for thought if they had it developed), but nothing to give them any clues as to who the owner might be.

Still, it had been a narrow escape. She'd sworn off intrusions for good after that.

As time passed, however, the urge had grown. Three weeks later, she was inside another house. It had been scary for a while, but soon the fear of being discovered had faded and she'd had no more problems.

So why, tonight, was her usual anticipation tainted by a shadow of dread?

Gillian parked in front of the house. Light shone through the closed draperies of the living room, but that was normal;

most people had timing devices to activate a lamp and make their homes look occupied while they were away.

She shut off her engine and headbeams, and got out of the car. As she walked around to the passenger door, she eyed the next-door houses. The one with the realtor's sign was dark. The other had lights on, but no car in the driveway. The owners might be home, but there was a good chance they were out enjoying themselves.

Ten o'clock on a Saturday night was the ideal time for Gillian to make her entries: too early for most people to return home from movies or dinner parties; not so late that her arrival, if noticed by a neighbor, would draw much suspicion.

Especially not the way she was dressed.

Gillian opened the passenger door. She took out her purse and suitcase, and walked casually toward the front porch, confident that anyone who might spot her would assume she was a legitimate visitor. Burglars, after all, do not usually wear heels, a skirt, and a turtleneck sweater.

If questioned by a neighbor who'd been alerted that the owners were off on a trip, she would simply claim to be the niece who'd come to house-sit. That had happened a few times. Usually, they bought the story. If not, Gillian was ready to cover herself. "Uncle Henry insisted that I—"

"No Henry lives here."

She would frown. "Sure. Henry Wadsworth."

Assured that no Henry Wadsworth resided here, she would act perplexed and show the suspicious neighbor a slip of paper on which she had written Uncle Henry's name and address. The neighbor would then explain that she was at the wrong address. "This is 8322, not 3822." Grateful for having her error pointed out, she would depart.

Tonight, Gillian had no use for the slip of paper on which she had reversed the first two numbers of this address. Nobody questioned her. She saw no one on her way from the car to the porch.

The light above the front door was dark. She listened for

a few moments and heard no voices from inside. Ringing the doorbell went against procedure. Though that was a good way to make sure nobody was home, the sound of a doorbell could sometimes be heard by neighbors. Also, it went against the logic of her cover; a niece coming to house-sit would hardly ring the doorbell.

Setting down her suitcase, Gillian opened the mailbox. It was empty except for a flier. She quietly lowered the lid.

The porch was an L-shaped concrete slab with a waist-high wall, and extended around the corner of the house. Its front was concealed from the street by a pair of geraniums. The house windows that looked onto the porch were dark.

Gillian carried her suitcase and purse around the corner and set them down. From there, she could see the high redwood fence that ran alongside the property. The next-door house had a single story, and only the very tops of its windows were visible above the fence. Lights shone through the windows.

It was all right, though. Not only were the curtains shut, but anyone inside would have to stand on a chair to see over the fence.

After slipping out of her shoes, Gillian stepped barefoot to the low wall and peered down. In the space between the house and the fence was a driveway that extended from the gate to a two-car garage. The porch was elevated leaving a drop of about six feet from the top of its wall to the driveway. There was no opening at the rear of the porch wall. She would have to jump.

Gillian opened her skirt and stepped out of it. She folded it, set it on the edge of her suitcase, then pulled off her sweater. Shivering in her gym shorts and tank-top, she opened her handbag and removed a small leather satchel. Then she climbed onto the side wall of the porch and pushed off. Her feet slapped the pavement, a quiet sound that could certainly not be heard inside the neighbor's house.

She walked quickly up the driveway, noting that all the windows along this side of the house were dark. At the rear

41

Richard Laymon

was a sliding glass door, then more windows. The concrete slab of the sundeck had a single lounge, a glass-topped table, a Weber grill, and a square platform surrounding the covered hot tub.

Gillian stepped around the corner of the house. She walked along the dewy grass strip between the wall and the fence, checking the windows and listening for sounds from inside. The last two windows showed light through their curtains, undoubtedly from the same source that illuminated the picture window she'd seen from the street. On this side of the house, there was no gate at the front.

Completing her rounds, Gillian felt sure that the house was deserted. She returned to the rear deck.

At the sliding door, she took a small flashlight out of her leather case. Shining its beam downward through the glass, she checked the runner. No rod had been placed there to prevent the door from being opened. She inspected the inside handle. It was one of those with a simple lever. A downward flick would disengage the lock.

With the flashlight clamped between her teeth, Gillian started to work. An open square of duct tape on the glass in front of the lock lever. A circle of tape stuck to the center for use as a handle. A careful line with her glass cutter along an inside border of the tape. Three more slices through the glass, completing the square. A few gentle taps at the edges. Finally, a pull at the tape in the center. The square of glass came out.

A cinch, Gillian thought.

She set the small section of glass on the table.

Reaching through the opening, she lowered the lock lever. She removed her hand and pulled the aluminum handle. The door slid open with a low, quiet rumble.

Gillian left her leather case on the table. She entered the house. The warm air had a closed-in, stuffy heaviness; one more indication that nobody was home.

Shining the flashlight around, she saw that she was in a den or recreation room. It had a couch, a couple of easy

42

chairs, lamps and tables, a television with a large screen and VCR, a stereo, bookshelves along the wall in front of her and a built-in bar at the other end of the room. The floor was hardwood.

Very nice, Gillian thought.

Especially the bar and the VCR.

Pointing her flashlight at the bookshelves, she found that the owner had an extensive collection of tapes for the video recorder.

Gillian turned around and went through a doorway. Ahead was the dining room. To the right was another entryway. She stepped through it and found herself in the kitchen. After a quick look around, she backtracked, passed the door leading into the den, and entered a hallway on the left. A short distance down the hallway, she came to a wide arch that opened onto the living room. She switched off the flashlight. Then she peered around the corner of the arch. Satisfied that the room was deserted, she continued her search.

Just beyond the arch, she found a closet, then a bathroom. Farther down the hall, on the left, was a small room with exercise equipment. Squinting into the darkness, she saw a Nautilus, treadmill, rowing machine and weights, a mat on the floor and a wall of mirrors.

Then she came to the bedroom. Standing close to the open door, her back pressed to the wall, she held her breath and listened. No sounds came from the room. She wiped her sweaty hands on her shorts. Flashlight still off, she stepped away from the wall and moved in front of the doorway.

In spite of the closed curtains, the room had a dim gray glow. Gillian peered at the bed. Its cover was flat except for the bulge of pillows near the headboard.

That's that, she thought.

Suddenly exhausted, she sagged against the doorframe.

End of Phase One, she told herself. You're safely in and nobody's here.

Of course, someone *could* be here, hiding. It was unlikely, though. So unlikely that it wasn't even worth worrying about.

Even if all the other indications were misleading, the stuffy air of the closed-up house was sure proof.

After a while, Gillian thrust herself away from the door-frame and walked toward the bed. She turned on her flashlight. Though it was aimed at the king-sized bed, a bright beam streaked across the ceiling.

She flinched and looked up.

Mirrors. Mirrors on the ceiling above the bed.

Well now, Gillian thought. Whoever lives here must be quite a sport.

Turning around, she found the light beam ricocheting off mirrors on the wall. Even the shut door of the closet had them.

Grinning, Gillian went to the bed, sat on it, and gasped as she sank into the mattress. Waves rolled back against her rump.

A *water bed!*

This is going to be terrific.

She flopped down on the undulating softness, felt herself rise and fall on the gently moving surface, stared up at her reflection in the mirrors.

She'd been in a few houses with water beds but none with mirrors like this. It would be strange, trying to sack out with images of herself on the ceiling and wall.

The sport who lives here must get quite a kick out of looking at himself . . . or herself. Could be a woman, she thought. But definitely not married. Definitely on the make.

Her curiosity aroused, Gillian went to the closet and opened it. The inside of the door had a necktie bar. On the floor were men's shoes. The hanging clothes were shirts, slacks, and sport coats.

Our Narcissus, she decided, is definitely a guy.

Gillian shut the closet. Beyond the end of the bed was a bureau. She could inspect its contents later. Beside it was another television. This TV, like the one in the den, had a VCR attached.

Leaving the room, Gillian went to the front door. She

opened it, looked around, then stepped out on the porch. She gathered up her shoes, clothes, purse and suitcase, and carried them into the house.

Then she headed back into the den. She spent the next few minutes gluing the square of glass into its original place in the door. She taped it there to hold it while the glue had a chance to set. Then she packed up her tool satchel and entered the house.

She locked the sliding door.

In the living room, she opened her suitcase and took out her burglar bar. She extended its telescoping rod, fitted its V-shaped end under the doorknob and jammed its other end against the carpet at a wide angle.

"All right," she said. "The house is mine."

Chapter Six

Rick woke up. The tent was dark. He pulled an arm out of his mummy bag and fingered a tab at the side of his wrist-watch to light the digital numbers. Eleven-fifty. He grimaced. He'd been asleep less than two hours, and now he felt wide awake.

Bert, in her own bag alongside his, breathed slowly in and out. She was deeply asleep, gone, and Rick felt abandoned.

Trying to find a more comfortable position, he rolled onto his side. The rubber mat under his bag helped a little, but it was thin and the cold earth was unyielding. Too much weight bore down on his shoulder, upper arm and hip.

They'll fall asleep before I do, he thought.

He rolled the rest of the way over and crossed his arms beneath the makeshift pillow of his rolled coat. This was bet-ter; the ground felt fine under his thigh muscles. But he was pressing down hard on his lower ribs. His penis, sideways against his groin, felt mashed. He turned slightly to relieve the pressure. Now his knee pushed against the ground and there was more weight on the left side of his ribcage. After a while, the knee and ribs began to ache.

Muttering, "Shit," he rolled onto his back again and gazed at the slanted walls of the tent.

This is madness, he thought. I could be home in my own soft bed, instead of out here in the wilderness scared out of my gourd. Like last time . . .

He listened to Bert's slow breathing, and resented her. This was all her fault.

"Get off it," he told himself. "You didn't have to come. And she's been great."

Rick wished he'd had a couple of shots before turning in. He'd been reluctant, however, to let Bert find out that he'd brought the bourbon along. She might not complain, but she would certainly disapprove. She *did* complain about her parents' drinking, whose cocktail hour had stretched into two hours on the several occasions when she and Rick had dined at their house. She didn't complain to them. She complained to Rick later on. By implication, her comments seemed directed at Rick since he had matched her parents drink for drink. "Can't people have a good time," she would say, "without trying one on?"

Rick had seen opportunities to sneak a couple of slugs after dinner tonight when Bert left camp to gather firewood. But he'd resisted the urge, knowing that she would smell it on his breath later when they made love.

I should've brought vodka instead of bourbon, Rick thought. Hell, she would've smelled that, too. Its odor is faint compared to bourbon, but distinctive.

He thought about the bottle. It was near the bottom of his pack.

They had left their packs outside the tent, resting atop slabs of rock on the other side of the campsite and covered with ponchos.

Not only was his bourbon out there, but so was his revolver. A lot of good the gun would do them some forty feet from the tent, but Rick didn't want Bert to know about that, either. The gun was a double-whammy; she hated firearms in general, and Rick bringing one on the camping trip would probably be seen as an act of cowardice.

If I'd had a gun the last time . . .

Maybe I should've told Bert the whole truth this morning. Giving her that sanitized version probably just made me look yellow—like I was a kid back when it happened, scared of my own shadow.

Rick had never told the whole truth about that camping trip to anyone.

When they first came upon the lake, Rick had wanted to keep moving. It was a deep shade of blue, itself beautiful, but trapped in a landscape of such desolation that Rick felt the skin crawl on the back of his neck in spite of the heavy sun.

Steep canyon walls loomed over the lake on three sides. High up were gray stretches of glacier shaded by overhangs so that they probably never melted completely, year after year. There were a few scraggly patches of foliage on the rock walls, trees stunted and twisted into grotesque shapes. Otherwise, the slopes were bleached tumbles of broken granite.

The trail down from Windover Pass led to a small oasis that looked alien in the midst of the otherwise bleak surroundings. The oasis, a shady clearing near the lake shore, had a campsite.

A *nice* campsite, probably added onto over the years by many people who had stopped there after the exhausting trek down from the pass. There was a stone fireplace with a heavy steel grill that must've been brought in by mule. Surrounding the fireplace were several flat-topped rocks that could be used as either seats or tables. Here and there were walls of stone, no doubt constructed to hold back the winds that must rip through the canyon at night. The site even had a few flat areas, mostly near walls, that looked as if they had been carefully cleared of rocks and leveled.

Dad swung his backpack to the ground and stretched. The

armpits of his tan shirt were dark with sweat. "Fantastic, huh?" he asked.

"I don't like it," Rick said.

"What's not to like?" Dad asked.

"This place gives me the creeps."

"It is a little . . . barren," Mom admitted. "They built those walls. The wind must be awful."

"Well, folks, it might be a long trek to the next decent spot. Even if we move on, there's no guarantee we'll find any place better than this. Might even be worse."

"It's still pretty early in the day," Mom said.

Dad showed her the topographics map, pointing out what lay ahead. Mom grimaced. "I guess we stay," she said.

They set up camp, pitching the larger tent in the flat area between two of the stone walls, setting up Rick's tent in a naturally sheltered area beside a high clump of rock. After arranging their gear, they rested for a while. Dad sat on a rock near the shore and smoked a corncob pipe. Mom sat cross-legged under a tree and read, and Rick lay down inside his tent. The tent was hot in spite of the shade, but he liked being enclosed, hidden away from the bleak landscape.

Later, Dad suggested that they take a hike to "explore the environs."

Rick wanted no part of the environs. "Let's not and say we did," he suggested.

"Stay if you want," Dad told him. "We probably won't be gone more than an hour."

"Mom, are you going, too?"

She crawled out of the bigger tent, stood up and nodded. She had changed into a tube top that wrapped her breasts and left her midriff bare, and cut-off jeans so short that the ends of the front pockets hung out below the frayed leg holes. She had abandoned her hiking boots for a pair of ragged tennis shoes. "You want to come," she asked, "don't you?"

Rick certainly did not want to stay by himself. "Sure," he said.

They started out, Dad leading the way. It soon became

clear that his plan was to hike entirely around the lake. Though the lake was not large, maybe a couple of hundred yards from one end to the other, the shoreline trail petered out on the other side of a rushing stream just beyond camp. After that, the lake was bordered by rocks: tilted pale slabs, chunks the size of cars, piles of smaller blocks, some that wobbled or slid underfoot.

In spite of the rough terrain, the going wasn't difficult. Rick felt amazingly light and springy in his sneakers and without the burden of his pack. He leaped from rock to rock, strode easily across slanted sheets of granite, hopped over crevices.

Mom, just ahead of him, sometimes looked back to see how he was doing.

He watched her feet, and stepped where she stepped. Now and then, his gaze wandered higher. Her slender legs looked dusky through his sunglasses. Her shorts were cut so high in the rear that he could see the creases where her buttocks joined the backs of her thighs. Isn't she wearing panties? he wondered. He felt himself getting hard, and guilt swarmed through him.

She's my mother, he warned himself.

Not really. His real mother had left Dad when Rick was six. Two years later, Dad married Julie.

That doesn't mean you can get the hots for her, Rick thought.

But sometimes he did. He just couldn't help it.

He looked away from her. He watched the rocks in front of his feet.

Soon, however, his eyes found their way back to her. He stared at the faded seat of her shorts, at the way the curves under her rear pockets took turns rising and falling with the movements of her firm rump as she walked. He stared at the exposed crescents of her buttocks. There was little more than a narrow strip of denim passing between her legs. If she got high enough above him, maybe he would be able to see up inside the shorts and—

50

No Sanctuary

Rick yelped with surprise as his foot came down. Rock was supposed to be there, but wasn't. He glanced down. Saw his shoe and jeaned shin drop into a crevice. Tried too late to push out with his other foot. Fell forward. Shrieked out his pain as the bones snapped.

Mum threw her arms around him, catching him in time to prevent the bones from ripping through muscle and skin. Then Dad was there. They eased his leg out of the fissure and lowered him onto the rock.

They both knelt over him. Dad, who never seemed to lose his calm, had a frantic look in his eyes. Mom's face was twisted with fear. "Are you okay?" she asked. "It's not broken, is it?"

Rick, teeth clenched in pain, nodded.

"Let's get those jeans off," Dad said.

As Mom unfastened his jeans, Rick noticed that her tube top was askew. It must've been pulled when she stopped his fall. On one side, a smooth half-moon of dark skin showed above the fabric hugging her breast.

He was in too much pain for the sight to arouse him.

But he remembered where he had been looking when he stepped into the crack.

He shouldn't have been looking there. It was dirty of him, even though she wasn't his real mother. The fall had been a punishment.

"I ruined everything," he muttered.

"Could happen to anyone," Dad said, and pulled the jeans down Rick's legs. His left leg, below the knee, looked swollen and slightly bent. Dad ran his hand along it. "There's a break, all right."

"What're we going to do?" Julie asked.

That was when Rick stopped thinking of her as Mom. It didn't seem quite so terrible to have gloated over a woman who was not Mom, just Julie.

"Hold his knee," Dad said.

Julie clutched his knee with both hands, and Dad tugged

sharply on his ankle. Rick flinched rigid as white-hot pain streaked up his body.

Dad fingered the shin again. "I think that set it. You okay?"

Rick nodded.

Dad stood up, looked around, apparently didn't spot whatever he wanted, then crouched and pulled off Rick's sneakers. Following his instructions, Julie pressed the soles of the shoes flat against both sides of Rick's shin. A little more of her nipple was showing. Rick forced himself not to look at it. He watched Dad instead. Soon, the shoes were strapped tightly into place with two belts.

"That ought to hold it," Dad said.

They helped Rick up. Julie suggested they support him under each arm and walk him back to camp, but Dad said that it would be easier, and less risky, if he carried Rick piggyback.

"You might hurt yourself," Julie said.

"You kidding? The man of iron?"

Dad didn't feel like a man of iron as he carried Rick over the rough terrain. He felt like oak, thick and solid and resilient. He wasn't even breathing heavily by the time they reached their campsite.

Instead of putting Rick down, he waded into the lake.

"What're you doing?"

"I want you to soak that leg for a while. The cold'll keep the swelling down."

"Do I have to?"

Dad crouched. The icy water soaked through the seat of Rick's cotton underpants, shocking his anus and biting into his genitals. Then the water numbed his legs. Julie, behind him, clutched him under the armpits.

"Okay, I've got you," she said.

Releasing his father, he eased backward against Julie. She lowered him deeper. Dad let go of his legs, then moved around to where Julie was. Together, they guided him closer to the shore. They found a flat rock for him to sit on.

Both legs were still submerged below the knees, but the

agony was gone. Rick felt as if his balls had been released from a vice. He took a deep breath.

Dad and Julie both stood in front of him, thigh deep in the lake. Didn't the water hurt *them*?

Julie had Rick's jeans with the crotch at the nape of her neck and the legs draping her front.

"You should probably soak that leg a few times a day," Dad said. He looked at Julie. "You make sure he does."

"You're going for help?" she asked.

"Don't see any way out of it."

"You're going to leave us alone?" Rick was stunned.

"There's no reason to worry. You've got plenty of food. Shouldn't take me more than about two days to reach the ranger station. They'll probably bring in a chopper."

"God almighty," Rick muttered.

"It won't be so bad," Julie said, and showed him a smile.

"Let him have some bourbon," Dad told her. "That'll help if the pain gets too bad. I'd better get a move on."

Rick and Julie both tried to talk him into staying the night, but he argued that there were still several hours of daylight and he'd better get to the ranger station as fast as possible.

They left Rick.

Turning sideways on his tiny island of rock, he watched his father pack a few things in his rucksack, kiss Julie good-bye, wave, and start striding briskly up the trail toward Windover Pass.

That night, the wind woke Rick. It howled and shrieked through the canyon. It shook the tent in spite of the protective stone walls on either side. He was glad that Julie had moved his sleeping bag into her tent, but she seemed to be sleeping through the uproar. His leg throbbed. He began to weep. The pain was bad, but the fierce noises were worse. He felt as if their presence had somehow offended a monstrous thing that dwelt in the canyon; it hated intruders in its domain and wanted to crush them. Finally, unable to bear the terror, Rick shook Julie awake.

"Huh? What . . . Jesus, what's going on out there?"

"Just the wind," Rick said, trying to keep his voice steady so she wouldn't know he was crying.

"Sounds like the end of the world."

"My leg hurts awfully bad," he said.

"Maybe we should break out the booze. Do you think that'd be a good idea?"

"I guess so."

"I could use some myself. What's going *on* out there?"

Rick rubbed his eyes. He saw Julie sit up in the darkness. A moment later, light stung his eyes. She had turned on the dry-cell lantern hanging from a joint of the aluminum tent poles near her head.

She crawled out of her mummy bag. She was wearing a T-shirt, baggy gray sweatpants and wool socks. She put on her down parka. "Right back," she said. On hands and knees, she made her way toward the front of the tent.

"Where are you going?"

"The bourbon's in my pack."

"Don't go out there," Rick said. There was a whine in his voice.

"I'd send you, but you're gimped." She opened the tent front and crawled away.

Braced up on his elbows, Rick stared at the shuddering flaps. He thought he heard a scream. Maybe it was only the wind.

Julie didn't come back. The packs were only a few feet from the tent. Even if she had trouble finding the bottle, it shouldn't take this long.

Suppose she *never* comes back!

He called out to her, but she didn't answer.

It got her! Whatever it was out there shrieking like a demon, it got Julie and ripped her apart and next it would come after Rick!

The tent flaps whipped inward and a scream stuck in his throat as Julie crawled in, her hair a tangle and the bottle in her hand.

"Where were you!" he raged through his sobs.

"Hey, calm down. What's the matter?"

"You didn't come back! I yelled and . . ."

"I was out there anyway so I took a pee. Calm down, for godsake." She sat cross-legged beside him and combed fingers through his hair.

Slowly, he regained control. He sat up, keeping his splinted leg straight inside his mummy bag, bending his other at the knee and turning so he could face her.

"Better?" she asked.

Rick nodded.

She unscrewed the cap of the bottle, took a sip, and handed it to him. He had tried wine and beer a few times before, but never whiskey. He drank some and winced. It tasted like medicine and scorched his throat, but then it felt warm and nice in his stomach.

"Like it?" Julie asked.

He wrinkled his nose. He took another swallow. "It's okay."

He gave the bottle to Julie and she drank. "Nasty out there," she said.

"I knew this was a bad place to stay."

"I wasn't too happy about it myself, but we didn't have much choice. We would've had to go over another pass to get out of here."

"I wish we had've." Rick accepted the bottle, took another swallow, and handed it back. His cheeks felt a little numb and there was a mild, pleasant fogginess inside his head.

Though the wind still howled and shook the tent, it soon stopped bothering Rick. It was outside and couldn't get in, couldn't hurt them. In here, talking with Julie and sharing the bottle, his worries slid away. He even found himself feeling glad that he'd broken his leg; otherwise, he wouldn't be here with her. Dad would be here instead, and Rick would be off alone in the other tent.

"When I get older," he said, "I hope I get to marry someone like you."

She smiled. "The booze must be getting to you."

"No, I mean it. Honest. You're really neat. For a mother," he added, just so she wouldn't get the wrong idea.

"You're pretty neat yourself. Even if you don't clean up your room." After capping the bottle, she placed it near the head of the tent and said, "We don't want hangovers in the morning. You think you'll be able to sleep now?"

"Maybe."

She took her parka and rolled it up. "Any more problems, just wake me up." She leaned forward and kissed him gently on the mouth. "Sleep tight," she said.

Rick settled down into his bag. He watched Julie reach up to turn off the lantern. A side of her T-shirt rose, showing a wedge of bare skin. He saw the way her nipples made the fabric jut. He felt a warm, heavy stirring in his groin.

The light went out. He closed his eyes. His mind held the picture of Julie reaching up toward the lantern. He knew he should feel guilty, but he didn't. He felt only languid and peaceful and pleasantly aroused. Soon, he fell asleep.

The next day, the men came.

There were two of them.

Rick was in his swimming trunks and wearing no shirt. He had just finished soaking his leg in the frigid lake. Julie, crouched in front of him, was using belts to strap the splints to his shin. She had made the splints yesterday, soon after Dad's departure, by chopping a length of dead branch into a pair of thin slats and padding each of them with one of Rick's undershirts.

Rick didn't hear the men coming. Suddenly, they just appeared among the trees behind the tent. He flinched. Julie looked up at him. "Someone's here," he said.

Julie made a final adjustment to the bindings, then stood and turned around.

"Morning," one of the men said in a cheerful voice. He and his friend came forward. He had a thick, shoulder-high walking stick. He wore a faded Dodger cap with sweaty blond hair sticking out like spikes around its edges. He wore sunglasses with silver lenses that hid his eyes. He looked as if he hadn't shaved for a couple of days. The sleeves of his filthy, plaid shirt had been cut off at the shoulders. A big sheath knife hung from the belt of his jeans.

His friend looked a couple of years younger, maybe eighteen. He was shorter and heavier, but not fat. His T-shirt bulged with muscles and was cut off just below his ribcage. For a hat, he wore an army helmet liner. Around his waist was a wide web belt with a canteen hanging at one side and a knife at the other. He wore plaid Bermuda shorts. He looked slightly ridiculous, but Rick didn't feel like smiling.

"You got some trouble there?" asked the thin one.

"My son broke his leg yesterday."

"Bad place for a thing like that."

With the help of a crutch Julie had made for him after preparing the splints, Rick pushed himself up. He stood beside Julie, most of his weight on his right leg, using the crutch for balance.

"We're getting along okay," Julie said. "Did you come down from Windover Pass?" she asked.

"Nope. Heading that way. Mind if we rest up for a minute?"

"Help yourselves."

They lowered their backpacks to the ground, but didn't sit down. "Nice camp," the lean one said. "Just the two of you?"

"My husband's around here someplace," Julie said. She looked off toward the outcroppings beyond Rick's tent. "Dave?" she called.

Rick, already concerned by the presence of the two men, was frightened by Julie's lie.

"I'm sure he'll be along in a minute. He just went after some firewood."

"Right." The lean man turned to his friend. "Dave went after firewood. How many packs you see?"

The stocky one smiled. "Just two. I'll just bet Dave hiked out to get help for the kid."

Rick felt as if his lungs were caving in. He swayed on his one leg and crutch.

It's okay, he told himself. They're jerks, but nothing's going to happen.

Julie shook her head. In a voice that sounded calm, she said, "My brother-in-law hiked out. Dave's just over—"

"Hey Dave!" the heavy one yelled. "Yoo-hoo, Daaavy! Where arrre you?" He shrugged. "Gosh, Jiff, I don't know where he could be."

Jiff, grinning, took a step toward Julie.

Julie's back stiffened. "Now don't . . ."

He barely moved, just reached his left hand across to the walking stick by his right leg and rammed it upward with both hands. The point caught Julie under the chin. Her head snapped back. Her arms flew up. She was still falling when Jiff pivoted and swung the staff at Rick. It smashed him above the ear.

There was a terrible, roaring pain in his head. He thought, I shouldn't have drunk so much booze last night. If this is what it means to have a hangover . . . Groaning, he opened his eyes.

He wasn't in the tent. Above him, the leaves of trees were shivering in the wind. He lifted his head off the ground, felt himself spinning, and twisted onto his side. The sudden motion shot pain through his head and leg. Vomit erupted out of him.

Good thing I'm *not* in the tent, he thought vaguely.

When he was done vomiting, he wiped his teary eyes. He pulled a handkerchief out of his pocket, blew his nose, and cleaned his mouth and chin. Then he sat up.

He saw Julie naked on the ground.

He remembered.

The men!

He looked around quickly, making his head whirl. The men seemed to be gone.

"Julie!" he yelled.

She didn't move. She was sprawled on her back a few yards away. She still had her knee socks on. And one shoe. Her blouse lay in a heap near her head. Her shorts were on the ground close to the shoe that was off.

Don't look at her, Rick warned himself. She's naked. God, naked. You might get turned on, and if you hadn't been looking at her yesterday, trying to see up her shorts . . .

As sick as he felt, and as guilty and frightened, he realized there was little need to worry about becoming aroused.

From where he sat, Rick didn't see any blood on her. But she didn't look right.

"Julie?" he asked again.

She's just out cold, he told himself. Like I was. That's good. Maybe she'd been unconscious while the men did things to her. They *must* have done things to her, or why were her clothes off?

When she woke up, she would know.

It'll be all right, Rick thought. I'll take good care of her. I'll cover her first. That's the first thing I'll do, so I won't keep looking at her.

Cringing as the pains in his head and leg punished him with burning throbs, he thrust himself up with his crutch. Another wave of dizziness came. He swayed, barely staying up as the ground tipped and turned. When the dizziness passed, he hobbled over to Julie.

She had a dark bruise where the walking stick had hit her under the chin. Her eyes were shut. Her lips and cheeks were crusted with something, as if white glue had been squirted around her mouth and dried. Rick wondered what it was. Then he knew.

Gagging, he turned his eyes quickly away from her face. But what he saw only added to his disgust and horror. The skin of her shoulders was bruised and dented from bites. Her breasts still held the imprint of fingers, as if they had been fiercely squeezed. Fingernails had left tiny, crescent-shaped impressions. Her nipples looked chewed. Rick covered his mouth and shut his eyes. But he had to look again. Lower, she was caked with dried blood and more semen. Rick had never seen that part of a woman before, just in a few pictures.

Embarrassment suddenly pushed its way through Rick's other agony. Even though he wasn't turned on, what if Julie woke up and saw him staring there?

He bent over and lost his balance. Though he waved an arm to steady himself, he knew it was useless. He flung the crutch from his other hand and reached beyond Julie as he fell. For a moment, he was braced above her like a bridge. But his left leg gave out as pain blasted up it. He collapsed. He fell on Julie.

He started to cry.

She was naked, and Rick had nothing on but swimming trunks, and he was lying on her. Her bare skin against him. He could feel the jut of her hipbone, her flat belly, her ribcage. He could feel a breast against this side, just below his armpit.

If she comes to now . . .

There was no movement under Rick.

No rise and fall of Julie breathing.

Of course she's breathing, he thought.

But she wasn't . . .

Rick's mind seemed to freeze. He shoved himself off Julie, rolled onto his side with his head resting on her outstretched arm. He saw his hand reach out as if it belonged to someone else. It curled around her throat. His fingers searched for the feel of blood pumping through arteries and veins below her jaw.

Then he was up on an elbow, sobbing as he shook Julie by the shoulder. Her head wobbled from side to side. He waited for her eyes to open.

They didn't.

They never would.

Chapter Seven

Gillian's first task, after securing the house, was to determine the name of its owner.

On the coffee table were several magazines: *People*, *Playboy*, *Los Angeles* and *Newsweek*. They had apparently been bought in stores, and bore no subscription labels.

Gillian went into the den. She shut the curtains across the glass door, then turned on a lamp. On top of the television, along with two remote control units, was a copy of *TV Guide*. It had a label with the address of this house.

The owner, therefore, was undoubtedly Fredrick Holden.

So, she thought, I'm house-sitting for Uncle Fred. Or is it Uncle Rick? I'd better just stick with Uncle Fredrick till I find out what he goes by.

With the lamp off, she stepped under the curtains and slid the door open. She carefully peeled off the duct tape she had used to hold the glued section of glass in place. She wadded it in her hand, shut and locked the door, turned on the lamp again, and tossed the tape into a waste basket she found behind the bar.

The bar had a refrigerator. Inside was a nice selection of soft drinks and beer, and a couple of jugs of wine. Gillian lifted out a jug of Blanc de Blanc. She chose a good-sized brandy snifter from a shelf of glasses, twisted out the bottle stopper, and filled her glass. She took a sip. The cold wine had a subtle, fruity flavor, and was not too sweet.

With the glass in one hand and her flashlight in the other, she went into the kitchen. The windows there faced the side of the house and the front porch, as she searched the kitchen in darkness except for the glow from outside. A bulletin board hung next to the wall phone. Some notes were pinned to it. Gillian decided to wait until morning to read the notes. Beside the bulletin board was a picture calendar. Flashlight tucked under her arm, she lifted the calendar off its small nail and carried it into the den.

She sat on a soft recliner chair, took a sip of wine, and studied the calendar. The top portion had a glossy color photo of a slender young woman posing beside a pool. She wore a string bikini and her skin was shiny with oil. Just what Gillian expected of a fellow who had mirrors on his bedroom ceiling.

The lower portion of the calendar was devoted to the month of June. Today was Saturday the 21st. The square block for the 21st had no writing on it. Neither did any of the squares for earlier in the week. On the 13th was written: "7:30 Stewardess; 9:05 Passion." The 7th had similar notations: "7:10 Elena, 8:50 Crazy." Gillian guessed that these were the starting times for double-features, the movie titles abbreviated. The rest of the dates for the month of June had no writing in their spaces. She glanced at July, then shook her head.

"You're no help," she muttered at the calendar.

Apparently, Fredrick Holden needed no reminders of when he was leaving on his trip or returning. Maybe Gillian would turn up some information later. She was in no mood to continue investigating the matter now. She wanted to settle in and relax.

No Sanctuary

One final chore.

After taking the calendar back into the kitchen, Gillian went to the front room. She stepped into her skirt again and pulled the sweater over her head, but decided not to bother with her heels. Car keys in hand, she removed the burglar bar and unlocked the door.

Outside, the night air was cool and fresh after the stuffy warmth of the house. The grass was dewy under her bare feet. Down the street, a car swung into a driveway. A man and a woman climbed out and walked toward their front door. Nobody else was in sight.

Gillian climbed into her car. She drove it to the end of the block, turned the corner, and parked at the first empty stretch of curb. She walked back to the house.

At the driveway, she stopped.

Something looked different.

She frowned. What was . . . ?

Light no longer glowed through the living room curtains.

The nape of Gillian's neck went tight.

Someone inside the house? Had someone been in there all along?

No. Probably the lightbulb burnt out.

But what if someone *is* . . . ?

She suddenly knew. Shaking her head and smiling at her foolishness, she checked her wristwatch. Eleven o'clock. Though she hadn't seen the timer, hadn't even bothered to look for it, the living room lamp was obviously equipped with one. It would be set to turn on the lamp after dark and kill it around bedtime.

Nobody in there after all.

Hearing the grumble of a car engine behind her, Gillian looked around. A Corvette. Slowing down as it approached.

Her heart lurched.

Oh Jesus, no!

But the car didn't swing into the driveway. It went by and turned onto the driveway of the house next door.

Gillian hesitated.

She must've been seen.

Okay, she thought. Fine. Great, in fact.

As the Corvette stopped in front of the gate at the far side of the neighbor's house, she cut across the lawn, heading for it. The engine went silent. The headbeam died. A man climbed out from the driver's door, swung it shut, and walked around the low front of the car.

"Hi," Gillian called.

"Hello," he said. He was slim, dressed in dark slacks and a sport shirt, and appeared to be in his mid-twenties. He had a friendly smile.

"I'm Gillian," she said. "Glad you came by. I'll be staying at Uncle Fredrick's place till he gets back. You know, house-sitting?"

"Didn't know he was gone," the man said.

"Well, I was afraid he might've mentioned he'd be away, and maybe forgot to tell you I'd be watching the place for him." She grinned. "Didn't want you thinking I was a burglar or something."

"You don't look much like one," he said. "I'm Jerry Dobbs."

Gillian offered her hand, and he shook it. "Nice to meet you, Jerry."

"From around here?"

"I've got a cramped little studio apartment in West LA. Which is why it'll be so nice spending a few days here."

"I can imagine. I was an apartment dweller myself till I scraped up enough to get this place. Hated every minute of it. Confining, no privacy . . ."

"Exactly," Gillian said. "Well, I'd better let you go. It was nice meeting you."

"Same here. Look, you need anything, just drop over."

"You mean like a cup of sugar?"

"Or company. Whatever."

"Thanks. Maybe I will." She backed away, raising a hand in farewell. "I'll see you around, Jerry."

"Right. So long."

No Sanctuary

Gillian headed across Jerry's lawn. She felt him watching, so she glanced over her shoulder and smiled, then continued toward the house. That had turned out great. Seemed like a nice guy, Jerry. If he'd been suspicious at all, he sure hadn't shown it.

Now, Gillian would be able to make herself at home without worrying about what the next-door neighbor might see or hear. A terrific development.

Inside the house she made her way through the darkness to a table lamp. After turning it on, she knelt on the floor beside the lamp that had gone off. She followed the cord, pulled the plug for the small plastic timer unit and inserted it into the wall socket. The lamp came on again. She turned off the other one.

After securing the door, Gillian carried her suitcase, purse and high-heeled shoes into the bedroom. She removed a few items from the suitcase, then packed her sweater and skirt.

She made a detour into the living room to pick up her wine glass.

In the bathroom, she had a few sips while she undressed and waited for the tub to fill.

She set the glass on the edge of the tub. She stepped into the water, sat down, and sighed with pleasure as the heat wrapped her to the waist. She stretched out her legs.

Flinched rigid as a bell jangled somewhere in the house.

Someone at the door?

Oh, Christ. And me in the tub.

She braced herself, ready to spring out, but the ringing came again and she realized it was the telephone.

A call. At this hour.

Her skin crawled. She saw goosebumps rise on her submerged thighs, felt her nipples tighten and pucker.

Calm down, she told herself. One thing's certain, it isn't for me.

Unless it's Jerry.

But it's not, she thought.

Each bray of the phone scraped her nerves.

It's not for me. That's the main thing. It's not bad news. Shit, there's nobody to get bad news *about*.

Maybe a neighbor, someone from across the street who saw me come in. Maybe just a wrong number.

At her apartment it was almost always a wrong number when it rang late at night.

Why doesn't it stop!

Gillian gritted her teeth.

Maybe an obscene caller, she thought. Maybe a burglar checking to find out if anyone's home before dropping by.

Maybe Fredrick Holden, calling in to ask what the hell I'm doing in his house. A pretty thought.

Gillian realized that a few seconds had gone by since the last ring. She sat motionless in the tub, her back rigid, her heart thudding, and listened. There was silence except for the slow drip of water near her feet.

Okay, she thought, he finally quit.

Or someone picked up the phone.

Charming idea.

Absurd.

She strained to hear a voice.

Your damned imagination is running haywire tonight. What are you, going paranoid? The house is empty, *empty*. Nobody home but me. The caller hung up, that's all.

Shit.

Gillian thrust herself up and climbed out of the tub. She rushed to the bathroom door, jerked it open, then ran dripping through the dark hall.

This is great. If someone *is* . . .

Even before she reached the kitchen, she could see the pale shape of a wall phone just beyond its entrance. Nobody there. Of course.

But the house had phones in the den and bedroom.

She reached for the handset. Stopped.

Drips of water trickled down her legs.

What if you pick it up and hear voices?

That's easy. You beat it the fuck out of here.

66

Or drop dead of cardiac arrest.

She snatched up the phone. A dial tone buzzed in her ear. Of course.

Still shaking, Gillian returned to the bathroom. She locked the door, then stepped into the tub and sat down. She took a few swallows of wine.

Now just relax, she told herself. Nothing's wrong.

She set aside the glass and lay back. The water washed over her, covering her to the neck, its warm caress soothing, but not enough to make the gooseflesh go away. She rubbed her thighs. The skin felt tender and achy at first, then better. She rubbed one arm, then the other. She massaged the back of her neck. She covered her breasts until the tightness faded and the flesh was smooth again. Letting her arms sink into the heat, she closed her eyes. She took a deep breath.

As the fear seeped away, a heavy weariness settled into Gillian.

She moved her arms and legs, sending gentle currents rolling against her body. Her mind seemed vague. She could almost fall asleep. The water bed would be nice.

She was back in her own apartment, lying on the sofa.

Feeling pleasantly warm, her limbs all lazy and limp. Suddenly, she was flotsam; drifting, floating beneath clear sparkling water. She felt so-ooo peaceful . . . Sunlight glittered like diamonds through the rippling waves above. Below, a mass of dark swirling weeds undulated in the current. Reaching up, but not *quite* touching her.

With a gasp of fear, she swam up toward the sunlight.

She was back on the sofa, the TV on, the sound turned low. Shadowy images flickered across her vision. Her eyelids closed . . .

And snapped open again.

In one limp hand she held a glass of wine. The wine was red and dark. Staring into its ruby depths she saw . . .

But the glass slipped from her grasp and fell to the floor.

Rising up on an arm, she looked down at it. Watched the stem snap away . . .

Click.

Smoothly. Neatly.

Like a slender neck, broken by a strong, practiced hand.

She stared at it for what seemed like an age. Then her eyes slid beyond the glass to the patch of spilt wine spreading around it.

Blood.

Whose?

Her face felt taut, expressionless. As if her skull was hard, molded wax. She glanced down at her arms, turning them over, this way and that. Studied her hands.

No blood there.

Her arms fell, heavily, and her eyes strayed down the length of her body. It came as no surprise to see that she was naked. Naked and glistening with sweat. It was so hot.

I need air!

She opened her mouth to scream but nothing came.

Then, like angry snakes, cords and wires whipped themselves around her ankles. Cutting into her flesh. At the same time, her wrists crushed violently together. She jerked with the shock and pain. Beads of sweat and blood eased out of her pores.

Aaaghhh!

A strangled scream broke from Gillian's lips.

And another one. Louder this time.

In a frenzy of fear, she kicked and floundered in the tub; her body thrashed, the water heaving around her like a storm at sea. Her wrists, mashed tight together, were thrust up high before her.

She came to with a jolt.

Her hands hit water, hard. With a tremendous splash, waves of it smacked her face, stung her eyes . . .

Ugghhh. How long had she been out of it? She shivered and shook her head, spraying droplets all around. The water was barely warm and goosebumps crawled all over her skin.

No Sanctuary

No blood. No cords. No wires.

"No panic, Gilly-babes. Just your friendly neighborhood nightmare," she muttered, clutching her arms across her breasts and shivering some more.

"So I dropped off in the tub. Lesson to be learned there. Never relax on the job, babe. Take a tub, sure. But *don't* fall asleep in it!"

Toweling herself dry, she dwelt on the mystery telephone caller. Who could it have been? She shrugged and slipped into a long, hooded terri-cloth robe she found hanging on the back of the bathroom door. Maybe she would never know.

Tying the belt tightly around her waist, she dug her hands deep into the pockets. A grateful smile curved her lips. So long, nightmare. Time for beddy-byes.

She felt warmer already.

Snuggling between the satin sheets on Uncle Fredrick's Amazing Wonderbed, she curled up into a fetal ball. Undulating gently with her movements, the bed reminded her of the bath she'd just climbed out of.

She still felt shaky after her weird experience.

After falling asleep in the tub.

That, and her scary dream or nightmare, whatever it had been. She told herself that similar slip-ups must never, ever happen again. Her intrusions were based on perfect planning. No, she prided herself on being the consummate strategist, right?

So no more sloppy hiccups. Okay?

She shuddered and shook her head, making the bed bounce some more. What if Fredrick Holden had come home early and found her hallucinating in his tub?

Yeah. *What if?*

Chapter Eight

When Gillian woke up in the morning, a mild breeze was stirring the curtains. She squirmed a little, enjoying the feel of the satin sheets sliding against her bare skin and the way the water-filled mattress undulated. Turning over, she saw herself on the ceiling. She drew the sheet away, stretched, and folded her hands under her head.

Fredrick Holden might have a few quirks, she thought, but she had to admit that the combination of water bed, satin sheets and mirrors was rather appealing. She wouldn't want to have such things herself, but they would be nice for the few days she hoped to stay here.

Gillian was in no rush to leave the bed.

Soon, she found herself sliding around, rolling, savoring the smooth feel of the sheet and the warm breeze from the window. She tried every position she could think of and watched herself in the mirrors, at first with simple curiosity about how she looked from the different angles. Then she

70

imagined a man being with her, a man admiring her display. He had the face of Jerry from next door. She twisted and writhed and contorted herself into erotic poses for his benefit, and suddenly blushed with shame.

For godsake, she thought, what am I doing?

She sprang from the bed. She was sweaty and breathing hard.

The blue satin bottom sheet, dark in places from her moist body, swelled and sank like the skin of something alive and panting.

Fredrick's Amazing Wonderbed. Too true, Gillian thought. Climb aboard, folks. See the astounding Miracle Mirrors transform you before your very eyes into lusting slaves of carnality.

Come one, come all.

Who're you kidding? Gillian thought. It's not the bed and mirrors, it's me.

Been alone too much.

She opened her suitcase, took out her white bikini and hurried to the bathroom. She dried herself before putting it on.

In the kitchen, she made coffee. While she waited for the pot to fill, she went to the den, opened the curtains, and slid the glass door wide. Most of the concrete slab behind the house was still in shade. The breeze felt good on her hot skin. She returned to the bedroom for her sunglasses and book, then poured herself a mug of coffee and stepped outside.

The redwood lounge chair needed a pad. She found one in a storage room alongside the garage. Then she sat down, crossed her legs, and drank coffee while she read her Simon Clark paperback.

When the mug was empty, she wandered over to the fence. On tiptoes, she peered into Jerry's back yard. He wasn't there. He had a big pool that shimmered in the morning sunlight, a patio set with an umbrella over the table, a couple of loungers and a barbecue.

It was against procedure, she reminded herself, to get involved with neighbors. It was risky. Too much danger of letting something slip. You make the brief, initial contact to allay their suspicions, then you stay away from them.

Curious that Jerry had wandered into her Wonderbed fantasy.

A little disturbing.

Disturbing, too, that she had hoped to see him when she looked over the fence.

The last thing you need is to get interested in some guy, she thought. All they do is mess you up.

Gillian went into the house for more coffee, then resumed reading until the mug was empty again.

She took the mug and book inside.

Then she went to the bedroom for her camera.

It had all started when Gillian was seventeen.

On her way home from school, she was walking past the deserted house when John Deerman called out to her. She stopped and waited for him to catch up.

"Look at this! Look!" He tugged a typed sheet out of his binder and waved it in front of her face.

She took it from him.

The title page of his term paper: "The Whiteness of Moby Dick." It had a big red "A" beside his name. The teacher had scribbled, "Wonderful job. A vast improvement."

"That's nice," Gillian said.

"Nice? It's *great*! I got an 'A'!"

"Somebody did." The "A" called for a ten-dollar bonus in addition to the twenty-dollar advance John had paid her for writing the paper. She held out her hand.

Smiling, John produced his wallet. "You're terrific, you know that?" As he slipped out a ten-dollar bill, a sudden gust of October wind snatched it from his fingers. Gillian made a quick grab for the tumbling bill as it fluttered past her face. She missed. It sailed over the battered picket fence.

"Shit!" John yelled.

Several yards beyond the fence, weeds in the overgrown yard snagged the bill.

"Don't stand here like a numbnuts," Gillian said. "Go get it."

"No way. I'm not going in there."

Gillian sighed, set her binder and books on the sidewalk, and rushed toward the gate.

"I wouldn't do that!" John called.

"Obviously," she said. The gate hung crooked, held up only by the single hinge at the bottom. She lifted it, shoved it inward, then ran through the weeds. She plucked the money off a sticker bush.

"Boy, that was stupid," John said when she returned to get her books.

"The only stupid thing was that you made *me* go after it."

"That's Mabel Brookhurst's place."

"So? Who's she?"

John's eyes brightened as if he were thrilled to meet someone who hadn't heard the story. "She was a lunatic. My dad's a paramedic, you know. He was one of the guys that went in and got her. She'd been dead like three weeks, hanged herself. The stink was so bad the neighbors had started complaining. That's how come she got found."

"Pleasant," Gillian muttered.

"They say there's no way to get the smell out. That's how come nobody's bought the place. And there's the writing. Dad said she'd written weird shit everywhere—all over the walls and ceilings. With a marking pen. You can't just paint over a marking pen, it comes right through the paint. So even if they could get rid of the stink . . ."

"What sort of stuff did she write?"

John shrugged. "Who knows? Weird shit. She was cracked."

"Didn't anybody read it?"

"I don't know. Dad didn't. I mean, the place *reeked*. He didn't stick around any longer than he had to."

"I wonder what she wrote," Gillian said.

73

Grinning, John said, "Why don't you go in and find out?"

"Sure thing," Gillian said. "You think I'm nuts?"

It was a Friday. Before her parents went to bed, Gillian told them she would be staying up late to watch TV. It was not exactly a lie. At that time, intrigued as she was about the writing Mabel Brookhurst had left on the walls and ceilings before hanging herself, she doubted that she actually had the courage to sneak over to the old house for a look.

After an hour of staring at the television movie, wondering about the Brookhurst house and trembling, she made up her mind. She left the TV on with its volume low. She turned on the light in the downstairs bathroom and shut the door to make it appear that she was inside—just in case one of her parents should come downstairs and wonder why she wasn't in front of the television.

In her bedroom, she changed from her nightgown into jeans, a chamois shirt and sneakers. She picked up her Polaroid camera and tiptoed downstairs and out of the house. In the garage, she found her father's flashlight and a screwdriver.

The walk to the Brookhurst house took no more than ten minutes. She stopped in front of it. Her mouth was dry, her heart thudding. She felt the wind under her shirt-tail, chilling her back.

Lights were on in some nearby houses, but she saw no one.

And no one sees me, she thought.

The Brookhurst house looked dismal. The weeds in front shifted and crackled in the wind. One of the front windows was broken, a star of blackness on the reflecting sheen of its pane.

I must be nuts, Gillian thought. I'm not going in there.

She walked past the crooked gate and kept on walking, and felt her fear slide away.

I'll just go back home and forget it. Nobody will ever know. It was a stupid idea.

Instead of relief, Gillian felt a sense of letdown.

No Sanctuary

What's the worst thing that could happen if I *did* go inside, she asked herself. The cops might get me. Can't be much of a crime, sneaking into an abandoned house. They'd take me home. I'd have some explaining to do, but Mom and Dad are okay. They'd think it was a weird move, but . . .

What's *really* the worst thing that could happen?

I'm not, for godsake, going to meet Mabel's ghost.

The worst thing, she finally decided, would be to sneak in and get herself nailed by some kind of creep or pervert. A deserted, run-down place like that, *anybody* might be staying there.

She began to feel the fear again. This time, she recognized that part of it, at least, was excitement.

Just watch your step, she thought, and get the hell out if there's any sign the place is occupied.

Gillian had already reached the corner of the block. She turned back. On her way toward the Brookhurst house, she watched the neighboring homes. Most of the draperies in the lighted windows were shut. Someone might be peering out a dark window, but she was willing to take the chance. If the cops grabbed her, too bad, but so what? A little embarrassment. She could live with that.

She swung open the gate and ran through the weeds to the side of the house. Ducking around the corner, she leaned against the wall and tried to calm down. For a few moments, she couldn't get enough air. This seemed strange to Gillian. She was in good shape; running such a short distance shouldn't have winded her at all. It had to be nerves.

Soon she was breathing more easily but her heart continued to race. Though she was no longer cold, she felt shivery inside. She noticed a tingling tightness in her chest and throat—a peculiar cross between pain and pleasure that she associated, somehow, with sliding down a rough hill on her rump. Her skin was crawly with goosebumps. Her nipples felt stiff and sensitive, alive to every touch of her blowing shirt. The inseam of her tight jeans pressed against her like a finger. The denim was moist.

For a long time, she didn't move. She simply leaned against the wall, hidden by a thick hedge along the neighbor's property line, and wondered what was going on with her body. It had to be a combination of fear and excitement—the thrill of doing something forbidden and a little bit dangerous.

I'd better get on with it, she finally told herself.

Easing away from the wall, she walked alongside the house. The weeds crunched under her feet. She crouched each time she came to a window. At the rear of the house was an overgrown yard.

She found a back door. Stepping up to it, she tried its handle.

The door was locked. Good. If it hadn't been, she might have given up, figuring that somebody else might be inside. She realized that she hadn't tried the front door.

Too late for that now.

With the screwdriver, she dug into the doorframe beside the lock plate. Bits of wood broke off. Splinters tore loose. Finally, she worked back the lock tongue and opened the door.

She entered the house.

The stale air was warm and had a faint, sweetish odor that Gillian found a little sickening, but not so bad that she needed to gag.

She was in the kitchen. For a while, she stared straight ahead into the darkness and didn't move. She heard the rush of her heartbeat, the sounds of her shaky, ragged breathing. She tried to hold her breath, but couldn't. She still trembled. The current sizzling through her body seemed even stronger than before; it made her ache for release, to cry out in terror or quake in orgasm.

Get moving, she told herself.

She turned on the flashlight and swept its beam through the kitchen. There was no writing. Maybe John had it all wrong.

Then Gillian stepped into the hallway. The ancient wallpaper, yellow with age and peeling in places, looked like the canvas of a crazed graffiti artist. So did the ceiling. Amazed, she swung her light beam along the multi-colored words and drawings.

All the drawings seemed to feature an obese woman. They were as primitive as the artwork of a four-year-old: bloated bodies, pumpkin heads with scrawls of orange hair and faces composed of bright slashes and circles, oval legs and arms, stick fingers. There were pictures with colors scribbled onto represent clothes. In many of the pictures, the woman was naked, with mammoth, pendulous breasts and huge red nipples. Here and there were drawings of a rump that looked like a pair of clinging balloons.

Must be self-portraits, Gillian thought. She felt a little sorry for the woman, but her pity was mixed with astonishment.

As if she had discovered a hidden treasure.

She read some of the scrawled messages:

> *Mabel Mabel, big as a stable,*
> *Finished her meal*
> *So she ate the table.*

> *I think that I shall never see—*
> *my feet!*

> *Blubber. Blub blub blub.*

> *It is no fun*
> *To weigh a ton,*
> *It is no fun at all.*
> *It'll take a crane*
> *As big as a train*
> *To pick me up if I fall.*

> *Deader is bedder.*

Richard Laymon

I have no kids,
No Mary or Bill.
It's just as well.

I have no kids,
No Bonnie or Jim.
If I had kids
I'd eat them.

Wingle wangle
Hang and dangle.

Why me?

Gillian didn't read anymore. She had brought her camera along, intending to take photographs of whatever she might find interesting in the house, but she wanted no reminder of this woman's torment.

She didn't explore the rest of the house.

She left.

Would've been fine, she thought as she walked home, if the woman hadn't put such depressing shit on her walls and ceilings.

What d'you expect? The gal committed suicide. You're lucky you didn't find something a whole lot worse.

Depressing.

Interesting, though.

Sneaking in that way, spying into her life.

Next time, don't pick a goddamn suicide.

Next time?

Gillian wanted to feel that way again, to feel as she did before the gloomy drawings and messages ruined it for her.

The next day, she called John on the telephone. "Guess what I did," she said.

"Finished my history paper?"

"I had a look inside Mabel's house."

"Sure thing."

"I wanted to see what she wrote all over the place."

"Yeah. And what did you find out?"

"She was fat. A blimp. Apparently, that's what drove her crazy enough to kill herself."

"I *knew* you didn't go in there. You kidding? She was nothing but skin and bones. Dad said she looked like one of those pictures you see of Auschwitz survivors."

"That's impossible."

"Hey, she was always that way. I used to see her around. She'd turn sideways, she'd disappear."

"No way."

"Ask anyone."

The revelation astonished Gillian. She couldn't get over it. Though Mabel's problem certainly seemed tragic, she felt as if she'd made an amazing discovery.

What if every house held strange secrets?

And even if they didn't, there was the thrill of sneaking in to explore.

That night, after her parents had gone to bed, she broke into the house of Ralph and Helen Norris, friends of her parents who were in Las Vegas for the weekend.

She felt a frenzy of fear and excitement.

She searched their closets and drawers.

Though she made no startling discovery, it didn't seem to matter. All that mattered was being there.

She tried their bed.

She took pictures and notes of every room.

What else? She wasn't ready to leave. Not yet.

She drank a cold beer and ate potato chips at their kitchen table, sitting in the darkness, hardly able to swallow because of her thudding chest.

Still unwilling to leave, she went into the master bedroom. There was a huge sunken tub. She filled it, took off her clothes, and climbed in. Except for the dim light from the window, the bathroom was dark.

I can't believe I'm doing this, she thought. I must be nuts. What if they come home and find me naked in their tub?

Richard Laymon

Hi, folks. I'm Goldilocks.

With a trembling laugh, she slipped down into the deep, hot water.

The Norris experience had been the start of something big. A life-changing event. The beginning of a series of adventures that led to a weird kind of addiction. It set in motion within her a yearning desire to discover the innermost secrets of other people's homes. In doing this, Gillian found an immense sense of fulfillment. A *needy* gratification that was almost sexual.

The highlight of it all, though—the cherry on top of the proverbial cake—had been bathing in the Norris's tub. After that, the ritual bath had been the highlight of every one of her intrusions.

Later. Two years and forty or so intrusions later, she'd tried to reason out, *why baths?* Why this fetish with other people's bathing arrangements? That first glimpse of the bathroom itself, the tub and the accessories that went with it: oils, shampoos, talc, deodorants, perfumed soaps. They all played an important part, leading up to the real climax. The shivers of excitement, the thrill of *invading* the inner sanctum of some unknown person.

Then. Easing into those hot bubbles.

As good as an orgasm.

The sensual release of some kind of mental climax. Lying naked and up to the neck in some guy's hot, foaming bubbles, she'd come, no problem.

Other girls had sex with strangers. Just for the thrill of it. Wham bam, thank'ya ma'am. And goodbye forever. No hassle. No hangups. No long-winded affairs to cool off, or drift into indifference. Two ships that passed in the night.

For Gillian, it was like: who needs a man when you can have it all in a stranger's tub?

You get it *off* in a hot tub? In somebody else's bathroom? D'you get all of your kicks this way? Like as in some kind of *titillation?* The whole experience is a *come-on?*

No Sanctuary

No shrink had heard of this one.

Climaxing under water.

Sure we're not talking *masturbation* here?

We're not? Er, well, Miss O'Neill. Must admit your problem *is* er ... rather unusual, to say the least. But hey. People get their kicks lotsa ways these days.

Maybe we should edit all of this down to one root cause. In your childhood, you were deprived of nice hot baths and have felt guilty about enjoying them ever since? A classic example of the "naughty but nice" syndrome!

It's not uncommon for people to become addicted to things they like, things with *forbidden* connotations. Things which are often socially unacceptable. Such as alcohol, drugs, certain foods. Shopping.

But hot baths ... ?

Mmmm-huh. I think we've found the answer to your problem, Miss O'Neill. Deprived childhood and no mistake. Good day to you. Oh, and please leave your check for $3000 with the clerk on your way out ...

Of course, she hadn't seen a shrink. First off, her little jaunts had not only "forbidden" connotations. They were illegal. Her intrusions were a criminal act. But she'd been addicted to them for too long to stop now. She knew that. *This thing will be with me forever*, she told herself. *Like some kind of disability*.

She'd tried to put a stop to it. Seriously. For weeks at a time she'd abstained. Then, like a reformed junkie offered a free trip, she'd feel the old familiar sequence moving neatly into action. Just like a clockwork train.

It was all there. Again. The adrenaline rush as she eased open the front door. The sweats, the soaring, nerve-wracking excitement, wondering if the house owner really was home. Upstairs taking a nap? On their way to the Speed-D-Mart for Aspirin? Or Pizza Hut for a takeaway?

Or would she be met in the hallway by the occupant? Fearful, trembling, finger poised. About to dial 911.

But she knew that, cool as ever, she'd pass off her intrusion by saying she'd mistaken the house number. She'd express frustration at her own stupidity. I'm *so* sorry . . . What*ever* must you think of me?

Yes, she was plausible, she knew that. She had her performance down to a fine art. After all this time she could play to packed houses. Fill theaters up and down the country. Her sudden warmth, charm, *ingenuousness*, would have people eating out of her hand in no time at all.

But it hadn't ever come to that.

So far, so good.

But only because she did her groundwork like a true pro.

Yeah, sure. She was good. Just as well, since her intrusions were food and drink to her now. A major part of the thrill was paying minute attention to detail—at every stage of the game. The reconnaissance, the illegal entry.

Then, the *prize*.

Eating and drinking *their* food. Watching *their* TV. Sleeping in *their* bed. And the kick of it all—entering *their* private domain. *Their inner sanctuary.*

Unknown to them.

She used their bathroom; their tub; their toilet. *And they knew fuck all about it.* She invaded their most private places without their knowledge.

That was the kick.

Gillian smiled softly. She didn't need the help of an expensive shrink to work that one out.

She got off on it is all.

Hey. Tubs she had known . . .

About sixty-six in total?

She could write a book.

Or a screenplay.

Miss O'Neill, talented winner of the Golden Goblet Screenwriter of the Year Award, please tell our viewers—your fans—which, in your experience, has been the most fascinating tub of all?

*　　*　　*

No Sanctuary

Her camera and notebook were ready. But instead of taking shots of Fredrick Holden's artifacts, as planned, she returned to the concrete sundeck and flopped back onto the lounge chair.

So, which *was* the most fascinating tub? Gillian thought hard about that one. But, damn it, she decided, she didn't need to give herself such a hard time. Because, like a flame among dying embers, one occasion stood out from all the rest.

Yeah. That one on Silverston. West of Studio City.

No shit, that's been the most fantastic tub so far.

She'd done her routine check. No one around. No snoopers. No dog-walkers. No mailmen . . .

The absence of human life, or of any other type of life on that street, come to that, was in itself unusual.

The house fascinated her from the start. The neighborhood was maybe too upmarket for her liking. But, in some strange way, she knew that the old place *needed* her.

And Christ, she knew about *need*, all right. She was here, wasn't she? Cruising around, searching for places to satisfy *her* need.

Looks like I've found it . . .

Too upmarket? Okay, Miss O'Neill, so break a few rules.

This one's going to be your special treat!

It was as if that lonely old house, set back against dark shadows, was crooking its finger and beckoning to her. She imagined its whispering voice, mingling and swishing with the windblown palms lining its path.

Hey, girl. Come on in. You want tales? I got tales a-plenty to tell—and a thousand secrets to share . . .

That clinched it. The white stucco house, detached and with around two, three hundred yards of driveway leading up to it, was her target for tonight. Tall, dark palms ran either side of the driveway. The rustling trees almost blocked out all of the remaining daylight until they looked like one long, dark, moving tunnel.

83

Leading to what?

The house. Secreted away in the background. Looming like a forgotten ghost; silent and forbidding.

Scary.

I must be nuts.

No possibility of nosy neighbors. Unless they used a pair of step-ladders, the tall yew hedges either side would obscure the driveway from view. And when she'd driven past earlier, she'd seen a For Sale sign sticking up out of next-door's front lawn. *That* house had looked dark and empty too.

The gravel leading up to number 1309 crunched loudly under her feet. This place, with its flaky, white-painted exterior, exuded an air of loneliness.

But not emptiness.

The driveway, the gardens, the long green lawn in front of the house, were neat and well-kept. A sure sign that a gardener or handyman had recently been at work. By the time she reached the three shallow steps curving up to the arched front door, she knew there was no one around to halt her progress.

In some strange way, this knowledge was a *certainty*.

Gillian smiled.

The house was hers.

Alarm system?

Yeah. Alarm system . . .

She looked around for tell-tale electronic devices. Wires. Anything.

Nope.

Crazy, but true. There were no alarm devices that she could see.

So, go for it.

She did.

Gaining access was easy. In the studded dark wood door a rectangular window gleamed. It was small, narrow and about two thirds of the way up: a nice stained-glass affair showing a white, stylized lily, cupped by two long green leaves. The background was bright blue. A quick glance around assured

her there was no one immediately in sight. Taking her small
leather tool satchel from her purse, Gillian paused for a moment, head tilted, listening intently to sounds from within.

Like someone running to open the door.

The click of a telephone being lifted off the hook.

Nothing.

She stretched out a length of duct tape and stuck it around
the window. She stuck a circle in the center of the window
to use as a handle. It's an old window, she thought with satisfaction. Should drop out okay.

She set to work with her glass cutter. When she'd finished
he tapped the glass. It came away in her hand.

Easy as drawing breath.

Too easy?

She reached her hand through the space and felt around
with her fingers. The door handle was just below the space.
It was large and heavy and she could move it up and down
with her fingers. But the door wouldn't give.

A bolt?

Yeah. She reached inside, felt below the window space and
found the bolt.

Slid it back.

It moved smoothly, in double quick time.

Freshly oiled.

Especially for her?

The door swung open.

Briskly, and with a pounding heart, she returned her tools,
and the small piece of window, to the satchel, slid it into her
purse and picked up her suitcase. She stepped inside and
closed the door behind her.

Taking her tools out again, Gillian worked quickly, re-
placing the window in the door and returning her tools to
the leather satchel. She placed the satchel into her purse.

Then looked around her.

Thirties Hollywood. That was her first impression. Maybe
not so big as some of those deco places out in the hills. But

in its own faded, still glamorous way, this one was just as tasty.

White marble entrance hall. Light streaming through looped drapes at the long windows either side of the tall white studded door. A white staircase rose before her. It branched off, right and left, each section winding upward and then back on itself. Both sets of stairs met on a white and chrome balcony, the entire width of the house. Just like the prow of a cruise liner.

The Busby Berkeley Babes.

Dick Powell and Ruby Keeler.

"Yessir," Gillian breathed. "The place has style, all right."

She shivered. It was this air of loneliness, inside the house as well as out. It hung about the place like some long-forgotten melody. It made her want to cry, it was so sad.

The emptiness made her think that maybe this house, too, was up for sale. But once again, she had this deep down certainty that it wasn't.

A quick check on all the rooms told her that the house *was* lived in. It was tidy; not a magazine out of place. Garden flowers were still fresh in the tall white vases.

Black and white studio shots of a blonde with cupid bow lips and provocative, dark-lashed eyes smiled archly from the walls. In one photograph, she was dressed up like Heidi, complete with pigtails, accompanied by a mustachioed guy in Bavarian fancy dress.

Gillian recognized the woman—though from where, she couldn't say. *Some old-time movie star. All alone with her memories. Alone, except for a maid coming in twice a week to keep the place straight . . .*

She inspected the first bedroom she came to. White quilted satin on a large, circular bed. Flimsy white drapes drawn aside from the heart-shaped quilted satin headboard. Flimsy white drapes at the windows, too. Built-in wardrobes. A curved white dresser covered in glass gewgaws and perfume and stuff. Matching nightstands stood either side of the bed.

A movie set from years ago.

No Sanctuary

Gillian stepped inside the adjoining all-white bathroom. And gasped with pleasure as her eyes took in the round sunken tub and ornate gold taps shaped like dolphin heads. Slender bottles filled with colored oils and unguents were set neatly at intervals around the rim.

Claudette Colbert in *Cleopatra*.

Only thing missing was a Nubian slave girl.

Excitement stirred, touching her spine with soft, seductive fingers. The tingly feeling teased her stomach and goose-bumps rose on her skin. She couldn't wait to undress.

But first off, had she missed anything? Like some vital clue telling her that the owner was home, after all? To be safe, Gillian called out, "Hello? Anybody home?"

If somebody answered she could always say . . . hell, what *could* she say? The usual excuses, like she'd been asked to call around, to check on . . . who? That she was a relative come to stay? All seemed woefully inadequate.

An escapee from the local psychiatric unit seemed more plausible, she remembered thinking.

Okay. Weak wasn't the word. Especially if she was discovered upstairs already. She'd have to come up with a pretty good answer. Bluff her way out of a tricky situation.

Or just make a break for it.

Let's hope it doesn't come to that.

Silence.

No reply.

Thank God.

She was safe. Although . . .

Do it now. Do it. I dare you . . .

The short hairs on the back of her neck began to rise.

Hey. Live life on the edge, Gilly baby. Why not?

She cocked her head. Listening for sounds. Any sounds.

None.

The familiar tingle of excitement teased her center. Her pubic mound throbbed until the ache became unbearable. A low giggle burst from her lips. She slipped off her shoes and undressed.

87

A flicker of fear came and went. *Wait*, a small voice whispered. *Forget the tub. Go explore. Make sure it's safe . . .*

Against her better judgment, she ran water into the tub. Steam curled into her face, making her gurgle with excitement. Selecting a long-stemmed container of bath oil, Gillian took off the stopper and poured it into the tub. Fascinated, she watched the amethyst fluid flow into the bubbling torrent.

The delicate scent of lilacs met her nostrils. Mmmm . . . Stepping into the fragrant water, she hummed a tune:

"Keep young and beautiful . . ."

Yeah. That was the most fascinating, the most luxurious, most memorable tub she'd *ever* taken.

All round, her most fascinating, memorable intrusion so far.

And the briefest, so it turned out.

Chapter Nine

Bert wasn't in the tent. Rick told himself there was no reason to worry, but he scurried out of his sleeping bag, needing to see her, needing to banish his sudden fear. He swept aside the tent flap.

She was nowhere in sight.

The fire crackled. Its pale flames fluttered in the morning sunlight. A distance beyond the fire were their packs. The ponchos had been removed and the red nylon top of Bert's pack was open.

Rick sat down just inside the tent and pulled on his running shoes. His fingers trembled as he tied the laces.

She's all right, he told himself. Probably down by the stream.

On her back. Wearing one knee sock.

Rick shook his head sharply to dislodge the thoughts, and winced. His head had a dull ache, thanks to the bourbon. He got to his feet, looked around, and walked across the camp-site.

She'll be down by the stream, he thought. When I get to

the top of the embankment, I'll see her. She's fine.

God oh God, why had he let himself remember all that last night? Over the years he'd become talented at turning his mind away from the memories whenever they started. But lying there in the dark tent, he'd dwelled on them, wallowed in them. He hadn't even tried to fight the memories.

He suspected that he knew the reason why—because he had a *need* to remember what happened last time. He was out here again. Probably a hundred miles from the place where Julie was murdered, but *here*, in the mountains, in the wilderness. He needed to relive the horror. He needed it fresh in his mind. A cautionary tale. Watch out, be ready, it could happen again.

Shaken by the memories, he had crawled from the tent last night, stirred the smoldering fire to life, gone to his pack and taken out the bottle and revolver. The pocket of his parka was deep enough to hold the revolver. Its weight felt good. He sat on a stump close to the fire and drank. The heat of the bourbon swept through him. He wished he had brought two bottles, not just the one. He had six more nights to go. He needed to hold back, to drink no more than a seventh of the bourbon, or he might run out.

But a seventh of a quart wasn't much at all.

There were bound to be nights when he wouldn't need to drink, nights when he would sleep through till morning.

Now is when I need it, he thought.

When a quarter of the bottle was gone, he forced himself to quit. Hoping that would be enough to help him sleep, he put the bottle away and returned to the tent. He rolled his parka into a pillow. In spite of its thickness, he could feel the revolver under his head. He didn't mind.

Nobody gonna fuck with us this time, he thought vaguely just before falling asleep.

Rick reached the edge of the embankment. For a moment he didn't see Bert and something clamped tight in his chest. Then he spotted her. She was off to the right, sitting cross-legged on a rock near the middle of the stream.

No Sanctuary

"Morning," he called, climbing down the slope.

She looked over her shoulder at him and smiled. "Afternoon," she said.

"Oh, it's not that late."

She got to her feet, hopped across the stream, and stepped into her sneakers. She was wearing baggy tan shorts and a white T-shirt. She looked fresh and wonderful. She came to Rick. He put his arms around her. She pressed herself against him.

"How come you didn't invite me to your party?" she asked.

She knew. Of course she knew.

"You were asleep," Rick said.

He felt her shrug.

"You didn't miss much. I woke up and couldn't get back to sleep. So I knocked back a few. They helped."

"The first night out can be tough," she said. "It'll get better."

"God, I hope so."

"Good thing I didn't light a match this morning, the tent would've blown up."

Rick laughed softly. "Sorry."

Her hands slipped inside the seat of his sweatpants. They were warm on his buttocks. "If you have trouble sleeping again, how about waking me up? I don't want you to suffer alone."

"All right."

She patted his rump, then stepped away. "Let's get some breakfast. I'm starving."

Back at the camp, Rick heated water on the fire for instant coffee. Bert dumped powdered eggs into her pan, stirred in water, and used her sheath knife to scrape chunks of meat off a bacon bar. She cooked the meal over the burner of her small propane stove.

Rick normally abhorred instant coffee. This morning, however, it seemed to taste great. He drank it eagerly while he lingered over the scrambled eggs with bacon.

And he watched Bert sitting on a log across from him,

91

eating from the pan. Her hair gleamed like gold over one ear where the sunlight fell on it. Her white T-shirt, so bright that it almost hurt his eyes to look at it, hung loosely over her breasts. Her nipples made it jut and he could see a hint of their darkness through the fabric. The pan was on her lap. Her legs, long and sleek, were stretched out and crossed at the ankles.

Finishing first, Rick got up and went to his pack. He took out his Polaroid camera.

"Come on," Bert said, "my hair's a mess."

"You look great. Just keep eating."

She shrugged and rolled her eyes upward. Rick took a shot as she lifted the fork to her mouth. With a buzz, the camera ejected the photo.

Rick crouched beside Bert and they watched the picture appear, faint at first, growing sharp, finally showing every detail in rich clarity. "I told you my hair was a mess."

"Now let's get one with your shirt off."

"Up yours."

"I'll wait till you go to change it."

"Who says I'm going to change it?"

Rick tried to keep his tone light. "You show through, you know."

She grinned. "Is that a problem for you?"

"I love it. But we might meet someone on the trails."

"Ah."

"Or you could put on a bra."

"If I'd brought one."

"I just don't think . . ."

"I know. You don't want some stranger getting an eyeful. Rather selfish of you, don't you think?"

"Yep." Not just selfish, he thought. Seeing her nipples through the shirt might give people ideas. Such ideas might lead to . . .

"Well, I suppose if it's going to bother you. But no pictures, or I'll change in the tent."

"A deal."

"Why don't you get some shots of the campsite before we ear it down?"

Rick obliged, then put the camera away.

They took the cook kits down to the stream. After cleaning hem, Rick remained to brush his teeth and wash. He returned to camp. Standing in a patch of sunlight, he changed ut of the sweatsuit he had slept in. Bert doused the fire and watched him. Then she pulled off her T-shirt, walked over o her pack, and took out the faded blue chambray shirt she ad worn yesterday. She buttoned it up, and gave Rick a coy mile as she fastened the button at her throat. "Is this modest nough for you?" she asked.

"Well, you don't have to overdo it."

She smiled and opened the top two buttons. "Okay?"

"Fine."

She went inside the tent. Rick watched while she forced er sleeping bag into its stuff sack. "Want me to do yours?" he asked.

If she started touching the things on his side of the tent, he might find the revolver in his coat.

"No, fine. I'll take care of it."

She crawled out.

Rick entered the tent, rammed his sleeping bag into its tiny ack, and brought it out along with his rolled parka. Bert tayed beside him, rearranging the contents of her backpack. Ie wanted to put the gun into a side pocket of his pack where : would be easy to reach, but that was impossible with Bert here. So he left it inside his parka. His sleeping bag went on op of it.

So much for easy access, Rick thought.

They struck the tent. They were both on their knees, folding it, when Rick heard voices. His stomach clenched. Head napping to the side, he saw three figures moving through he trees, coming down the trail that ran past their campsite. Ie looked at Bert.

She was watching them, too. Her hands were on the tent. he way her loose shirt hung toward the ground, Rick could

93

see the shadowed slope of a breast. He felt as if his head were being squeezed. He wanted to shout for her to button up, damn it! Then the shirt swayed back and concealed her breast as she raised herself.

She waved at the strangers. "Morning," she called.

Shit!

They might've gone on by if she'd kept quiet. Why did Bert *do* that?

The young man in the lead called, "Hi, there," and turned off the trail. He stepped between a couple of saplings and came toward them, followed by his two companions.

Bert stood up. She brushed dirt and pine needles off her knees.

Numb and shaking, Rick got to his feet. He forced himself to smile and say, "Hello" to the three approaching men.

Men? Boys. They were teenagers, seventeen or eighteen years old.

That's worse, he thought.

Three of them. God.

He strolled over to his pack, lifted out his sleeping bag, and set it on the ground. There were voices behind him, but he didn't listen. Fingers trembling, he plucked at his down parka, turned it until the pocket was on top. He slipped his hand in, pulled out the revolver and shoved its barrel down the front of his pants. He untucked his shirt, looked down at himself to make sure the gun handle didn't show, then took a cigar from his shirt pocket and faced the intruders.

They're not intruders, he told himself. Bert *invited* them over for godsake.

She was still beside the collapsed tent. The three guys stood in a semi-circle, facing her.

He ripped off the cigar's cellophane wrapper as he walked toward them. "Hello, fellows," he said, and clamped the cigar in his teeth.

As he lighted up, Bert smiled at him. "They spent the night at Mosquito Pasture," she said.

"Sure did," said the leader, smiling. He was bigger than

Rick and had a body that looked solid. "They damn near carried us off. Wally got messed up real good."

Wally, a fat kid in glasses who wore cut-off jeans that hung low and appeared ready to drop around his ankles, turned and pointed to red weals on the backs of his legs. He pointed out others on his neck, on the inner sides of his forearms and the crooks of his elbows. "They murdered me," he said in a dismal voice.

"Don't you have insect repellent?" Bert asked, sounding concerned.

"Who wants to stink?"

"That's a good one," said the third boy, a lanky, freckled kid in white-rimmed sunglasses and an olive green beret.

Wally sneered at him.

"Have you tried Cutters'?" Bert asked. "It doesn't smell bad."

Wally shook his head.

"I've got some left in my old bottle," she said. "Why don't you take it?"

"Gee . . ."

Bert headed for her pack.

Wally scratched the side of his neck and watched Bert. The leader watched her, too. Rick couldn't tell where the guy in the sunglasses was looking, but he could guess.

They were all three staring at the way she moved inside her shorts.

"How long you fellows been in?"

"Three nights," said the leader, still looking past Rick. He licked a corner of his mouth. Then he took a pack of Winstons from the pocket of his sleeveless shirt, shook out a cigarette, and poked it into his mouth. "Borrow a light?" he asked.

Rick slipped a book of matches from his pocket. He pictured the guy grabbing his hand when he reached out, yanking him forward and driving a knee into his guts. So he tossed the matches.

The guy caught them, muttered "Thanks," and lit his cigarette. He tossed the matches back to Rick.

"Where are you folks heading?" asked the one in sunglasses.

"Granger Lake," Rick said. He'd never heard of such a place.

"Yeah? That anywhere near the Pylons?"

"Is that where you're going?" Rick asked. "The Pylons?"

"Yeah."

Rick heard footfalls behind him. Bert was coming back, and the eyes that he could see were on her. She stepped past Rick and handed a squeeze-bottle to Wally.

"Thanks a lot."

In her other hand was a plastic tube. "Here, put some of this on your bites. It should help with the itching."

Wally nodded. He uncapped the tube, sniffed its opening and wrinkled his nose.

Bert let out her husky laugh.

"Can't smell any worse than your pits," the one in the sunglasses said.

"You and the horse you rode in on, Bugger." He started dabbing the pink ointment onto his bites.

"Bugger?" Bert asked, smiling.

"It's *Burgher*." He spelled it. "Luke Burgher."

"Also known as Ham, Cheese, and McDouble," Wally said, leering as he got in his digs.

"So it's Wally, Luke and . . ." Bert looked at the leader and raised her eyebrows.

What *is* this, Rick thought, a goddamn cocktail party?

The guy blew out smoke and said, "Jase."

"Jason?"

"Just Jase."

"He's sensitive," Luke said.

"You know," Wally said. "Jason. *Friday the Thirteenth*."

Bert smiled at Jason. "I didn't recognize you without the hockey mask."

He blushed. Then he smiled.

"I'm Bert. Nobody calls me Bertha and lives." She shook hands with Jase. The cigarette drooped in his lips, and his eyes glazed over as if she were holding his cock instead of his hand.

"My silent partner here is Rick," she said.

Rick nodded, but didn't offer his hand. Jase made a feeble smile, and his eyes stayed on Bert as she sidestepped to Wally.

"Bert," Wally said. He wiped his pink fingertip on his shorts, then shook her hand. He grinned and blushed. Watching, Rick half expected the kid's glasses to fog up.

She moved on down the line.

"Pleased to make your acquaintance, Bert," Luke said, and gave her hand a quick, stiff shake. Rather formal. Rather mocking, as if he thought she was weird for shaking hands with them all.

Good for him, Rick thought.

Wally resumed smearing goo on his bites.

"Are you guys heading up over Dead Mule Pass?" Bert asked.

"Yeah," Jase said. "How about you?"

"Same here."

Great, Rick thought. Why don't you break out the map and show them our whole route?

"Maybe we'll run into you up ahead," Bert continued.

"Yeah. Could be."

Next, she'll be inviting them to hike along with us.

"We'd better finish getting our stuff together," Rick said, "or we'll be here all day."

"Need a hand with the tent?" Jase asked, looking at Bert.

"We can take care of it," Rick said. "Thanks anyway."

Wally twisted the cap back onto the ointment.

"Better?" Bert asked him.

"Yeah. Thanks. And thanks for this." He patted the shirt pocket where he'd put the mosquito repellent.

"It was nice meeting you," Jase said. Then, he stepped over to the muddy ashes of the fire and tossed in his cigarette butt.

97

"Well," Bert said, "if we don't run into you fellows up ahead somewhere, have a real good trip."

Don't worry, Rick thought. We'll run into them again. They'll see to it.

"Yeah," Jase said. "So long."

"Nice meeting you," Wally said.

"See you around," said Luke.

"Take it easy, guys," Bert told them.

"Yeah," added Rick.

He watched the three turn away and head for the trail. Wally looked back and waved. Jase glanced back a couple of times. Luke didn't.

"Nice kids," Bert said.

"That remains to be seen."

She looked at him. "Did I miss something?"

"Hell, they were drooling all over you."

"Drooling?"

Rick nodded. For a moment, he couldn't see the three boys. Then they appeared on the other side of a rock cluster. "Looks like they're leaving," he muttered.

"Expect them to circle around and jump us?" She sounded amused.

"It's a possibility."

"My protector," she said, and patted his rump.

Rick was tempted to lift his shirt and show her what was in his belt.

Protector, all right.

He fought the urge. If Bert found out that he had a gun, she would go into shock.

She'll find out if I have to use it, he thought. Then she'll be damn glad I was scared and crazy enough to bring it along.

"Want to stand guard while I pee?" Bert asked.

"Why don't you wait a few minutes?"

The smile left her face. "They're gone, honey."

"Maybe."

Frowning, Bert gently stroked his cheek. "I wish you wouldn't worry so much."

"Me too."

"There's honestly no need for it. We're perfectly safe out here. We left all the nutcases behind in LA."

"I hope so."

"Anyway, my teeth are floating."

The trail looked deserted. There was no sign of the boys. "Okay, go ahead. But stay out of sight."

She turned away and walked toward her pack.

Rick shifted his attention from the trail to Bert until she wandered into the trees with a roll of toilet paper in her hand.

The moment she was gone, he rushed over to his pack. After a quick search, he found a T-shirt. He wrapped it around his revolver and stuffed them in a side pocket of his pack. He zipped the pocket shut, patted it, and felt the hardness of the gun inside.

Now he'd be able to get at it without taking his pack apart.

Still wouldn't be as fast as he'd like.

He only wished he could wear the gun on his hip.

Chapter Ten

Gillian took photographs of every room in Fredrick Holden's house for her scrapbooks. When shooting the bedroom, she was especially careful to avoid catching her reflection in the mirrors. In the past, she had sometimes taken pictures of herself, either in mirrors or using the camera's delayed timing device. Fortunately, she hadn't done that at the Farnsworth house, where the family returned home early and she left everything behind, camera included. After that, she stopped taking self-portraits.

Once every room of Fredrick Holden's house had been photographed to her satisfaction, Gillian began to investigate.

She started with the kitchen. The notes on the bulletin board by the phone provided no information about Uncle Fredrick's trip. There were scribbled names and telephone numbers, nothing of much interest.

The refrigerator was well stocked, but Gillian noticed that it held no milk or cream. A good sign. Fredrick had removed the perishables, not wanting to return home and find his refrigerator stinky. He wouldn't have tossed such things if he planned to be gone for only a couple of days. If Gillian could just find out the date he left . . .

The freezer section was full of goodies: steaks, lamb chops, chicken breasts, bags of onion rings and Golden Crisp Potato Nuggets, two sausage pizzas, chocolate-chip ice-cream, a box of tacquito hors d'oeuvres, and a dozen TV dinners such as veal parmesan, lasagna, fried jumbo shrimp, and lobster Neuberg.

Gillian decided she was hungry.

She turned on the oven, tore open a box of pizza, and slid the frozen slab onto the oven tray. After setting the timer for ten minutes, she took a lamb chop from the freezer and set it aside to defrost for dinner.

The pleasant odors of the pizza stole her concentration as she inspected the drawers and cupboards. When the dinger sounded, she opened the oven door. The heat washed over her. She breathed deeply of the rich, spicy aromas. The tomato sauce and cheese bubbled, but the crust needed to darken some more. Leaving it in the oven, she went into the bar and got herself a bottle of Corona beer.

She checked the pizza again. The rim of its crust was golden brown, nearly black in places, just the way she liked it.

She cut out several large wedges, put them on a plate, and sprinkled them with salt and pepper.

She ate outside, sitting cross-legged on the lounge chair with the plate on her lap. The sun felt uncomfortably hot on her bare skin. The pizza, in spite of its wonderful look and smell, was more of a disappointment than a pleasure.

If I'd wanted the taste of cardboard, Gillian thought, I would've eaten the box.

But the beer was cold and tasted terrific.

Her hand was wet from the bottle. She rubbed it over her shoulders, sighing as the cool moisture soothed her hot skin.

I ought to get Jerry to invite me over for a swim, she thought.

Forget it. No fraternizing with the neighbors.

She looked over at Fredrick's spa. The water in there was probably cool.

Later, she told herself. I have more snooping to do before I can flake out.

The second and third slices of pizza didn't seem as awful as the first. Gillian supposed that they *were* no less awful; that they only seemed better because she was growing accustomed to the lousy flavor.

When her plate and bottle were empty, she stood up. She was streaming with sweat and the seat of her bikini pants clung to her buttocks. She plucked the fabric away as she walked over to the fence. On tiptoes, she gazed into Jerry's yard. No sign of him. His pool looked delicious.

He should be in it, Gillian thought. *I* should be in it.

Back in the house, she peeled off her bikini, went into the bathroom, and took a brief, cool shower. It felt great. In the bedroom, she put on a lightweight sleeveless shirt that draped her thighs. She buttoned it at the waist, and returned to the kitchen.

She wrapped the left-over pizza in aluminum foil and put it in the refrigerator. It would make a decent snack, cardboard taste or not, for tonight when she planned to watch movies on the VCR.

With another beer from the refrigerator behind the bar, Gillian sat down at a small desk in one corner of the den. The top of the desk was clear. She searched the drawers.

Fredrick had left behind his checkbook, which seemed a little odd. The balancing was up-to-date. His account had a total of $1,248.60.

The last check had been written on June 20.

Friday.

Jesus!

Gillian grinned.

He was still in town on Friday, day before yesterday. I got here yesterday.

He'd stopped his mail, tossed his milk so it wouldn't go sour.

No Sanctuary

I bet I could stay two, three more nights. Maybe longer if I want to push it.

The check dated June 20 had been made out to "cash" in the amount of $2,000.00.

He took that kind of money, he might be gone *weeks*.

Just because he withdrew that much, Gillian thought, doesn't mean he plans to use it all for his trip.

She looked at the earlier stubs. Most of the checks had been written to pay supermarkets, auto insurance, the monthly mortgage, utilities and credit card companies. None of the checks had been made out to an airline or travel agent.

So he'd probably used part of the two thousand dollars to pay for his transportation to wherever he went.

Unless he drove.

His car is probably parked at the airport, Gillian thought.

She snapped the checkbook shut and slid it back inside the drawer.

Awfully strange that he left it behind. Who would go on a trip without taking his checkbook along?

With that kind of cash, who needs a checkbook?

In the same drawer, Gillian found Fredrick's savings account passbook. It showed a total of $156,835.46. "Not bad," she whispered. She had twice that in her own passbook and nearly as much tied up in stocks and bonds, but not everybody gets two wrongful-death settlements to build up that kind of nest egg.

Whatever Uncle Fredrick does for a living, she thought, he does pretty well for himself. Maybe he's a doctor or a lawyer.

He certainly had quite a modest house considering his income.

"You'd think he could afford a goddamn pool," Gillian muttered.

She put away the passbook and looked through the rest of the drawers. They held nothing of much interest until she slid open the bottom drawer and found a .357 magnum Colt Python. Whistling softly, she lifted it.

103

The thing was loaded.

Obviously Uncle Fredrick was prepared to blast away intruders.

That's me, Gillian thought.

Though she didn't expect to be taken by surprise, she saw no point in leaving a loaded gun around where it might be used on her.

She broke open the cylinder and tilted the barrel up. The cartridges slid out, dropping into her palm. She dumped them into her shirt pocket and returned the revolver to its drawer.

Finished at the desk, she wandered over to the bookshelves. Three of the shelves were taken up by boxed video tapes. Though tempted to explore the collection, she decided to wait until later and check them out when she was ready to settle down and watch a few.

The books looked fairly normal. At first. The reference collection included a set of the *World Book* encyclopedia, several atlases, a dictionary, *The People's Almanac*, *Gray's Anatomy*, and a couple of motion picture encyclopedias. He had several books about body-building, but none that might indicate his profession. Unless he's a photographer, Gillian thought. There were fifteen or twenty books on that subject, most of them expensive, large format and with glossy pages. Most of them featuring nude women.

His hardbound fiction ran toward best-sellers by Joseph Wambaugh, Robin Cook, Lawrence Sanders, Dean Koontz, Stephen King, and so on. He had rows of paperbacks, mostly suspense and horror novels.

And one entire shelf of non-fiction that made Gillian wonder about Fredrick Holden. She felt a chill on her back as she inspected the books: volumes about Jack the Ripper, Albert Fish, Ed Gein, Charles Starkweather, Richard Speck, the Boston Strangler, the Manson family, John Wayne Gacey, the Skidrow Slasher, the Hillside Strangler, and Theodore Bundy. Many of the books contained photographs of the dead victims.

What's with this guy? she wondered.

Maybe he's a suspense writer, she told herself, and just had these books around for reference.

Then where's his computer?

Maybe he's a true crime buff, into police procedure and that kind of thing.

Sure. What he is, he's crazy about homicidal maniacs.

And he's got a water bed. And mirrors all over his bedroom.

"I really picked a good one," Gillian muttered.

After sliding a copy of *Helter Skelter* back onto the shelf, she headed for the bathroom to wash her hands.

She was reminded of the Benning house, where Bill and Andrea had shelves of sex manuals, stacks of nudie magazines, an assortment of dildos and vibrators, various devices for which Gillian could only guess at the purposes, numerous oils and lotions, and erotic wardrobes: transparent negligees, G-strings (Bill's with a leopard-cloth pouch that opened like curtains), loin cloths, frilly garter belts, leather undies and bras, and bras with open fronts.

Gillian had inspected the Bennings" collection, intrigued and a little embarrassed. Though she'd considered trying out some of the devices and clothes, she'd found the idea more repellent than exciting.

She'd washed her hands after touching the things, just as she was washing her hands now.

All you touched this time were books, she thought as she rinsed off the suds. Hardly the same.

But what kind of person would enjoy reading that kind of junk?

Gillian recalled the uneasy feelings she'd had last night before even arriving at the house. Were they premonitions? Nonsense.

How about the way she reacted when the telephone rang? Phones had rung at odd times when she was staying at other places, but she hadn't panicked.

It was as if a shadowy corner of her mind knew she'd picked the wrong house this time.

"Bullshit," Gillian said. She dried her hands and stepped into the hall. "So what if the guy's a little bent."

That's what keeps it interesting, she told herself. Discovering the hidden quirks.

She took her Minolta from the bedroom and returned to the den and touched the books again. After arranging them on the floor with their front covers showing, she snapped a close-up. She put them away. Just to be thorough, she then grouped the photography books on the floor for a shot, then the body-building books.

That, she thought, takes care of his peculiar reading habits.

In books, at least.

The search for Fredrick's magazine collection took about two minutes. She found it in the bedroom in the bottom drawer of his nightstand, pretty much where she expected it to be. The magazines were neatly arranged in two stacks. True-crime magazines.

Kneeling on the floor, Gillian lifted out half a dozen. Most of the covers featured a woman in peril, usually sprawled at the feet of a man. Only the back of the man was shown. The woman invariably gazed up at him with terror in her eyes. She was dressed in scanty undergarments or a revealing negligee or a torn blouse. More often than not, her hands were tied.

Gillian looked through a few of the magazines. The stories had lurid titles: "Weird MO of the Sorority Killer," "Death of the Gang-Sex Beauty," "Rampage of the Peeper." There were grainy photos of murder weapons, cops investigating cases (usually in wooded areas), apprehended killers and their victims (before and after).

The advertisements seemed as strange as the stories. They pushed pamphlets revealing the secrets of how to build the body you've always wanted, how to earn big bucks at home in your spare time, how to become a detective, how to hypnotize girls "Secretly!" so they'll obey your every command.

There were several ads for trusses. Other ads urged readers to buy pellet guns, tear-gas guns, "authentic badges" and "durable, reliable" handcuffs.

Gillian had seen such magazines at news-stands, never suspecting they contained such garbage: stories to titillate you with the details of sex killings (including hints on police procedure to help you avoid capture), followed by those ads.

The crime books in the den were sophisticated literary endeavors compared to these rags.

Who reads this shit? she wondered.

Fredrick Holden, for one.

He's starting to look like a real sicko.

Gillian lifted more magazines out of the drawer. More of the same.

Then she came to the sex magazines.

"Surprise," she muttered.

Already feeling disoriented and revolted by the crime magazines, Gillian could only stand to look at a few of these. The photos didn't depict beautiful women in seductive poses.

The last magazine Gillian inspected dealt with bondage and sado-masochism. Then men and women pictured wore chains and leather. Some wore black leather masks that made them look like medieval executioners. The victims were tied spread-eagled to a bed or shackled to a wall or suspended from a ceiling beam. Gillian flipped the magazine shut. She closed her eyes and took deep breaths.

She felt as if she had descended into a dark world of perversity.

A world in which Fredrick Holden loved to wallow.

Any *more* nasty little secrets? Gillian wondered. She bent over the drawer and glanced at the covers of the remaining magazines. Most of those near the bottom of the drawer appeared to be S&M. She left them there.

She spread half a dozen of the crime magazines on the bed and took a photograph. She did the same with several of the sex magazines. After putting them back in the drawer, she returned to the bathroom and once again scrubbed her hands.

Enough goddamn exploration for one afternoon, she thought.

Keep it up, you might find something *really* nasty.

She gave a sour laugh. In the mirror above the sink, her face looked a little bloodless, her eyes glassy. There were specks of sweat above her lip. She hadn't taken pictures of the S&M stuff at the bottom of the drawer. Hadn't wanted to.

She felt nauseous. Needed fresh air.

Gillian changed into her damp bikini, grabbed a bath towel, and went to the den. She took a beer from the refrigerator behind the bar.

The hot concrete sundeck hurt her feet as she turned toward the spa. Setting her beer and towel aside, she started to remove the cover.

She hesitated.

So you really want to go in this guy's hot tub? Especially after that *dream* . . . God only knows what's gone on in it . . . who might be in the water.

Yuck.

She picked up the cold bottle of beer and took a drink.

Maybe I should get the hell away from here, she thought, while the getting is good.

"Hey there!"

Gillian whirled around.

Chapter Eleven

"Why don't we take a breather?" Rick suggested.

Bert grinned along with her frown. "You can't be pooped again already . . . a strong fellow like you."

"Must be the altitude."

"Okay. Five minutes."

He stepped backward to a waist-high boulder, eased his back down, and sighed as the straps went loose on his shoulders. The sigh was for Bert's sake. He'd found the hike rather easy so far and his occasional pleas for rest stops had nothing to do with the effort of lugging his pack up the trail. His only motive was to slow their progress, to avoid overtaking Jase, Luke, and Wally.

So far, fine. He hadn't seen them since that morning.

The boys had had a fifteen-minute lead by the time the tent was rolled, the packs were ready, and they started out. Fifteen minutes, Rick quickly realized, was too short a gap. Bert didn't hike with a leisurely stroll; she took long, sure strides that ate up the trail. Though Jase and Luke might be fast on their feet, Wally had seemed like the type who would hold them back. Rick felt sure that, without the frequent stops, they would've caught up with the boys by now.

There was also the possibility that the boys would take it slow or even stop and wait to make sure of another encounter with Bert. If that was their game, Rick's delays would only postpone the meeting, not prevent it.

Rick opened a side pocket of his pack and took out his plastic water bottle. He unscrewed the cap and took a drink, then passed it to Bert. The shadow of her bush hat left her face as she tipped back her head. She shut her eyes and drank.

"I'm wondering if we really want to go over Dead Mule Pass," he said. "Are we locked into that?"

"It's the route I planned," she said, and returned the bottle to him. "That's how we'll make a circle and get back to the car without backtracking. What've you got against Dead Mule Pass other than its name?"

"Sounds like a tough climb."

"That's a good one. All of a sudden you're pooped at every turn and worried about a little climb. Aren't you the same guy who did a 10K run last month?"

"That was different."

She lifted an eyebrow. "I *am* onto you, y'know. You don't have to pretend with me. Took a while, but I figured it out after about the third rest stop. You just don't want us running into our friendly neighborhood teen trio."

"Maybe."

"Maybe, my ass."

"It's your ass I'm worried about," he said, forcing a smile. "And other nearby areas."

"You still think they want to jump my bones."

"You think it hasn't crossed their minds?"

Bert shrugged. "I suppose it probably has. That hardly means they'll try it, though. There's an enormous gap between wanting something like that and actually trying it."

"Maybe. I just think we're better off avoiding those guys. I mean, we're out here in the middle of nowhere and they've got us out-numbered. Why tempt fate?"

"Rick, they're three guys on a camping trip. They seemed perfectly normal to me."

"Even Jase?"

She hesitated. Frowning, she said, "Jase I could do without. If I were alone out here and he showed up, I might be a little concerned. But you're with me, and Jase has Burgher and Wally in tow. Those two guys wouldn't try anything."

"If they thought they could get away with it, they might."

"Would you? Suppose the situation were reversed, and you're out here with a couple of buddies and run into someone like me? Would you and your pals try to rape me?"

"Of course not."

She put a hand on his thigh. "Sure about that? You're talking as if it's inevitable that all guys would try it in a situation like this."

"It would occur to most guys. It would occur to me, I'm sure. But I wouldn't do it."

"Why not?"

Rick shrugged. "Aside from being a decent guy with moral scruples, I suppose I'd be chicken."

"Afraid the cops'd get you?"

"That'd be a major deterrent. Thing is, and why I'm so worried, this area isn't exactly teeming with fuzz. We're pretty much beyond the reach of the law out here. A guy could get away with most anything." Rick went cold inside. "Especially if he didn't leave witnesses."

"Plot thickens," Bert said. "Now we're talking murder."

"You rape someone, you don't want a prison stretch, nobody knows you did it except you and the victim. Even if you're not a cold-blooded killer, you're scared. The thrill is over and you realize what you've done—the consequences if you get caught."

Bert's fingers tightened on his thigh.

"You take these three," he went on. "Jase wouldn't kill us out of panic. He'd be more likely to do it for kicks, or just to be on the safe side, or just for the hell of it."

"You don't even know the guy," Bert muttered.

111

"I know his type. Burgher, he seemed aloof. The rational sort. He'd see the logic of eliminating us and that might override his qualms about it. Wally, he'd panic. He'd no sooner get his pants up than he'd start seeing himself getting gang-raped in prison."

Bert looked into his eyes. "You're scaring me," she said.

"I just think we need to realize the—"

"I mean *you're* scaring me. What the hell is going on inside your head? We meet three guys who don't give us any trouble at all. Next thing you know, you've got them raping me. Jase kills us for kicks, Burgher kills us because it makes good sense, and Wally kills us so he won't get sodomized in prison. My Christ! Your imagination is revolting."

"I read the newspapers," he muttered, stunned by her reaction.

"Sounds to me like you're projecting your own fantasies onto those guys."

"My fears," he said.

Her eyes seemed to soften. "Oh, Rick." Her hand lifted to his face, gently stroked his cheek. "I shouldn't have dragged you out here, should I?"

"I was doing all right till those three came along."

"Doing all right? That's why you got yourself shit-faced last night?" Her tone was sympathetic, not accusing.

"I didn't get shit-faced."

"Maybe we'd better hike on back to the car and get out of here."

"Hell," he muttered.

"It's no good if you're a basket-case the whole time. It isn't fair to you."

"I'm sorry. I promised myself that I wouldn't ruin things. But I won't get this stuff out of my head."

"I'm the one who pushed you into this. I knew you hated the idea." A corner of her mouth curled up. "Guess we should've gone to Maui after all."

"I'd feel awful if we quit," he said.

"You'd feel worse if we stayed. Besides, you might be right

112

about those guys. I mean, I don't really expect them to attack us or anything, but just the fact that they're around—truth is, I've had some of the same thoughts as you."

"Really?"

She nodded. "My thoughts didn't go quite as far as yours. But it crossed my mind that Jase might talk the others into jumping us." Her smile widened. "In my version, they thumped you on the head with a rock, but I fended them off with my knife."

"Always the optimist."

"That's me. Anyway, all things considered, I won't be too disappointed if we leave."

"I guess we could head over to Lake Tahoe, check into a nice hotel . . ."

"Nothing to wear."

"They've got stores."

"Sounds good to—"

Her voice stopped.

Rick heard faint, distant talking. Fear clamped his chest. He handed the water bottle to Bert. Standing, he slipped his arms from the pack straps. He turned to his pack, reached for the side pocket where he'd put his revolver, and pulled at the zipper with trembling fingers. It was half open when he realized that the voices were female.

He glanced at Bert. She was watching him. With a shake of his head as if he were confused, he shut the zipper. He took the water bottle from Bert and slipped it into the other pocket.

"Afraid they'll try to bum our water?" Bert asked, grinning.

"Exactly. Wouldn't be sanitary." He rested against his pack again. He still heard the voices, but he saw nobody on the trail.

"From the sound of them," Bert said, "they're either girls or sissies."

They were girls. They came striding, side by side, around a bend in the trail.

The one on the right looked up, saw them, smiled and

113

said, "Howdy." The other, flushed and panting, nodded a greeting.

"Hi there," Bert said.

"Hi," said Rick.

"Let's take a load off," the girl said to her haggard friend. She stepped to the side of the trail across from Rick and Bert, swung her pack down, and boosted herself onto a hip-high shelf of rock. The other girl kept her pack on. It scraped against the vertical block of stone as she sagged. Her rump met the trail and she stretched out her legs. She sighed.

Her slim legs were tanned, her shins mottled with trail dust that had turned dark on her sweaty skin. She wore faded blue gym shorts and a gray T-shirt that read UCSC. Her shirt had a wet V, wide at the crew neck and narrowing as it descended between her breasts. Her chest rose and fell as she fought to catch her breath. The bill of her ballcap was tipped upward. A fringe of blond hair clung to her forehead and glossy wisps curled around her ears. In spite of her grimace and sunglasses, Rick could see that she was a beauty.

"From Santa Cruz?" Bert asked.

"I shoulda boogerin' stayed there," said the one on the ground.

The one sitting on the rock laughed. "We just got done with finals," she said.

"Great way to start the summer break."

"Andrea isn't used to this sort of thing."

"Neither am I," Rick said.

"I love it." The girl swept off her straw cowboy hat. Her thick, brown hair was pinned up except for bangs that fluttered in the breeze. Unlike Andrea, she looked cool and dry. She wore no sunglasses. Her brows were thick, her eyes bright green. Though she lacked Andrea's delicate features, she had a fresh, athletic look that Rick found appealing.

She tossed her hat. It landed on her pack, slid off, and dropped onto the trail. Leaning back, she braced herself with straight arms. She was wearing a yellow blouse. The sleeves were cut off, and it was unbuttoned and tied below her breasts. From the yellow cord across the gap, Rick guessed that she was wearing a bikini. Her flat belly was tanned. She wore jeans, the legs cut off so high that the ends of her front pockets hung out white against her thighs.

The way her jeans looked disturbed Rick. For a moment, he didn't know why. Then he remembered that Julie had worn jeans like these, cut so short the pockets showed. He'd been watching her instead of the trail.

My fault, he thought as a warm wave of shame swept through him. If I hadn't been trying to see up her pants . . .

It's not my fault, he told himself. She shouldn't have worn something like that if I wasn't supposed to look. A guy will look. Any guy will look. It was her fault more than mine.

". . . your car we parked next to this morning," the girl in the cut-offs was saying. Rick realized he had missed some of the conversation.

"A blue Pontiac?" Bert asked.

"Yeah, that's the one."

"So you just got in this morning?" Rick asked.

"Seems like a century ago," Andrea said. Still on the ground, she had slipped out of her pack straps without Rick noticing. Her gray T-shirt was dark around the armpits. She was no longer panting. "Bonnie doesn't believe in resting. You ask me, I don't know what's the big rush."

"I thought we'd make it over the pass today," Bonnie said, "but that's starting to look doubtful. There's a lake just this side, though. Fern Lake? I suppose we'll wind up there. What about you?"

Bert shrugged. "We're not too sure at this point."

"Are you going over the pass?" Bonnie asked.

"We might head back," Bert told her. "I'm not feeling too swift."

Bonnie frowned. "That's too bad. You might just pack it in?"

"We're considering it."

"That'd be a shame, you came this far."

"Sounds like a good move to me," Andrea said. She raised

115

one knee and folded her hands around it. Her other leg was still extended. Through the gaping leg-holes of her shorts, Rick saw her shadowed thigh. He looked away.

Bonnie had her ankles crossed.

"There are some guys up the trail," Rick said. "You may run into them."

"Guys?" Bonnie asked.

"Three of them," Bert said. "They're probably about your age."

"Oh great," Andrea muttered.

"What sort of guys?" Bonnie asked.

"How many kinds *are* there," Andrea said.

Bonnie uncrossed her feet and swung a boot sideways as if to knock her friend in the head. She missed. "Did they seem all right?" she asked Bert.

"I guess so."

"They're not a contingent from Stanford," Rick said, with a smile in Andrea's direction. Bonnie threw him a challenging look. He could've been mistaken, but he thought it said, *Get off my patch, mister. And lay off Andrea. She's mine.*

Andrea looked up at Rick and wrinkled her nose. "They're a contingent from like where?"

"The Youth Authority."

"I'm gonna barf."

"They aren't that bad," Bert said. "One of them did seem rather hard, but the others were okay. We had a chat with them back at our camp. They didn't give us any trouble."

"Sure they didn't," Andrea said. "You've got *him*."

"Rick," he told her, pleased that the girl believed his presence had prevented trouble.

"Yeah, you had Rick."

"How far ahead are these guys?" Bonnie asked. Leaning forward, she hunched over and put her hands on her knees. The front of her blouse bunched outward. Rick saw the side of her left breast. The yellow bikini looked too small to hold it all.

"Who knows?" Bert said. "We've been stopping a lot.

They might be half an hour up the trail, maybe farther."

"Or they might be just around the bend," Rick said.

"Just what we need," Andrea muttered. "Hassled by a trio of cretinous thugs."

"Who says they'll hassle us?" Bonnie said.

"They're guys, aren't they? No offense, Rick," she added, and grinned up at him with one side of her mouth. "I'm talking mostly your basic teenage toad. They got just one thing on their minds, and we all know what that is. Fucky-wucky."

"You're gross," Bonnie said.

"But perceptive." Andrea twisted her head around and peered up at her friend. "You think these guys are gonna just ignore us, we meet up with them?"

"You can level them with your tongue."

"Yeah, that'd be sure to save the day. Get the scrotes pissed at us." She turned to Rick. "Maybe the four of us oughta stick together for a while. You mind us tagging along?"

"They're leaving," Bonnie reminded her.

"Oh, yeah. Shit soup. You guys sure about that?"

"It's not definite," Rick said.

Bert looked at him. "We'll have to discuss it," she said. "If we change our minds, we won't be far behind you."

"Well," Bonnie said. "We'd better get moving." She leaped from her perch, picked up her hat and dusted it off. "If we don't see you again, have a good trip back."

"Thanks," Bert told her. "You too."

"I was just getting comfortable," Andrea complained, reaching behind her for the pack straps.

Bonnie lifted her pack off the trail without apparent effort, swung it onto her back, and slipped her arms through the straps.

Andrea struggled with hers. First, she clutched both straps and tried to rise from a squatting position. That didn't work, so she lurched forward onto her hands and knees, then thrust herself up.

"So graceful," Bonnie said.

Grimacing, Andrea rubbed her hands on her shorts. They left dust smears on the faded blue fabric. She turned her palms up. "Never gonna be clean again," she muttered.

"The pleasures of roughing it," Bert told her.

"Yeah. You guys really serious about leaving?"

"We'll see," Bert said.

Andrea grinned at her. "Want to loan us Rick for a few days? We'll make sure we get him back to you in good condition."

She caught Bonnie's sour look and rolled up her eyes in a gesture of mock despair.

What's with the attitude all the time, Bonnie? Can't take a joke? Loosen up for godsake, we're on vacation here.

Rick laughed. "I could go for that."

He was joking. Almost.

Bert slapped his leg. "Sorry," she told Andrea, "I'm afraid I can't do without him. He's my love-slave."

The girls, including Bert, laughed it up.

"Real cute," Rick said, smiling but embarrassed.

Still laughing, Bonnie and Andrea raised hands in farewell, turned away, and began striding up the trail. Rick and Bert watched until the two girls disappeared around a bend in the trail.

"Nice kids," Bert said.

"Yeah."

"So what about it?" she asked. "Do you still want to split?"

"I don't know," Rick said. "Maybe not."

Bert looked amused.

"You have to admit, they change the picture somewhat. In terms of the guys," he added.

"I'd say so," Bert agreed. "Substitute victims. If the boys are so inclined. Which would let us off the hook."

"They must be out of their gourds, coming out to a place like this. Two girls."

"Dykes," Bert said.

"You think so?"

She laughed. "Maybe. On the other hand, maybe not. Not

fully fledged yet, anyway. Borderline in my opinion. Bonnie's the pushy one and Andrea's playing hard to get. But don't quote me on that. And I don't think they're out of their gourds. They're probably safer out here than they'd be on the streets of Santa Cruz."

"That's not saying much."

"So what are we going to do?" Bert asked.

"I think they're worried about running into the guys."

"Of course they are. You made the fellows sound like escapees from a chain-gang."

"What do *you* want to do?" Rick asked.

"Let's stay. We'll give the girls a good long lead. The guys can jump them and fuck their brains out, and be too pooped to care by the time we go by."

"Sometimes," Rick said, "you're very strange."

She contorted her face and rolled her eyes.

"Does this mean you think we should join up with them?" Rick asked.

"I'm not thrilled by the idea, but I guess it makes sense. I get my camping trip, the girls get our protection, and you get to continue drooling over a couple of nymphets young enough to be your daughters."

"I wasn't drooling," Rick protested. "And I'm not that old."

She arched an eyebrow.

Rick grinned. "Maybe we'd better forget it. I just might lose control and go for them."

"I'm worried."

"Obviously."

"You get the urge, buddy, just remember something."

"What?"

Smiling, Bert gently squeezed him through the front of his pants. "They ain't me." She let go and patted his leg. "Come on, we'd better catch up with the children."

Chapter Twelve

Jerry Dobbs was smiling at Gillian over the top of the fence. "Sorry," he said. "Did I startle you?"

"That's all right." The jolt of alarm she'd felt at first hearing his voice faded, but her heart still raced from the shock of it. She managed a smile.

"A little warm today for the hot tub, don't you think? How about coming over here and joining me in the pool? I was just about to go in myself."

Gillian, surprised and delighted by the offer, didn't hesitate. "That sounds great."

"Come around to my driveway, I'll open the gate for you."

"Be right there," she said.

His face disappeared, and Gillian went into the house.

She knew she was breaking her rule against fraternizing with neighbors, but she didn't care. Ever since meeting Jerry so briefly last night, she'd hoped to see more of him. He must've felt drawn to her, also. A guy doesn't invite just anyone over to use his pool.

I'll have to watch what I say to him, she cautioned herself.

Wouldn't do, at all, to slip up and let him find out I'm not Fredrick's niece.

Fredrick, the sicko.

The house, though pleasantly cool after the heat outside, seemed forbidding to Gillian as she hurried toward the bedroom.

She dreaded the thought of spending another night in it.

I won't, she told herself. After I leave Jerry's, I'll pack up and get out of here.

In the bedroom, she set her beer bottle on the dresser and slipped into sandals. She turned to the wall of mirrors. And shook her head in dismay. The bikini was little more than cords that tied at her hips and behind her back and neck. Strung from the cords were flimsy, meager swatches of snug white fabric. Gillian felt naked. This was an outfit for wearing in private, not in front of strangers. She had a modest one-piece swimsuit for beaches and pools, but it was back in her apartment; she hadn't foreseen any need to bring it along.

That's because you don't go swimming with neighbors, she thought. Right.

She considered changing into shorts and a T-shirt.

He already saw me in this. He'd think I'm nuts.

With a sigh, she put on her shirt as a cover-up. The shirt was long enough to drape the scanty bottom of her bikini. She buttoned it, brushed her short hair, then picked up her beer bottle and headed for the front door.

She removed the burglar bar. Having no key, she left the door unlocked.

She walked across Jerry's yard and found him waiting at the open gate of his driveway. He was lean and dark. Instead of trunks, he wore an old pair of tan corduroys with the legs cut off.

"Glad you could come over," he said.

"Who could refuse a swimming pool on a day like this?"

He shut the gate. Gillian walked with him toward the rear.

"Enjoying the house-sitting?" he asked.

"It sure beats staying in my little apartment."

121

"Does your apartment have a pool?"

Gillian nodded. "I never use it, though. There could be thirty people watching you from their windows. Not to mention an assorted variety of tenants who might decide to join in the fun."

"Yeah. Know just what you mean."

His pool was shimmering and clear, its surface flat in the still afternoon.

"Feel free to dive in," Jerry said. "I think I'll get myself a beer. Could you use another?"

Gillian squinted at her bottle. It was half-empty. "Sure, why not?"

She sat at the table under the shade of its broad umbrella while Jerry went into the house. She sipped her beer. Her hand trembled slightly and she felt her heart thumping. She looked at the house. From the rear, it seemed similar to Fredrick's.

Bet it doesn't come with a collection of sick magazines, she thought.

Or mirrors on the ceiling.

Not that I'd mind the mirrors.

She wished her heart would slow down.

Take it easy, she told herself. Relax.

The rear door slid open and Jerry came out with a bottle of beer in each hand. He sat at the table. He pushed a bottle across to her.

"Beck's," Gillian said, reading the label. "I like it."

"What's that you're drinking?"

She slid the bottle toward him. "Corona. Have some. It's okay, I don't have any diseases." As the words came out, she felt herself blush. That's certainly laying the cards on the table, she thought.

Jerry drank from her bottle and nodded. "I'll have to pick up some of this stuff." He passed it back to her.

She drank the rest of it. "Uncle Fredrick has good taste in beer," she said. "I can't say the same for his taste in reading matter."

"Oh?"

Careful, she thought. "He seems to go in for some pretty gruesome stuff."

"I guess we all have our quirks."

"Does he seem all right to you?"

Jerry shrugged. "I'm embarrassed to admit it, but I really don't know the man at all. I've said hi to him a couple of times when we've crossed paths, but that's about the extent of it. He keeps to himself pretty much. So do I. Comes from all those years of apartment living, I think. The less I see of my neighbors, the better."

"That's why you poked your head over the fence and asked me over," Gillian said, smiling.

He laughed. "That's different." He took a drink of beer and flinched slightly as the bottle dripped water onto his chest. Gillian watched the clear bead trickle down his skin, leaving a shiny trail. He smeared it with the flat of his hand.

"Are you on vacation?" he asked.

"Me? I'm on permanent vacation," Gillian said. "I don't do much in the way of work."

"How nice for you. Wealthy family?"

"Dead family."

His eyes widened.

Gillian felt a little shocked herself. Why am I telling him the truth about my family? she wondered. Would've been easier to lie. She always lied about her background.

"I shouldn't be flippant about it. I'm sorry. But it's been a few years and I usually don't . . . I usually just make up a story. The fact is, my parents were killed in a traffic accident. A deputy sheriff's car lost its brakes while it was in hot pursuit of a robbery suspect and smashed into them. My parents' attorney filed a wrongful-death suit on my behalf, and it was settled for a good sum. I'm pretty well set up." Gillian shrugged.

"I'm sorry about your folks."

"Well, thanks. What is it that you do?"

"I design computer programs."

"Ah, you must be a brain."

"That's me." He laughed and took a drink of beer.

"What kind of programs?"

"I specialize in weapons systems."

"You mean like for missiles?"

"Something like that."

"Yikes. Guess I'd better stop asking questions or you'll put the FBI on me."

"That's right." He set down his bottle. "Well, I'm about ready to go in for a dip. How about you?"

"Sure." Gillian lingered at the table, taking another sip of beer while Jerry rose from his seat. He hitched up his shorts and turned toward the pool. Gillian pushed her chair back. He looked around at her. "You don't have to wait for me," she said, and crossed a foot over her knee to remove a sandal. Nodding, Jerry headed for the deep end of the pool. Gillian slipped off her other sandal and stood up. She slowly unbuttoned her shirt. As Jerry dove, she took it off. She draped it over the chair and stepped quickly to the pool, watching him skim beneath the surface to the opposite side. He was just coming up for air when she leaped. She hit the water in a shallow dive. For an instant, the chill was an agony. Then it felt good as she glided along through the silence. Her fingers touched the tile wall. She bobbed to the surface and stood. The water covered her to the shoulders.

She spotted Jerry near the middle of the pool, treading water, watching her. "I missed your dive," he said.

"Too bad. It was a ten."

"Let's see you go off the board."

"Thanks, anyway."

"I'll go first."

"I'm not stopping you."

He swam to the side and boosted himself up. His sodden shorts hung low. Gillian saw a pale band of skin where his tan stopped, the top of his buttocks. He tugged the shorts up as he walked toward the diving board. Pausing at the end of the board, he rubbed his hands together. "I'll now perform my world famous triple somersault."

He bounced on the board, springing higher and higher, his firm body shining in the sunlight. Suddenly, he tucked and hugged his knees. Gillian winced as his head barely missed the tip of the board. Midway through the first somersault, his back slammed the surface. A geyser of white water exploded.

He came up grinning foolishly, and Gillian clapped. "Bravo!" she called.

"Do I get a ten?"

"I'll give you a three on the grounds that you survived at all."

"Okay. Let's see how an expert does it."

"I don't know."

"Come on. I'm you can do better than me."

"I'm not much into diving."

"You're too modest."

That's about right, she thought.

Jerry side-stroked to the opposite side of the pool. Facing Gillian, he boosted himself up and sat on the edge. He grinned and wiped the water from his eyes. "I'll make you a deal. One dive will get you a steak dinner tonight. Barbecued by the master chef, me. How about it?"

"Shameless bribery," Gillian said.

"Naturally, the offer includes cocktails and hors d'oeuvres."

"What about dessert?"

"Ice-cream, followed by after-dinner drinks."

"And all I have to do is one dive off the board?"

"That's all."

"How come you're so eager for me to go off the board?"

"So I can get a good look at you," he said.

His smile vanished. "And so you can stop being nervous about your bikini."

"You noticed, huh?"

"Yep. You came over here in a shirt. That was my first clue. Then you kept it on."

"I don't usually parade around in something like this."

"But remember, I've already seen you in it."

"You took me by surprise."

"Nevertheless, the damage is done. I've seen what there is to see."

Gillian grimaced.

"I think we'll both enjoy ourselves a lot more once you get over the self-consciousness. You can stop worrying about what I might see, and I can stop worrying about *trying* to see what you're hiding."

"Makes sense," she muttered. She rolled her eyes upward and sighed. She wished she had left the shirt back at the house. Drawing attention to her timidity had turned out to be even more embarrassing than if she had simply shown herself from the start. "I feel like an idiot," she said.

"Don't. There's nothing to be ashamed of. If I were in your place, I would've been reluctant, myself, about going over to a stranger's pool in an outfit that exposed every intimate detail of my anatomy."

The remark stunned Gillian for an instant. Then, bursting into laughter, she cried out, "You bastard!"

He rocked, clutching his knees and grinning, delighted.

Gillian whirled around, still laughing, and thrust herself out of the pool. She strode toward the far end, scowling over her shoulder at him. "Every intimate detail, my ass!"

"That's included!" he called. He wasn't laughing anymore. His smile was slipping. He stared at her.

Gillian looked away from him.

It's all right, she told herself. Plenty of women wear as little as this to the beach. Why should it bother me?

Her wet feet slapped the concrete. Water trickled down her body. The cling of the bikini kept her terribly aware of how little there was of it. Her breasts, though firm and not very large, jiggled and swayed as if they were bare. Without looking down, she knew that her nipples were erect and that the fabric of the bikini was too flimsy to hide the fact.

At the end of the pool, she turned toward the diving board. Jerry was still sitting with his legs in the water. He was gazing straight ahead.

He's not even looking at me!

Gillian felt a mixture of relief and annoyance.

She stepped onto the diving board. Jerry kept staring into space.

She walked to the end of the board. It was springy under her feet. She stood straight, toes curled over the edge, and waited for the board to stop moving.

What's with this guy? she wondered. He bribes me to climb out of the pool so he can get a good look at me, and then it's like I'm not even here.

"Yoo-hoo," she called.

His head turned. "Oh," he said, as if mildly surprised to see her.

"Welcome back."

"Guess I was daydreaming for a second there."

"Gee, thanks. I thought you couldn't wait to ogle my marvelous, semi-nude body."

His eyes slowly roamed down Gillian. "And a fine body it is," he said. "Now, let's see if you can top my dive."

"That'd be tough," she said. What do you want? she asked herself. Do you want him to gape and pant in awe? Lick his lips? Drool? The bastard *could* show a tiny bit more interest.

Maybe he's gay.

Wouldn't that be a joke?

With a sigh, Gillian hopped. Her feet hit the board. She leaped as it flung her up. Soaring over the pool, she arched toward the sky, bent quickly at the waist and touched her toes, then straightened her body and knifed down into the water. When her fingertips brushed the bottom, she pushed herself away and glided to the surface.

Jerry held up both hands with their fingers spread. "Definitely a ten," he said. "I had no idea I was in the presence of a champion."

"I think it was a seven," Gillian told him. "But thanks."

"I knew you looked familiar. I saw you in the Olympics."

"I'm not that good," she said.

"Could've fooled me. And you claimed you weren't into diving."

"It was an easy one."

"Well, don't stop now. Let's see another."

"Okay, one more." She boosted herself out of the pool. "Don't expect anything spectacular," she cautioned him. "I'm a little rusty."

She was standing at the end of the board before she realized that she had forgotten to be self-conscious about her bikini. Jerry was watching her. He had an eager look on his face.

What the hell, she thought. He thinks I'm a great diver.

She bounced high, tucked, somersaulted, and went in straight and clean.

Jerry was clapping when she came up. "An artist!" he proclaimed. "A virtuoso. You could win trophies for that kind of performance."

"I've got a few," Gillian admitted, treading water just in front of his submerged feet.

"I don't doubt it. Let's see another one."

"I think two's enough," she said. "I don't want to press my luck. Next time, I might belly-flop and embarrass myself."

"Just one more?" he asked.

What's the point of refusing? she thought. He really wants to see me dive again, and I've got no good reason to disappoint him. "Okay," she said. "One more, and that's it. For now, anyway."

"Terrific."

Instead of crossing the pool to climb out where she had before, she swam to Jerry's side. He watched as she placed her hands on the edge next to him and thrust herself up. Gillian stayed there for a moment, braced with stiff arms. She saw him glance at her breasts, then look into her eyes.

128

"I'll do a really hard one this time," she said. "My grand finale."

Jerry made a thumbs-up sign.

Gillian swung her leg up, climbed from the pool, and hurried to the diving board. She walked out to the end of it, stood motionless until the board stopped shaking, then did an about-face.

Her back to the pool, she stood erect with her arms at her sides. She jumped, bounded straight up, came down again and bounced higher. On the third leap, she shot herself away from the board, did a quick somersault and snapped rigid, coming down fast with the board at her back and her arms stretched toward the water.

She had an instant of stabbing fear when she realized she had come out of the tuck too late.

Her head missed the end of the board. So did her upper back. It caught her just above the buttocks. She gritted her teeth as the board pounded her, scraped her and knocked her forward. She glimpsed her bare legs kicking against the pale sky. Then the water blurred her view.

She blew out air through her nose. Plunging toward the bottom of the pool, she wondered how badly she was hurt. She clawed at the water.

Then she felt a hand on her back. The hand found her arm and pulled her. She reached out and grabbed the side of the pool. Jerry was beside her.

His face looked pale. "My God," he gasped, "are you okay?"

She shook her head. Her heart was slamming with fear and her throat felt clamped tight. Tears filled her eyes. She crossed her arms on the tiles, and rested her face on them. Jerry's hand gently rubbed her back.

"I'm sorry," he whispered. "I'm so sorry. I shouldn't have made you do it."

"It's what I get . . . for showing off."

"Damn, I bet that hurt."

"I feel . . . like I got . . . kicked by a mule."

"You ever been kicked by a mule?"

"Don't be a wiseguy." She managed to swallow. She took a deep breath. She wiped a wet forearm across her eyes, then reached down and carefully fingered a raw area near the top of her right buttock. She could feel loose edges of skin that had been peeled down. Her left buttock was in better shape. It felt battered and slightly scuffed, but not flayed.

Suddenly alarmed, Gillian reached lower. Her bikini pants.

"Oh shit," she muttered.

"What?"

"I lost something."

"Don't worry about it."

"Easy for you to say," she told Jerry. She thought she was done crying, but her voice broke and her eyes flooded. "*Damn* it!" she gasped.

"I'll find them for you."

Jerry was no longer beside her. She wiped her eyes and turned around. He was far below the surface, kicking his way toward the bottom of the pool.

Gillian pushed away from the edge. She swam toward the shallow end, then stood. She was shoulder-deep. She peered down. The water blurred the view, but not enough.

Jerry was swimming toward her, well below the surface, the white rag of her bikini pants fluttering in his grip.

She drove her hands down quickly to cover herself.

Jerry veered off. So he has his eyes open under there, Gillian thought. Wonderful.

He swam toward the left, moved past her, and stood up. He lifted her pants out of the water. "Here you go."

He looked into her eyes. He didn't look down.

Gillian uncovered herself. She took the garment from him. The cords on both sides dangled, torn loose from the seat. "It's ruined," she muttered.

"You can't put it on?"

She shook her head. She sighed. She felt as if she might burst into tears again.

"I'll get you something to wear," Jerry said. He turned

away, waded to the side of the pool, climbed out, and hurried across the sundeck to the rear of his house.

While he was gone, Gillian moved to the pool wall. She pressed herself to it, feeling the slick tile against her belly and hips and pubic mound and thighs.

The initial pain had been replaced by a dull ache. Even the skinned areas no longer hurt much.

What hurt was the humiliation.

It wasn't much different from the time, a few years ago, when she got plastered at a party and barfed on the floor in front of everyone.

That was worse, she decided. This time, at least, it was an accident. It wasn't exactly my fault.

If I hadn't been showing off . . .

Jerry came out of the house with a blue terri-cloth robe. "This should do the trick," he said. He dropped it onto the pool deck in front of her, then turned away.

Gillian climbed out, hoping he wouldn't take advantage of the opportunity to look at her. She put on the bulky robe, and belted it shut. "Okay," she said.

He faced her. He was frowning. "Better?" he asked.

Gillian nodded. "Thanks."

"You really caught it."

"Yeah. I noticed. Thanks for pulling me out."

"Do you think you need a doctor? I could drive you to an emergency room."

"No, it's not that bad. I'll have an ugly ass for a couple of weeks, that's all."

Jerry smiled a little sadly. "It's a shame for something that gorgeous to get banged up."

Heat rushed to Gillian's face. "I'd better get going," she muttered. Stepping over to the table, she slipped into her sandals and picked up the shirt she had worn as a cover-up.

"You'll come back for the barbecue, won't you?"

"I don't know, Jerry."

"You earned it. The hard way."

"I don't know. This is all . . . pretty embarrassing."

131

"Yeah, I guess it would be." He lowered his voice. "Look, the invitation stands. I'd really like you to come over. But I'll understand, if you'd rather not."

"If I do come, are you going to make me dive?"

He looked up at her. "Certainly. If you won't dive, forget it. Stay home and starve."

"What time do the festivities start?"

"Say five?"

Gillian nodded. "We'll see. I'll bring you back your robe, anyway."

He walked with her to the gate, and opened it. "I'm awfully sorry you got hurt."

"I'm awfully sorry I lost my pants."

"I'm not."

"Screw you, buster."

He patted her gently on the arm. She stepped through the gate and walked down his driveway, trying hard not to limp.

Chapter Thirteen

"I think we should push on," Bert said. "It's still early, and Dead Mule Pass is only two miles."

"Two miles straight up," Andrea pointed out. "I don't know why we want to push it. This looks like a perfectly good place to spend the night."

Rick thought so, too. The lake was surrounded by trees, and the shady place where they'd stopped was close to the shore and had a rushing stream nearby. There were flat areas where they could pitch their tents, a ring of stones for a campfire, and sawn-off logs for seats.

Nobody was using the seats. All four had dropped to the ground and were resting against their packs.

"Let's go on," Bonnie said, looking up from a map spread across her legs. "It shouldn't be more than a couple of hours to the top. We'll come into a whole string of lakes just on the other side of the pass."

"Bug squat," Andrea muttered.

Bert smiled at her. "Look at it this way. If we don't go over the pass this afternoon, we'll be hitting it first thing in the morning. Wouldn't you rather get it over with?"

"Maybe it'll flatten out overnight. Maybe we'll die in our sleep. Maybe . . ."

"What do you think, Rick?" Bonnie asked.

"Yeah, Rick," Andrea said. "How about it? Which'll it be, the Bataan Death March with yours truly more than likely turning toes up along the way, or a pleasant afternoon relaxing here by the lake, possibly going in for a dip?"

"Well," he said, "it's two against one."

"Make it two against two. I'll give you my first-born."

"No fair bribing," Bert told her.

"It's nice here," Rick said. And it would be very nice indeed if the ladies decided to take a dip in the lake. "Also, the chain-gang is probably up ahead somewhere. I'd prefer not to run into them."

"Right," Andrea said. "We stay here, we won't meet up with The Three Thugateers."

"But I think we should keep moving," Rick finished.

"Stabbed in the back!" Andrea blurted.

"Sorry. I just think it'll be nice to get the hard part over with."

Sure I do, he thought.

He wanted to stay here. But Andrea wanted to stay and Bert didn't. He had to side with Bert, damn it. Because Andrea was young and beautiful, and it wouldn't look right if he didn't.

"Guess I'm out-numbered," Andrea said. "You guys'll regret it when I drop dead of heat prostitution."

"Prostration," Bonnie corrected.

"You die your way, I'll die mine."

They got up, shouldered their packs, and hiked up the path that led from the lake to the main trail, leaving the shade behind. Ahead was the barren, rocky side of a mountain with switchbacks zigzagging up its slope and no top in sight.

Rick supposed that Jase, Luke and Wally were up there someplace. But he wondered if he had misjudged them. If the

uys had any plans for staging a confrontation, they probably
ould've done it by now.

Unless they're biding their time, he thought, waiting for
ust the right opportunity.

Maybe waiting for nightfall.

If we'd just stayed at the lake, we might've lost them for
ood.

There are four of us now, he told himself. We've got them
ut-numbered. That should give them second thoughts. But
he temptation might be greater. Three gals instead of just
ne. Three times the temptation. Might be too much for
hem. Take me out of the picture, they'll have a field day.

Hell, they might not even know about Bonnie and Andrea.
I hope not.

Bonnie, in the lead, came to the first turn in the trail. She
ounded it and kept walking, facing them now as she started
p the next level. She swung her arms. Her stout legs took
owerful strides. She looked as sturdy as a tugboat.

Andrea, behind her, hesitated when she reached the turn-
ng place. Tilting back her head, she peered at the trail and
ared her upper teeth. Her chest rose. Rick could almost hear
er pained sigh as her chest deflated. Clutching the straps at
er shoulders, she leaned forward and started trudging. Her
egs looked too slim and frail to support her under the weight
f the big pack.

Bert, just in front of him, seemed neither as fragile as An-
rea nor as solid as Bonnie. Lithe and graceful, that was Bert.
ick watched her slender legs swing out, watched the way
he seat of her loose tan shorts moved with each step.

Here I am, he thought, one guy with the three of them.
Not bad. Better make that two of them, though. Count Bon-
ie out. Try anything with her, you'd probably get a right
ook for your trouble. Or a rock to the head. Good looker,
hough. So, count your chickens, Ricky baby, it's not all
ad—three gals and one guy. Know some dudes who'd give
heir eye teeth . . .

If I just didn't have to worry about those other guys . . .

and make sure Bert doesn't catch me eyeing the other two
Especially Andrea. Wouldn't mind seeing a lot more of tha
one. And she's available, looks like. Maybe she's straight afte
all.

Bert looked back at him. "You hanging in okay?" sh
asked.

"No problem. How about you?"

A corner of her mouth twitched. She turned around an
walked backward. "It's starting to get to me," she admitted
She took off her hat and rubbed a sleeve across her brow
Fringes of hair were clinging in damp curls around her face
Her faded blue shirt was dark around the collar. All but th
lower two buttons were unfastened. Her skin in the opening
gleamed as if it were oiled. She was breathing hard, and Ric
could see a glossy patch of skin below her sternum throb witl
her pulsebeat.

"Maybe we should take five," he said.

"Let's keep at it a while longer. Gotta get this over with.
With a wry smile, she shook her head and raised her arm
pointing at something behind Rick.

He looked around.

Bert was pointing at Fern Lake. It looked clear blue an
cold below them. "And to think we could be there righ
now," she said. "Maybe Andrea had the right idea."

"No pain, no gain."

"Wise-ass. Why didn't you talk me out of this?"

"Would've looked like I was siding with Andrea."

"Long as that's all you do with her."

"She's an eight, you're a ten."

Bert huffed out a laugh without much breath behind it
"I'd say she's more of a six, but that's in the eye of the be
holder." Grinning, she turned away.

She walked slowly, staying a few strides ahead of Rick
Even though the hike was beginning to take its toll on her
she could easily have passed Andrea. She was probably eve
capable of leaving Bonnie in her dust, if she had the incli
nation. Ever since they had joined up with the girls, however

136

Rick had kept to the rear and Bert had remained in front of him like a barrier. When Andrea slowed down, Bert slowed down even more. When Andrea stopped to rest, Bert stopped too, and the three of them waited until she was ready to move on.

Protecting her interests.

Just as well, Rick thought. It keeps the burden off me.

If Bert went on ahead at her normal pace, he would need to choose between trying to keep up with her (and letting Andrea disappear behind him), or staying back with Andrea (which would look as if he were choosing to desert Bert). Either way, it would've been lousy.

This was better.

A lot to be said for hiking behind the three of them. Nice view.

Too bad they aren't naked, he thought. On the other hand, that'd be rough. Then I'd feel compelled to take over the lead. The front view could be far superior to the rear. Rick smiled. Every silver lining has its cloud.

Be worth the effort, though. Plug on ahead. No pain, no gain. Get up in front for the view. Walk backward the way Bert was doing a while ago, careful not to fall on your ass or step off the side of the mountain. They'd be hiking toward him single-file.

Rick stopped smiling.

They'd still have on their hats, their socks and boots. They'd still be lugging their packs, the straps pulling their shoulders back and thrusting their breasts forward. Their breasts would jiggle and bob as they walked. Their skin would gleam with sweat. Their muffs would be powdered with trail dust.

"How about a little fucky-wucky?" Andrea called to him.

"Don't be so gross," Bonnie told her.

He asked Bert for permission. "Long as I'm first," she replied. Then all three gaped in alarm. Rick whirled around. Jase smashed his head with a rock.

He came to. The guys were gone. The girls lay sprawled

along the trail in motionless heaps. He rushed down to them and crouched over Bert. Her throat was split as if slashed by a razor. She had blood in her open eyes. Whimpering, Rick backed away and tripped over Bonnie. He rolled off her without looking and found himself on his hands and knees, staring at Andrea. She was staked to the trail, spread-eagled. Her neck was a pulpy red stump. Her head was between her legs, peering at him over the bloody mat of her pubic hair.

"It's all right." It was Bert's voice. He opened his eyes. His head was on her lap. Her throat was healed. She was in her clothes again, though her shirt gaped open and he could see the side of a breast above his face. She was mopping his forehead with a cold, wet rag.

Andrea and Bonnie were also alive again, both kneeling beside Rick. They wore clothes, but no packs. They were staring at him.

He suddenly had to vomit.

He lurched up and scurried away on hands and knees, but didn't get far before spasms wracked him and he heaved. When he finished, he crawled backward away from the mess. He turned around and met Bert's gaze. She looked worried.

"What happened?" Rick asked.

She shook her head. "I heard you groan. I looked back just in time to see you fall flat on your face."

"Christ," he muttered.

Bert passed a water bottle to him. He gulped the cold liquid.

"What was it?" Andrea asked.

Yeah, he thought. What was it? Exhaustion? Dehydration? The heat? He'd been feeling just fine before it happened. Having quite a pleasant, erotic daydream and suddenly it turned on him, twisted into something hideous.

As if all his worries about Jase, Luke and Wally had blasted to the surface and knocked him out.

Some kind of paranoia attack?

A premonition?

Rick felt a sudden chill.

That old John Newland show, *One Step Beyond*. People were always having dreams or visions foretelling disaster. ESP.

I've never had any ESP.

This was just my imagination taking a nose-dive.

"I don't know what happened," he said. "I guess I just passed out."

"Did you feel it coming on?" Bonnie asked.

"No, I was fine." He shrugged. "I feel all right now."

"We'd still better rest for awhile," Bert said. Putting a hand on his shoulder, she guided him down. He stretched out on the trail and lay his head on her lap. She smoothed the damp cloth over his brow.

"Maybe we'd better turn back," Bonnie said.

"If we'd stayed at the lake in the first place," Andrea said, "this wouldn't have happened." She sounded angry, as if she held Bonnie and Bert responsible. "He could've fallen over the friggin' side and broken his neck."

"I'll be all right," Rick protested. "We can go on in a minute."

"We're still a long way from the top," Bert told him. "I think Bonnie's right. We should go back down to the lake. We can tackle this again first thing in the morning when everybody's fresh."

"Before it gets so hot," Bonnie added.

"Really, I . . ."

"It's settled," Bert said.

Rick closed his eyes.

We're going back down to the lake, he thought. I wanted to stay there in the first place.

He wondered if a scheming corner of his mind had staged the nasty little skit in hopes of getting the group to turn back. Slap Rick off his feet, everyone gets worried, hy-ho, hy-ho, it's back to the lake we go.

It's what you wanted. It's safer there. The guys are up ahead, and it's the guys you want to avoid, so it's all working out great.

139

Great, except I conked out like a wimp, then barfed right in front of everyone.

Shit.

Way to go, Ricky-babes.

Hearing movement, he opened his eyes. And figured he saw a shadow. A darting figure disappearing behind a rock.

Gone.

A scrawny leafless tree dipping over the rock made short jagged patches of shadow.

He peered into the shimmering heat. Nothing but rock and goddamn tree. He groaned, snapped his eyes shut and shook his head. When he opened them he saw that Bonnie and Andrea were both on their feet, turning away from him. Bonnie strode up the trail toward her pack. She must have thrown it down and come running back when he passed out. Andrea's pack was next to Bert's, only a couple of yards away. As she went to it, Rick lifted his head off Bert's lap, hoping to orient himself because they didn't seem to be on the trail.

They were at one of the hairpins where the trail turned back on itself. One wing of the trail stretched downward along the mountainside, one angled upward to meet another juncture far beyond the place where Bonnie was swinging her pack off the ground. Rick raised his eyes. The side of the mountain seemed to go on forever. The higher switchbacks were barely visible, faint pencil lines zigzagging upward.

He looked at Andrea as she sat down. She leaned back against her pack and stretched out her legs. She folded her hands behind her head. The side of her gray T-shirt, from armpit to waist, was dark with sweat. Turning her head, she smiled at Rick. "Too bad you didn't flop a little sooner."

"I don't think it's something to joke about," Bert said.

"Who's joking? Felt like I was crawling up the bunghole of the universe. A couple more minutes, they could've renamed it Dead Andrea Pass."

Rick smiled at her, then put his head down. Bert's hip bone was against the nape of his neck. She turned slightly, and the knob went away. She felt good under his head. He pressed his face against her, then winced and turned away as the hot belt buckle stung his nose. Bert laughed softly. "Not your day," she whispered.

Nice view, though, he thought. If her shirt was open about one more inch, he'd be able to see her left nipple. If Andrea and Bonnie weren't around . . .

You'd better just forget about the goddamn nice views, he warned himself. They get you into nothing but trouble.

Bonnie appeared. She swung her pack to the ground not far beyond Rick's feet, then sat down on a boulder with her back to the mountainside.

"That lake does look nice down there," she said.

"Too bad we're not in it," Andrea muttered. "But at least we don't have to—"

"What?" Bonnie asked.

"Something flashed up there."

Bonnie twisted around and tilted her head back. "Where?"

"Way up. There it is again."

Rick felt a clutch in his chest. He sat up, scooted himself around in the dust until he was beside Bert, and searched the mountainside.

He too saw the flash. It was followed by a second blink of brilliant glare. Double-barreled, he thought.

"It's the sun hitting something," Bonnie said.

"A piece of glass?" Bert suggested.

"How about binocular lenses," Rick said.

Bert moaned and started to fasten a button.

"Cripes," Bonnie muttered.

"Those fuckheads are *spying* on us!" Andrea blurted. "Spy on *this*, you jack-offs!" She jammed her middle finger into the air.

Bonnie saw her do it. "Don't!"

"Maybe it's someone else," Bert said.

"I don't care who it is," Bonnie said. "They shouldn't be watching us with binoculars."

"Scumbags."

"It's them, all right." Rick had hoped that the boys didn't

141

know about Andrea and Bonnie. But they knew. And they were very interested, or they wouldn't be studying the group with field glasses.

Andrea got up. She walked in front of Rick and sat down near the end of the lower trail, her back to a cluster of rocks so she would be out of sight from above. "Aren't gonna get their kicks looking at me," she muttered.

Bonnie shoved herself off the boulder and squatted. "Maybe we ought to start down."

Bert nodded. "I don't like this at all."

You and me both, Rick thought. "Let's get moving."

Chapter Fourteen

Gillian woke up. She was sprawled on the water bed. Lifting her head off the pillow, she looked at the alarm clock on the nightstand. Three-twenty. That left more than an hour and a half before it was time to go over to Jerry's.

If I'm going, she thought.

She groaned as she climbed off the undulating bed. Her back ached, and her rump felt stiff and sore. Standing up straight, she turned her back to the wall of mirrors. She looked over one shoulder. Her right buttock had a three-inch band of shiny red near its top. Some curls of white skin rimmed the lower edge of the scrape. She picked at one of the larger pieces, thinking she might peel it off like the dead skin after a sunburn, but pulling it hurt so she stopped. The left buttock, now so raw, looked as if someone had taken a hard swipe at it with sandpaper. The skin around both abrasions had a rosy glow. That's where the bruises will come, she thought. That's where I'll be black and blue.

Could've been a lot worse, she thought.

The rosy glow suddenly spread. Even her face took on a deep red hue.

God, why couldn't I just get bashed up? Why did I have to lose my pants?

Talk about your Stupid Human Tricks.

Jerry was good about it, though. Hell, he was terrific.

He really wants me to come over.

And I told him I'd bring his robe back.

She lifted the robe off the foot of the bed where she had tossed it before flopping down. It was still damp inside. She didn't see any blood on the dark blue fabric, but maybe she ought to throw it into the washing machine, anyway.

She tossed the robe down, stepped into her sandals, and slipped into her shirt. The shirt felt fine. The way it draped her rear end, it didn't even touch the wounds as long as she stood very straight.

When she bent over to pick up the robe, the shirt fell lightly against the raw place. It stuck to moisture there when she straightened up. She plucked it away, thinking she had better bandage that side, at least.

First, I'll throw this in the wash.

She carried Jerry's robe outside.

On her way to the laundry room, she looked at the high redwood fence and listened for the splashy sound of swimming. There was only silence from the other side. Maybe Jerry had gone inside. Or maybe he was stretched out, sunbathing.

I might still be there, she thought, if I hadn't crashed and burned.

She saw herself lying on one of his loungers. She felt the heavy heat of the sun, and then Jerry's hands sliding over her skin, spreading oil on her back and legs.

It might have gone that way, she thought. With a sigh, she entered the laundry room.

In spite of the light coming in through the curtained windows, the room seemed dark after the brightness outside. Next to a large basin stood a drier. On the other side of the drier was a top-loading washer. A nearby shelf held a collection of detergents and bleaches.

No Sanctuary

Gillian lifted the lip of the washing machine and peered inside. The drum appeared to be empty. She stuffed Jerry's robe inside, sprinkled it with soap powder, and closed the lid. She changed the temperature setting to cold, and turned the dial to regular. The machine started with a rush of shooting water.

Jerry'll think I'm terribly domestic, she thought, returning the robe to him all freshly laundered.

Smiling, she looked away from the washing machine. At the end of the room stood a white-painted cabinet. Its doors were shut.

Normally, Gillian's curiousity would have been whetted by the sight. She would've hurried to inspect the contents.

But the urge wasn't there.

She realized that she'd had enough of Fredrick. She didn't want to inspect anymore of his possessions, didn't care to discover anymore of his secrets.

She left the cabinet unexplored and went out the door.

Walking into the driveway, she angled toward Jerry's fence.

Don't be a ditz, she told herself.

Why not?

On tiptoe, she peered over the top of the fence. The pool was deserted. Jerry was nowhere to be seen. Feeling a small tug of disappointment, Gillian turned away. She cut across the driveway and entered the den through its sliding glass door.

In the bathroom, she searched the medicine cabinet. She found adhesive tape and a roll of gauze. And three straight razors, one with a scrimshaw handle depicting an old-fashioned sailing ship. She picked that one up. Holding it carefully, she fingered a trigger-like lever and the blade flashed up.

She grimaced and muttered, "Yook."

Fredrick Holden *would*, she thought, have a collection of straight razors. They way his taste seems to run, he probably daydreams of slicing up naked women.

145

Maybe he does slice up naked women.

Goldilocks and the homicidal maniac.

Cute thought, that.

She looked closely at the white handle of the razor. Any bloodstains? Didn't seem to be.

She set the razor down on the edge of the sink, then took off her shirt. There was only enough gauze to make a bandage for her main scrape, so she didn't need the razor to cut it off the roll. Lucky me, she thought. She folded the netty fabric into a pad. Then she stripped off two lengths of tape to secure its edges. She used her teeth to rip the tape off the spool.

I could've gotten by, she thought, without even touching the damn razor.

She picked it up and carefully folded the blade. She put it back into the medicine cabinet, set the remaining tape inside and shut the mirrored door.

Her face in the mirror looked flushed. Specks of sweat glistened on her forehead, under her eyes, over her lip. A hand towel hung from a bar beside the sink, but the thought of wiping her face on one of Fredrick's towels was repulsive.

She used her shirt to mop the sweat off her face.

Then she stepped in front of the full-length mirror on the bathroom door. She turned around. Peering over her shoulder, she pressed the bandage into place.

She put on her shirt as she walked to the den. She went directly to the bar, opened the refrigerator, and took out a bottle of beer. After a few swallows, she sighed.

Now what? she wondered.

The washing cycle wouldn't be finished yet.

She wished she could take her suitcase out to the car. That way, there would be no need to return here after leaving Jerry's house tonight. But he might see her carrying it out.

I'll get it all ready, she decided, and leave it by the door when I go over. Then I'll just have to reach in, grab it, and take off.

Beer in hand, she stepped around the end of the bar and

glanced at the digital clock on the VCR. Three thirty-eight. Christ. Only eighteen minutes had gone by since she woke up from her nap.

Give yourself about twenty minutes to get ready, you've still got an hour to kill.

Read? She felt too restless to read.

So watch the tube, she thought.

She wandered over to the shelves and looked at Fredrick's collection of video tapes.

Should've known, she thought, as she started to read the titles: *Maniac, Texas Chainsaw Massacre, Halloween, Friday the 13th, 2000 Maniacs, Psycho, Dressed to Kill, Badlands, Visiting Hours, Mother's Day, Body Double, Sleepaway Camp, Return to the Valley of the Dolls, Ten to Midnight, The Ripper, I Spit on Your Grave*, and a lot more. Gillian had seen several of the movies in Fredrick's collection. Most of them featured nude women and nasty murders.

This guy has a real bent, she thought.

Crouching to inspect a lower shelf, she found some titles that were more to her liking: *Back to the Future, E.T., Star Wars, Alien, The Howling, The Snows of Kilimanjaro*, and about a dozen others. She'd never seen *The Howling*. She'd enjoyed the book, and the movie was supposed to be good. There wouldn't be enough time to watch all of it, but she could take a look at the first half, then rent the tape later and watch the rest back at her apartment. So she slipped its case off the shelf and carried it over to the television.

The VCR was a different make from hers. She studied it for a few moments, then turned on the television, pressed a button marked Power and another marked Play. The machine came on. She took her beer to the easy chair and sat down.

The movie opened with a young woman standing under a shower. She turned slowly, humming as she soaped herself and the camera roamed her body.

Werewolf victim number one, Gillian thought.

She was a little surprised by the explicit nudity. They even

147

showed a close-up of the girl's vagina as she stroked it with a sudsy hand. The picture quality was poor, too. It looked grainy and cheap.

Suddenly, the shower curtain shot open. The girl yelped in surprise as a hand grabbed her hair and jerked her backward. She fell over the edge of the tub and landed with a slap of wet skin against the tile floor. Kicking and whimpering, she was dragged out of the bathroom by her hair.

The screen went dark.

Against the black background appeared the words: *Torture Slave*.

What's going on? Gillian wondered. She glanced at the plastic box on the floor. It clearly belonged to *The Howling*, not something called *Torture Slave*.

Credits were still showing on the television. Screenplay by Tryon Cleaver, directed by Otto Keller. Obviously pseudonyms created by guys with terrific senses of humor.

Must be some kind of porn, Gillian thought.

The credits ended.

The girl from the shower was hanging by her wrists from ropes attached to ceiling beams in the living room of a house. She squirmed and screamed while a man in black clothes stood nearby. His back was to the camera. He was facing a fireplace, holding a wrought-iron poker.

Gillian muttered, "Oh, shit."

She rushed from her chair, stopped the tape and ejected it. Her hands trembled as she placed the cassette into the box labeled *The Howling*.

What kind of sick crap is this? she wondered.

She stepped over to the shelves and scanned all the titles on the three rows of video tapes. No *Torture Slave* in the whole collection.

She slipped the cassette back into its place and pulled out *Star Wars*. She opened the box. The cassette inside had no label at all.

She took it to the television. Crouching there, she inserted it in the VCR and pressed the Play button. For a few seconds, the screen was blank.

Then a young woman inside an elevator approached its opening doors. Before she could step out, two thugs in leather jackets rushed in, knocking her backward. She slammed against the rear wall of the elevator. Laughing, one of the men tore open her blouse. The other yanked her skirt up.

Gillian stopped the show. She ejected the cassette and took it back to the shelves.

Probably *E.T.*, *Back to the Future*, and the rest of them in this section of Fredrick's collection were more of the same. The popular titles on the containers were camouflage for his secret library of sick videos.

Where did he even *get* such things? Gillian wondered. Maybe he ordered them through one of those S&M magazines he kept in his bedroom. Did they come packaged as legitimate films? That hardly seemed likely. Pretty expensive, though, if he bought all those popular videos just for their cases.

The guy's loaded. He can afford to squander money when he has that much of it.

Why would he even bother? He could keep the things in a closet, or something. Maybe he enjoys having them hidden in plain sight. His little secret.

A guy like this, his mind's warped. He probably has plenty of strange games. I'd just as soon not run into anymore of them, Gillian thought.

She wondered if she should get her camera and snap some photos of his video tape collection. She didn't much care to have such a reminder; it would be like taking a little of Fredrick the Gross home with her. On the other hand, she already had shots of his book and magazine collection—with the exception of S&M and child porn. If she left without taking pictures of his tapes, she might regret it later. Besides, she had time to kill.

She went to the bedroom for her camera.

149

I don't have to put any of these in my scrapbook, she thought. Just throw them in the back of a drawer if I don't want to look at them. But at least I'll have the things.

Back in the den, Gillian removed *Psycho*, *I Spit on your Grave*, *2000 Maniacs*, and several more from the shelf of legitimate videos and arranged them on the floor. She took a close-up showing their covers. As she put them away, she wondered if even these were what they seemed to be. Probably. But she opened the case of *I Spit on your Grave*. The label on the cassette inside had the same title. So the psycho/slasher movies were for real. Naturally.

Crouching, she took down a dozen of the videos with the phony cases. She spread them on the floor, took a shot, and returned them to the shelf.

She wondered when she'd find time to put all this down into note form—but maybe she wouldn't want to; the pictures would speak for themselves. She returned to the bedroom with her camera and put it into the suitcase. The clock on the nightstand showed five minutes after four.

The washing machine had probably stopped by now.

Gillian hurried through the house.

I won't wait for five o'clock, she decided. As soon as the robe's in the drier, I'll come in and get ready. By the time I'm set to go, the robe should be pretty dry. Jerry won't mind if I show up a little early.

Outside, she resisted the urge to peer over the fence again. She walked straight to the laundry room. The washing machine was silent. She opened the lid, reached inside, and lifted out the heavy, sodden robe. She dropped it on top of the drier.

Bending over, she opened the drier's door.

And groaned.

Fredrick had gone off and left laundry in the machine.

Just what I want to do, Gillian thought. Touch his stuff. At least it looks dry.

Reaching into the drum, she pulled out a washcloth, a shirt, some white socks and a few pairs of brightly colored bikini underpants. She tossed them on top of a drier beside Jerry's robe. When she dragged out a large blue bathtowel, the machine was empty.

Except for a book.

It was oversized, with a brown leatherette cover, and looked like a photo album.

So what's it doing in the drier? Gillian wondered.

She supposed that Fredrick had put it there as a precaution, to save it in case the house burnt down while he was away.

She removed it, set it on top of the drier, and stuffed Jerry's robe into the machine. She closed the door. She pushed a button to start the drying cycle.

Then she stared at the album.

My big chance, she thought, to see what Fredrick looks like. A guy with mirrors all over his bedroom would probably have quite a collection of photos featuring himself.

It's more likely crammed with Polaroids of his girlfriends in the raw. That would be his speed.

Do I really want to find out? I doubt it.

Gillian left the album on top of the drier, turned away, and walked to the laundry room door. She stepped outside into the sunlight. Then she halted. She sighed.

If I look in the album, I'll regret it.

She muttered, "Shit," turned around, strode to the drier and picked up the album. Holding it under one arm, she walked quickly to the lounge and sat down. She rested the book on her crossed legs and opened it.

There were no photographs on the page. Pressed beneath the clear plastic sheet was a newspaper clipping. There was nothing to indicate the name of the paper or the date. Gillian read the story.

U of A CO-ED VANISHES

Foul play is suspected in the disappearance, Saturday, of 19-year-old Candice Fairborn, a University of Arizona co-ed, from her apartment on Spring Street.

According to police authorities, the roommate of Miss Fairborn returned to the ground-floor apartment Sunday evening after a weekend outing to find a rear window open. Further investigation led to the discovery of an upset lamp in the victim's bedroom along with the torn remnants of her nightgown.

Being sought in connection with the disappearance is Miss Fairborn's former boyfriend . . .

The story continued, but Gillian didn't bother to finish it. She turned the page. And found another clipping.

MYSTERY BODY GREEN BAY HOUSEWIFE

The partially decomposed body discovered Thursday by hikers in the Bagley Rapids area has been identified as Kathy Ellen Warnack, the 22-year-old wife of Ronald Warnack, who disappeared from their Jackson Avenue home on August 4.

According to the coroner's report, the slain woman had been sexually molested and died of multiple stab wounds . . .

Gillian had a tight, cold feeling in her stomach.

Why did Fredrick Holden keep these clippings? Why, indeed?

Her hand trembled as she turned the page.

GRISLY DISCOVERY

Saranak Lake—The remains of an unidentified female were found Saturday in a densely wooded area north of Saranak Lake . . .

She glanced at the next page. Eighteen-year-old Pam Jones had vanished from her parents' home in Park Ridge while they were out playing bridge. On the next page was the story of Maggie Drukker, a twenty-three-year-old housewife who disappeared from her New Orleans apartment while her husband was working the graveyard shift at the airport.

The raped and mutilated body of a Seattle secretary was found in the woods near Salem, Oregon, two weeks after her disappearance.

Remains, partially devoured by wildlife, were found in the bayou and identified by dental charts as belonging to Maggie Drukker, who had disappeared from her New Orleans apartment on November 2nd.

Page after page, the stories went on. Young women mysteriously vanishing from their homes or apartments. Corpses found in secluded, wild areas. On four occasions, stories of the discovered bodies matched earlier stories of disappearances. Gillian turned several pages and came to one without a clipping. The remaining pages of the album were bare.

She turned back to the final story.

MISSING TEEN FOUND SLAIN

Underhill—The raped and savagely mutilated body discovered Friday by hikers in the Smuggler's Notch area of Mt. Mansfield has been identified as that of 17-year-old Rhonda Bain, who was abducted May 24 from her parents' home in Burlington.

The nude corpse of the teen was found . . .

Gillian didn't read the rest of it. Numb and confused, she flipped to the front of the album. She counted the clippings. Twenty-six of them.

She looked again at each.

Most of the stories contained references to locations. Some of the areas were unfamiliar to Gillian, but she knew enough geography to realize that the disappearances and murders had taken place in states all over the country.

None in California, though. That was interesting.

She shut the album and stared at it.

153

Why, for godsake, did Fredrick Holden have a scrapbook like this?

Yeah, why?

Why do I keep my photographs and stuff?

To look at them and remember.

Chapter Fifteen

"You guys should get first choice of where you want to set up your tent," Bonnie said.

"I think we'll do some scouting around," Bert told her. "You can have this campsite. I'm sure we'll find a good one."

Rick felt something collapse inside. Oh no, he thought. Bert, no.

Andrea pulled a boot off and looked up, perplexed. "What do you mean?" she asked. "You aren't leaving, are you?"

"There's plenty of room here," Bonnie added. "There's no reason to go."

"I'm sure we won't go far," Bert said. "You girls didn't come out here to be stuck with us."

"And vice versa," Andrea muttered.

Bert didn't respond to that remark. "Maybe we can get together later on, tell stories around the campfire or something."

"Whoopee." Andrea looked at Rick. "I thought we were all going to stick together."

"Yeah. Well. I guess it doesn't really matter. We'll be close by, in case anything happens."

"Nothing's going to happen," Bert said. "I'm sure Jase and the others are over the pass by now." She turned to Rick. "Why don't we leave our packs here until we find a place? No point in lugging them around anymore than necessary."

Andrea peeled a sock off her foot and threw it down.

Rick followed Bert to a path near the shore of the lake. "There are probably a lot of good campsites," she said.

"This one has the stream. We want to have running water, don't we?"

"Maybe we'll find another stream."

They walked only a short distance before Rick spotted a clearing with a fire ring. "Let's check this place out," he suggested.

Bert scanned it from where she stood. "We can do better," she said.

It's too close to the girls' camp for her taste, Rick thought. Great. Wonderful. Shit.

They kept walking. Soon, they came to a clearing with a built-up fireplace that had a grate. There were logs for seats, even a makeshift table. The area had high clusters of rock on three sides that would provide a natural barrier against the wind.

It was probably not much more than a five-minute hike from the girls' camp.

"This looks perfect," Rick said.

"Not bad," Bert agreed. "Why don't we keep going, though? There's no big hurry. Maybe we'll run into something even better if we keep looking."

"Okay."

"Maybe we'll find a stream."

They found a stream.

But not before they had rounded the end of the lake.

Standing on a small rise, they stared down at it. The stream by the girls' camp was a trickle compared to this. The wide band of water rushed down over bare rocks, white and frothy in places; in other places gleaming like clear glass. Not far from where it spilled into the lake, the stream formed a wide pool.

"Oh, this is fabulous," Bert said.

Rick tried to spot the girls' camp. He couldn't. The stream emptied into an inlet with a rim of rocky, wooded land across the front. There was only a narrow opening between a high outcropping on the shore and the end of the sheltering arm. Bert couldn't have found a more secluded spot. And there was a camping area on the other side of the stream, down near the inlet.

She smiled at Rick and squeezed his hand. "Come on." She led him down the slope. She had a spring in her step. She really loves this place, Rick thought. And he couldn't blame her. But it was too far from Andrea and Bonnie.

When they reached the stream, Bert stopped at its edge. She stood there, turning her head, smiling as she watched it rush and swirl. It sounded like a strong wind, and a hint of coolness seemed to rise off its surface.

"What do you think?" she asked. She looked eager. And she looked ready for disappointment.

"It is nice," he admitted.

"I know we're a long way from the girls, but this is *so* beautiful and we'd have it all to ourselves. It's the kind of place I was hoping we'd find, even before we started out."

"Okay," Rick said.

"You *want* to camp with the girls, don't you?"

"No, of course not. It's just that we told them . . ."

"We don't owe them anything. Hell, we spent the whole day with them. We didn't come on this trip to have a four-some. We came to be with each other."

"It's just that I'm worried about them."

"The guys are long gone, Rick. The girls don't need our protection."

"No, I suppose not. I *said* we could stay here."

"Your heart wasn't in it. Do you *want* Andrea? Is that it?"

"Don't be ridiculous."

"Because if you do, just say so. I'll camp here, out of your

157

way. Maybe we can even get Bonnie to come over, so she won't . . ." Her voice snagged. Her eyes glimmered wet. She turned away.

Rick put his hands on her shoulders. "For godsake, Bert."

"I'm sure she'd be . . . more than happy to oblige you."

"It might be nice," Rick said. He felt Bert stiffen under his hands. "But she isn't you."

"Oh, I'm sure she has pretty much the same parts."

"So do a Volkswagen and a Rolls-Royce."

"Christ, you're going *automotive* on me?"

"Four wheels and an engine, but there's a difference."

"You don't even have a Rolls-Royce."

"Got you."

She sniffed and rubbed a shirtsleeve across her nose. "Yeah, you got me. Still want me to move in with you?"

"Will you?"

"No. But I'll think about it." She turned around. Her dirty, tear-streaked face wore half a smile.

"Your mascara ran," Rick said.

"What mascara?" The other half of her smile came up.

"You need to wash your face."

"Thanks, buster. You seen yourself lately?" She kissed him on the mouth. "Anyone for a bath?" she whispered.

"We'll freeze our nuts off."

"You may."

"We'd better get back," Bert said. "The girls might think we're lost and come looking. If they see you like this . . ."

"They'd go apeshit, but they'd be tough out of luck. I couldn't get it up now if my life depended on it."

"Wouldn't bet on that," Bert said.

He felt her hand.

"Ah, I was right." She patted his belly. "But enough of this. We'd better get dressed."

She sat up. Her back was speckled with grit. The smooth face of the rock still bore her wet imprint.

They both stood. Rick used his open hands to brush off

her back and rump. Then he turned around, and she did the same for him. "For a man," she said, "you have a very nice ass."

"Well, don't beat it to death."

She squeezed it and stepped away.

When they were dressed, they crossed the stream, leaping from rock to rock, and made their way down to the campsite. The shaded clearing had a fireplace with a grate, and a good flat area where they decided their tent would go.

"Looks fine to me," Rick said.

"Any more qualms about abandoning the girls?"

"They'll be all right."

"Would you feel better if we asked them to come over here? I'm not willing to give up this place, but if they want to bring their stuff over . . ."

"You've sure changed your tune."

Bert shrugged. "I guess Andrea doesn't seem like such a big threat anymore."

"I guess she wouldn't," Rick said.

Bert reached forward and clasped her hands behind Rick's neck. "So, what do you think? Should we allow them into our nice little hideaway?"

He slipped his hands inside her open shirt. He curled them over her breasts, lightly caressing the smooth skin and stiff nipples. "I don't think so," he said. "They'd just be in the way."

"Let's bring our packs over." She tipped back her head and squirmed against his moving hands.

"What's the hurry?"

"I want to . . . lie out on the rocks again . . . while the sun's still on them."

"That's certainly worth hurrying for."

She swallowed. "Thought you might think so."

Rick drew the front of her shirt together and fastened the middle button. She released his neck. Her hands glided down his shoulders, then dropped away.

He followed Bert across the clearing and up the rock slabs

159

to the stream. They hopped across it. The flat surface on the other side, where they had made love, was dry now.

Rick remembered how her wet skin had been cold at first, and stippled with goosebumps.

Then he remembered what his mind had done.

How could he have let himself imagine such things?

It had been Bert under him, but sometimes it was Andrea, Andrea naked on the trail to Dead Mule Pass, but not dead, not decapitated, alive and writhing, gasping and clutching at him as he rammed; and then she was Julie sprawled beneath him in nothing but her knee socks, Julie his stepmother, but she was no more dead than Andrea or Bert and those were her hands tugging at his buttocks to urge him deeper into her wet, hugging heat. Rick had thought, this is wrong, this is bad. But he couldn't help it. He loved it. He was having Bert and Andrea and Julie all at once.

It's these damn mountains, he thought, ashamed now that he'd allowed such fantasies to take hold. It's the mountains and not enough sleep last night and hiking all day in the heat. It's what happened with Julie all those years ago. It's Jase and Luke and Wally and knowing what they'd do to the women if they got the chance. Or is it what *I* would like to do to them?

Hadn't Bert suggested as much this morning?

You're scaring me, she'd said. *What the hell is going on inside your head?*

Your imagination is revolting.

Sounds to me like you're projecting your own fantasies onto those guys.

Yeah? And what was I projecting when we caught them spying on us with their binoculars? Was that my imagination, too?

But you have to admit, he thought, your imagination's been throwing some real curves lately. Some wild stuff. Dreaming up that slaughter on the trail, turning Bert into Andrea, which was bad enough but understandable; turning her into Julie, which was sick.

Need to get home. All this will stop when I'm home.

God, we almost turned back this morning before the girls came along. We'd be home tonight, or at least out of the damned mountains, maybe in a hotel at Tahoe, but I had to open my big mouth and talk Bert into staying. To watch out for the girls. To *watch* them, more like it. Had nothing to do with protecting them.

What did I think, I'd get in their pants? Fat chance of that, unless I bashed in Bert's head . . .

Or slit her throat.

"Oh my God!" Bert gasped. She stopped abruptly and grabbed his arm.

Rick felt a surge of dread that she'd somehow read his mind. His face burned. She's not psychic anymore than I am, he told himself. And I'm not. That trail massacre was mind garbage, paranoia, not a premonition.

But it came roaring back through his head—the sprawled naked bodies, the mutilations, the death—when he saw what Bert was pointing at.

Jase, Wally and Luke.

The three were crouched side by side among the rocks of an outcropping that jutted into the lake.

They had their backs to Rick and Bert.

The way they peered over the top reminded Rick of old westerns, of outlaws waiting to ambush a stagecoach.

"Those bastards," Bert muttered.

Rick pulled her off the path and into the trees, where they couldn't be seen if the boys should turn around.

"Those assholes are spying on the girls," she said. Her eyes looked fierce and unafraid.

"Close up, this time."

"Can you imagine? If that was them with the binoculars, they actually came all the way back down."

"Obviously liked what they saw."

"The nerve of those . . ." A red hue washed over her face. "You don't think they watched *us*, do you?"

Rick shook his head. "No. They don't know where we are."

161

"They would've, though. If they'd known."

"Yep."

"I'd like to rip out their eyes."

"It could come to that," Rick said. "They might not be happy, just looking."

"We'd better do something. Maybe we can sneak up and take them by surprise."

"And then what? I forgot to bring my black belt." *And my revolver's in my pack*. "I don't think this is the right time to confront them. We'd be . . . catching them red-handed. I don't think they'd like that at all."

"Screw what they'd like."

"If they feel cornered, they might decide to go for broke and have at us. I seriously doubt that we'd come out on top. Let's just stay out of their way. If we circle the lake, we can come around from the front and join up with the girls, and those three scums won't know that we're onto them."

"That makes sense," Bert said. "Yeah. That's what we'll do."

"Guess we can write this place off," Bert said when they came to the stream. "Now we've gotta stick with the girls."

"Maybe we can all come over here."

"Doesn't matter," she muttered. "It's no good now, anyway."

"I'm sorry."

She shrugged and looked at him. "It was nice, though, wasn't it?"

"Fantastic."

"At least we had that."

They hiked through the trees, staying away from the shoreline path, until they heard faint splashing sounds. Then Rick led the way to the edge of the lake. They ducked behind a deadfall and peered out through the rotted limbs.

"Oh great," Bert said. "Just great."

Andrea and Bonnie were directly across the lake from

hem, knee-deep in the water near the shore. Bonnie, in her
ellow bikini, was bent over and splashing herself. Andrea, in
black bikini, stood closer to the shore, rigid and hugging
er chest as if she were freezing.

Rick turned his eyes to the jut of rocks where the boys had
een. He couldn't see them.

"So where are the guys?" Bert asked.

"Still there, probably. Enjoying the view."

"Nice of the girls to be so obliging."

"They don't know they're being watched," Rick said.

Bonnie waded farther out. The water climbed her stout
egs. Her lips peeled back in a grimace when the cold lapped
er groin. She turned to face Andrea. She spoke, but Rick
ouldn't quite make out her words. When Andrea replied,
er voice carried clearly across the water. "Yeah, sure it's not
o bad. Tell me that when you're pissing icicles."

"Come on," Bert said. "Let's get going."

Rick glanced toward the rocks. This time he did see a
hadow. Small. Fleeting. Even imagined a low, cackling
augh. He exhaled slowly and shook his head in disbelief.
What was the *matter* with him? The place was giving him
he creeps, that was the matter. At least The Three Thuga-
eers were flesh and blood. He could handle them okay. But
kinny shadows? No way.

Bert was moving forward. Had she seen him staring at the
ocks like some crazy lunatic? In case she had, Rick said, "I
wish the guys would show themselves."

Andrea turned around and waded toward shore. Her hips
wayed. Her small, firm rump flexed with each step. Her bikini pants were low enough for Rick to see the shadow of
cleavage between her buttocks.

"Quit stalling," Bert said. "You're no better than those
eeping Toms."

"I just hope they don't do anything but look," he said.
"We'd better get over there fast."

"Before the girls get dressed," Bert added.

She *is* psychic.

163

*   *   *

With Bert in the lead, they stayed away from the shore, and only pale bits of the lake were visible through the dense trees to the right. A few times, Rick heard the girls' faint voices. There were occasional splashing sounds.

Finally, Rick saw bright orange in the distance. "Looks like a tent," he said.

Bert nodded.

They made their way into the clearing. Their own packs were on the ground near the side of the tent. The girls' packs were propped up against rocks, and open. Rick saw no one, not even when he turned toward the lake. He felt himself knot up.

Oh my God, he thought.

We would've heard shouts, he told himself.

Not necessarily. If the guys took them by surprise . . .

He headed for his pack.

"Going for your camera?" Bert asked. The smile fell off her face when she saw Rick's expression. "What's wrong? You don't think . . . ?" Her head snapped toward the lake. "Bonnie?" she called. "Andrea?"

"Over here," Bonnie called from the direction of the lake.

"You guys get lost or something?" Andrea asked.

Bert looked relieved. She glanced at Rick and rolled her eyes upward.

"False alarm," Rick muttered.

He followed Bert to the lake shore and they found the girls on a sunlit slab of rock that slanted gently into the water. They had their towels beneath them. Bonnie was sitting up, hands on her raised knees, looking over her shoulder as they approached. Andrea was stretched out, face resting on her crossed arms. Her bikini top, untied so the strings wouldn't leave marks across her back, was pressed between her body and the towel. The side of her breast was bare and pale. Rick forced himself to look away. He glanced to the left. The cluster of rocks where the boys had been lurking was farther away than he had supposed—maybe fifty yards off. With the binoculars, though, they'd still have a fine view.

"Don't look around or anything," Bert told the girls. "Try not to show any reactions."

Frowning, Bonnie turned herself around to face them.

Andrea lifted her head. She glanced from Bert to Rick.

"The guys are here," Rick said.

"You're shitting me," Andrea muttered. "*Our* guys? The chain-gang?"

"They're down the shore a ways," Bert explained. "Or they were, when we saw them about half an hour ago. They were hiding behind some rocks, watching the two of you while you were in the water."

"*Jesus.*"

"You're serious?" Bonnie asked. "They're right here at the lake?" She kept her eyes on Bert. Rick admired her restraint in not trying to spot them. "They were *way* up the trail above us," she said. "They came all the way down just to . . ."

"Must've really liked what they saw," Andrea said.

"Where are they?"

Bert turned so her body would block the boys' view, raised a hand to her belly, and pointed.

Bonnie still didn't look that way. Andrea tried, twisting her head to look over her shoulder and rolling just a bit. Her right breast unmashed and lifted partway out of the limp bikini. Bert sidestepped into the path of Andrea's view. Unable to see past her, Andrea eased down again. She picked up the ends of her bikini strings, bent her arms up high behind her back, and started to tie them.

"To get over there," Bonnie said, "they had to go right past us."

"You know, this really sucks." Andrea finished tying her bikini. She sat up, adjusted her top, and crossed her legs. "Do you realize how much this sucks? These scrotes came all the way down the trail. They were almost to the *top*. They came all the way back down and snuck past and spied on us like a bunch of fucking voyeurs. And we're not supposed to know they're around. What are they planning on, anyway? They obviously aren't gonna leave, not this late in the afternoon. It not only sucks, it's extremely creepy."

"Aren't they going to pitch tents or build a fire or anything?" Bonnie asked.

"If they do that," Rick said, "they'll give away that they're here."

"What they're gonna do," Andrea said, "is keep hidden and sometime during the night they're gonna move in."

Bonnie looked up at Rick. "What are we going to do?"

He thought about the gun in his pack.

"I'll tell you what I think," Bert said. "Why don't you two get into some clothes, then the four of us will take a walk and pay the guys a visit."

Andrea grinned. "Fuckin' A, right!"

Bonnie looked grim. She nodded. "Yeah, let's face the bastards."

"I agree," Rick said. "If there's going to be trouble, better to get it over with. While it's still light out and we can see what we're doing."

"What *they're* doing," Bert added. "And let's not go empty-handed."

Chapter Sixteen

"Damn it," Bert said. "I have to pee."

"Pick a tree," Rick told her.

She scanned the woods around the clearing. "What about our three friends? I certainly don't need an audience."

"They're probably still near the place where we spotted them. I don't think they'd come in close. Not while it's still light out."

"Want to come along?"

"I thought you didn't need an audience."

"You don't have to watch."

How do I get out of this? he wondered. The girls were inside their tent getting dressed. Bert going off to urinate would give him just the chance he needed to grab his revolver out of the pack.

Bert reached a suitable clearing, well away from the trail, bent over her pack and took out some toilet paper and a small plastic shovel. She frowned. And bent her head to get a closer look at what she saw on the ground.

A paw print. A large one.

"My God," she breathed, almost forgetting why she was here in the first place. Her stomach lurched and a warm patch began to spread between her legs. She clamped her muscles tight to stop the patch getting any bigger.

Bert rocked back on her heels. Trying to come to terms with what this new danger would mean to them. She leaned forward to examine the palm-size pawmark imprinted in the sand.

Relatively new. A few hours old at the most. Another one, to the right of the first, lay about eight inches ahead. She looked back and saw two more.

"My God," she whispered again. Cougar, by the look of it—and one helluva size. It's in the vicinity. Or was last night. Just passing through? Or is this its patch?

No sign of it now, anyway. She got to her feet. Slowly. Thinking, one cougar and you got more cougars . . . Great. That's all we need. Should've listened to Rick and gone to Mauii instead.

Scooping up her pack, paper and trowel, Bert raced back to Rick.

"Hey," she panted, pulling up short. She took a couple of deep breaths to steady the tremor in her voice. "Looks like we got company, Rick. Big cat type company . . ."

"Oh yeah?"

"Sure. Come see for yourself. I know cougars are around in the mountains, the Rockies, mainly. But let's hope this is a one-off that's strayed from home . . ."

She tried, but she couldn't convince herself that this cougar was a one-off. One vacation she'd helped out at a feline breeding center in Rosamund. From her time there, she'd learned enough about big cat behavior to know that there was probably a mom cougar, and a bunch of kitty cougars holed up in the rocks somewhere near.

Rick followed her back to the clearing.

Apart from coyotes and maybe the occasional wolverine,

he'd discounted other wildlife. Keep to the track, he'd thought. No problems if we keep to the track. But if it looks like we got mountain lions tracking us down as well as the teen trio, then maybe it's time to bring out the gun . . .

"We better keep our eyes peeled. For cats—and for The Three Thugateers," Bert said. "And tell the girls, too. Better safe than sorry. Anyway, we keep to the main trail, cougars won't bother us."

"Okay. But you said we shouldn't confront the guys empty-handed," Rick said. "What did you have in mind?"

"Weapons." She patted the sheath knife on her belt and eyed Rick's. "The girls have knives, too."

Rick opened the side pocket of his pack. He pulled out the T-shirt and unwrapped his revolver.

Bert gazed at it. "My God," she muttered.

"Just in case there's real trouble," he said. He lifted the back of his shirt and pushed the pistol under his belt. Its barrel slid down cool between his buttocks. He let his shirt-tail hang out to conceal the bulge.

"I don't believe this," Bert said.

"I knew you wouldn't like the idea. That's why I kept it out of sight. But it'll do us a lot more good than knives and a hatchet."

"You wouldn't shoot anyone?"

"If we're attacked . . . This isn't fun 'n games, Bert. We've got to be ready to protect ourselves."

"But a gun."

"They've got knives, too, you know. You actually think we'd stand a chance if it came to a fight?"

"I don't want anyone getting killed."

"As long as it's them and not us."

"You and Dirty Harry. Maybe we shouldn't take any weapons at all."

"Are you looking to get yourself gang-raped? Or chewed up by a cougar?"

"Yeah. Cougars." The color drained from her face.

"It'll stay in my belt unless they try for us."

"Promise?" she asked in a small voice. "You won't wave it in their faces and threaten them?"

"They'll never know I have it. If I pull the gun, it comes out firing."

"Don't let the girls know about it, either. Andrea—she might start something with the guys if she knew you had it."

"It'll be our secret. You and me."

"I wish it was just *your* secret."

"Well, now at least you know we've got some protection."

"A real comfort. You didn't happen to bring along a nuclear warhead?"

"Wouldn't fit in my pack."

Bert sighed. "Let's go. My teeth are floating."

He followed her out of the clearing. They leaped the small stream. A distance beyond it, he stopped and Bert went ahead. She stepped behind a tree. Rick heard her belt buckle, the rustle of fabric as she lowered her pants.

She didn't take it well, he thought. But at least she didn't go ape. She'll be damn glad I've got the gun if things get so bad that I have to use it. The look on her face when I mentioned getting gang-banged. Hell, she'd probably use it herself before she'd let that happen.

Give the gun to *her* if she's so afraid of what I'll do with it.

I don't think so. No, I don't think so. Not such a hot idea. She might not even know how to fire the thing, and even if she did, she might chicken out until it's too late. Too late for all of us.

I'll just keep it, thanks.

Just let them try something, they'll be dead meat.

Dead meat.

The words had a chilling ring to them.

Rick began to tremble. His breath hissed through his clenched teeth.

If I'd had a gun last time, Julie would still be alive. They wouldn't have fucked her and killed her. I'd have blown their heads off and saved her and we wouldn't have been alone together until Dad got back with help and Dad wouldn't have acted like *I'd* killed her and he wouldn't have turned into a drunk and killed himself and my life wouldn't have turned to shit.

All because I didn't have a gun.

Well, I've got one now.

Bert came out from behind the trees, fastening her belt. When she saw Rick, her face darkened. "What's wrong?" She looked around as if expecting to spot the guys.

"Everything's fine," Rick said.

"Is it?"

"I'm just worried about what might happen."

"What's to worry about? You've got your equalizer."

"Thank God."

They returned to the clearing. The girls were out of their tent. Both had changed into jeans and jogging shoes. Bonnie wore a sweatshirt, Andrea a red plaid shirt with long sleeves. It looked too big for her, and it wasn't tucked in.

"Do you have knives or something?" Rick asked.

Nodding, Bonnie patted a bulge in a front pocket of her jeans. Andrea lifted the front of her shirt. Sheathed at her hip was a hunting knife with a staghorn handle. "Bonnie has a tomahawk we could take along," she said.

"It's my brother's old Boy Scout hand-axe. But we probably shouldn't take it with us. I mean, we don't want to look like we've come to do battle."

"I agree," Bert said. "I think we should just play it very cool."

"Maybe you should do the talking," Rick suggested. "You were good with them this morning."

"Okay."

"And no mouthing off," Bonnie told Andrea.

"You think I'm stupid?"

"You flipped them off, didn't you?"

"That was different. They were ten miles away." She scrunched up her face and said, "Uh-oh. You don't suppose that's why they came down? Maybe I pissed them off and they came down to pound the shit out of me."

Her tone was half joking, but Rick could see that the possibility had her worried.

He'd read, last month, of a motorist being killed because he gave the finger to the driver of a pickup truck that cut him off. The pickup stopped, blocking the road. The driver got out, pulled the man from the car, and beat him to death with a tire iron.

"I'm sure your gesture didn't help the situation," Bonnie said.

"I doubt if that's why they're here," Bert said, and Rick nodded in agreement.

"Good. Glad of that. So all they want to do is fuck our butts off."

"Hilarious," Bonnie muttered.

"Come on," Bert said. "Let's get it over with."

She led the way. Rick followed. His leg muscles felt soft and shaky. Everything, he realized, felt soft and shaky, as if his skin was filled with jelly.

"Oh, and incidentally," Bert murmured, over her shoulder, "I came across cougar tracks when I went for a pee back there." She glanced at the girls' faces and saw that she had all of their attention. "Just thought you ought to know."

"Should we whistle a happy tune?" Andrea asked.

"Should we shut up?" Bonnie suggested.

"Everybody wearing clean panties?"

Rick heard a soft whack.

"Hey!"

"Just cut it out," said Bonnie. "There's nothing funny going on here."

"Why don't you lighten up." Andrea sounded hurt. "Just because we're walking toward our imminent defilement and demise, you don't have to be so fucking *tense* about it."

Rick looked back. "We'll be okay," he said.

Andrea made a grim smile. "Encouragement from the male. You ever hear the one about the Lone Ranger and

Tonto? They're surrounded by an Injun war party, they're out of ammo. The Lone Ranger turns to Tonto and says, 'Looks like we're gonna buy the ranch.' And Tonto, he says, 'What you mean *we*, white man?' "

We're not out of ammo, Rick thought. He wanted to lift his shirt-tail and let her see the revolver, but he'd promised Bert to keep the gun secret from the girls.

It would ease their minds, knowing.

But Bert was right. If Andrea knew about the gun, she might become very brave and make matters worse.

"We'll be all right," he said.

"Yeah? You got an Uzi or something?"

"No, but I'm good with my dukes."

She smiled. "That's consoling."

"Is this banter absolutely necessary?" Bert asked.

Rick faced forward again. "Just trying to keep up the morale of the troops."

Her eyes flashed. She looked shaky. Rick realized, suddenly, that he no longer felt loose and shivery inside. "The banter helps," he said. "Why don't I take over the lead."

Bert nodded. She stepped aside. Though the late afternoon was mild and they had been walking in the shade, she was wet. Honey-colored curls were stuck to her forehead. Her face and neck looked slick. The sides of her pale blue shirt were dark. Rick saw that she had buttoned it all the way up. He stopped in front of her.

"Are you okay?" he asked.

A corner of her mouth twitched. "Maybe we should turn back," she said. "The more I think about it . . ."

"Why don't I go on ahead," Rick suggested. "You and the girls could wait here. There's no need for all of us to confront those creeps."

"I'm not going to let you do it alone," Bert said.

"Besides," Bonnie added, "we don't even know for sure where they are. Or the wildlife, and I'm talking cats, here, for that matter."

"Yeah," Andrea said. "What if you go on your own, and the guys, or the cats, jump the rest of us?"

"The bastards are probably up near those rocks," Rick said, pointing. He deliberately didn't mention cats. They hadn't actually *seen* a cougar anyway, so in his opinion, The Thugateers posed a more immediate danger.

The rocks suddenly seemed very close. There it was again. Whoever, *whatever* it was, ducked out of the way, behind another rock. It wasn't one of the teens. Too thin, too wiry. Too spindly. What the hell was it? Good thing he'd got the gun.

For godsake, what *is* it about this place?

One thing's for sure. *Little House on the Prairie* it ain't.

Too right . . .

Best not alarm the girls till I know the score about our mystery stalker.

"We'd better all stick together," Andrea said. "It'll be four against three. Even if some of us are of the female variety, it doesn't mean we're helpless."

"And we've got our knives," Bonnie added.

"We'll stay together," Bert said.

Rick kept going. She moved on behind him. He felt her hand rub lightly for a moment between his shoulder blades. Then it was gone.

He walked along the shoreline path, closer and closer to the rocks where the boys had been crouching to watch Bonnie and Andrea. He saw no heads among the rocks.

They would've seen us coming by now, he thought. They probably took to the trees. We may not find them at all.

He passed the rocks, and looked back at the place where they'd been.

Gone.

Bert touched his shoulder. He snapped his head to the left.

Jase was sitting on a log beside the fire ring of a campsite not far from shore. He wore jeans and no shirt. He was star-

174

ng at them. A cigarette hung from a corner of his mouth.

Luke was stretched out on a sleeping bag in a patch of sunlight. His hands were folded under his head. He wore sunglasses and jockey shorts. His skin looked almost as white as his underwear, except for a cluster of zits in the center of his chest.

Wally, sitting cross-legged in the shade, was stripping the wrapper off a Mars bar. He still wore his cut-off jeans and camouflage shirt.

"Hi there," Jase said as Rick entered the clearing. Bert moved up beside him, and he heard the footsteps of the girls to the rear.

Wally looked up from his candy bar. A smile spread across his broad face. Luke propped himself up with straight arms and crossed his outstretched legs at the ankles.

"Thought you people would be on the other side of the pass by now," Jase said.

"We thought you would, too," Bert told him.

"Nope. When we got to this place, we decided to flake out."

"Wally was whining about his feet," Luke said.

Wally, chewing on his candy bar, nodded agreement.

"So you didn't go up the mountain at all?" Bert asked.

"Nope. Been here since about noon."

"Funny. We walked right by this place a couple of hours ago and you weren't here."

"Don't know how that happened."

"Must've been while we were gathering firewood," Luke said.

Rick glanced at the pile of kindling and branches near the fireplace. He hadn't noticed it when he and Bert had looked at the campsite earlier. But he was certain that the boys' packs hadn't been here either.

They're lying, he thought. Of course they are. They'd been the ones with the binoculars high up on the trail, and they'd come back down because of the women.

"Are you going to introduce us to your friends?" Jase asked.

"Tweedle-dee and Tweedle-dum," Andrea said.

Luke grinned.

"The friendly type," Jase said, and mashed his cigarette under his boot.

"I don't like being spied on," Andrea said.

"Shut up, would you?" Bonnie muttered.

"Has somebody been spying on you?" Jase asked.

"Sounds like she means us," Luke said. "Do you mean us?"

"Who do you think I mean, anus-face?"

"Woooo."

Bert whirled around and glared at Andrea. "Would you *please* stop it?"

"You people must have us mixed up with someone else," Jase said, all innocence. "We haven't been spying on anyone. We've just been hanging out, relaxing. Isn't that right, Wally?"

Wally swallowed and nodded. His face was bright red.

"Isn't that right, Luke?"

"We have simply been minding our own business. Frankly, I find myself disgruntled. Not only are we being unjustly accused, but my face has been maligned by this vicious wench."

"I think *you're* the one getting spied on," Wally blurted.

"Indeed. I believe they came here for the sole purpose of ogling me in my dainties."

"Nothing there to ogle," Andrea said.

Wally whooped. Jase's thin lips turned up. Bonnie squeezed Andrea's shoulder, making her grimace for a moment before she knocked the hand away.

With a thumb, Luke hooked out his waistband and peered down the front. "Oh yeah," he said, "something there all right. Want to see?"

"That's about enough," Rick said.

The elastic snapped down. Luke grinned at him.

"I don't know what you guys think you're up to, but I'd

ggest you pack up your stuff and get out of here," Rick
id.

Jase narrowed his eyes. "Hey, man, it's a free country. You
n't like us here, *you* move on."

"And have you follow us there, too?"

"We haven't followed you anywhere. We were here first.
ou don't like it, tough."

"We're not leaving," Bert told him. "We're staying exactly
here we are—and I'm sure you know where that is. We saw
u looking at the girls from those rocks by the shore. Now
re's the thing. Stay away. Don't come anywhere near our
mp, or else."

"Oooo, I'm trembling," Luke said. "I'm so scared I just
n't know *what* to do."

Jase sneered. "I don't know what your problem is. You
me in here like gangbusters, calling us names, telling us to
t out of here, threatening us. Where do you get off, huh?
e didn't do shit to you. Sure, we took a look when those
o were swimming. Why not? It's a public lake. They want
go swimming, we got every right to watch. So we watched,
what? I tell you, the view wasn't all that terrific. As for
aying away from your camp, you can bet on it. Give me
e good reason why we'd *want* to go near your camp."

"They probably think we want to molest them," Luke said.

"Wishful thinking," Jase said.

Wally, staring at the ground, chuckled.

"Just stay away," Bert said. "We don't want any trouble."

"You stay away from us. We're not interested. You gals
t the hots, you'll just have to settle for him." He looked at
ick. "I'm sure he'd be glad to . . ."

"Shut your face," Rick snapped.

He felt a tug on his arm. "Come on," Bert said. "Let's get
t of here."

"Yeah," Jase said. "Take him away before he loses his tem-
r and hurts me."

Rick stepped backward as Bert pulled him. Bonnie turned
vay from the boys. Andrea, still facing them, slipped her

177

knife out of its sheath and pointed it at Jase. "I'm gonna b
watching for you shitheads," she said, then turned around.

They walked toward the shoreline path.

The boys began taunting them from a distance.

"Oooooo," from Luke.

"Now they're threatening us with weapons," Jase said. "W
oughta get the cops on them."

"What cops?" Wally asked.

"That's right, there ain't no cops out here."

"Oh, dear!" Luke blurted. "Who, oh who, shall save u
from this tribe of paranoid Amazons? Are we damned? Is th
all she wrote? And me without a will!"

"Hey," Wally said, "you should've shown them your dick.

"Wally's getting brave," Rick muttered.

"They wouldn't have known what it was," Luke said. "Any
way, I didn't want to turn on that fag who's with them."

Rick looked over his shoulder. The trees were in his way

"What a bunch of crotch lice," Andrea said.

"Keep your voice down," Bonnie told her.

"They can't hear me."

"How many dykes does it take to screw a fag?" Wally
voice. Yelling.

"I don't know, how many?" Luke.

"*Three*, you dork! Two to hold him down and one to hol
him up!"

"The guy's a wit," Rick said.

Bert, walking beside him on the path, suddenly stoppe
and turned around. She glared toward the trees concealin
the boys' camp. Suddenly, she shouted, "*I gave you my mo
quito repellent, you fat tub of lard!*"

Rick looked at her, amazed.

"Well, I did," she said. A corner of her mouth turned u
Rick patted her rump.

They heard nothing more from the boys as they hiked bac
to camp.

Chapter Seventeen

"Is something the matter?" Jerry asked.

What could possibly be the matter? Gillian thought. I've just spent last night and today in the house of a rapist, a psycho, a homicidal maniac.

She shrugged her shoulders.

"You seem a little distant."

She forced a smile and waved across the patio table at him. "I'm all right here. No more than, oh, four feet away."

"Didn't like the dinner?" he asked.

"It was awful. That's why I gobbled it down like a sow."

"Are you saying it was swill?"

Gillian laughed softly.

In spite of his little joke, Jerry still looked concerned. "Is it something I did?"

"No. For heaven's sake. You've been great."

"If you're still upset about this afternoon . . ."

"It's not that. So I lost my pants in your pool? Big deal, huh? Yeah. Cripes." She picked up her mai-tai and drank the last of it. "It's Fredrick Holden."

"Who?"

Gillian realized that she had slipped. Maybe it's Freudian, she thought. Maybe I want to tell him the truth, the whole truth. And what would he think of me then? The girl's a lunatic who gets her jollies playing Goldilocks.

"Uncle Fredrick," she said. "I've found some things that have me worried."

"That's right, you mentioned this afternoon about his gruesome taste in books."

"It's more than just books. I had some time to kill before coming over and thought I'd take a look at one of his video tapes. I put one in his VCR. It was supposed to be *The Howling*. That's what the case said. It turned out to be some kind of sicko sado-masochistic shit called *Torture Slave*. I just watched a minute of it. The thing was vile. I mean, I've seen a few porno movies in my time. But this was different. This was like something they don't carry at the corner video shop. I did some snooping, and he's got a whole bunch of movies like that. They're all hidden inside cases for stuff like *Star Wars* and *E.T.*"

"How well do you know your Uncle Fredrick?" Jerry asked. He sounded worried.

"Not very well," Gillian said, surprised and glad that he hadn't made any jokes about wishing she had brought the tape along with her.

"Has he ever tried anything with you?"

She shook her head.

"It seems pretty odd that he would ask you to house-sit for him. He must've known that you might look at some of his videos. They weren't hidden? They were right out in plain sight?"

"On the shelves in his den."

"Apparently, he didn't care if you looked at them. Maybe he *wanted* you to look at them."

"Why would he want that?"

"I'd hate to speculate. I mean, he's your uncle."

Sure he is, Gillian thought.

"How long is he supposed to be away on this trip of his?"

"He told me he'd come back Thursday," Gillian said.

Jerry frowned at her. "I think it might be a good idea for you to get out of there. I think you should leave right away, go back to your own apartment and stay away from the guy."

"Trying to get rid of me?" Gillian asked.

"I'm serious. If those films are as bad as you say, he isn't just a normal horny guy who enjoys skin flicks. And the fact that he left them out for you to see . . . I don't like it. I don't think you should stay in his house. He might be planning to come back early, and . . . and I don't think you should be there when he does."

And Jerry doesn't even know about the scrapbook, she thought. Just the movies are enough to make him fear for my safety. Tell him about the scrapbook . . .

And he'd probably want to call the police.

And it would all come out that I'm a criminal. No thanks.

"As a matter of fact," she said, "I already made up my mind to leave. I'm all packed up and ready to go. Hell, I'd be gone now except I had to collect on your bribe of dinner."

Gillian stood up, lifting her plate and glass off the table. "Come on, let's take the dishes in."

He loaded his hands and followed her into the kitchen. Three trips later, the patio table was clear. Gillian opened his dishwasher.

"No way," Jerry said. "These can wait. Would you care for an after-dinner drink?"

"Trying to get me sloshed?"

Jerry stepped up behind her. He put his hands on her shoulders. The feel of them seemed to radiate down her body. The force of her reaction surprised Gillian. Is this the first time he's touched me? she wondered.

If you don't count towing me to poolside after my crash.

"How about coffee?" he asked.

"I was just kidding about you trying to get me drunk."

"I know. I'd rather have coffee myself. I'd hate to spend the rest of our evening in a drunken stupor."

"Me too."

He gave her shoulders a gentle squeeze, then stepped away and began to prepare a pot of coffee.

Gillian turned around. She leaned back against the counter. Its edge pressed her an inch above the abrasions. She wasn't in pain there, just a little tender. She watched Jerry.

He had dressed nicely for the dinner. He wore a neatly pressed, short-sleeved plaid shirt that was very much like the blouse that Gillian had decided to wear. His slacks were white, the same as Gillian's shorts. He wore topsiders, she wore sandals.

"Do you realize we match?" she asked.

He smiled. "I noticed." He dumped scoops of coffee into the filter.

It felt good to be with him.

She wished she could tell him her secret.

Maybe someday, she thought.

Don't count your chickens . . .

"There's a pen and notepad by the phone," Jerry said. "In case you want to give me your phone number." He glanced over his shoulder at her. "I don't even know your last name. I looked you up under Holden, but you weren't there."

"He's my mother's brother," she said.

Jerry's tried to find me in the telephone book. He wants my number. He doesn't want to lose me after I leave tonight.

God. All right!

"I'm O'Neill," she told him.

"Gillian O'Neill. Nice."

She stepped over to the telephone. On the pad there, she wrote her name, address and telephone number.

You're really giving it away, she thought. *You broke the fuck in next door*. He'll be able to tell the cops exactly where to find you.

It won't come to that. Probably.

So what if there's a risk?

While standing by the phone, she copied his number off

182

the sticker. She tore it from the bottom of the paper and tucked it into the pocket of her blouse.

Soon, the coffee was done. They took their mugs outside and sat at the table by the pool.

It was dusk. Darkness was not far away.

"I love this time of the evening," Gillian said. "It's so peaceful."

"Yeah." Jerry sipped his coffee. "We used to go out after supper for some bounce-or-fly on the street in front of the house."

"I did that. Didn't get up to bat very often, though. I wasn't much of a catch."

"I bet you were a good catch. I have the feeling you were something of a tomboy."

"Oh, hell yes." She drank some more coffee. It was hot and good. "I could knock a ball a mile. I just couldn't lay my mitt on it."

"Do you still like to play ball?"

"You being a wiseguy?"

Jerry smiled and they lapsed into silence. It was getting darker now.

"And now? I mean, what do you do now?" he asked.

Here it comes. Story time again, folks.

"Do? In my spare time? Well, I don't play bounce-or-fly, that's for sure!"

Jerry raised his eyebrows. Did he detect a challenge in her tone? If so, he wasn't sure he wanted to pursue the matter of her spare-time activities anymore. They had something good going here, and he didn't want to mess up.

She winked, threw him a quizzical smile and said, "I scribble."

"Scribble?"

"Sure. I scribble. Anything that comes to mind, really. Anything and everything. I have this wild, untamable imagination, and when I get bored with life, I just, well . . . scribble . . ."

"Okay. So you scribble. Do you often get bored?"

183

"Yep. Pretty often."

"You bored now?"

"Nope."

"Good. I would hate to think . . ."

"Jerry. Stop it. I'm having a great time. You're the perfect host," she laughed. "And I couldn't be less bored. Honestly. So please, let's drop it."

Jerry laughed. "As a matter of fact, I was thinking we might head over to a park sometime. I could pitch, you could hit."

"Like after dinner some night? That'd be neat. Of course, if you're into reliving childhood games, there never was anything as good as hide-and-seek. The hiding part, that's what I liked. Forget being 'it.' I loved to run off and duck into places that were small and dark where they'd never find you. It was always a little scary if you found a good place. I remember how my heart used to pound. Like I was afraid I'd get grabbed by something while I was waiting."

"It was always such a let-down," Jerry said, "when they gave up looking."

"Right. It's not that you wanted to be found, but you didn't want to be abandoned."

"Remember what a drag it was when you'd hear your parents calling your name? You knew it was time to go in."

"That's one of the great things about being an adult. Nobody to stop your fun." Gillian's heart started pounding hard. "Speaking of fun," she said through a tightness that had suddenly squeezed her throat.

Jerry raised his eyebrows and waited.

"Why don't we go swimming?"

He beamed. "Hell, yes. What about your injury, though?"

"I'm just skinned a little. The water will probably feel good."

"Great. But wasn't your bikini wrecked?"

"I'll go in in my skivvies."

"Skivvies?"

"My bra and panties. If you will." She shrugged and smiled.

She took a sip of coffee. She had trouble swallowing it. "That sound all right to you?"

"This is the same Gillian O'Neill who was here this afternoon and didn't want to be seen in a bikini?"

"Not exactly," she said. "This is a Gillian who's gotten to know you better."

"And who's had a few mai-tais."

"I'm perfectly sober. Somewhat sober. Besides, it's dark now. Of course, if *you're* too bashful . . ."

"I'll go in and get the towels," he said. He took a final drink of coffee, then pushed his chair away from the table, got up, and went into the house.

Gillian was relieved that he'd left. She suspected that he'd gone for the towels as a ploy to let her undress in privacy. Decent of him. She had thought she would have to strip in front of him, and had rather looked forward to it, but this made it easier.

She stood up. With trembling hands, she unbuttoned her blouse and took it off. She folded it and placed it on the seat of her chair. Then she stepped out of her sandals. She lowered her shorts, stepped out of them, and dropped them onto her blouse.

The warm breeze roamed her body. She felt naked. Looking down at herself, she supposed that the black bra and panties were no more revealing than her bikini had been. Though the bra had lace cups, the darkness of the night prevented much from showing.

Still, she thought. This isn't a bikini, this is undies.

Jerry might have been right about the mai-tais.

Too late to back down now.

Who *wants* to back down? she asked herself.

She felt daring. It reminded her of the way she used to get when she broke into houses. The feverish thrill of the break-ins had diminished over the past couple of years, so that recently it had been little more than a faint stir of excitement. Not like this. This was intense. Her heart was slamming. Her mouth was dry. Her nipples ached under the soft touch of the bra. Her panties were clinging in front.

She looked at the lighted kitchen door. No sign of Jerry.

Reaching back with one hand, she peeled off her bandage. She set it down on her shorts.

Then she stepped to the edge of the pool and dove in. The cold of the water was a harsh shock for an instant. Then it felt fine. It felt better than fine, caressing her everywhere as she glided along below the surface. When her fingertips touched the tiles at the far side, she came up.

She swam toward the shallow end. Finding the bottom with her feet, she stood up. The water covered her to the neck.

Jerry opened the sliding door and stepped out, holding towels in his arms. "You're already in," he said. "I missed the show."

"Tough toenails," Gillian said. Then she gritted her teeth to stop the tremor in her jaw.

Jerry dropped the towels onto the table. "So you just get to stay in there and watch me?" he asked.

"That's the picture."

Shaking his head, he sat down on a chair and took off his shoes and socks. Then he stood and removed his shirt.

"Maybe you could turn on the patio lights," Gillian suggested.

"Yucka yucka," he said. He unbuckled his belt, opened the waist button of his trousers, and slid the zipper down.

"We could use some stripper music," Gillian said.

He pulled his trousers down.

Gillian thought he was wearing boxer shorts, but a white cord hung over the elastic waistband.

"That's a swimming suit!" she blurted. "Cheat! Cheat!"

Jerry shrugged. "No reason we should *both* embarrass ourselves."

"Creep! Heel! Scab!"

Laughing, he said, "Okay, okay," and pulled down the trunks. He was wearing something white and scanty.

"Is that a swimming suit, too?" Gillian asked.

"Nope. I swear."

"Better not be. We had a deal."

"How do I know *you* don't have a suit on?"

"Just have to take my word for it."

Turning away, he walked toward the house. He stopped at a switch plate on the wall. His arm went up. The water surrounding Gillian was suddenly illuminated by lights below the surface.

She looked down at herself. Her breasts and bra were distinct in the shimmering light, the lower areas of her body slightly blurred.

"How's that?" Jerry called, his hand still on the switch. "Or would you prefer it dark?"

"This is nice," she said.

He walked toward the pool. He stopped at its edge and rubbed his hands together. "How's the water?" he asked.

"It won't kill you."

Balancing on one foot, he crouched a bit and dipped his toes in. The light from the pool fluttered on him. He looked lean and strong. His brief shorts hugged his hips. His penis, bulging against the thin fabric, looked as if it might thrust its way up through the waistband.

He seemed very nonchalant as he took his foot out of the water and rubbed his hands together again. Doesn't he realize? Gillian wondered. Of course he does. And he knows I'm watching. He must want me to see, want me to know he's turned on.

He took a deep breath, then leaped from the side in a low powerful dive that took him far out over the water before he knifed in with barely a splash. He was a pale streak below the surface for a moment. Then he came up at the wall and gripped its edge. "Not bad," he said, "after the first shock."

Gillian nodded. She didn't trust her voice. It would probably come out shaking.

Jerry stayed where he was, hanging onto the edge of the pool several yards away.

Gillian stayed where she was, too.

This is silly, she thought. Say something. Do something.

"Let's see one of those fancy dives," Jerry said.

"Oh, sure thing." She was right. Her voice shook when she spoke. "You just want me to lose my pants again."

"Never crossed my mind." Jerry pushed himself away from the wall. He kicked and stroked his way slowly backward, but he headed straight for the other side instead of approaching Gillian.

Don't just stand here like a jerk, she told herself.

Leaning forward, she left her feet. She did the breast stroke toward the deep end, keeping her face out of the water and gazing at Jerry as she glided closer to him. He had stopped short of the wall. Treading water, he watched her go by.

"That isn't your bikini," he said.

"That's right." Under the diving board, she turned around to face him. She kicked hard, reached high, and caught an edge of the board with one hand. Pulling herself up, she clutched the other side of the board. She hung there, out of the water to her waist. The air felt chilly on her wet skin.

Jerry stared at her.

She let go with one hand. Dangling under the board, she pawed her side with a floppy hand, stuck her chin out, and grunted like an ape.

Jerry didn't crack a smile.

"You're not amused?" Gillian asked.

"Me Tarzan," he said, and lunged at her.

Gillian yelped. She clutched the board with her other hand, pulled herself up and raised her legs. She kicked water at Jerry. He grabbed one of her ankles. "Don't you da—!" He tugged. She lost her hold. Dropping rump-first, she took a deep breath.

She kept her eyes open. At first, she saw only white froth. Then Jerry was above her. His eyes were open, too. His mouth was shut, but curled up at the corners in a mischievous grin.

He was above her, not touching her, just gazing down and

grinning. He waved. Then he twisted around and began swimming away, still under the surface.

Gillian went after him.

She gained on him.

She grabbed his foot. A pull sent her rushing forward over the backs of his legs. She hooked the fingers of her other hand under the band of his shorts, but let go as he rolled and looked up at her.

His impish grin was gone.

He reached up to her. His hands stroked the sides of her head, slid down along her neck and caressed her shoulders. Gillian ran her hands lightly down his forearms.

Letting go of him, she swam forward. She felt his touch all the way down her body as she glided over him. The she twisted around and stood and gulped air.

Jerry came up.

They faced each other.

The water was as high as Gillian's neck.

Jerry moved into her arms. They held each other. They were both gasping, and didn't kiss.

"Tarzan," she said. She looked into his eyes. His wet lashes made tiny points.

"Jane?" he asked.

"Gillian and Jerry," she whispered.

She hugged him tightly. He was warm and smooth and hard.

Chapter Eighteen

We just need to get through tonight, Rick thought as he lay in his sleeping bag, staring up at the slanting walls of the tent.

After dinner, Bert had taken out her map. She had studied it with her flashlight while they sat around the campfire, and found a route that would lead them around the foot of the mountain, avoiding the trail up to Dead Mule Pass. "We can wait and make sure the creeps are on their way up to the pass. Then we'll take this trail, and it'll be the last we ever see of them."

"Unless they come back down again when they realize what we're doing," Andrea said.

Bonnie got up from the log where she'd been sitting, and crouched behind Bert to look at the new route. "I don't know," she said. "That would take us right to the edge of the wilderness area. Look at that road. The trail runs almost over to it."

"Afraid we'll get hit by cars?" Andrea asked.

"It's just a crummy little dirt road," Bert said. "Not like we'll be back in civilization."

"I guess this is better than having to cope with those jerks."

"Who are probably gonna jump us before long."

"For godsake, Andrea."

"She has a point," Rick said. "It's all well and good to make plans for tomorrow, but the main thing is getting through tonight."

"They could be watching us right now," Andrea said, gazing into the darkness beyond the campfire. "Just waiting for the right moment to make their move."

"What are we going to do?" Bonnie asked. "We've got to turn in sooner or later."

"We'll just have to post guards," Rick said. "Can you two hang in for a couple of hours?"

"Sure," Bonnie said.

Andrea nodded.

"Stay by the fire and keep watch while Bert and I get some sleep. Then we'll relieve you, stand watch for a couple of hours, and get you up for another turn."

"Funzies," Andrea muttered.

"Whatever you do," Bert said, "stay together."

"Right," Rick agreed. "Nobody should go off alone for any reason."

"Not even to pee," Bert said. "If you have to do that, stay close to camp. Better yet, don't even leave the clearing."

"And let out a shout if anything starts to happen."

Rick had considered giving the revolver to them before he and Bert turned in. He decided not to. That way, he would still have the final control over everyone's safety. Though the tent flaps were down, they weren't zippered shut and neither was the mosquito netting. He was fully dressed except for shoes. He could be out of the tent, gun in hand, at the first sound of trouble.

He wished he could sleep. Bert had dropped off almost at once. At first, he had been able to hear the hushed voices of the girls. Though their words were masked by distance and the rushing sound of the wind, at least the talking had assured him that everything was okay. During the past half hour or so, however, he hadn't heard them at all.

He heard the wind. He heard the crackle and pop of the campfire. Sometimes there was a soft crunch like a footstep near the tent, which could have been a pine cone or limb hitting the ground; could have been almost anything—including a footstep.

Mr. Shadow Man?

The girls are fine, he told himself. They just ran out of things to talk about.

They'll come along pretty soon to wake us up for our turn.

Rick pulled his arm out of the sleeping bag and checked his wristwatch. Ten forty-five. Their turn at standing guard wasn't supposed to start until eleven-thirty. He returned his arm to the warmth of the bag.

Maybe the girls fell asleep, he thought. Sure. Bonnie's sitting on a log, Andrea on a rock. They might drowse a little, but they aren't going to conk out.

What if the cougar shows up? Nosing around for a late-night snack . . .

Why don't you just crawl out of your bag and take a quick look?

What if they're not there?

He pictured them sitting close to the fire while Jase, Luke and Wally crept up behind them. Arms hooked the girls across the throats and jerked them backward off their seats. Choked, unable to shout for help, they were dragged away from the camp. Taken far off into the trees.

They're right outside the tent, Rick told himself quickly before he could start imagining more. Nothing's happened. It's all in your mind.

He slipped the revolver out of the boot near his head and sat up. The fluttering light of the fire was faintly visible through the translucent tent flaps.

He squirmed out of his sleeping bag, picked up his rolled parka, and crawled to the front of the tent. There, he parted the flaps a bit and peered out through the gap.

192

Bonnie and Andrea were sitting by the fire, Andrea leaning forward to add a stick to the blaze.

I *knew* it was all in my mind, he thought.

You didn't know any such thing.

Rick put on his parka. The warmth felt good. He slipped into his jogging shoes and tied their laces. He put the revolver inside his coat and clamped it against his side. Then he crawled out.

Bonnie saw him coming and looked at her watch. "You're early," she said.

"Couldn't sleep, anyway. How's it going?"

"No problem," Bonnie said.

Andrea grimaced. "No problem if you don't count freezing your ass numb."

"Stick it in the fire," Rick suggested.

"Then she complains about the rivets in her jeans burning holes in her butt," Bonnie said, smiling.

"You can't win," Andrea said.

"Well, I'll take over the watch. You two can go ahead and sack out. That should thaw you out," he told Andrea.

"What about Bert?" she asked.

"I'll let her sleep for a while." He sat down on a flat rock, leaned forward, and held his hands out over the fire "No point in both of us suffering."

"I'm not sure there's a point to any of this," Bonnie said. "They haven't tried anything yet. Maybe we've just blown this whole thing out of proportion. You know? I mean, who's going to look the other way if he's seen a couple of gals in bikinis. And, when you think about it, that's really all they did, isn't it?"

"They didn't come all the way down the mountain," Andrea said, "just for a closer look."

"They claimed they were never up there."

"They lied."

"It's very possible they won't try anything," Rick said, trying to sound as reasonable as Bonnie. "But we should be prepared in case they do. All it'll cost us is a little discomfort.

I think that's preferable to letting our guard down and hoping for the best."

Andrea nodded her agreement. "I don't want to wake up and find a strange cock in my—"

"Cut it out," Bonnie said.

"That's the first thing I'd do."

Bonnie shot her a sour look and Rick grinned. "Anyway, I'll keep watch. So you won't have to worry about that."

"Are you just going to let Bert sleep?" Andrea asked.

"Might as well."

"I'll stay for a while then."

"What about your frozen ass?" Bonnie asked.

"I think somebody should stay out with Rick, don't you? If he's alone, he can't cover his back."

"Whatever you want," Bonnie said. "I'm turning in. And if you're asking, I'd advise you to do the same, Andrea."

"Yeah, sure. See you soon, Bonnie."

After Bonnie was inside her tent, Andrea got up from her rock. She turned her back to the fire and bent over. Her jeans were tight and faded, their rear pockets frayed. There was a butterfly patch over her left buttock. "Pardon the view," she said, looking over her shoulder at Rick.

"View's not bad."

She rubbed her seat with both hands. Then she stood up straight and turned around. "It's true about the rivets, you know. They heat up really fast. I've probably got little red burn spots on my butt." She sat down again and pushed her hands into the pockets of her puffy down vest.

"Don't your arms get cold?" Rick asked. They were covered only by the sleeves of her plaid shirt.

"They're all right. How long have you and Bert been going together?"

"A few months."

"Live together?"

"Not yet."

"Oh yeah? Who's the holdout?"

"She's not ready to give up her independence."

"Where've I heard that before?" Andrea smiled. She looked beautiful, her eyes shining, her face burnished in the trembling glow of the firelight, glossy curls hanging across her forehead from under the edge of her stocking cap. "How come you let her talk you into this torture-fest they call back-packing?"

"She had her heart set on it. I didn't want to disappoint her."

"That's about the way I got into this. Bonnie got the god-damn call of the wild, and talked me into coming along. Too bad we all didn't run into each other a lot earlier. Those two sourdoughs could've kept each other company and left us out of it."

Rick smiled. "Those are the breaks."

"What would you like to be doing right now, if you weren't stuck out here in the armpit of the universe?"

"Ideally. Maybe sitting at home with a drink, watching a good movie on the VCR."

"Yeah. All right. What kind of movies do you like?"

"All kinds. Thrillers, mostly."

"I knew a guy who lived off campus and had a VCR. All he ever played on it were sex movies. The idea was, I was supposed to get turned on and go crazy."

"Did it work?"

She smiled. "Maybe. How about Bert? Does she like to watch that kind of stuff?"

"She'd rather do it than watch."

"Well, lucky you. Does she see . . . other guys?"

"Not that I'm aware of."

"What about you?"

"I'm not into guys."

"You know what I mean."

Rick's heart quickened. Good Christ, he thought. Don't jump to conclusions, maybe she's just curious. "I haven't," he said. "It . . . hasn't come up."

"It has now," Andrea said.

"She might wake up." His voice came out hoarse.

"That's a chance we'd have to take. We could go off into the trees."

"What about our three friends? Not to mention maybe mountain lions on the prowl?"

Still smiling, Andrea stood and brushed off the seat of her jeans. "I can see you're not ready for this. But it's gonna be a long night. If you change your mind, you'll know where to find me." She nodded toward her tent.

"Bonnie's in there."

"She won't tell. In fact, I'm sure she'd be happy to keep watch later on. We could use the tent."

"I don't know."

"Think about it," she said. Then she turned away. She strolled across the camp, bent down, and crawled into her tent.

For a long time, Rick sat motionless.

He stared at Andrea's tent.

Then he got up. He went to his pack and took out the bottle. When he returned to the fire, he sat on the rock where Andrea had been. That way, her tent was behind him so he wouldn't have to look at it.

He opened his parka, took out the revolver, and rested it on his lap. Then he unscrewed the cap of his bottle and drank. The bourbon heated a path down his throat, spread warmth through his stomach.

You're going to stop thinking about Andrea, he told himself.

He thought about how she had looked sitting across from him in the firelight. He remembered the way she had rubbed the seat of her jeans and he could almost feel her buttocks through the warm denim. He had half expected her to show him the marks that she suspected the hot rivets had put on her rump. If the rivets felt so hot, were they pressing her bare skin? Wasn't she wearing panties? He wondered if she had taken off her jeans before getting into her sleeping bag. Maybe she had taken off everything, and was lying awake, naked in the snug warmth, waiting for him.

No Sanctuary

If you change your mind, you'll know where to find me.

I'm not going to change my mind. Not the right place. Not the right time. There's Bert. And you never know when those three scumbags might come sneaking out of the trees.

Rick looked quickly over his shoulder. He scanned the darkness behind him. Then his gaze lingered on Andrea's tent.

When their time for watch comes up, he thought, she'll probably stay inside, expecting me. How am I going to handle that?

Maybe I won't tell them when it's time. Maybe I'll just stay here all night.

He turned again to the fire. He took another drink and looked toward the dark bushes. A rustle. Then the crack of breaking twigs. His head snapped forward, eyes riveted to the bushes. His breath came in shallow gulps.

Christ. My nerves are shot.

Another swig.

And another rustle. More of a flurry this time.

Birds?

Not in the dark.

The Thugateers? Jase, Luke—but not Wally, the scrote'd be asleep.

Who then?

Rick held still for a while.

No more rustles.

Silence.

Thank God.

Then, *"Drink is the devil's curse! 'Tis Satan's brew to be sure. It poisoneth the soul!*

"Repent, sinner, and mend thy ways afore it's too late . . ."

The words hissed loudly in Rick's left ear.

It was *that* close.

He twisted away and rolled off the rock. Hit the ground and lay there. Gasping for breath. Panting with fear. Choking on the pall of fetid breath that still warmed his cheek. It was wet with spittle. Uhhh . . . He rolled over, heaving and grunting with disgust. Slashing at his face with both hands.

"God almighty!"

Outlined in the darkness, a man dressed in animal skins stood astride Rick's body, his bony arms akimbo on his hips. Atop his head was the head of a coyote, flaps of gray fur hanging and winging about his shoulders. The coyote's mouth hung open, showing teeth and a lolling tongue. There were dark holes where its eyes had been.

The weird headgear swung back and forth as its owner shook with rage. Rage? Rick couldn't distinguish. Laughter? Yeah. The bastard was laughing. High-pitched squeals of glee.

A sweaty, hormonal *animal* odor swept up Rick's nostrils as the creature side-stepped away from his body and skipped backward.

"What . . . *who* in hell are you?" demanded Rick. The god-damn bastard was right about the Devil's brew. I *am* seeing things—I gotta be!

"Angus is the name. Dearly beloved son of the Right Rev. John Brown McTavish! I was brought to this wilderness fifty years ago to preach the good Lord's word. Aye. Praise be to the Lord. A-men!"

With a manic cackle the creature lifted a scrawny arm above his head, crooked the other at his hip, did a quick jig and then vanished, cackling, into the night.

The bottle was three-quarters empty. Rick held it toward the fire and shook it, watching the amber fluid swirl.

So that's what it was. Stalking us. A bastard preacher-man gone ape. My God . . . The fuckin' cotton-pickin' lunatic . . . Aawgghh . . .

Better cut it out or I won't have any left for tomorrow night.

He stood up. The revolver slid off his lap and dropped, its muzzle pounding his left foot. He winced at the sudden hurt, then bent over and picked up the weapon. He carried it in one hand, the bottle in the other. Bending over his pack, he put away the bottle.

He stood up straight. He breathed deeply. The chill night air smelled of pine. Just like a Christmas tree lot. He was a kid, and he'd gone with Dad and Julie to the Lopez Ranch to pick out a tree. They wandered through a maze of spruce and pine. Their breath made white plumes. Julie wore a down vest. Her jeans had a butterfly patch on the seat. Her jeans were cut off so high that the bottoms of her rear pockets hung out. Odd that she would wear such pants on a night like this. Odd, but nice.

Julie slipped in sideways between two trees, and vanished. Rick stayed with his father. Together, they inspected a silver spruce to see if it had any bare spots. It looked good. "Go find your mother," Dad said. "We'd better get her approval."

Rick squeezed his way through the trees, smelling their rich scent, feeling their limbs run like soft, cool brushes against his body. He came out the other side.

And almost tripped over Julie's leg. She was sprawled on the ground of an aisle between the rows of Christmas trees, naked except for a single knee sock. Bert lay nearby, the handle of a knife standing upright in the center of her chest. Reeling, Rick staggered sideways. His bare foot (why was he naked?) came down on Bonnie's belly, slipped into a gash and sank deep into her warm guts. With a gasp, he pulled his foot free and stumbled to the other side of her body before falling. He landed on his hands and knees between Andrea's spread legs.

Jase and Luke were on each side of him, holding Andrea by the ankles. Wally was sitting on her face.

"Go to it," Jase urged him.

"You killed her! You killed them all!"

"You did," Luke said.

"All your fault," Wally said, and bounced on Andrea's face, his blubber shaking.

"No!" But Rick looked down at himself. His body was slick with blood, his penis erect.

199

"What are you waiting for?" Jase asked. "Go to it, pal."

"Don't worry about Bert," Luke said. "She'll never know." He chuckled.

NO!

Rick was on his knees, doubled over, his forehead pressed against the cool damp mat of the forest floor. He pushed himself up. The revolver was clamped between his thighs. He wrapped his hand around its grips, and stood up. His legs had pins and needles, and he was barely able to keep himself up.

The campfire had burnt down to a heap of glowing embers. He looked at Bert's tent, then at the girls' tent. Then he scanned the dark trees surrounding the camp.

He wondered how long he'd been out of it.

Must've been a long time, or his legs wouldn't have fallen asleep like that.

What if Jase and Luke and Wally had come while he was . . . was what?

What the hell was all that, anyway? he wondered.

An hallucination? A nightmare? A premonition?

And Angus, the mad preacher. A fantasy? Or the real thing?

His heart started thudding hard. He licked his dry lips.

He walked to the remains of the fire, crouched there and tossed sticks onto the embers. White smoke rose off the sticks like thick steam. The wind shredded the smoke and cast it away.

With a sudden *whup*, flames erupted.

Firelight shimmered on the front of the girls' tent.

Rick stood up, trembling. He switched the revolver to his left hand and wiped his right hand dry on the leg of his pants. He fingered the handle of the knife sheathed at his hip.

He glanced at Bert's tent and half hoped to see the flaps bulge and Bert crawl out, ready to join him on the watch— and in time to stop him.

He turned toward the other tent.

Were they both asleep in there? Or was Andrea still awake, waiting for him?

He pictured the way they had looked on the ground in the Christmas tree lot, all three of them, and Julie—naked and dead. *Go for it*, Jase whispered.

Taking the revolver into his right hand again, Rick stepped around the fire and walked away from its heat.

Chapter Nineteen

Monday June 23

Jerry had said, "Why don't you stay here tonight? We'll ge
your stuff out of your uncle's place and bring it over."

"Right now?" Gillian had asked.

"Maybe not *right* now."

They were both naked in bed. He was lying on his side
propped up on an elbow, looking at her body in the candle
light while his other hand rested open on her hip, fingertip
moving ever so slightly in the curls of her pubic hair. Gillia
was on her back, hands folded beneath her head. She fel
worn out and wonderful.

"In a little while," Jerry said.

"I might not be able to walk," she told him.

He laughed softly.

"I'm serious. You ruined me. I might need a wheelchair.

Gillian wished, now, that she had taken him up on th
offer. She didn't want to leave her suitcase in Fredrick Hol
den's house overnight, and now Jerry was asleep.

But she had been lying there, peaceful and weary, his fingers toying with her hair, feeling too good, too full, too ruined to move—even the short distance toward his side of the bed so she could get away from the cool, wet place on the sheet.

We *should* go over now, she had thought. Get it over with. Then I'll never have to set foot in that maniac's house again.

She had been about to tell Jerry, but his hand moved. His fingertips slid and her breath snagged.

"Are you really ruined?" he whispered.

She took a hand out from under her head. She touched him. Then she rolled toward him, smiling, shaking her head, nudging him onto his back. Straddling him, she held his shoulders and eased herself slowly down. His warm thickness spread her, slid in deeper and deeper, filled her. She sighed and shut her eyes. She felt his hands close gently over her breasts.

All thoughts of going next door for her suitcase were gone.

When the thoughts came back, she was lying on top of Jerry. Her cheek was against his shoulder. She felt spittle at the corner of her mouth. Lifting her head, she wiped her mouth and saw a shiny area glimmering in the candlelight where she had drooled on his shoulder in her sleep. She rubbed it off gently with the heel of her hand. He didn't wake up.

He'll probably wake up when I climb off, she thought.

His arms had been around Gillian just before she'd fallen asleep, but now they were out to the sides, as if they had simply dropped onto the mattress when he'd conked out.

His legs were still straight together between her legs.

His penis had been inside her, and she could feel that it was still inside her, but not very far.

Pushing at the mattress with her hands and knees, she carefully raised herself.

She felt a pulling sensation.

Permanently stuck, Gillian thought, and smiled.

Though it still took a slight pull that stung Gillian and

must've hurt Jerry as well, she freed herself without waking him.

Maybe I *should* wake him up, she thought. He said he'd go over with me.

Working her way slowly backward, she stopped when his penis was just below her face.

I could wake him up in a way he wouldn't mind at all, she thought.

Just let him sleep. I can take care of this myself.

She kept backing up until her knees found the end of the bed. Then she climbed off.

Only stubs were left of the candles on the dresser and on the nightstands to either side of the bed. Gillian tiptoed from candle to candle, and puffed out each flame.

She entered the lighted hallway and followed it to the kitchen. A clock on the kitchen wall showed 2:38.

Lord, Gillian thought. How did it get so late?

She slid open the back door. The pool still shimmered pale blue in the darkness.

How did it get so late, indeed?

We must've been in the pool more than an hour after the Tarzan Jane business.

Gillian walked to the far side of the pool. Squatting there, she picked up her bra and panties, Jerry's briefs. They were still wet.

She remembered how the garments had hit the concrete deck with sodden splats when they were tossed from the pool. And the feel of Jerry when she first embraced him naked in the water. And the sudden urgency, and how he had entered her and she had wrapped her legs around him and he had walked her to a corner of the shallow end and she had stretched out her arms and hung onto the edges of the pool until it ended fast with a quaking inside that made her cry out.

The memory of it left her a little breathless, a little aroused.

She stood up with the undergarments in her hands. Wring-

g them out, she walked to the pool corner where he had
ken her, where he had held her for so long afterward and
here she had finally said, "Now what'll we do for fun?" Jerry
iggested playing Marco Polo, a water version of hide-and-
ek.

So they had played that game for a while, taking turns as
le blind searcher, as the quarry. The hiding reminded Gil-
an of how it had been when she was a kid, but this time she
oked forward to being found. The kisses. The touching.
Vhich grew more intense as the game progressed until fi-
ally they climbed from the pool, rubbed each other with
wels as they shivered in night air that had seemed terribly
old, and went inside to the bedroom.

The air now seemed warm. It's because you're not soaking
et, Gillian thought.

She went to the table. She draped the undergarments on
le back of Jerry's chair.

Her bandage was still on top of her piled clothes. She had
early forgotten about the scrapes. The worst of the two had
iused her a few pains during the night when Jerry touched
by accident or when it rubbed too hard against the sheet,
ut those had been only minor irritations, whispers in the
oisy crowd of competing sensations.

She fingered the bad scrape. It felt dry, a little stiff, as if
l that time in the water had leached out the wound's mois-
ire. So she left the bandage off. She stepped into her white
horts, fastened them at her waist, and put her blouse on.
uttoning it with one hand, she took the bandage into the
itchen and tossed it in the waste container.

She went to the bedroom. In the faint light from the hall-
ay, she could see Jerry stretched out on the bed. He looked
s if he hadn't moved a muscle.

I could just leave the suitcase, she thought. We could go
ver in the morning. Jerry had said he would take a floating
oliday—no pun intended.

I don't want it hanging over my head, she decided. We'll
ave better things to do when we wake up.

She walked back down the hall, moved carefully through the dark living room, and opened Jerry's front door. She unlocked it so she could get back inside. Then she stepped out and quickly pulled it shut.

The grass was dewy under her bare feet as she crossed the lawn. She stayed close to the front of Jerry's house. Fredrick driveway was empty.

What did you expect? Gillian asked herself. Did you think he'd come home while you were at Jerry's?

It was a possibility. She knew that she would've heard his car pull into the driveway if he'd returned while she was the pool. But Jerry's bedroom was on the other side of the house. From there, she couldn't have heard it. And she hardly been listening for it. And she'd been asleep part of the time.

But the car wasn't there.

Fredrick Holden was still on his trip—maybe on one of his killing sprees.

Which will come to a quick stop, Gillian thought, once I've sent his scrapbook and a little anonymous note to the police.

She stepped onto his driveway. Its pavement felt warmer than the grass.

She glanced quickly up and down the block. Most of the houses were dark except for a few porch lights. She saw no one, and no cars moved on the street.

She came to the walkway that led to the front door. Its painted surface would be slick under wet bare feet, so she moved carefully even though the dew on her feet had mostly been blotted off while she crossed the driveway.

That would be just the thing, she thought. Take a slide and bust your keester.

No more than one crash and burn per day, please.

She climbed the stairs to the stoop.

She realized that she was gritting her teeth and trembling. The night was warm and she wasn't even wet. So knock off the shakes, she told herself. What are you, scared or something?

thing? What's to be scared of? Oh, nothing much.

Shit, no.

She gripped the door handle. Her thumb depressed the leaf-shaped metal tab and she heard the latch draw back. But she didn't open the door.

She licked her lips.

Do it, she told herself. Get your damned suitcase and get the hell out of here. Grab it, you'll be back in Jerry's house in about fifteen seconds, maybe eight if you put on the old spring.

She took a deep breath.

Maybe I should wait for Jerry, she thought.

Damn it, the suitcase is right at the door. All I have to do is reach in. Maybe one step into the house, that's all. Then I'm home free.

She swung open the door.

The house was dark. It was supposed to be. Fredrick's timer was set to shut off the lamp at eleven.

Her suitcase was a dim shape on the floor, just far enough inside so the opening door wouldn't knock against it.

Exactly where she'd left it.

No sweat.

Glad I didn't wake Jerry up for this.

She stepped over the threshold, took one more step, bent forward and reached for the suitcase handle.

A pale hand shot past the edge of the door, snatched Gillian's wrist, and swung her stumbling forward into the dark. The suitcase tripped her. She knocked it over and fell across it.

The hand on her wrist was gone.

The front door thudded shut.

She scurried forward, knees on the suitcase, then on the carpet. She started to push herself up, but someone landed on her back, smashing her down flat. Her breath blasted out. She turned her head in time to prevent the front of her face from pounding the floor, and pain flashed through her cheek-

207

bone and jaw. Then something—a fist?—struck the other side of her face.

She wondered vaguely what was happening. Somebody's been waiting behind the door?

Not . . .

She couldn't think of the name. The owner. Not him. Not him! A burglar? She'd left the door unlocked.

Another punch smashed the side of her face.

The weight left her body. Fingers dug into her armpits and she was lifted. Her knees rested on the floor for a moment. Then she was hoisted higher, jerked backward against a body, swung around and pulled, heels dragging along the carpet. Out of the living room. Into the hall. Through a doorway.

The hands thrust her away and let go. She flapped her arms, grabbing at the darkness for a moment before she hit the floor flat on her back. A dim figure leaped past her sprawled body.

She squinted when light stabbed her eyes.

Through a tingling in her ears, she heard a man's voice. "Oh, you're a beauty, a real first-rate beauty."

She raised her head. A man was standing near her feet, smiling down at her. He looked younger than thirty. He looked clean-cut with his short brown hair, white knit shirt and blue slacks. There was glee in his smile and eyes.

It's him, Gillian thought. Oh Jesus.

"I'm glad you dropped in," he said. "I've been waiting for you. Knew you'd be back."

He unbuckled his belt and slid it out of the loops of his slacks. He doubled it.

"Does anybody know you're here?"

Gillian shook her head. She raised her knees.

"Answer me."

"No," she gasped. "Nobody knows."

"Where were you tonight?"

"No place."

"Not what I wanted to hear," he said, and rushed forward, swinging the belt.

Gillian flung up her arms. The belt snapped against her, lashed her arms and belly and legs as the man danced around her, bending and whipping. She rolled over and covered her head. The belt smacked her back and buttocks. She shivered with the stinging pain. She heard herself whimpering, making sharp sucking sounds each time the belt hit her.

He's not going to stop, she thought. He's . . . enjoying himself.

When he pranced past her head, she reached out and grabbed his ankles. She tugged, but he stayed up and lashed her harder than before, the belt whistling and slapping her sides and rump. Lurching forward, she tried to bite his ankle. He tore himself free and leaped backward in time to avoid her teeth.

"Ooee! A fighter! I'm gonna have fun with you."

Dropping to his knees in front of Gillian, he grabbed her hair. She yelped and felt as if her scalp were being ripped as she was jerked up.

They were both on their knees, facing each other.

His fists were tight against the sides of her head, clenching her hair.

His face was blurry through Gillian's tears, but she saw that he was still smiling. He had slobber on his chin.

His hands shot down. They snatched the neck of her blouse and yanked. The front flew open and he peeled the blouse off her shoulders, tugging it halfway down so it pinned her arms at her sides.

He stared at her breasts. His eyes were so wide they seemed lidless.

"Where were you tonight?" he asked.

"I . . . went . . . for a walk."

"Bad lie." He pinched her nipples and twisted them. As pain streaked through her, she realized vaguely that he had let go, and then she saw a fist floating up from his side. It seemed to be coming at her very slowly and she thought that

209

she should have no trouble at all ducking it, and then it crashed into her face.

The telephone was ringing. Gillian felt a rush of terror.

I won't answer it, she thought. If I don't pick it up, Mom and Dad will be all right. Just ignore it. It'll stop.

It didn't stop.

She sat up in bed.

The handset was in its cradle. Blood streamed from both ends. Puddles of blood were spreading over the top of the nightstand.

"No!" she cried out. "Stop!"

The phone kept ringing. The blood began to dribble off the nightstand's edges.

Then the handset leaped from the cradle and flew at her. It sprayed her face with blood. It wrapped the cord around her neck. She started to choke. She pulled at the cord, but it tangled her hands, bound them.

The mouthpiece pressed against her mouth, spouting blood down her throat as the cord strangled her.

Then the receiver mashed her ear. "Your turn," whispered the voice of the phone. "Your turn now."

Gillian jerked awake.

But the nightmare didn't stop. She *was* being choked. Her hands *were* bound. She struggled in the darkness, trying not to panic. The cord at her throat kept tightening. But when she straightened her arms, it loosened. She sucked air into her burning lungs.

A surge of motion tipped Gillian.

Something was vibrating under her. She could hear an engine sound and the hiss of wheels spinning on a road.

I'm in a car.

Her eyes saw only black. She blinked them to make sure they were open.

On a car floor. The back seat floor? she wondered. But no light. None at all. And no driveshaft bump under my side.

Gillian's legs were bent. She began to straighten them, very

210

slowly in case the movement should tighten the rope across her throat. Though she could feel that her ankles were tied, there didn't seem to be any line connecting them to her neck. She unbent her knees a little more. A wire snagged one of her feet.

A tail light wire? A brake light wire? One or the other.

Gillian knew where she was.

In the trunk of Fredrick Holden's car.

Her heart started slamming, pumping pain into her head, making her battered face burn.

Oooh, I'm gonna have fun with you.

Chapter Twenty

Rick wished, once again, that he had brought the bottle with him. He was shivering. His neck was stiff, and the rigid muscles seemed to go right up into the back of his skull, squeezing pain into his head. The bourbon might have helped. On the other hand, he would have polished it off a long time ago, probably during the first hour of his vigil, and he would've ended up totally plastered; it might've even been enough to knock him out.

I'd be no good to anyone, he thought, zonked out of my gourd.

Yeah. But what good is this, anyway?

This is doing a lot of good, he told himself. It's the one sure way to keep those bastards from sneaking out of the woods and jumping us. And it got me away from Andrea, away from temptation.

Rick was seated on the ground with his back against a tree trunk, the revolver resting on his lap.

He thought about his visit from the preacher-man.

Jeez, what a performance!

The bastard was mad as a coot but most probably harmless. Christ, he'd been out in the wilderness for fifty years or more. Enough to turn anybody crazy . . .

Through a gap in the bushes ahead, he could see Jase, Luke and Wally in their sleeping bags. If the boys had a tent, they'd decided not to use it. They'd sacked out around the fire.

The fire had still been flickering when Rick arrived. Later, nothing remained except a red glow, though sometimes a flame had climbed out of the rubble like a fatally wounded survivor, quivered in the darkness for a little while, and died. Even the glow had faded out, finally. For the past hour or so, the fire had been dark and smokeless.

Rick needed no firelight. He could see the shapes on the ground better without it. The night was cloudless and pale. Where direct moonlight made it through the trees (and a patch of it fell on his left knee), Rick thought it was almost bright enough to read by. It layered everything it touched with a milky hue. And it touched the sleeping figures of Jase, Luke and Wally. They were mottled with patches of dingy white. And totally black everywhere else, as if they didn't exist at all except where the moon found them.

All three had seemed to be asleep when Rick arrived, and they hadn't moved since, except to alter their positions slightly. One of the bags would bulge when a body curled up or rolled under its surface, would jut when a knee pushed it up.

From the size of the mound, Rick knew which bag held Wally. Jase and Luke were in the other two, but he didn't know which was which. Even when the fire had been going, he hadn't been able to tell them apart. One wore a hooded sweatshirt, the other a dark stocking cap, and their faces had been turned away or half buried in their sleeping bags.

Though he couldn't tell which body was Jase, which Luke, all three of the creeps were accounted for. They were right here, asleep, and they wouldn't be sneaking over to the other camp as long as Rick kept watch.

213

The watch, he had realized long ago, was probably unnecessary.

Several times, he'd almost convinced himself to quit and return to camp.

But maybe, just maybe, their plan was to get up in the dim hours before dawn and attack when they could be certain to catch everyone fast asleep.

They'd overpower us before we knew what was happening.

You don't have to quit, Rick told himself now. You could just hurry over to the camp and take some aspirin (and grab the bottle?) and come back.

This headache's going to kill me if I don't do something about it.

Rick lifted the revolver off his lap. Slowly, he drew in his legs. He got his feet beneath him, pushed himself away from the tree trunk, and started to rise.

A sleeping bag flipped open.

Rick dropped to a squat.

Peering through the gap in the bushes, he saw moonlit bits and pieces of a person sitting up. It was the kid in the hooded sweatshirt. He couldn't make out whether it was Jase or Luke.

His heart hammered, pounding spikes of pain into his head.

Thank God I didn't leave, he thought. This is it. This is when they make their move.

The kid pulled his legs out of the bag. He seemed to be wearing gray sweatpants. He twisted around, picked up a pair of boots that had been left near his head, and started to put them on.

Though Rick heard only the wind, something must've disturbed Wally's sleep. Maybe the other kid had spoken, or maybe it was just the sound of his movements. The big mound shifted and Wally raised his head.

There were voices too soft to understand.

Wally started getting out of his bag.

"DON'T MOVE!" Rick shouted.

Both heads snapped toward him and the person in the third sleeping bag sat up fast, the bag still around his shoulders. Rick lunged forward through the bushes, arm stretched out, revolver jerking from side to side as he aimed from target to target.

Wally squealed and threw his arms around his head.

"Holy fuckin' shit!" Jase's voice, sharp with alarm. He was the one in the sweatsuit.

Luke sat motionless, all but his head enclosed in the bag.

Rick halted about two yards from Wally. He stood with his feet apart, knees slightly bent. He clutched the wrist of his gunhand.

"Christ, don't shoot!" Wally bellowed.

"Just nobody move. Nobody move a muscle."

"What the fuck are you doing?" Jase blurted. "You nuts? What is this?"

In a calm voice, Luke said, "I believe this is what is known as a pre-emptive strike."

"What the fuck are you talking about, Burgher?"

"This poor deluded son of a bitch believes that we have designs on his harem."

"Aw jeez," Wally said. "Aw jeez, I knew we were gonna get it. We shouldn'ta looked at 'em. Jeez."

"We didn't do nothing, mister," Jase said. "I don't know what your trouble is. So we looked at them. What's the big deal?"

"It wouldn't have stopped with looking," Rick said. "And you know it."

"See a shrink, pal."

"Stop it, Jase," Wally whined. "He's gotta *gun!*"

"So what're you gonna do, mister, shoot us?" There was bluster in Jase's voice, and there was fear.

"All depends," Rick said.

"If we wanted to violate your ladies," Luke said, "why haven't we done it? You'll note that we were peacefully sleeping until a few moments ago when you barged in."

"Your two friends were already up."

"I was gonna take a fuckin' *leak*," Jase said.

"Me too. I just woke up 'cause Jase was messing around, and I had to go."

"Don't give me that shit," Rick said. "I know what you were going to do."

"You're nuts, man." Jase wrapped his arms around his chest. "It's *cold*. Who'd want to slip it to those babes when it's this cold? You've gotta be kidding."

"I wouldn't rape a person even if it was hot out," Wally said in a small voice. "You'd go to prison. And besides, I just wouldn't do it."

"On top of which," Luke added, "I left my condoms at home. I most certainly wouldn't jeopardize my health by using a bare tool on strangers."

"Yeah," Wally said. "Me too. God, you could get AIDS or something. You could die."

"That's right," Jase said. "Whatever those babes got, we don't want it. They're all yours. So go on back and ream 'em out."

Rick aimed the revolver at him. "Shut up," he said.

"You aren't gonna shoot."

"Don't *say* that!" Wally blurted.

"I think you'd better leave now," Luke said.

"If you're not," Jase said, "I'm gonna have a smoke."

"You've broken the law," Luke went on while Jase got to his knees, turned away and crawled over his ground cloth toward his pack. "You've come into our camp and threatened us with a gun. I think, if we were to tell a ranger about this incident . . ."

"Don't *say* that!" Wally shook his head. "We aren't gonna tell, mister. Honest. We'll keep our mouths shut."

Jase, hunched over his pack, looked over his shoulder. "That's for sure," he said. "We talk to the cops, it'll probably be *us* that gets jammed up. Who're they gonna believe, you or us?"

"Right," Wally said. "We won't tell. No way."

Jase poked a cigarette into his mouth. He stood up, turning

his back to Rick. "So what're you gonna do? Gun us down? Shoot our dicks off . . . ?"

"*Jase!* Don't *say* that!"

What *am* I going to do with them? Rick wondered. Have them tie each other up? That'd be stupid. They could work themselves free in a while, no matter how well they might be tied. Then they'd be more dangerous than ever. Maybe just make them pack up and hike out of here. I could stay with them partway up the trail. But what's to keep them from turning around and coming back? Maybe just knowing that I've got a gun. Wally, for sure, wouldn't dare come back. But the others might. Maybe I should just keep them covered until morning. When Bert and the girls wake up and find out I'm gone, they'll come looking. They'll come armed. Then there'll be four of us, and . . .

Jase whirled around. His arm flew up. Something in his hand flashed in the moonlight, and he threw it. A knife shot at Rick, flipping end over end.

He started to duck.

Pain crashed through his head. His vision exploded with lights. He staggered and fell. His back hit the ground.

Someone was on him, sitting on his chest, wrenching the gun from his hand. "Okay fucker." Jase's voice. A harsh whisper. Rick's vision cleared and he saw Jase raise the revolver, ready to whip it across his face.

Wally grabbed Jase's wrist. "Hey, don't. We got him."

"Let go my hand."

Wally released it.

Jase stood up, straddling Rick. He was gasping for breath. He aimed the revolver at Rick's face and thumbed back the hammer.

"No!" Wally cried out.

"Jesus!" Luke yelled.

"He's got it coming," Jase said, and fired.

The explosion slammed Rick's ears. The bullet kicked a spray of forest scrap against his cheek.

*   *   *

"Come on out," Jase called.

Rick was on a rock near the campfire, sitting where they had placed him only a few minutes ago. Luke had already started the fire. It blazed brightly now, and Rick felt its warmth on his face.

Wally was standing on one side of him, Jase on the other.

Jase raised the gun overhead. "Come on," he called again. "We can hear you gals sneaking around out there. We've had enough fun 'n games, so stop fucking around."

"Get out of here!" Rick yelled.

"You shut up," Jase told him.

"I'm coming in." Bert's voice.

"Don't!"

A shape slipped out from behind a tree beyond the clearing. It moved forward, footsteps quietly crunching on the forest floor. It was Bert. She came into the firelight and stopped on the other side of Wally's empty sleeping bag.

She wore the pale blue warm-up suit and wool socks she had slept in. She wore no shoes. A knife in her right hand hung at her side.

"Call in the other two," Jase said.

"There's no need for them."

Luke tossed more twigs onto the fire, then rose from his crouch and faced her. "Bert, right?" he asked.

She nodded.

"Bert, we've got the gun. That means we're in control. We can do *whatever* we want. So when Jase tells you to call in the other girls, the prudent move on your part is to follow instructions."

"They haven't done anything to you," she said. Her voice was low and steady.

So damn brave, Rick thought. He could see the fear in her eyes, but she wasn't giving in. She had walked right into their camp and now she was standing up to them. He wished he could go to her and put his arms around her. He wished he could make all of this stop.

I had my chance. I blew it.

Now Bert will be the one to pay.

"Call the girls in," Jase told her again.

"No way. Let's go, Rick."

Wally clamped a hand on his shoulder.

"Nobody goes anywhere," Jase said.

Bert scraped her lower lips across the edges of her teeth. "What do you want?"

"Three fuckin' guesses."

"We want to discuss the situation," Luke said, "with everyone present. We don't enjoy the idea of having those two jungle warriors creeping around out there."

"You just want to 'discuss the situation,' " Bert said. "Sure thing. Have your discussion with me." The knife came up from her side. She held it in front of her belly, blade straight out. "Who wants first try?"

Jase didn't say a word. He left Rick's side and stepped around the fire.

"Run!" Rick cried.

She spread her feet slightly. The knife in her fist circled as Jase approached her.

"Jeez," Wally said.

"I wouldn't," Luke warned.

Jase stopped in front of Bert. "You're a dope," Jase told her. "But you've got balls." He reversed the revolver. Holding it by the barrel, he offered it to her.

Looking perplexed, Bert took the gun from him.

"Your fuckin' boyfriend here paid us a visit with this thing. He shouldn't be allowed to play with guns. Now how about you call off your troops, take this dork out of our face, and go back to your own camp so we can get some fuckin' sleep around here?"

Bert nodded.

Wally let go of Rick's arm. Rick stood up, stepped around the campfire, and followed Bert out of the clearing. They reached the shoreline path.

Bert suddenly hurled the revolver.

"No!"

It was too late. The handgun tumbled against the pale moonlit sky and dropped with a heavy splash into the lake.

She turned to Rick. "We're better off without it," she said. "I'll buy you a new one when we get home."

"It's all right," he muttered, and took her into his arms. He held her gently against him. She was warm. He felt her fingers stroking his hair.

"I was so scared when I heard that shot," she said.

"I didn't fire it. They took it away from me."

"That's when you got the lump on your forehead?"

"Jase threw a knife. Just the handle got me, I guess. But they took the gun from me."

"Well, I love you anyway."

He kissed her, and they were still kissing when sounds of footfalls approached. They eased apart. Bonnie and Andrea came out of the trees.

Bonnie had a hatchet in her hand. Andrea had a knife. Apparently, neither girl had wasted time getting dressed. Bonnie was in her socks and a pale body stocking that clung to her like skin and made her look naked. Andrea wore her down vest and skimpy dark panties. She was barefoot.

They were in a sour mood. Cross, as if they'd had an argument that had almost, but not quite, simmered down. They were still fired up. The atmosphere around them bristled with tension and they looked just about ready to use their weapons on anybody who said a wrong word.

Rick glanced from one to the other and realized that Andrea had indeed expected him to join her. She'd lain in her sleeping bag, naked or just in her panties, and waited for him.

Bonnie had known this, and had probably kicked up about it.

Flattering. But he'd managed to stay away. And he was glad. He had Bert. Bert was all he ever really wanted, better than he deserved. He'd been stupid even to consider . . .

"They just let you go?" Andrea asked.

"We were watching," Bonnie said. "But we couldn't hear what was going on."

"They never meant us any harm," Bert explained.

"What were you doing there?" Andrea asked Rick. "My Christ, we heard a shot and . . ."

"Let's get back to camp," Rick said. "I'll explain everything."

"Yeah, let's," Andrea said. "I'm colder than the left tit of an Arctic witch." She turned away. She started to run ahead of them, and Rick didn't bother watching.

He took hold of Bert's hand. "There's something," he said, "that needs to be told."

Rick built the campfire to a high blaze while the others were in their tents. They came out one at a time after dressing for the early morning chill, and sat down around the fire.

Bert sat on the log beside Rick. She put an arm around his back.

"First," Rick said, "I want to thank all of you for rushing to my rescue. It took a lot of guts, and . . . I really appreciate it. The thing is, apparently no rescue was necessary. There never was any danger from Jase or Luke or Wally. That was all in our heads. In *my* head."

"They did spy on the girls," Bert reminded him.

"But like they said, who wouldn't? You take any normal guy, and he's not going to turn the other way if he has a chance to look at some attractive females—especially if they're not wearing much. It wasn't any crime."

"They came all the way down the mountain," Andrea said.

"They denied that," Bonnie reminded her.

"If they did come down," Rick said, "we don't know for sure that it had anything to do with us. But I thought they planned to rape and . . . when I collapsed on the trail, I was having some kind of dream or vision that they'd killed all three of you. And I had another dream like that tonight while I was on watch. I was afraid it might be a premonition or something, a warning—so I could stop them sneaking in here."

"You start telling us you're psychic," Andrea said, "I'm gonna shit right here and now."

"I've never been psychic."

"Thank God. 'Cause if those were premonitions . . ."

"He said they weren't," Bonnie told her.

"No, all he said was that he'd never been psychic. That doesn't mean you can discount the possibly that those visions of his—"

"Andrea also believes in extra-terrestrial life forms, ghosts, astrology and Ouija boards." Bonnie shook her head and grinned. "Not to mention Tarot cards—and don't believe her when she says she isn't psychic. She is." She looked meaningfully at Andrea.

"Remember the time you said that dummy Marion Dahl was gonna be off sick and wouldn't be in class the next day and she was? Sick, I mean."

"I keep an open mind, that's all. I don't disbelieve shit just 'cause people tell me it's supernatural nonsense."

"I don't think there was anything supernatural about the tricks my imagination was playing," Rick said.

"I sure the hell hope not," Andrea said.

"I mean, it's pretty obvious at this point that Jase and the others never meant us any harm."

"You were worried all along," Bert said, "about making this trip. Even before we ran into those three guys, you were a nervous wreck. Then, when they showed up, it all seemed to focus on them. You were convinced they were trouble long before you ever had those—hallucinations, or whatever."

"Yeah. I guess I expected history to repeat itself." He saw confusion in Bert's eyes. "I didn't tell you everything," he said, "about what happened on that other camping trip." He looked at Andrea and Bonnie. "The last time I went camping was when I was fourteen. I've already told Bert about it. How I broke my leg and my father left me to go for help. What I didn't tell her before was that my stepmother was with us. Julie. She stayed with me. And a couple of guys came into the camp. They knocked me out. They raped and killed Julie.

They did it while I was unconscious. When I came to, the two guys were gone. Julie was naked on the ground and she was dead."

"Jesus," Bert muttered. "I wish you'd told me."

"I've never told anyone."

Bert shook her head. Her eyes glimmered wet in the firelight. Her hand moved up Rick's back and curled around the nape of his neck. "It must've been so awful for you. I'm so sorry."

"Anyway, that's why I brought the gun along. I got Julie killed, but I wasn't going to let it happen to you. Then when we met you two," he said, glancing at Andrea and Bonnie, "it was all part of the same thing."

"You couldn't save Julie," Andrea said, "so it's like you wanted to save all of us—to make up for it."

"Something like that, I guess."

"Heavy," Andrea said.

"If I'd known what happened before," Bert said, "I never would've talked you into this."

"You were so eager. I didn't want to spoil it for you. Besides, I had no idea I'd suddenly turn into a total paranoid. That other was a long time ago. I figured I'd be able to handle being in the mountains again. But when we got here, it all came back fresh as if the years in between just folded up. Then Jase and his pals walked into the camp. That's what the others did, just walked into camp and the next thing I knew Julie was dead. The way I saw it, it was all starting over again. But this time I was ready and I had a gun and nobody was going to get hurt except the guys."

"And I threw away the gun," Bert muttered.

"You *what*?" Andrea blurted.

"I threw it in the lake."

"Holy limping Jesus."

"It's all right," Rick said. "We're better off without it. I could've . . . I came pretty close to shooting those guys tonight. And they were innocent."

"Innocent my ass."

"They're creeps," Bert said, "but they're not rapists or killers."

"That remains to be seen," Andrea said.

"They had my gun," Rick told her. "They could've done whatever they wanted. All they did was hand it over to Bert."

"We really misjudged those guys," Bonnie said.

"*I* sure did," Rick said, "and I think the rest of you caught it from me. It was contagious. I was so obsessed with this thing."

"For good reason," Bert told him.

"If I'd just . . . really thought about it rationally. I mean, the odds against something like that happening twice . . . It almost *couldn't* happen again with odds like that."

"You hear about the guy who got caught trying to take a bomb with him on an airline flight?" Andrea asked. "They said to him, 'Are you nuts? You could've killed yourself and everyone else on the flight.' He told them it didn't have a detonator, so they said, 'Then what's the bomb for?' He said it was a safety precaution. He said, 'You ever hear of *two* bombs on a plane?' "

Nobody laughed.

"Cute," Bonnie muttered.

"The odds."

"We get it," Bonnie said.

Bert rubbed the back of Rick's neck. "Are you about ready to turn in?" she asked.

"Yeah."

"Does this mean we're not going to stand watch anymore?" Andrea asked.

"What's the point," Bonnie said.

"I guess I'll stay up for a while, then. Make sure nobody sneaks up on us and . . ." She stopped herself. She shrugged. "I'm not very tired anyway."

"Suit yourself," Bonnie told her. "But there's really no point."

"Maybe not. But it can't hurt to be careful. Rick did have those visions."

"Just the daydreams of a disordered mind," he said, smiling a bit.

"Besides," Bert said, "the odds."

"Yeah, the odds. Did you know it's a common misconception that lightning doesn't strike the same place twice? It does hit the same place twice. Frequently."

"On that cheerful note," Bert said, "goodnight." Rick told the girls goodnight, and followed her into the tent.

As they lay close together in the darkness, Rick said, "Yeah. 'Nother thing. I met Angus, our friendly neighborhood preacher-man, earlier. Says he's lived out here fifty years. Caught me drinking the 'devil's brew' and told me to repent of my wicked ways, or else. He's out of his gourd. A real freak."

"Angus?"

"Yes. The bastard that's been following us around—never mentioned him before. All I'd seen was his shadow. Thought it was part of my general paranoia. But he sure scared the shit outa me tonight. Jumping out like that. Turns out he's just your average harmless maniac. I guess."

He started to tell Bert the whole story but she rolled over and put a finger to his lips.

"Tell me about Angus tomorrow," she said.

Chapter Twenty-one

Gillian had thought it wouldn't last long. Half an hour, maybe. Just long enough for Holden to take her up into the hills, probably somewhere along Mulholland, where he'd find a secluded area and open the trunk and do what he had in mind.

This can't be happening.

It's happened to a lot of others. It happens all the time. This time, it's my turn. I'll be dead. After he's done with me.

It's impossible.

Gillian knew it was possible.

Not inevitable, though, she told herself. It's not over yet. It doesn't have to turn out that way. Maybe he'll get a flat, or the cops will stop him, or . . .

The wires at her feet.

She explored them with the toes of her right foot—the foot on the bottom. There seemed to be a central cable stretched along the front of the trunk. Small clusters of wires ran off it. These, she thought, must be attached to the car's right rear lights.

No Sanctuary

Cops will stop a car with dead lights.

Though her feet were bound together tightly at the ankles, she was able to spread them open as if they were hinged at the heels. She clamped the main cable between them. She pulled at it, trying to work the wiring loose without a struggle that might make the rope across her throat go tight.

You'll never break the connection this way, she realized.

Stop screwing around, this is your life!

She ripped at the cable. Newspapers whispered and crackled beneath her as she slid. Her knees pounded the front of the trunk. The rope dug into her throat. She jammed her hands down to give herself slack, bent forward slightly, felt the rope rub between her legs and buttocks, felt the pressure ease across her throat, and kicked back with both feet. The cable gave. It didn't flop loose, but Gillian was certain that some of the small wires running off to the lights must've popped free. She pictured the car moving along the road, the lights dead on its right rear side.

Now if we just get pulled over, she thought.

They didn't get pulled over.

And Holden didn't stop in a secluded place in the Hollywood Hills to finish with her.

They would've been there by now.

Hours had seemed to go by after Gillian's struggle with the wiring.

Lying on her side had become unbearable after a while, so she had experimented with moving and found to her surprise that she could lie on her back. By angling herself across the trunk, she was actually able to stretch her legs out. The rope at her throat seemed more like a nuisance than a threat. She had figured out that it would not choke her so long as she kept her back straight and her arms stretched down. But the rope made it impossible for her to reach the knots and work on them. That's what it's for, she knew.

In bits and pieces over the hours, during short periods of time when she could focus her mind, Gillian had assembled

227

the puzzle of what Holden must've done after she lost consciousness in his house.

First, he stripped her naked. Probably fooled with her. He would, wouldn't he? Yeah. Maybe even fucked her, though she had no way of knowing, not after the condition Jerry had left her in. When he finished messing with her, he tied her up. Oh, he must've got some extra jollies from that, running the rope down from her hands, centering it so it went right into her, turning her over and pulling it up so tight she could actually feel it against her anus, then looping it around her throat so it would choke her if she struggled. Her arms must've been bent just a little while he did all that; otherwise, she would've been strangled by now. He probably left some slack on purpose, not wanting to have her die in the trunk and miss the fun. Then he bound her ankles together.

Somehow, he got her to his car. His car hadn't been in the driveway when Gillian went to his house. Maybe he'd put it into the garage. If that's where it was, he'd simply carried her out the back door to the garage, opened up the trunk, and dropped her in. Maybe took out the spare tire first to make more room, and spread newspapers on the floor of the trunk before putting her in. Newspapers that could be removed later, and burned to destroy any evidence that might be left behind: blood, semen, hairs, the kind of stuff cops vacuum out of a suspect's trunk and put under a microscope and use in court. Holden had read a lot of books. He knew about such things.

What had he done with her suitcase and clothes? Probably brought them along. He wouldn't be stupid enough to leave them in his house. When they got where they were going, he would burn them or bury them or just leave them by her body. Took his scrapbook out of the suitcase, of course. He'd probably searched her suitcase while she was at Jerry's. Must've been a shocker to find the scrapbook and realize she knew his secret. If he'd had any ideas about letting her live, that had put a stop to them. He'd probably had no such ideas, though. How could he pass up a chance like this—to have a victim walk right into his house? Like getting a surprise gift. Which he couldn't wait to unwrap and try out.

Only try out, though. His own house was no place for really having fun. Not for a careful man like Holden, who traveled out of state to find his victims, who never even killed them in their own homes or apartments but took them out to wild areas where their bodies wouldn't be found for days or weeks, or at all.

So where's he taking me? Gillian wondered.

Someplace far away, she thought, or we'd be there by now.

She wondered if it was still night. After sunrise, it wouldn't matter so much about the dead lights. Maybe she had nailed a brake light, but what good would that do?

Where *is* he taking me?

From the smooth, steady ride and the engine sounds, she guessed that they were on a freeway—had been on a freeway most of the time.

We're going very far away, she thought, and then felt herself slip away again.

She woke up gasping with fear and bathed in sweat.

Sweat?

The air in the trunk felt warm. She couldn't remember it being warm before. She could remember shivering sometimes and wishing she had clothes on, or at least a sheet to cover herself. The warmth meant sunlight.

It's daytime.

She wondered what time they had left Holden's house. Maybe three or three-thirty in the morning? There was no way to be sure, since she'd been unconscious, but he'd probably been quick to get on the road. The sun would start heating things up by seven or eight. If it was much later than that, the trunk would probably be a lot hotter.

So we've been on the road about four hours, maybe longer.

If he headed south, we're well into Mexico by now. East, we're in Arizona.

"Crucify me on a cactus," she heard herself mumble. "Ha ha." No joke. She could see herself on one of those saguaros that stood in the desert like a mutant man with upraised arms. She felt nails in her palms, the spines piercing her back and buttocks and legs. The sun seared her bare skin. She heard her skin sizzling like bacon on a skillet. Squinting through the glare of the noon sun, she saw Holden smile and drop to his hands and knees and crawl toward her. Bones littered his way—glaring white skulls, ribcages, parts of a dozen bodies or twenty. The bones clinked and clattered as Holden scuttled through them. Some dissolved into white powder that puffed, and he was crawling through a cloud of bone dust. When he emerged from the cloud, he was no longer Fredrick Holden. He was a tarantula, fat and furry and half a foot across. And scurrying toward Gillian's feet. Gasping, she tried to move her feet away from it. Skeleton fingers held her feet to the hot desert ground. She couldn't move. The spider climbed onto her bare left foot, walked up the skeleton hand at her ankle as if the finger bones were the rungs of a ladder. It moved up her shin. It sat for a moment on her knee as if resting. Then it began crawling up Gillian's thigh, and she screamed.

The scream snatched her away from the horrors in the desert. She was in the trunk again, panting. When she opened her eyes, they both burned as if someone had flung saltwater into her face. She realized it was sweat.

The trunk was very hot. The black air felt like a heavy blanket pressing down on her, suffocating her.

I won't suffocate, she told herself. This trunk isn't airtight. I'll just cook.

I must've been out a while, she thought.

She was drenched. Even lying motionless, she could feel runnels sliding down her body, tickling her. The newspapers felt sodden under her back. She rolled onto her right side. Sweat must have been clinging to her skin in tiny beads like raindrops, standing in pools in the hollows of her throat and navel. It cascaded off her when she rolled. She heard it spill onto the newspapers.

The change of position helped. Much of the paper peeled

off her back with the turn. A sheet of it still adhered to her buttocks, but there was nothing she could do. She lay there motionless, her eyes shut tight to keep the sweat from stinging them. The trickles continued. Her legs, pressed together, felt as if they were lathered with hot butter. Only her mouth was dry. Her tongue touched dry flakes along her lips.

The floor of the trunk suddenly tipped beneath her. She flinched and choked herself on the rope and quickly bent her knees, rumpling the papers but stopping her forward roll.

The car's going uphill, she thought. Up a steep hill.

It had moved up and down many times before, rocking her slightly, but never anything like this.

He's taking me into the mountains, she thought.

Chapter Twenty-two

Rick jerked awake as something smacked the wall of his tent. He lifted his head. The blue tent was murky inside with daylight. He thought a pine cone must've fallen. But then the tent was struck twice more, and other objects, missing, thumped the ground outside.

Bert moved, rubbing him, and he looked down at her. "What's going on?" she whispered.

"They're throwing stuff."

The sleeping bag's zipper was on the other side of Bert. He couldn't get to it without crawling over her, so he started to squirm out the top. Bert rolled away from him. He heard the zipper slide with a sound like ripping fabric.

"So long, Rick the Prick!" Jason's voice. It came from a distance. "So long, cunts!"

Rick was half out of the bag, sitting up, his hand on the knife propped upright inside his hiking boot. Bert had slid out the open side. She was on her elbows. At the sound of Jase's voice, she stopped trying to get out.

"It *hasn't* been nice knowing you!" Luke called.

"FUCK YOU AND THE HORSES YOU RODE IN ON!" That one came from Andrea. From nearby. Her tent?

Bert shook her head.

There was distant, derisive laughter from the boys.

Rick sat motionless, waiting. Bert didn't move either. She was still stretched out, lying half across her empty sleeping bag, propped up on her elbows, naked to the knees. Her feet were still inside Rick's bag. Her breasts rose and fell as she breathed.

"I guess they're gone," Rick finally said.

"Good riddance to bad rubbish." Smiling, she lay back and folded her hands behind her head. One of her feet stroked the side of Rick's leg. "I hope that's the last of them."

"We'll take that other trail."

"And make sure, first, they're really going up to Dead Mule Pass." Bert took her legs out of Rick's bag and stretched them out on top of it. "It's hot in here. Must be late."

He flipped the sleeping bag off his hot legs. The air felt good on them. "When Jase handed the gun to you, it changed everything. That . . . I think that pretty much shattered my obsession with Julie and the rest of it."

"God, if I'd known what you went through. I feel like such a jerk for forcing you into this trip."

"It was probably good for me. I *know* you've been good for me."

"We don't have to go on, though. If we turn around, we could be back at the car this afternoon. Would you rather do that?"

"I don't know. I think I'll be all right now. And I'd hate to cheat you out of the rest . . ."

"I wouldn't mind. This hasn't exactly gone the way I'd hoped, anyway."

Rick nodded. "Bet you didn't expect it to be this exciting."

"Or this crowded."

"Well, now that Jase and his pals are gone . . ."

"That only leaves Andrea and Bonnie."

"Maybe we ought to split up with them." That, Rick knew,

233

was what Bert wanted. Strangely, the idea of leaving the girls behind didn't disturb him. He felt no disappointment. Andrea was a temptation and she had offered herself to him. If she were gone, he could stop struggling against the urge to take her up on it. And he could be alone with Bert.

"They're nice and everything," Bert said. "Andrea's kind of a kick."

"She's sure got a mouth," Rick added.

"But it's like having guests. Even if you like their company, they're in the way."

Rick suddenly had a thought that made his heart quicken. "How about this?" he asked. "We'll have a leisurely breakfast, tell the girls to go on without us, and then we'll get all our stuff together. And we'll hike around the end of the lake to our stream."

"You mean, stay there?" Her voice was eager, her eyes bright.

"All day. And we'll pitch our tent down by the inlet and spend the night. Does that sound okay?"

"It sounds perfect. Too good to be true."

"But true," Rick said.

Chapter Twenty-three

The ride became a torture as the heat in the trunk grew worse and the car climbed and dropped and made sharp turns, sliding Gillian over the newspapers, trying to throw her forward and back, the rope squeezing her throat each time she flinched at the sudden movements.

It can't go on much longer, she thought.

We're in the mountains. We'll stop soon and he'll let me out.

Let me out. No! God, what am I going to do!

The car slowed abruptly, throwing Gillian onto her back. Her knees flew up. Her left knee bumped the lid of the trunk before she could straighten her legs.

She felt the car make a sharp turn. Then it began moving forward. It was no longer on pavement. On a dirt road? The floor of the trunk shuddered under her back, shaking her, sometimes bouncing her roughly.

It won't be long now.

I'm sorry, Jerry, she thought. I shouldn't have left without you. But then he might've gotten you, too, so maybe it's better this way.

Knowing that she would never see Jerry again, Gillian felt a twist of sorrow and loss.

It's not over yet, she told herself.

Then the car stopped and the engine went silent.

Gillian felt a change inside herself as if a switch had been thrown. She no longer felt the stifling heat, or the pains of her bound and battered body, the awful fear. Her heartbeat thundered. She shivered. She felt *cold*. Even her mind felt cold. And sharp.

He's gonna have to work for it.

The trunk lid swung up. Daylight poured down on Gillian, blinding her. Cool air lapped her burning wet body. The air smelled of pine and damp earth. Squinting, she peered out. The opening was about three feet high. Beyond it, she saw the green of trees and a few pale patches of sky. Fredrick Holden wasn't there.

He must've used a trunk release on his dashboard.

Gillian heard the soft sound of a breeze whispering through the woods. There were birds singing, chirping, squawking. She even heard the flutter of wings. The whiny buzz of a mosquito.

Where is he?

She heard a footstep. It made a quiet crunching sound on the ground. Then there were more footsteps.

He's coming!

He stood over the trunk and stared down at her.

Didn't do anything, just stared as if entranced by the look of Gillian stretched out in his trunk, naked and gleaming with sweat, tied up and helpless. His mouth hung open. Gillian could see his chest move as he breathed rapidly. He closed his mouth, licked his lips and swallowed. Then he rubbed a forearm across his mouth.

"All mine," he muttered as if to himself. "Allll mine."

He bent over the trunk. His hands swirled over Gillian's slick skin as if he were fingerpainting.

Go ahead. Enjoy the hell out of this. I'll get my turn.

The hands slid on her shoulders, circled and kneaded her breasts, swarmed over her belly and down her thighs, slipped between her thighs and slithered there, delving around the rope. Then they roamed up her body again and lingered on her breasts as if he couldn't get enough of the slippery way they felt, especially when he squeezed them.

"Untie me," Gillian said. Her voice came out in a dry, raspy whisper. "I'll do wonderful things to you."

He slapped her face hard.

Then he rubbed his hands on his shirt. They left dark stains on the pale fabric. His right hand dropped out of sight below the edge of the trunk. It came back with a knife.

It was a huge knife with a long, broad blade. A bowie knife?

Leaning over the trunk, he cut through the rope around Gillian's ankles. The edge of the blade scraped lightly along the side of her calf and kept moving higher. Goosebumps crawled over her skin. She tried not to shiver. She couldn't help it. She wanted to clamp her legs together, but that would push the blade into her thigh.

He's gonna ram it right up into me.

No, he won't, she thought. He can't have blood in his trunk. Even the newspapers wouldn't hold it all. He's smart enough to know that.

The knife turned. The point lightly traced its way up the hollow where her leg joined her groin, followed it to her hip.

The knife rose above her. Holden kept it in his hand while he wiped his mouth again with his forearm. Then it came down slowly and Gillian thought he was going to free her hands. The blade pressed, instead, against her pubic mound. She saw his arm make a sawing motion, but she felt no pain. He's cutting the rope, she realized. That's all.

That's all?

She felt the rope part. Her hands were still bound together, but now she would be able to raise them without choking herself.

And my feet are loose, she thought.

He'd take me easily in a fight, but I can make a run for it.

Holden pressed the blade to her throat. With his other hand, he reached behind her neck. He grabbed the rope and yanked it. Gillian felt as if she were being scorched by the streaking rope, but then it was out from under her.

Holden clutched the end of it with his left hand. "Up," he said, and tugged it like a leash. Gillian sat up. Sweat streamed down her body, dripped off her chin and breasts. Sodden newspapers clung to her back.

With his rope hand, Holden peeled the papers off. "Out," he said. His command was followed by another tug. Gillian winced.

Bracing herself with forearms on the edge of the trunk, she turned and got to her knees. She had papers on her rump. They stayed stuck to her while she swung a leg out of the trunk. Her knee found the bumper. It slipped off when she put her weight on it. She squirmed on the edge. The rope at her throat was yanked, and she tumbled out, rolling. The bumper hit her side. She bounced off it and slammed the ground . . . and reached up and caught the rope and jerked it. Holden yelped. His arm snapped forward. The end of the rope flew from his hand.

Gillian flipped over. She rammed the fists of her tied hands against the ground and thrust herself up, and was almost to her feet when Holden's kick caught her hip and sent her hurling sideways. She crashed against the rear of the car. It knocked her away. She fell and rolled and tried to keep rolling but Holden pinned her down with a shoe on her belly.

He stared down at her. He was breathing hard. He rubbed his lips again with his forearm.

Then he stomped.

Pain blasted through Gillian.

Wheezing and dazed, she was only vaguely aware of Holden picking up the rope, of how he pulled it and how she crawled, and how he picked her up and braced her against a tree trunk. By the time her mind cleared, it was too late.

Holden no longer held the rope. She couldn't see where it was, but she felt it around her neck, against her right ear, against the side of her head. Its other end, she knew, must be tied to a branch above her.

She tried to grab for it.

Something stopped her.

She looked down. She was wearing a black leather belt. It was cinched tight around her waist. Her bound hands were lashed to it with rope—probably some of the rope that Holden had cut off her feet.

When did he do that? she wondered.

I must've been out for a while.

She looked around. The car was a few yards away, its trunk and driver's door still open. But she didn't see Holden anywhere.

Soon, she heard him tramping through the woods.

He came into the clearing. His arms were loaded with twigs and sticks. He gazed at Gillian and walked toward her.

Jesus, he's gonna burn me at the stake like a witch!

But he dropped the bundle a safe distance away from her. He cleared an area surrounding it. He gathered up all the newspapers from the trunk of his car and stuffed them into the heap of wood. He found the paper that had come out of the trunk on Gillian's rump. The breeze had tossed it into a bush, where it waited for him, snagged.

He touched a match to the pile.

I knew he'd do this, Gillian thought.

The papers had been spread in the trunk like papers at the bottom of a bird cage—to catch her debris so the cops would have nothing to find if they ever searched. Now, the papers were being burnt.

He won't be putting me back in the trunk.

I'll be left here.

Panic blew through Gillian like a frigid wind.

"You can't *do* this!" she cried out. "Please!"

"Shut up or I'll cut your tongue out."

She snapped her mouth shut. She sucked air through her nostrils. The air was acrid with smoke.

Holden walked slowly to the car. He opened a rear door

and pulled out Gillian's suitcase. He carried it to the fire, set it flat on the ground, and opened it.

On top were the white shorts and plaid blouse she had worn to Jerry's. Holden held the blouse over the fire until flames started crawling up its tails. Then he dropped it into the blaze. He picked up her shorts and tossed them onto the flames. As the white fabric curled and blackened, he looked over at Gillian. "What were you doing in my house?" he asked.

"You told me not to talk."

"I changed my mind. Talk. What were you doing there?"

"I just break into houses," Gillian said. "I stay in them when people are away."

"What for?"

"It's exciting."

He laughed. "*Real* exciting, this time. You must be crazy or something."

"Look who's talking."

"You think I'm crazy?" He looked amused by the idea. "I'm not crazy. I just do what any guy'd do if he had the guts."

"Bullshit."

"Yeah, you'd be surprised." He lifted out her tank-top and gym shorts and tossed them into the fire. "Isn't a man alive doesn't take one look at a piece like you and want to rip her clothes off and fuck her brains out. They just don't have the guts or they'd do it. Me, I do it."

"Then you kill them," Gillian said.

"Dead girls tell no tales. How long you think I'd last if I let them live?"

"You enjoy killing people—and hurting them?"

He grinned and threw her skirt into the fire. "Just part of the game. Have to break some eggs if you're gonna make an omelet."

"You could get any woman you want. You don't have to do it this way. You're handsome and rich."

240

"Rich, huh? You're a little snoop, aren't you?" He tossed her heels into the fire.

My sandals are still at Jerry's, Gillian thought. So are my panties and bra. All that he'll find of me when he wakes up.

"You know what they say," Holden told her. "Money can't buy happiness."

"It'll buy a lot of women."

"Whores. Riddled with disease. Who wants that? I'm real particular who I touch." He took a plastic bag out of the suitcase, opened it, and pulled out Gillian's bikini. The bag shrank on the fire and burst into flames. "What'd you do, use my hot tub?"

Gillian nodded. She couldn't let him know that she'd been in Jerry's pool.

"Wore a bikini in the hot tub. That's a laugh. You're a very modest young lady."

"That's me," she muttered.

Holden dangled the bikini top over the flames. Steam rose off its damp fabric. He dropped it, then rubbed the pants on his face. "Mmmm, delicious."

"You're a pig."

"Oink oink," he said, and laughed. The pants fluttered down into the blaze. He took her camera out of the suitcase and held it toward her. "What's this for?"

"Dental floss."

"You babes are such a riot. If you aren't screaming and weeping and pleading, you turn into wise-asses. There oughta be a bounty on you." He opened the back of the camera and removed the film cartridge. "You got pictures of my place in here?"

"Develop them and find out for yourself."

"You're a real prize, you know that? Where do you get off, breaking into a man's private domain and taking fucking *snapshots*?"

"Where do you get off, killing people?"

"Right between my legs, hon." He dropped the film into the fire. "Seriously, you took pictures of my place?"

"I take pictures of all the places I stay. I have albums full of them."

"No kidding. And you think *I'm* crazy."

"Yeah, a madman."

"Mad is right. But not crazy. If I was crazy, you think I could've done thirty-two babes without ever even getting *questioned* by the cops, much less busted? You think a crazy man would do that?"

"If he's smart."

Black, greasy smoke curled off the film.

"At least you're right about that," Holden said. "I *am* smart. Take you, for instance. They find your body out here, *if* they find it, they aren't gonna know who the fuck you are, much less where you came from. I mean, they won't even think of *looking* in the goddamn San Fernando Valley. Hon, we're more than three hundred miles away. If they do find you, they'll think you're from San Francisco or Sacramento or some damn place. We're so far away you won't even turn up in the LA papers."

"That'll make it tough to keep your scrapbook current," Gillian muttered.

He laughed. "Oh, I'll manage. There's this news-stand in Hollywood, carries papers from everywhere. What were you gonna do, give my scrapbook to the cops?"

"If you're so smart, you shouldn't have kept it around."

"Shit, it's not evidence. It sure would've made them look at me, though, wouldn't it? I'm lucky I got back when I did."

"Who'd you kill this time out?"

"Oh, a real sweetie. Linda Ryan." He had lifted a handful of socks and panties out of Gillian's suitcase, but he held onto them and stared past the fire. "A real beauty. Sixteen years old. Spotted her leaving a 7-Eleven and followed her home. That was what, Thursday? Friday night, her folks left her alone. She was a fighter, too. Like you." He turned his head and smiled at Gillian. "But she cried and pleaded at the end. You will, too."

He tossed the clothes into the fire, then gazed at Gillian

for a long time. He rubbed his forearm across his mouth. "I'm gonna have real fun with you."

He got off his knees, picked up the suitcase, and dumped the rest of its contents into the fire. For a few seconds, the flames were covered by clothing and her leather toilet kit and handbag. Then they broke through, crackling and blazing high.

He kicked the camera into the fire.

He turned the suitcase in his hand, inspecting it, apparently undecided about its fate. Then he carried it to his car, leaving his knife on the ground by the fire. Gillian quickly jerked up her knees. The rope stopped her, squeezed her throat. She swung, keeping her neck muscles tensed. Blood seemed trapped inside her head. She felt as if her face were swelling up, as if her eyes might pop from their sockets. Shooting her legs down, Gillian stood up straight and gasped for breath. She looked toward the car. Her vision was dark as if clouds had covered the sun.

Holden was swinging her suitcase into the backseat.

He came back to the fire, apparently unaware of Gillian's attempt.

Squatting, he picked up the enormous knife. He poked the fire with it, shoving some unburnt rags into the leaping flames. Then he used the blade to separate some fiery brands from the main pile. They formed a smaller pyre at his feet. He eased the broad blade into the midst of the flames and rested the handle on the ground.

He left it there.

Oh, Jesus.

Standing up, he faced Gillian.

"Hey," she gasped. "Come on."

Grinning, he pulled off his shirt. His torso was lean and tanned and muscular. He tossed his shirt to the ground.

He wore no belt. His belt was strapped around Gillian's waist.

He unbuttoned his slacks and lowered the zipper and his rigid penis sprang out and someone not very far away yelled,

Richard Laymon

"*Pick it up, man. What's the matter, you got lead in your ass?*"

The livid color drained out of Holden's face. He tucked his penis in. He zipped his pants and buttoned them and whirled around. He grabbed his knife out of the small fire. He snatched up his shirt.

The shirt fluttered, clamped in his teeth, as he ran at Gillian.

He swung the heavy blade. It thunked the branch above her head. The rope dropped in front of her like a dead snake. Holden grabbed it, then let it go. His shoulder rammed Gillian's belly. She folded over him.

He ran with her.

His shoulder pounded her guts, keeping her breathless and unable to yell for help.

Her face was against his bare back.

She saw the brown wooden grips of a revolver above the waistband of his slacks.

She reached for it with her bound hands.

And almost got it.

Please!

Holden flung her into the trunk of his car and slammed the lid shut.

Chapter Twenty-four

"Let's take a breather," Bert said, and sat down on a rock shelf beside the trail.

Rick sat down beside her. When he leaned back, the sloping rock took the weight of the pack off his shoulders.

"Whatever happened to your cigars?" Bert asked.

"Want one?"

"Maybe a puff of yours."

Rick slipped free of the straps. He stood up, turned around, and opened a side pocket of his pack. The pocket was partly open where he'd kept his revolver. He found matches and the pack of cigars. Sitting down, he unwrapped a cigar and lit it. He took a few puffs, savoring the sweet aroma of the smoke.

Then he passed it to Bert.

She poked it into her mouth and wiggled her eyebrows.

"Hooray for Captain Spalding," Rick said.

She blew smoke in his face and handed the cigar back.

"Funny," he said. "You don't look worn out, weary, exhausted and pooped."

"I've picked up some of your tricks."

"Isn't necessary, though. I don't want to run into the girls anymore than you do."

"It's been nice without them."

"It was even nicer by the stream," he said.

"Yeah. Can't win. I feel like we're getting dumped on right and left." She leaned back. The rear brim of her Aussie hat bumped her pack. The hat slid down her face. She caught it, held it on her thigh, tilted her face into the sunlight and closed her eyes. "It would've been so wonderful."

"It *was* for a while."

"Yeah," she muttered. "Before a bunch of assorted goons put in their appearance."

That morning, after dressing, they had left the tent. The girls weren't up yet. And they still weren't up when they returned from the stream where they'd washed and brushed their teeth. Back in camp, they built up the fire, made coffee and a fine breakfast of scrambled eggs with chunks whittled off the bacon bar. As they finished eating, Bonnie came out of her tent.

"Andrea's zonked," she said. "Didn't get much sleep last night."

Rick felt himself blush. I didn't do anything, he told himself. He wondered if Bonnie had still been awake when Andrea returned to the tent after making her offer. Had Andrea told her about it?

"Just woke up long enough to say goodbye to our friends?" Bert asked.

"That's about it. I'll get her up, though. We don't want to keep you waiting."

"That's all right," Rick said.

"We're going to head over to a place we found on the other side of the lake," Bert explained, "and spend the day there."

"I thought we were going to take the trail that bypasses the mountain."

246

"We'll be staying behind," Bert said.

Bonnie nodded. Rick thought he caught a brief look of relief on her face. "Well," she said, "I guess we'll go on. Andrea might not be too happy about it, but . . . you two didn't come out here to have us in your hair."

"We've enjoyed traveling with you," Bert said.

"Yeah," Rick said.

"It's certainly been an adventure," Bonnie said.

"Sorry about that," Rick told her.

"Well, I think if you hadn't been with us, those guys really might've started trouble. So thanks."

They were folding their tent and Bonnie was sipping coffee by the fire when Andrea appeared. She got to her feet in front of her tent and stretched in the sunlight. She wore her faded blue shorts and her gray T-shirt. "You guys look like you're about ready to hit the trail," she said.

"They're not going with us," Bonnie told her.

Frowning, she walked over to them. "What's the deal?" she asked.

"Bert and I are planning to camp at a place we found on the other side of the lake," Rick said.

Andrea looked hurt. "What's the problem?"

"No problem," Bert assured her. "The guys are out of the way, and . . ."

"I thought we'd all stick together. I mean, we're even *parked* in the same place."

"Well," Rick said, "we want to have some time to ourselves."

She stared at him.

In the moment that their eyes met, Rick felt as if she were asking if he really wanted to leave her, was this Bert's idea, did he *have* to go, did he understand what he would be missing?

"So, it's *adios*, huh?" she asked.

"Not for a while," Bert said.

Andrea returned to the fire. She sat there with Bonnie,

sipping coffee and talking quietly while Rick and Bert finished packing.

Shouldering their packs, they went to the girls. "Guess we'll be on our way," Bert said.

Bonnie stood up and shook hands with her, then with Rick. "It's been nice traveling with you."

"Same here," Rick said.

Andrea stood up. "We don't even know each other's full names," she said. "I'm Andrea Winston, this is Bonnie Jones."

"I'm Bert Lindsey," she said, and shook hands.

Andrea offered her hand to Rick. He held it briefly as he introduced himself. "Richard Wainwright."

"If either of you ever get down to LA," Bert said, "make sure to look us up. We could get together for dinner or something."

"We're in the San Fernando valley," Rick said.

"And you're in the phone book?"

"Yep."

"Well," Andrea said, "who knows? Maybe we'll see each other again some time."

Rick followed Bert to the lakeside trail. There, he looked back and waved. Andrea had a strange look on her face. A knowing smile.

My Christ, Rick thought, she's going to show up at my door. Maybe next week, maybe next month.

His heart raced with the prospect.

Maybe she'll forget my name, he told himself.

She won't.

I'll just treat her as a friend, and . . .

What if it's over with Bert by then? What if we've broken up?

What if we break up and Andrea *doesn't* come along?

Her name is Winston. I can always find her through the university at Santa Cruz.

Why am I thinking this nonsense? Everything's great with Bert.

But you never know.

Bert, ahead of him, looked to the left. Rick saw that they were passing the clearing where Jase, Luke and Wally had camped.

Won't ever see *them* again, he thought.

"We forgot to give our names to The Three Thugateers," he said.

Bert smiled back at him. "What an oversight! How will they ever manage to look us up?"

When she faced away again, Rick looked over at the lake. He pictured himself diving for his revolver. Probably wouldn't find it, anyway, he told himself. And Bert wouldn't be too pleased if he tried. He kept walking.

Soon, they rounded the end of the lake and climbed to the top of the rock slope overlooking the stream. "Do you feel like a dip?" Bert asked.

"Do I look like one?"

She laughed. They crossed the stream, hopping from rock to rock, then made their way down to the clearing by the inlet. There, they put down their packs. "This time," Bert said, "we'll have towels."

"And let's take a sleeping bag with us," Rick suggested. "That was hard on my elbows and knees yesterday."

They found their towels and placed them on top of Rick's sleeping bag roll. Sitting on a rock, Bert took off her boots and socks. She stood up and stepped out of her shorts and panties. She left her shirt on, and Rick stayed in his jockey shorts.

On the way up to the stream, Rick stayed behind her. He watched her long bare legs. He watched the way her shirt-tail swayed and fluttered, giving him glimpses of her shadowed rump. The stolen glances, he realized, were somehow even more enticing than when she was naked.

Just don't fall and break your leg, he thought. We don't have the revolver anymore.

He pictured Julie on the ground. He felt a rush of fear.

Isn't it ever going to end?

Not while we're in the mountains.

This'll be great, he told himself. Yesterday over here was great. Nothing to worry about. The guys are gone.

They reached the side of the stream at a place where the water tumbled down off a ledge and formed a pool. Rick turned around slowly, scanning the area.

"Checking for voyeurs?" Bert asked, smiling.

"We're really out in the open."

"That's what's nice about it. Didn't bother you yesterday."

He turned toward the lake. Only patches of blue were visible through the trees. The tops of nearby trees blocked his view of the trail leading up to Dead Mule Pass. The same trees, he supposed, would prevent anyone on the trail from seeing them, even with binoculars.

"Don't worry about it," Bert said.

"What, me worry?" Rick spread out the sleeping bag. Bert dropped the towels onto it.

He stood up and went to Bert and kissed her. Her arms went around him.

The feel of Bert soothed his fears, melted his cold tightness.

He stroked her back, slid his hands down and under the draping tails of her shirt. He caressed the smooth mounds of her buttocks. He ran his hands up her back. As he curled them over her shoulders, Bert stretched the front of his elastic waistband and dragged his shorts down around his thighs. He felt her cool, gliding fingers.

Moaning, he lowered his hands. He squeezed her rump, but it slid out of his hands as she crouched. She pulled the shorts down to his ankles and he stepped out of them. He felt a gentle kiss. Her tongue lapped the underside of his shaft. Then her lips opened and slid down him. She was wet and tight and she sucked.

Then she was rising. Rick felt air on his wet penis. He opened her shirt and spread it wide before she squeezed herself against him and her slick mouth joined his lips.

Soon, she eased back a little. She gazed at Rick as he

250

slipped the shirt off her shoulders. She reached back and shook the sleeves down her arms. The movements made her breasts shake slightly. Rick caressed them. He bent down and licked a jutting nipple. He pressed it between his lips. He opened wide and filled his mouth with her breast, tongue swirling over the springy nub. He felt her trembling fingers in his hair. He moved to the other breast and took it in, and as he sucked he put a hand between her legs. She spread her legs to make room for it. He slipped fingers into her. She squirmed and clenched his hair.

She pulled his hair gently and he let his head go back, the breast sliding out of his mouth. His fingers kept stroking. Bert's hips kept moving in a slow, languid way as she rubbed herself on his hand. Her mouth hung open. Her eyes had a vague look for long seconds, then seemed to focus on Rick's eyes. She moved his hand away as she lowered herself. He felt the light touch of her fingers on his penis, guiding him. She sank lower, taking him in, sheathing him. He went to his knees. Then he was all the way in, buried in her hugging warmth. She wrapped her arms around him and thrust her tongue into his mouth.

His knees hurt, but he didn't care. Bert was tight against him. They were locked together in a hard embrace. They were joined by his penis and her tongue. They had made love many times before, but somehow this time was different. He felt the difference. He didn't think about it, but he knew it was there. She wasn't his girlfriend or his lover. They were two parts of the same person and he felt a surge of joy that didn't overwhelm his passion but fired it instead.

Bert gasped into his mouth. Her tongue pushed in more deeply. He pulled at it and clenched her buttocks. She was motionless against him, but inside she clutched and squeezed him and seemed to be sucking him up. He fought to control himself.

She started to whimper. And then she shuddered against him and Rick gave up trying to hold back. He quaked, his penis far up into the center of her, suddenly jerking and pulsing, pumping out his semen, throbbing hard until he was drained.

When it was done, they stayed together, panting for air. Bert rested her chin on his shoulder. Her hair tickled his cheek. Her hands lay on his back, almost heavy, as if she were too spent to lift them. Spent or not, she kept certain muscles contracted to hold him inside her. He caressed her buttocks.

Later, she placed her open hands on the sides of his face and looked him in the eyes. "Could we stay like this forever?" she whispered.

"Maybe."

"Might be hard on the knees."

"What knees?"

She laughed, her nipples moving against his chest. Then she kissed him lightly on the mouth. Her vagina tightened, giving him a friendly farewell squeeze that brought a fresh stir of arousal so that he was growing hard again as she slid off him.

Bert duck-walked backward and sat on the sleeping bag. Her knees were red. She brushed them off. The grit left her skin pitted. Rick stood up. One of his knees popped when he straightened it. He bent over and rubbed them.

"We've got matching knees," Bert said.

"Should've used the sleeping bag. That's what it's here for."

"Any port in a storm," Bert said.

Rick limped and sat down beside her. He put an arm around her back.

"When are we going to take that dip?" she asked.

"I think I'd rather rest for a while before I brave the freezing waters."

"Then rest," she said. She turned him and guided him. He lay down on the sleeping bag, head on Bert's lap. Her legs were stretched out. She was leaning back, braced up on her arms. She smiled down at him. "Close your eyes."

"Are you kidding?" He turned his head and kissed the hot skin below her navel.

Bert stroked his hair.

His gaze roamed up the sleek bare slope of her body, studying her flat belly and the curves of her ribs, lingering on the smooth undersides of her breasts, on the twin rumpled disks of darker skin with jutting posts of flesh in the center of each. He looked up the valley between her breasts, at the hollow of her throat, at the soft sweep of her collar bones, her shoulders, her slender neck. Her face. She was smiling down at him.

"This may be as good as it gets," he said.

"Oh, I don't know. As good as it gets was maybe ten minutes ago."

"Think so?" Rick asked.

She shook her head. "Not really. It's all part of the same thing, isn't it."

His heart suddenly quickened. "I love you, Bert."

Her smile died. "I love you, too," she whispered.

She pressed her lips together. Her eyes shimmered . . .

"FOULNESS! STENCH!"

Bert gasped and flinched rigid at the sudden shouts. Rick lurched up. Prancing on a rock slab beside the stream no more than twenty feet above them was Angus, waving a large wooden club overhead.

"FILTH OF SATAN!"

Bert twisted away from the stranger. She flung an arm across her breasts, glanced up at Rick with shocked eyes, and looked back over her shoulder at the wild man.

"Angus . . ."

Rick sprang to his feet, his heart slamming. He had an urge to laugh—or scream, he didn't know which. His old buddy, the King of the Wild Frontier. Savior of souls. Christ. What a time to show up. The bastard. That coyote's head, with its mouth hanging open and those teeth an' all—no wonder he'd given Bert such a fright.

Rick didn't believe this was happening to them.

This is mad!

Angus hopped up and down like a crazy thing, shaking his

stick, the coyote head bouncing but not falling off.

"MAGGOTS! GET THEE GONE!"

"Get out of here, you damn lunatic!" Rick yelled.

"ANGUS MOUNTAIN KING! GET! NAKED INTER-LOPERS! VERMIN! TURDS!"

Angus ducked and skipped aside as a rock shot by, barely missing his head.

Rick looked at Bert. She was on her knees, reaching for another rock. She grabbed one and reared up.

"WHORE!"

"Crazy old fart!" she shouted, and hurled the rock at him. It struck his bare knee, just below the hem of his animal-skin robe.

He scurried backward.

Rick crouched. He picked up some of the chips of rock and joined Bert in throwing them at Angus.

The old man retreated up the slope, shaking his stick and shouting over his shoulder, "SICKNESS! DEFILERS! PUKE AND PISS!"

A rock thrown by Bert skimmed the top of his head. His coyote hat flew off. Suddenly, he looked a sorrowful sight; his straggly gray beard shook and trembled as he mumbled more profanities. He dropped to his hands and knees, grabbed the hat by its snout, scurried up and ran. Soon, he disappeared among the trees near a bend in the stream.

Rick and Bert faced each other. Her face was ashen, her eyes wide. "That, I presume, was Angus the Mountain King. You never did get around to telling me the whole story last night . . ."

"Yeah, sorry. I should have prepared you for that. I told you, he's a maniac, a freak. But, on the whole, probably harmless. Probably gets off on watching folks doin' what comes naturally . . ."

Bert was not convinced. She was still pale and Rick could see she was shaking.

"Let's get out of here." She hurried into her shirt. She tried to fasten the buttons while Rick put on his shorts. Her hands trembled too much so she gave up.

They rushed down to the clearing. In minutes, they were dressed and packed.

On the shoreline trail, they hiked fast and looked back often. They reached yesterday's campsite. The girls had already packed up and gone.

Bert stopped by the dead remains of the fire. She was breathing hard. Her shirt was still open. She lifted its front, baring her midriff, and knotted the ends together. "Should we head for the car?"

"If you want to."

"Don't *you?*"

"It was awfully nice before the Wild Man of the Mountains dropped by."

"What *is* he? What really makes him tick? He's out of it, sure. And gets his kicks spying on other people. Yuck. What a sicko."

"He's a hermit, I guess. Mad as a hatter."

"Don't mention hats. My God." She took a deep breath and shook her head.

"I *suppose* he was probably harmless."

"A High Sierra shopping cart man," Bert muttered.

"I wonder if he would've bothered us again."

"What, you want to go back and find out?"

"I hate to leave that place."

Bert looked into his eyes. "It wasn't the place, it was us."

"That's true. But the place was special, too."

"He ruined it."

"Maybe we can find somewhere else."

Bert raised her eyebrows. "Does that mean you don't want to leave?"

"I guess that's what it means. We ought to be able to find another nice, private place."

"That one didn't turn out to be so private."

"It was for a while."

"What have we got here, a convert?"

255

"Apparently. Why don't we take the trail you picked out yesterday?"

"The one the girls are taking?"

"We'll walk slowly."

"They can't be very far ahead of us," Bert said. "We weren't gone all that long."

"If we run into them, we do. But we won't stay with them. I want to find a place where we can be alone."

"Pick up where we left off?" Bert asked.

"Before the rude interruption."

"Fine with me."

Rick twisted the burning stub of his cigar against the rock by his hip. Then he rolled the remains between his thumb and forefinger, crumpling the cigar to flakes of brown leaf that drifted down onto the trail.

He looked at Bert. She was beside him, leaning back against her pack, her legs stretched down to the trail. Her hat with its one side turned up rested on her thigh, held there by the weight of her curled hand on its brim. Her belly was the color of dry sand. It had light, downy hair that was almost too fine to see. Her shirt was tied below the swell of her breasts. Her mouth was open slightly. Specks of sweat glistened above her lip and below her closed eyes. The hair across her forehead shone golden in the sunlight and moved as the soft breeze blew through it.

Maybe she was simply resting. Maybe she was asleep.

Rick decided not to disturb her.

There was no reason to hurry.

He felt perfectly content. So far, it had been one helluva trip, he reflected, and in some strange way he was sorry that it was all over. Back in civilization he wondered if they'd still feel the same way about each other. The same way as they did now.

Wide open spaces—and a touch of danger—did funny things to people. Heightened their senses. Made them think things they wouldn't normally think—or feel. What if . . .

well, suppose Bert didn't feel the same about him when she hit the real world again.

What if . . .

He hoped not. He sincerely hoped not.

Meanwhile, he was quite content. He wouldn't mind sitting here all day, he thought. Just looking at her . . .

Chapter Twenty-five

It was late when they woke next day. Ten-thirty. No nymphets invaded their space. No teen thugs. No Angus. They were alone. Just as they'd planned from the first, a vacation together, away from it all. Rick lay back and thought how different things would've turned out if only it had stayed that way.

No Andrea to disturb his dreams. No Bonnie to give him the snake-eye. Yeah, so they could *still* have met up with The Three Thugateers. And Angus, the Wild Man of the Mountains. In an ideal world, he supposed he and Bert could have handled all four of those dudes. Could've and would've, most likely.

With some help from my trusty equalizer . . .

Rick frowned. Not for the first time did he bitterly regret Bert having tossed his gun into the lake. Oh well, at least we have our knives—and I suppose in an emergency we can hurl a nifty rock or two.

Bonnie's hatchet would've been useful . . .

Bert's eyes were closed, but she was smiling.

No Sanctuary

"You thinking what I'm thinking, honey?"

"Mmm . . . maybe. Just depends. What *are* you thinking?"

"That I could murder a coffee. And a long lazy swim."

"Oh great!" Rick said. "And bring the wrath of that god-damn Angus down on our heads again!"

Bert faced him and leaned up on an elbow. She was naked, happy and smiling. The forefinger of her free hand traced slow circles on his chest.

"Hey. Ricky baby. Think positive. That's all over now. This is us, remember? We're on vacation and having a great time. Come on lazybones, let's go. Race you to the coffee pot!"

She swung back the flap of her bag and stretched luxuriously. She could afford to—as of right now she had him all to herself. Rick watched her smooth tanned back and the way her arms twisted provocatively above her head as she stretched. He reached out to touch her skin, then gave a sigh of resignation and let his hand drop. Plenty of time for that later.

Sins of the flesh!

Whoa boy, for a moment there you sounded like our lunatic preacher . . .

"Go on, get the coffee going, woman, and let a man get dressed in peace!"

They were alone now. Together. He savored the thought like a kid with a special Christmas toy. He had this all-over warm feeling because he knew they both cherished the *joy* of being together—the *tenderness* of it.

Nothing else mattered.

They'd been through hell and come through the other side okay. From here on in it's vacation time, folks.

Enjoy!

They heated up and drank what was left of last night's coffee. It tasted gritty, bitter. Like something from the bottom of a lion's cage, but hey, what the heck? Right now it was nectar from the gods.

"Let's just mosey around awhile before we set off back on

the trail," Bert said. "Let's live a little; enjoy ourselves. Might as well, since we're here."

"Suppose we meet up with Angus?"

"Then we'll turn right around and get back on the trail again. Whatever. C'mon, Rick. We can't keep saying *what if?* We're two responsible people. Innocent people, doing what hundreds of other responsible, innocent people do every year. Hit the trail and enjoy this great big beautiful country of ours!"

He held up his hands and said, "Okay, okay. Let's do it."

It was hot on top of the ridge. The blinding sun scorched their heads, despite the hats they wore. Rick checked his wristwatch. Two forty-five, near enough. They'd been on the back-of-beyond trail an hour and a quarter. Before that, they'd lingered over coffee, eaten beans and a couple of oaty breakfast bars. Then they'd spent some time in the stream. He sure could use that cool stream water right now. He imagined himself naked, scooping it up in cupped hands. All sparkling and cold. Sluicing down over his head, his shoulders, chest, and trickling all the way to his feet.

"You thinking what I'm thinking?" Bert asked.

"Probably. It's goddamn hot up here." He swatted away a bunch of mosquitoes swarming around his head. They parted, and came back for more. Persistent little bastards. Sizing him up for grub. He splatted one on his arm. It squelched red. *His* blood, he guessed. Or maybe Bert's. Or . . .

Bert pointed to a finger of pale gray smoke curling skyward. It came from a cabin, halfway down the other side of the ridge. "Who'd live in a place like that? Kinda isolated don't you think?"

They stared at the cabin. It was a dilapidated place, sprawling in an untidy heap, part hidden amidst the tall dark pines. It looked like a good place not to visit.

* * *

So who suggested it might be an adventure to take a closer look? Rick couldn't remember. Whatever. At the time, it seemed okay to investigate and discover who needed isolation so desperately as to put up sticks out here in the wilderness.

On the way down Rick decided that it was a bad idea, breaking in on somebody's solitude like this. But Bert insisted. "It's an adventure, Rick. We *are* on vacation after all, aren't we?" The way she looked at him, all innocent and eager, almost made Rick change his mind. Trying hard to convince himself, he reasoned that, time-wise, a slight detour wouldn't make a major difference. And they didn't exactly have a deadline to meet . . .

They descended at a slow jog, their packs bumping on their backs, propelling them forward.

"Did anybody mention climbing back up the mountain with these packs on our backs?" Rick muttered, under his breath.

The cabin was old; fifty, sixty years old, Rick reckoned. And it was in bad repair. The filthy rag stretched across the front window looked as if it'd hung there since the year dot. A broken-down rocker with a greasy plaid cushion propped up on its seat stood on the rotting porch.

The bad feeling Rick had had before suddenly got worse. He climbed the wooden steps and looked at Bert, poking around, pushing open the cabin door which was already ajar. The door had a small window in it. Its glass was stained with grime. A around hole had been rubbed in the dirt.

A peephole.

Bert's curiosity got the better of her; she was about to step inside.

"Bert . . ." he began.

A manic whoop cut through the stillness, then tapered off into a coy giggle. The giggle ended in a humorless titter.

Angus.

Who else?

Appearing from the far end of the cabin, making his way

slowly along the porch toward them. Head cocked like a wary animal.

Angus with a gun this time. An old hunting rifle held loosely but, Rick saw, with the practiced ease of an expert. It hung cocked in the crook of his arm.

King of the Wild Frontier or Preacher Man. *Which is he today?* Rick wondered. *Whatever, the guy means business . . .*

Bert, taken off guard, backed up against the doorframe. Her face had paled. A look of defiance had the twist of fear that was already teasing her gut.

"Hi Angus," she managed, cheerfully. "Care to give two weary travelers a drink of water?"

The coyote skins, even in this heat, shook around the preacher's shoulders. His bony chest was naked. Roughly stitched skin trousers covered his bowed legs. He let out a bark that Bert took to be laughter. She blanched again, hearing the triumphant ring to it.

"Yeah," Rick bluffed. "We were just passing by and thought you might offer us a drink—then we'll be on our way . . . On the other hand, no worries about the drink. We'll just be on our way. Bert?"

"Why yes," she chirped. "We'll be on our way. Er . . . have a nice day, Angus!"

Suddenly they were looking down the barrel of the preacher's gun. His face was screwed up alongside.

Easy does it . . . Rick's eyes signaled the message to Bert. Catching his drift, she nodded imperceptibly.

The gun jerked toward the cabin door.

"Get on it, get on in there, my fine, young travelin' friends."

Angus at his most amiable. Most wily.

A bullet clicked home.

Angus at his most persuasive, most *lethal*, Rick decided.

They turned and trouped in through the doorway.

First thing they noticed was the stench. Rotten food, human smells and something else; gamey, putrid. Couldn't make out what it was. Angus jostled them to a deal table. It was stained with coffee, food and God knew what else. The surface was cluttered and cracked with age.

Sweeping aside the dirty crocks, stale food and other debris, Angus made one end clear. He jerked the gun again.

They slid out of their packs and sat down.

Taking the rickety spindle-back chairs either side of the table, Bert had her back to the door. Rick faced her. Angus took his place at the head of the table, to the right of Bert, and eased himself into a wooden armchair. The rifle rested across his bony knees.

A moment's silence. Then Angus snatched off his hat and tossed it to one side. It landed in a mangy heap on the cabin floor. His head was bare, but for a few long gray hairs crawling through patches of thick, yellow scales. Grinning, he made his scraggly beard wiggle at them, and tapped the tabletop with a bony forefinger. Bert stared in disgust at the finger's long, grimy nail, noting that all of his nails were black—and curved, like the talons of a giant bird of prey.

"Put 'em down, right here!" he ordered. "That's it. You heard me right first time. Them huntin' knives you got tucked away in there."

They didn't want to do it, but right at this moment there wasn't a hope in hell of playing it any other way. Angus held the aces. And the gun.

Slowly, they unfastened their belts and placed the sheathed weapons, and the looped belts, side by side at the center of the table. Angus leaned over, raked them in and dropped them into his lap.

Rick and Bert remained poker-faced. Wouldn't do to let the bastard see that taking their knives was any major deal.

"Well, now," Angus smiled craftily, looking from one to the other. "Ain't this fine an' dandy. Just the three of us. Sitting here like old friends." He settled back into the curve of his chair and smiled some more.

Way too big for a skinny runt like him, Bert thought. It's built for a bigger man . . . She glanced around the one room cabin. Seated on her side of the table, she didn't have to move her head to do it.

A tousled bed with grimy, greasy covers stood in the top right corner. The filthy ticking pillow skewed sideways, half on, half off the mattress. Bert's eyes followed the pillow downward. To a huddle of dark canvas stashed beneath the bed. A loop or a strap had strayed from the pile. It lay curled like a snake on the worn wood floor.

A breath of fear flicked at her throat.

Over the brass-knobbed headrail hung a framed picture of Christ on the cross. Bert figured it probably served as a reminder to Angus to keep up the Lord's good works. She pictured him jumping out at them yesterday. Screaming insults and vile words.

No chance he'd forget, she reckoned.

To the right, sunlight filtered through a dirty rag-draped window. In the corner stood a large store cupboard. Its dark veneer had been polished at some stage of its life, but not anymore. She looked at the dull, wormy wood and reckoned it must be at least a hundred years old. An heirloom.

Like the dresser, with its heavy, carved shelves towering above the good-sized set of storage drawers. The whole thing filled most of the cabin's facing wall. Religious bric-a-brac and faded sepia photographs in brass frames littered the shelves and top surface of the drawers.

Bert's eyes lingered on a picture of a small, gentle-looking woman standing by the side of a seated, autocratic man. Both were laced up to the chin in Victorian-style dress.

In particular, she studied a photograph of a young girl with mournful eyes. She wore a crocheted shawl and stood with one arm across the shoulders of a small, pixie-faced boy with blond curls.

Family photos.

Was Angus that small boy?

An old Indian blanket thrown roughly over a wooden rail came next. Bert reckoned it could hide another door. Or a secret store of weapons, maybe. Her mind worked overtime.

If Angus got caught off guard, Rick could tackle him. I could rush the blanket, grab a gun or something, and we could shoot our way out . . .

Yeah. Pigs might fly.

Her eyes slid around to the left, taking in the plastered walls scarred at intervals by brown floral wallpaper. A section of the left-hand wall, the far side of one of the cabin's three windows, hoasted a rogue's gallery of faded heads.

Clerics of long ago. Much of a muchness: dog collars, around wide-brimmed hats and pursed, pained expressions. Different images of two men, it appeared. One, the elder, had a full bushy beard and mean eyes. The other had the same mean eyes, but was younger and clean shaven.

Father and son.

To her left, by the remaining window, stood a brownstone sink. Next to it, a lit stove made tiny spitting, crackling noises. It exuded a malodorous stink. The ash can beneath the stove was catching gobs and spills of grease. The falling grease made dark holes in the mounds of fine gray ash.

"You interested in my pictures, whore? Them there's my daddy an' my granddaddy. Both good men of the cloth. Preachin' the Lord's word all of their lives . . .

"Yessir . . . they wus good men, my daddy and my granddaddy. Men a mother could be proud of. Ridding the world as they did, of SCUM LIKE YOU!"

"You bastard . . ." Rick caught Bert's warning look and snapped his mouth shut.

"No offense. No offense . . ." Angus said, with a lewd smirk at Bert.

"Gotta keep on doin' the Lord's work."

He carries on like this, I'll kill him, thought Rick.

Interpreting his thoughts, Bert gave a small frown, and shook her head.

Angus was gone. Oblivious to the mental dialogue of his captives, he nursed his rifle lovingly against his chest, his bony fingers caressing the hard steel. He began rocking to and fro. The knife belts in his lap shifted and chittered. The sound roused him from his reverie and he continued his story.

"My daddy and his daddy afore him were strong Scottish Presbyterian. Ministers of the cloth, both. Back in Perthshire, Scotland, my granddaddy ministered to his flock of good folk . . . and kept them free from sin. A-men.

"Jist as the good Lord woulda wished.

"When he died, my daddy took over. But, in a wee while, that same flock turned on my daddy, so they did . . ."

His attention wandered again. Mumbling to himself, he looked up and stared for a long time at a brass crucifix hanging over the door.

Rick coughed. "And then what, Angus?" He looked at his wristwatch. "Whoa. So late? We really must be moving on. What d'you say, Bert?"

Relieved that Rick had broken the tension, Bert said, "Yes, sure thing. We better get going. Mustn't keep the girls waiting, must we, Rick? Promised we'd be back before dark."

In a flash, Angus was on his feet. The knives fell to the floor with a clattering *thunk*. He gripped his gun and shoved it at them with both hands.

"SIT DOWN, FILTH! I haven't finished yet. You ain't goin' nowhere till I've had my say!"

They all sat down. Angus gave them another crafty smile and resumed his story.

"First off, you can't fool me. Them girls broke camp a while back. They on their way to somewhere else by now. That means you're on your lonesome. Two lost sheep who've gone astray!" He giggled at his own words, then fell silent, his loose, wet lips pulsating gently beneath his beard. Testing the effect of the pun on his audience.

He leered slyly at Bert.

"See, now, where wus I? Yep. Then my daddy heard that there was a need for God's ministers over here in the United States of America. So we came over in a sailing ship. My daddy, my mammy and Maire and me. We traveled across the seas to this great country and finally dropped anchor, so to speak, in the Tehachapis.

"My daddy preached an' he preached till he was blue in the face. He loved his flock, oh my, how he loved them people. Mammy would cry and say that there was no need for him to love and care for them so much. 'Specially the young 'uns. She was there, she said—he didn't need no more love . . .

"And then he got to lovin' Maire. The Lord's wishes, he swore. An' my Daddy, he allus carried out the good Lord's wishes. Praise be to the Lord. A-men."

If I keep him talking, looking my way, Rick thought, *Bert could break out before he gets a chance to use his gun. I could overpower him. And we could be on our way.*

As if.

"Anyways. One night, them good church folk held a meetin' and a whole contingent of them marched over to our house and told my daddy to get out. They said he wus evil. Not fit to be a man of the cloth, they said.

"Daddy told them to go away and he closed the door, right in their faces. Went straight in to Maire's room and loved her some more. I could hear her pleadin' an' cryin.' She wus saying, *Daddy please don't. Don't Daddy, you're hurtin' me . . .*

"When Mammy went in, she found my sister Maire dead in her bed. A seizure, so my mammy said. She ran out into the night a-screaming for help and daddy got his gun, the one that's setting on my knee this very minute, and shot her dead.

"My daddy and me gathered up a few family treasures, took to the hills, 'n built us this mighty fine cabin, so we did. My daddy told me we were poor wanderers, a-travelin' the wilderness with only wild things for company. Jist like the Lord Jesus Christ, he said. Only we stayed more 'n forty days an' forty nights. We stuck it out for much longer. All of my daddy's natural born life, turned out . . .

"An' I been here since my daddy passed on. Lookin' after God's creatures and spreadin' the word. This 'ere mountain

267

country is my *home*. It gets a bit lonesome sometimes and I don't have much truck with outsiders . . . but, it's my home . . ."

"That's it." Rick stood up. So did Bert. Grabbing their packs, they started for the door.

A gunshot whined and hit the roof.

"No you don't. Filthy swine! Foul defilers! I'm not yet done with ye. REPENT AND BE SAVED!"

He marched them through the door, out onto the stoop and around to the back of the cabin.

Chapter Twenty-six

Bert's heart sank when she saw where they were headed.

Toward a cage-like pen made from tough, pine staves about twelve feet high and bound together by stout twine.

Angus danced around them, herding, prodding, maneuvering them together with his rifle. The cage door was open.

"Ready and waiting," Bert muttered.

An almighty crack descended on Rick's head and a gasp shot from his lips. He groaned, folded and went down on all fours.

What the. . . . ?

All in a day's work for Angus. Suddenly, he was business-like; prodding Rick with the rifle butt, kicking and pushing him into the cage.

Fuck.

Rick slid along the dirt floor, lurched to his knees and tried to stand. His legs gave and he crashed, face down, into the mat of foul-smelling straw.

Angus darted behind Bert and poked her sharply in the back. She stalled. Another vicious poke sent her sprawling onto the floor of the cage. Angus cackled to himself as he quickly secured the cage door with a strong plait of twine.

"Rest awhile my travelin' friends!" he simpered. "Rest and repent ye of your sins. Praise the Lord!"

"Shit, shit, shit," wailed Bert. She stood with her hands rattling the staves in angry frustration.

Rick got to his feet. "Okay," he panted. "He's got us for now. But we'll get out. No sweat." He wasn't sure how, but they'd make it. If it was the last thing he . . .

This is too ridiculous for words. We're two intelligent, professional people. Doing nobody any harm. All we ever wanted was to be left alone . . .

This can't be happening to us. It can't. I won't let it . . .

Rick bashed the palings with a clenched fist. All the way down one side of the cage, the staves shook in unison. A blinding pain shot through his skull. And his fist. The pain in his head was bad, but now his fist . . .

He cursed. They both needed his two hands to be in working order. Trust him to go and get a loused-up fist . . .

The crack on his head, from the rifle butt had raised a fair-sized lump. He groaned and pictured a bottle of Jim Beam, standing on the bar, back in his apartment. A glass, half filled with sparkling rocks was ready and waiting. The amber fluid glinted seductively, beckoning to him . . .

Rick closed his eyes against the screeching pain in his head. Oh, for anything, but *anything* vaguely alcoholic, preferably straight from the bottle. And aspirin. Got some in my pack.

Angus, would you mind fetching me some water and aspirin? The aspirin's in my pack, by the way.

Christ, give me strength.

When that fuckin' turd leaves us alone, we'll find a way out of his goddamn cage.

"Rick," Bert said quietly. "Look at this." She pointed to a heap of canvas humps in the corner of the cage.

"Backpacks. Old backpacks, Rick." She looked at him and the same thought passed between them.

"Huh. Kids who never got around to repenting . . ." Rick said.

"Looks that way."

"Probably butchered and got eaten for breakfast."

Rick's watch told him it was six o'clock already. "We rest up till dark. Okay?" he whispered. "Meanwhile, we'll figure out a way to escape."

Bert was near to tears. "Oh, sure, Rick. What d'you suggest? Please Angus, let us outa here 'cos we want to go home now?"

Rick hadn't got an answer. Yet. They couldn't climb over the staves. Too high, too pointed and far too dangerous. They couldn't try to shake the staves loose from their moorings either. Angus might be watching.

When it got dark, they'd find a way.

They sat together, their backs leaning against the palings. They felt *defeated.*

Bert huffed loudly. "I'm so hot and sticky. Can't take my shirt off; our friendly fuckin' neighborhood creep'd probably get off on it."

"Rest while we can, Bert, that's about all we *can* do."

As the shadows lengthened around the cage, they fell silent and dozed a little.

A low, throaty snarl brought Rick to his senses.

He lay stretched out on the floor. Eyes closed.

Christ. His head hurt.

What in the name of Jesus happened to us these last few hours?

He remembered this morning, so long ago now, sitting and staring at Bert, thinking that he could do that all day.

Hell, I shoulda just done it. Stayed there. All day.

Bert?

Where *is* Bert . . .

Rick's hand shot to his head. It felt like it had been kicked around a baseball pitch, non-stop. He groaned and let his hand drop to his side. Easier that way. Just lying there.

Eyes open now.

Staring at the night sky . . .

Another low snarl. More like a warning growl, Rick thought. It was deep, throaty and seemed like it was sending him a message.

Coming to getcha, white man . . .

Okay. Here I am . . .

He watched the clusters of stars above.

Constellations.

Asteroids.

Planets.

They were all up there, in the yawning blackness.

He moved his head—first to one side, then the other.

The lump on it throbbed like crazy. He lifted his left hand to feel it.

Ouch . . . maybe I should have a brain scan . . .

A gut-wrenching stench brought him to. A den of *lions*?

He sat up.

Flashes of pain shot fresh stars into the hurt already there. He groped his eyes with a hand and saw more bright lights.

Fuck stars. I got big, blinding asteroids.

Rocking to and fro, he remembered where he was. And why.

Small, stifled sobs caught his attention. They broke off, snagging in their owner's throat. Sobs and wails of frustration.

Louder this time.

"Bert?"

"Rick . . ." she sniffed. "Thank God you're awake. You passed out."

"Yeah. My head's killing me."

"Rick, I've not heard Angus for a while. But I've heard his playmates . . ."

A low warning snarl was joined by another. And another. And another in a higher key. Then a sharp yelp as if its owner had received a hefty swipe.

"Yeah. Cougars, Rick. They're here and they're close . . ."

272

Rick staggered to his feet and moved forward, hands held before him. God, it was dark.

And that fuckin' *smell* . . .

His outstretched arms touched palings. Placed about four inches apart. He fingered the twine holding them together at intervals, and tugged at the staves.

God, I need a drink. My mouth's like the bottom of a lion's cage. Nice choice of words, Rick. Go to the top of the class.

The staves had been hammered in firmly. Too firmly. There was no moving them. No tools to loosen them with either. Rick's heart sank.

"Wooden bars all around and goddamn mountain lions waiting for our skins," he muttered.

"If we could just loosen the staves, perhaps I could slip through . . ." Bert muttered, testing each one to see if she could work it free.

A blinding light slashed through the darkness. Covering their eyes against it, the preacher's high-pitched giggle rang out.

"Welcome to 'Braeside' chapel of rest for all ye who are heavy laden. You're very welcome indeed to lay down your weary bones and tarry here for a wee while."

The r's were strongly pronounced—a bizarre parody of a Scottish accent. A pious greeting you might expect from a preacher's wife.

Angus stood outlined in the yellow glow from the doorway. A gnome-like figure, hopping from one foot to the other in excitement. He held a lighted candle in one hand.

"So that's what was hiding behind the blanket," Bert muttered. "Not weapons. Not stove-wood. Another door."

Another peephole.

Angus was wearing his coyote hat again. It swung about his shoulders as he giggled. Over his free arm he nursed the old rifle. He still hopped from one leg to the other like a maniac.

Scuttling forward, the flickering flame lit up the dog snout

273

from underneath. His straggly beard was in serious danger of going up in smoke.

Angus glared at his prisoners. His eyes, gleaming through the holes in the coyote head, darted gimlet sparks in their direction. His beard moved up and down as he cackled and jibbered an endless stream of profanities.

"Rick," Bert whispered. "What is this screwball gonna do with us?"

Angus hurried past their cage. "Here, kitty, kitty, kitty . . ." he called softly into the darkness.

A volley of mild growls and snarls came back.

The preacher turned to look at Bert over his shoulder. "Does that answer your question, *whore*?" he simpered, with sneering emphasis on the last word. "My kitties haven't had a good meal in quite a wee while. Not since the last godless sinners passed this way. Hee, hee . . ."

"He's crazy."

"Bert, hold on. Don't say anything to spook the guy."

Bert's eyes flashed with impatience. "What d'ya think I'm nuts or something?"

Rick grinned and kept his eyes on Angus.

Yeah. The guy *was* crazy. But crazy like a fox, and Rick knew he had to be just as clever. Get into his mindset and play him along at his own game.

"He's got our knives, so we can't get physical," he whispered. "Maybe if we talked him into opening the gate to this place, we could rush him."

Right on cue, Angus set the lighted candle down on the grass. Then, like a magician performing his best trick, he fumbled at the waist of his trousers and with a flourish, produced two knives. Still in their sheaths. He held them by their belts, one in each hand, and jiggled them in the candlelight.

"You'll not be needing these little beauties. Filth! Defilers!" he taunted, throwing the belts down onto the grass.

"Okay, Rick. Do your stuff. Start talking," Bert muttered.

The cougars milled around in the background. Getting restless. Snuffling, giving sharp little whines.

274

No Sanctuary

Peering through the darkness, Rick and Bert could see them pacing around in their compound—another "cage" of strong, supple staves bound together by twine—about five yards from their own. The cats' noses pointed skyward. Sniffing out the human scent. Slinking around their pen, one after the other, their powerful tails swinging low and threatening.

The cats were hungry—and impatient. Most of all, hungry.

"He's out of his gourd," Rick hissed back. "You can't reason with a madman. We'll just have to play it by ear. There's got to be a chance to break out, somehow."

He hoped to God there would be. They'd have to make a desperate move soon or they'd wind up dead, for sure. Sweat streamed from his armpits. If it weren't so damned hot.

And still.

Like the unbearable calm you get before a storm.

The moon was a smooth around disc, hanging high in the soft night sky. Rick watched it and wondered if they'd be around to look at it tomorrow night. He grunted in disgust. Because of that stupid, damnfool idea of theirs, they were here, imprisoned in the preacher's stinking back yard.

In this clammy, stench-ridden hell-hole.

"Rick, look at this," Bert pointed to the ground. A shard of glass, picked out by the moon, glimmered gently in the dark soil.

Rick screened her body with his. Bert bent to pick up the glass. She retrieved it quickly and stood up.

"Probably left by the last weary travelers," she mouthed.

Wonder what happened to them?

Don't ask . . .

Pressing the piece of glass to her lips, she breathed a silent "thank you" to the last occupants of the cage.

Angus had his back to them, facing the cats, mumbling and whining exaggerated words of endearment. He'd left the candle burning by their cage. He seemed in a world of his own, but his rifle was still cocked and resting on his left arm.

King of the Wild Frontier.

Behind him in the cage, Rick was gripping staves, shaking

275

them back and forth. Looking up now and again to make sure Angus was still talking to the animals.

He was.

No joy with the staves, though.

Firm as rocks.

Bert followed suit and suddenly hit paydirt. One of the staves jiggled about in her hand. They exchanged triumphant glances. Bert bent down to see if she could work another one loose.

Yes.

She began working on the twine with the glass shard.

Rick was having a hard time with his staves. He'd only worked his way through six by the time Angus quit his conversation with the cats.

Shit.

"Not much longer now kitties. Come sun-up, you'll have the biggest breakfast you've eaten in a long, long time. You all, and me both—we'll have us a mighty toothsome meal!"

Still working on the twine, Bert watched him from behind the bars. From where she was standing, Mr. Preacher-Man looked like he was in serious need of some sleep. He may be a lunatic, but he was old and frail. Should be tucked up in his flea-ridden rags by now.

Sweet dreams, turd bastard . . .

She worked on the twine some more.

Yes!

It had come free in her hand. A quick wrench and she'd cleared the stave from its moorings. Adjusting her balance, she held it poised like a spear; threw back her arm and zoomed it through the air, straight at Angus.

His rifle fell to the ground.

"Ha!" he shrieked, clutching his hat and side-stepping out of the way.

"BITCH! WHORE! FILTH! You'll rue the day you did that . . ."

He tailed off as Bert bent down and slid her body easily through the eight-inch gap. With a yell, she bent and grabbed the stave again and thrust it deep into his bare shoulder. Blood spurted and spilled down the fur skins.

Looks like a wounded animal, Bert thought.

But instead of going down, he plucked out the stave, threw it to the ground and kicked it aside, blood still pouring from the gash. He came for her, slowly but surely, his arms spread wide. She caught the evil glint in his sunken eyes. He reminded her of a snake mesmerizing a rabbit.

And for a moment she *was* mesmerized.

Rick saw what was happening.

Zombie-like, Angus moved forward. Through the gaping holes, his eyes were mean and menacing . . .

Feverishly, his bony fingers worked at the front flap of the skin trousers. They fell loose and he shook them down, stepped out of them and kicked them out of the way. His skinny body glistened with blood and sweat. The hole in his shoulder still pumped blood.

His horny erection jerked in anticipation.

Rick found a stave that moved in his grasp. He wrenched it around until it came free. He'd already cut through the twine with the glass shard.

The space between the two poles was too narrow for his body. He pushed. Tried to force his way through but couldn't quite make it.

Shit!

Bert screamed "Rick!" as Angus knocked her to the ground.

He leapt on top of her, his filthy dog furs swinging over her body. The fur got in his way, so he grabbed his hat by the snout and flung it to the ground. Rick caught sight of the preacher's pate, gleaming in the moonlight and ludicrously sprouting long gray hairs from its scaly patches.

Blood still ran freely from Angus's shoulder. It flowed down through Bert's blue chambray shirt and onto her chest. Her arms were sprayed and spattered with blood as she struggled to free herself.

With rising hysteria, Bert felt the man's strength. He was thin, old, but wiry and *incredibly* strong. Tearing open her shorts, he dragged them, and her panties, down her failing legs. Then, like some greedy, parasitic vine, he coiled his own corded, bony ones around her. She struggled violently against his vice-like grip and, still under him, managed to force her knees up against his bony chest.

She screamed again. "Rick, I can't fight him—he's so strong! *Get him off me! Pleeease!*"

Her voice rose hysterically. Through it all, she could hear the cougars mewling and whining with excitement.

The second stave broke free from its moorings. Rick tossed it away and forced himself through the gap. He'd made it! Rushing forward he flung himself at the slobbering, quaking figure jerking up and down on top of Bert. It was shoving, panting, making small whimpering noises.

Rick fought back vomit as he landed on top of them.

God, the bastard's doing it. He's raping her.

Rick wrenched the jibbering preacher away from Bert and threw him off her.

Angus's back hit the ground hard. He grunted and whimpered with the shock of it. Eyes, wide-open, bulged out of his head, and his slack, slobbering mouth worked behind the blood-flecked beard. Rick stared down at the emaciated body. Still writhing in some kind of ecstasy, glistening with the exertion. The wormy penis was a thin, sharp spike, refusing to lie down. A long stream of semen slimed from it to Bert's bare leg.

"Aaarrgg!"

Released, Bert rolled away from the conflict, tears of revulsion streaming down her cheeks.

The crud tried to fuck me . . .

But he didn't make it in.

Nearly did, though.

God. How did we get into this fucking nightmare? Why aren't

we in some expensive hotel in Maui? Why are we here in this . . .
this stinking hell-hole?

The preacher's breath came shouting out in snarls and
pants as Rick slashed him across the face with the back of his
damaged hand. White hot pain seared Rick's knuckles. But
he couldn't stop. Again and again he brought his fist back
and forth across the bony skull.

Blood, his and the preacher's both, clotted the filthy beard
and spattered the ground around them.

Slowly, Bert stood up, dragged up her panties and fastened
her shorts. Then squirmed as she saw the semen on her legs.
Plunging her hand into her shorts pocket, she found a wad
of tissue and rubbed vigorously at the mess. First one leg and
then the other.

Satisfied she was as clean as she could get, she tossed the
soiled paper and turned her attention to Rick.

"He's gone, Rick. You're only hurting yourself more. Let's
go. Jesus, Rick, just let's go."

She saw tears of rage and revulsion falling down Rick's
face. He looked up at her. "Christ, Bert. We didn't *need* this.
The sicko tried to fuck you, Bert. I mean, how did this thing
HAPPEN?"

Nursing his shattered hand, he rose to his feet. She
wrapped an arm around his waist and they turned to go.

Rick staggered and fell from a terrific blow from behind.
Bert nearly went with him.

Regaining her balance, she whipped around and came face
to face with a cougar. White muzzle, dark mask, pale golden
eyes. Up so close she saw the spittle drooling from its teeth
and felt the heat of its rancid breath.

Jesus. A big one. Granddaddy of them all.

A group of maybe four tawny bodies milled around the
compound. The roughly made barred gate had swung open.
The cats saw it and filed through at a trot.

Coming their way.

Rick stayed on his knees. No choice, the cat's front paws

were holding him down. He felt its steaming hot breath in the nape of his neck.

A wet, flashy tongue investigated his ear.

Bert's heart sank faster and she felt sweat ooze from her armpits. *Oh my God*, she panicked. *What shall I do? I should know, but I can't think straight . . .*

Then, like watching an old movie, a childhood memory reeled through her mind. She saw four lions sitting upright on big round drums in a circus ring. A fat ringmaster in red coat and white breeches faced one of the lions. He held a whip which he kept flicking at the beast. The lion pawed the air, trying to grab the whip . . . The other lions grumbled, became restless. Angry roars broke out. She remembered her ten-year-old self thinking what a goddamn stupid thing to do . . .

IDIOT. This is *not* a traveling circus.

This is for real! Out of the corner of her eye she saw the hungry way the cat was nuzzling Rick's neck. Do it, girl.

Do it.

She did it.

Bending quickly, she grabbed the bloodied stave from the ground. Momentarily distracted, the cat growled and lunged for her. But she had the stave now, held like a spear, above her head. She leapt out of the cat's reach and did a little war dance, to keep it distracted.

She gained its full attention.

The cat reached her easily in a single bound.

As it roared and swiped at her, she thrust the stave deep into its gaping maw. The cat fell back, shaking its head, gurgling blood. Sprays of it spurted from its mouth. Drenching her hair, face, body and legs. As it shook its head, more red spurted onto her—and all over Rick.

The cat pawed the ground, withdrawing from them, padding backward, uttering strangled, whimpering noises. Still shaking its head, trying to free the stave.

Its paws worked at the wood but the stave didn't budge. With a final roar, the cat twisted over and lay panting on its side. The stave had gone through the throat and was poking out the other side.

"Come on!" Bert shouted.

Momentarily, the other cats had retreated, watching, lynx-eyed, from a distance. But they were really excited now. Creeping forward, they sniffed and butted the head of the fallen cat—then, one by one, smelling fear in the air, their noses lifted. Their interest in Rick and Bert was swift, sudden.

They closed in for the kill . . .

Bert gripped Rick's arm.

"The knives, Bert," Rick panted. "They're around here someplace."

"Oh, leave them, Rick." Frowning, she looked around in the darkness. By some miracle there they were, close to her feet, belt buckles glinting in the moonlight. Where Angus had thrown them.

She bent down, hooked them up and grabbed Rick's good hand. Why she snapped her head around at that moment, she couldn't say. But she did, and saw a head, half buried in the dark clumps of grass. It was a woman's head with tousled brown hair and an eaten face. Most of the face was gone, but one eye remained. Wide open. It stared at Bert.

Swaying with shock, Bert clung tightly onto Rick's hand. They both legged it through the cabin door and slammed it shut behind them.

For a moment, they leaned back against the door, acutely aware of the roaring cats on the other side. The door shook as heavy paws pounded and tore at the wood.

Kicking the Indian blanket out of his way, Rick made a grab for one of the wooden chairs and stashed it against the quaking door.

Angus!

Bert reached up for a quick peek through the small window in the door. It was misted with grime but she could still see the preacher.

Alive. Only just.

He was on his back, his bare, spindly legs curling against

his chest. His arms were up, vainly shielding his head.

Come sun-up, you'll have the biggest breakfast you've eaten in a long time . . .

A strong-looking cat, a young male, was taking powerful swipes at him, rocking his body back and forth, moving him around like a rag doll. The other cats were spiteful, restless; prowling around impatiently, swiping at each other. A couple pushed their noses in, but instinct kept them from going for the kill. The big male would take his share first.

The cat nosed around the man's upturned butt and sniffed its way through the slowly cycling legs. Then gave all of its attention to the soft genitals . . .

The preacher's puny erection had died long since.

Piercing screams told them when the cougar made its first strike. The big male dealt with the innards, shaking its head like a cat with a rat, until the bunch of steaming gut stretched like elastic and broke free from its moorings.

Another shake and the cat dragged the bloodied entrails outside of the body, gathering the hot, dripping mess into his powerful maw. It nosed upward, a jaw-full of the dripping trophy glistening yellow in the dawn light.

Gobs of dark blood dripped from the prize, down the cougar's chops and made slimy trails on the grass. The cat lay down, took the kill between its paws and started to eat.

Curls of warm mist rose up from around the feast.

In seconds, Angus was covered in a roiling mound of tawny bodies, each hungry cat fighting for its share of the kill.

Don't hurt me, Daddy, please don't hurt me . . .

Too late. Deed's already done . . .

The cats squabbled among themselves, each fighting to tear off its own share of the preacher. One, its nose bloodied from the kill, carried a dark skinny arm between its jaws. It moved away from the others and settled down to devour its trophy.

"Oh, God . . ." breathed Bert. "The guy was horrible—sick and mad. But he didn't deserve to die like this . . ."

No Sanctuary

Rick wanted to vomit, but the carnage happening before them was like a magnet. He couldn't tear his eyes away.

"Show's over, Rick," Bert said. "Let's go before I barf all over the place."

"Yeah, you're right. Let's get outa here," he agreed.

They hurried through the cabin, fastening their belts as they went and adjusting their hunting knives. They found their packs where they'd dropped them earlier and thrust their arms through the straps.

It was sun-up by the time they hit the trail again and they didn't stop until they'd reached the fork in the path. They were exhausted, breathless, but at least they were alive. They had their packs—and their knives.

"I just wish I hadn't seen that eaten head, Rick. That coulda been us, y'know? Thank God *we're* still around to tell the tale," Bert said.

"You can say that again." Rick's injured hand was painful and he wondered how long it'd be before they hit the stream again. He could use some cold water to ease the pain and the swelling.

". . . could use a beer, too," he muttered.

"And me."

"Yeah, one for the road and how 'bout a nice juicy burger on the side." He gave a faint grin.

"Christ. Have a heart," Bert grimaced. "On the other hand, maybe don't have a heart. Too soon to talk offal after the slaughter-fest down at Chez Angus, don't you think?"

Gratefully, they looked deep into each other's eyes and Rick felt a sudden surge of joy. It sure was good to be alive.

"C'mon," he said. "Let's put some miles between us and this crazy place."

Chapter Twenty-seven

After parting company with Rick and Bert, the girls fell quiet. Trudging on in silence, they already felt lonesome. The goddamn *emptiness* of this whole terrain was getting to them so much, it was scary.

Andrea spoke first. "I don't know that we did the right thing, Bonnie. Maybe we should have insisted we all stay together."

"What are you, nuts or something? They practically told us to go our own ways. Or weren't you listening to those people?"

"Sure, I know that. But I could've persuaded Rick. Y'know?"

"Yeah. I bet," Bonnie sneered. "You made a fool of yourself back there with Rick. You know that, Andrea, don't you?"

"You mean you were jealous of the way he came onto me?"

"Jealous? You *threw* yourself at him. Practically handed yourself to him on a plate. I'm surprised Bert didn't kick up about that. I admire her. She's got a lotta patience, that woman!"

"Oh yeah? Then how come if he loved her so much he invited himself to my tent? Answer me that, why don'cha?"

"Let's not go over that particular scenario anymore, Andrea. *Puhlease!* You're so hung up on yourself I'm surprised you don't have an orgasm every time you look in the mirror!"

Andrea plumped herself down on a smooth slab of rock. She edged out of her pack and swung it to the ground.

Holy Moses. Was she *pooped*!

And what's more, she didn't like the way the conversation was headed. She could do without all this shit about her and Rick.

With a sigh, she flipped off her ballcap and wiped her brow with the back of her hand.

"Bonnie Jones. If you don't stop handing me insults like this, I ain't goin' nowhere with you. It's too darn hot to argue and I don't know why we're traveling by ourselves, anyway. We coulda gone on ahead of the others—or trailed behind. We needn't have gone *with* them . . ."

Andrea was almost whining now. She mopped her brow again.

Then lifted the hem of her gray T-shirt, bent her head down and wiped all of her face with it. It didn't help much; sweat was still rolling down her cheeks.

Bonnie tried to reason with her. "Okay, okay. But you heard them say they'd rather travel alone. Rick specifically said they wanted some time to themselves.

"And if it helps, I don't know why we had to come out here into the boonies, anyway. Come to think about it, it was a dumb thing to do. But we *did* discuss it, Andrea, before we set out. When we had taco and fries and cola at Pepe's Pitstop, the day you took your social history books back to the library and they were overdue. Remember? We talked it over and agreed that a week's vacation by ourselves, *alone* in the Sierras, would clinch it."

Andrea sniffed at the front of her T-shirt.

God, it stinks. After this is all over, I'm gonna toss this thing in the trash, no kidding.

She screwed up her eyes and peered at Bonnie, standing before her, hands on hips, with her back to the sun.

"Clinch what?" she asked suspiciously.

"Whether we could make it together, dummy. Christ, Andrea. Don't make me spell it out."

Bonnie huffed in frustration and edged her way out of her backpack. Pushing out her chest, she bent at the knees and lowered the bulky pack to the ground. She collapsed on the smooth rock shelf beside Andrea, stretched out her sturdy legs and examined the toes of her boots . . .

Okay. Let's take it slowly. From the top.

With a small sigh of resignation she began, "Look, Andrea, you know how I feel about you. I just hoped that . . . you know . . . a little time spent together and you'd begin to feel the same about me, too."

Bonnie warmed to her subject.

"I mean, you seemed to get off on me, at the first. Now you go all girly and start making out with the first goddamn available male you see."

Andrea sounded repentant. "Sorry, Bonnie. I've been a grade-A idiot, I know. But I can't help myself. Maybe . . . well, the thing is, maybe I'm not cut out to be a dyke, after all."

She traced circles on her smooth, tanned knee. Bonnie watched her do it and thought how much she'd like to take her in her arms.

I mean, make the sparks fly.

Float her boat until she screams for more.

Hell. She was no fucking expert at dykedom herself.

What experience had she had? She only knew that from age fifteen-ish she'd been significantly different from the other girls in class.

Always awkward around guys, she'd never actually dated one—not that she'd ever been asked. Wouldn't have gone with one even if she had.

Neither was she in awe of guys. Not like the other bimbos,

describing in ecstatic terms how they'd been to the movies/
the game/the beach with this fantastic guy etc. etc . . .

Instead, she'd always aimed to come out top. The guys
didn't like that. At college she'd always had to be *better* than
they were. Better at everything, sport, science, cultural studies—all of that . . .

And then there was that, well . . . call it an exploratory
fling, if you like, with Deena Alvarez, her Cultural Studies
tutor.

Dark, sensuous Deena.

She of the sensational body, full, voluptuous breasts and
nipples like dark, ripe berries.

Okay. She'd been too wary; scared that she wouldn't make
the grade. And in the end she'd come away feeling totally
exasperated with herself. Embarrassed. Pissed off. In a nut-
shell, she was just too damned inexperienced. The demanding
Deena had eventually gotten impatient with her—she, and
her fumbling, inadequate responses. Within a week Bonnie
had been out on her ear with a bunch of insecurities as high
as the Empire State.

And Deena moved onto that *total* dork; the dumbest of all
dumb broads, Caroll Helliman.

Bonnie flushed at the memory of that particular put-down.
Yeah. That really had been a swinging blow to her pride and
dignity. She knew she was better at most things, including
sex, than that slut Caroll, who acted no better than cheap
trailer trash, with her minis up to her ass and those fancy
low-cut blouses of hers. Plus a gnat-size brain that got no
further than the color of her lipstick. Jeez, Deena musta been
desperate.

Caroll's folks were loaded, though. They were in real estate. Had a hunk of their own the size of Disneyland. But,
no matter how many sackloads of dough they had, Bonnie
decided, it'd never buy "class" for their sleaze of a daughter.

What the hell. She'd bounced back from that and had had
a smoldering affair with raven-haired Lindy Carson, nubile
daughter of one of the night porters at UCSC.

That went sour when she caught the lovely Lindy naked and cavorting in the shower with half of the college baseball team. From then on in, it had been "no way, Jose" for Bonnie. Sex was off the menu.

Romance was for the birds, so to speak.

Then along came Andrea. Fragile, elegant, graceful Andrea, with her upturned nose, glossy blond hair and slender legs that went on forever. Yeah, Bonnie decided. Andrea was the one for her, all right.

Now, here on vacation in the Sierras, the question had to be asked. *Was* she the one?

I'll work on her some more. She doesn't play ball, I'll find somebody else who will, thought Bonnie, knowing that if Andrea didn't come across now, she might as well chuck it in.

Plenty of others out there.

May well be, but there's only one Andrea.

It's make or break time.

"Bonnie . . ." Andrea twisted her hands, looking slightly embarrassed.

"What is it? You can't stand the sight of me? You wanna phone home and ask your Mom if it's okay to be a dyke? What's the problem, Andrea? Spit it out."

Andrea spat it out. Slowly and with feeling.

"You know how I get these hunches sometimes . . . like *premonitions*?"

Jesus Christ, that's all we need . . . Three teenage fuckin' hoods. Now we get a message from beyond.

"You have mentioned them before. Go on."

"Well," Andrea twirled a strand of sweat-damp hair around her finger.

She was obviously ill at ease. Bonnie prepared herself for some bad news.

"What would you say if I said don't let's go back by way of Dead Mule Pass?"

Andrea picked at the hem of her T-shirt, uncomfortable, knowing that Bonnie was staring at her, open-mouthed.

"I just get this feeling, Bonnie," she went on quietly. "It's a really strong feeling that we should take another route."

Andrea slipped off the rock and faced Bonnie. Then, reaching out, she caressed Bonnie's shoulder. The touch was gentle and timid, like the flutter of a small bird. With mounting impatience, Bonnie shrugged it off.

"Please," Andrea said in a small voice. She knew she would cry in a minute if Bonnie didn't say something nice to her.

Like, *It's okay. You're with me. I'll look after you.* Or, *Don't mind me, I didn't mean what I said about you and Rick.*

Instead she got a gesture of bored resignation from Bonnie and, "Er . . . okay. If that's what you want."

Bonnie slid off the rock and hunkered down to open her pack.

Pulling out a well-thumbed map of the Sierra Nevada mountains, she spread it on the rock before them and began to trace out another route.

"There isn't another recognized route to Mulligan Lake," she announced eventually. "We could go up this ridge, here, and then drop down, by-passing Dead Mule Pass. But it's out of the way; we're not likely to meet many other backpackers along there. You get into trouble on the Mulligan Lake Route, and you'd see other hikers and maybe a ranger on patrol to help out.

"Sorry, but the way I see it, Andrea, the main route is the only way to go."

"Damn."

"But we're not likely to hit a problem, are we? I mean, the terrible trio have gone their own way by now. And the mad preacher is probably rounding up repentants somewhere else."

"*Please*, Bonnie."

"Hey. Somebody's gotta act responsible around here. We can't go wandering off down some lonesome ol' trail nobody uses. Nobody except those with no business on the official route, that is. Talk sense!"

"Okay," Andrea lifted her chin defiantly. "Don't say I didn't warn you."

She swung up her pack, shrugged her arms into the straps and adjusted her load. Bonnie followed suit. She glanced sideways at Andrea's self-righteous expression.

"Okay. Okay," she said, with a dramatic sigh. "We'll do it the hard way. Main route to Mulligan Lake, it isn't. Trail of the lonesome pine, it is."

Bonnie stomped on ahead. She wasn't happy about choosing the ridge route. They had their knives, and could throw a mean rock if trouble broke out. And she still had her brother's hatchet . . . But what if one of them broke a leg or fell into a crevasse—anything could happen.

And probably would, she thought, gloomily.

One of them had to stay behind, they could get chomped by a goddamn cougar.

"You're not happy with this, are you, Bonnie?"

Andrea was striding out, abreast of Bonnie now. She took a peek at Bonnie's set face.

"The hell I'm not happy with it. But, my mystic munchkin, if you've got a funny feeling about reaching Mulligan Lake by the tried and tested, we'll go the ridge route. No problem. The map says it's the quickest route anyway, so that's one consolation."

They were climbing now; a cluster of pines up ahead told them that the trail—*what trail?*—began right here. They kept on trucking. This way, they'd soon get through and back to their vehicle in no time.

Not worth hassling about.

Who needs the main route anyway?

They pressed on up the rough grass track. Then, "Bonnie, are you hearing what I'm hearing?"

Bonnie stopped and listened.

"Yeah, guys' voices," she replied.

"What d'you reckon? Men or boys?"

"Haven't the foggiest. Whatever they are, they sure sound as if they're whooping it up."

Andrea stopped, hand on hip, and listened some more. The whoops got louder. Men. A group of men, *gotta be backpackers* were headed their way. *But they sound more like hooligans than your average hiker*, she thought.

More shouts. Bursts of coarse laughter rang out through the trees ahead. The voices:

"Hey, Wilbur. I fancy a bit o' skirt! How 'bout you?"

"You'll be lucky 'round these parts! Don't see no skirt hereabouts. Can you see anything that vaguely looks like a skirt, from where you're standing, Bud?"

"Not from where he's standin', he can't. He's busy takin' a leak!"

"Aw, leave it out, Wilbur. Go get yourself another beer."

Loud guffaws echoed through the dark trees.

Bonnie and Andrea tensed as they heard footfalls coming toward them on their left, through the forest undergrowth. The footfalls got closer, but they still couldn't see the guys.

Then, "Shoulda brought that Nicole along. She'd oblige us, all three. Yessirree. An' then ask for more!"

They heard whoops of laughter, lewd, suggestive. Then it simmered down to muffled, low-key banter.

Andrea and Bonnie couldn't quite hear what was being said.

The next gust of laughter seemed a helluva lot nearer to where they were standing. Holding their breath, they looked at each other, wondering what to do.

" 'nother can of beer, Wilbur?"

"Sure, Dean, chuck it across . . ."

The slap of a hand catching a beer.

"They're shit-faced . . ." Bonnie whispered. "But it sounds like maybe they're settling down. Taking a goddamn rest. And we've got to walk along the path, right past them—there's no other way!"

"So what? We just ignore them. Pretend we haven't seen them and just, well, just walk on by . . ."

"Oh yeah. Great. Andrea, haven't you learned your lesson yet? We got rid of The Three Thugateers, now we meet up with a second bunch, with bells on this time. We had enough hassle with the first lot. Now we got these wiseguys who look as if they mean business. Serious business. And sounds like they're gagging for it, too. And you say *walk on by*? The $64,000 question is, sweetcakes, will they *let* us 'walk on by'? You bet your sweet life they won't!"

Bonnie fumed under her breath. She snatched off her straw hat and fanned her flushed cheeks with it. Andrea could be a real *dork*, sometimes.

"Hey! What have we here? Guys, come on over. Think we just found ourselves a coupla playmates!"

The speaker appeared to the left of them. Right out of nowhere. *Must've been walking through the trees, caught sight of us and then side-stepped out onto the path.*

More like they knew we were here and were coming to get us the whole time.

How could they? We haven't even reached them yet.

The guy leered at the two girls. He was drunk and it showed. His chunky red face creased into an idiot smile as he sized them up. He waved a can of beer in his left hand. A hunting rifle hung loosely in the other. He wore a red check shirt gaping open, one side tucked into blue jean pants. The other side hung down his thigh.

Thick, black hair covered his barrel chest.

Shit-faced, Bonnie muttered to herself.

A hootnanny hillbilly, straight out of *Deliverance*.

The guy's unsteady legs were thrust into tan cowboy boots. He'd appeared on the path, suddenly, out of the patch of pines. The girls gasped as they saw how near to them he really was. About five yards away and weaving in their direction all the time.

Answering shouts and a couple of disbelieving grunts came from the goon's buddies.

"You're shitting us, right?"

"Get your backsides on over here and find out!"

One shouted back that he'd be along when he'd had a pee.

Bonnie grabbed Andrea's arm.

"Okay, let's run for it!"

"You bet . . ."

Mashing their hats well down onto their heads, they turned tail and ran back past the pines and onward down the grass track. Their packs pounded their backs like lumpy lead weights.

Dead Mule Pass, here we come!

"Hey, come on back here, now . . . We won't hurt you none. Jest want to be friendly like. Come on back, y'hear?"

The thick voice taunted them over the rapidly growing distance Then, in a sing-song voice that sounded loud and close, "Don't know what you're missin'!"

He was on them.

Right behind and closing in.

Must be one of those gun-happy, bit cat killers with nothing better to do, Bonnie thought in disgust. Probably a whole bunch of them back there. Trackin' down mountain lions, drinkin' themselves shit-faced first, to get their courage up.

The girls stumbled over the rough grass, regained their footing and picked up speed again.

But the guy was still close enough for them to hear him grunting for breath as he chugged along.

Must be fit. I'll give him that, Bonnie marveled. Must've flown down that track . . .

A gunshot cracked overhead.

Then, "Christ Jesus! Aawwgg . . ."

Bonnie paused and looked back.

Their tormentor lay sprawled headlong on the track.

She saw him wave a fist in their direction, his red, swollen face mouthing obscenities.

She hurried along after Andrea.

*   *   *

The girls got away while the going was good. They reached the rock they'd been sitting on earlier and took the trail to Dead Mule Pass. Andrea seemed to have forgotten her objection to this particular route. They pounded along for a while, then slowed up slightly, figuring they'd cleared enough distance between themselves and the guys on the ridge to make a clean getaway.

Even so, they decided it was better not to linger.

They strode steadily down the track for some twenty minutes before Andrea spoke. She was almost breathless and her words huffed from her lips in short bursts.

"That was a narrow miss . . . Couldn't take anymore hassle from rampant males. Had enough of them to last me a lifetime . . . Men are such chauvinistic PIGS. Thinking that every woman is fair game. AND, that no problem at all, women are just standing around WAITING for them to get into their knickers . . . God, they're such SHIT-heads!"

Bonnie slowed down to catch breath. She smiled philosophically.

"Yeah. Carried on past those guys and we'd have been dead meat for sure."

"Bonnie . . ."

"What is it?"

Silence.

Bonnie waited for her to say her piece.

"I'm sorry. *I'm sorry*." Andrea muttered, shame-faced. "I never get things right, do I?"

"Go on! You're not doing too badly. You're a bit of a girl, is all." Bonnie humped her pack more comfortably on her back and turned to smile at Andrea.

Relieved that their earlier tension seemed to have gone, Andrea responded eagerly. A nice warm feeling passed between them.

Thirty minutes farther down the trail they called a halt.

They were parched and badly needed a reviving sip of water—cold would have been nice, but they were more than

eady to settle for warm. Twisting out of their packs, they
umped them onto the grass and flung themselves down
longside.

Eventually, their breathing became easier, more measured.
ying there together, in silence, they relaxed. The herby fra-
rance of the warm grass beneath them felt good. Through
alf-closed eyes they watched the cloudless sky overhead and
stened to the distant stream, tumbling and gurgling through
he rocks.

The sound reminded them that they hadn't taken that
rink yet. Hadn't had one since they broke camp this morn-
ng. Struggling to a sitting position, they unfastened their
acks and brought out their water bottles. Taking long, lei-
urely swigs, their tension drifted away and they felt, for the
rst time in hours—days, it seemed—that danger was now
vay behind them. Andrea yawned and they both stretched
ut again on the warm, rough grass It smelled sweet and
lean.

"Sure you don't mind coming along this route, after all?
n spite of your premonition?" Bonnie asked, chewing on a
talk of grass. "No option, y'know. With those creeps block-
ng our path."

"I probably got it wrong way around in the first place,"
Andrea replied cheerfully. "My premonition could've been
varning me against taking the lonesome pine route, not this
ne. Could've misinterpreted the message. In which case,
ooks like everything's turned out okay!"

"And what about Rick? Still lusting after him?"

"Goddamn it, Bonnie. Gimme a break. I'm sorry I made
fool of myself, believe me. But Rick's history. He's no dif-
erent than the rest . . . Really."

She found Bonnie's hand and gave it a squeeze.

"Could be," Bonnie murmured, hardly daring to believe
he way things were going. "Anyway, don't you dare say sorry
gain . . ."

Leaning up on her right elbow, Andrea turned to face her.

Looking deep into Bonnie's eyes, she leaned over a little and kissed her gently on the lips.

Then on her cheeks, her forehead, and, as Bonnie closed her eyes, Andrea touched her lids, gently, with her lips. Then her mouth again. She was more demanding this time.

With a faint gasp of delight, Bonnie twisted quickly and came on top of her. Then, shifting her weight off Andrea, she leaned away and lifted up the soft gray T-shirt. She sighed when she saw Andrea's small, perfectly formed breasts. They were smooth shiny mounds, the color of milky coffee. Her nipples, exposed to the warm, balmy air, grew hard and pert as she looked at them.

Bonnie drew away from Andrea and lay, head resting on one arm, looking at her.

No need for words.

They were together now. That's all that mattered. Wasn't this what their vacation had been about? Finding each other?

They'd found each other all right.

Now, all they wanted was to get away from this place . . return to Santa Cruz and get on with their lives. Together.

Bonnie felt the joy grow inside her; it blossomed until she could contain it no longer. Their eyes met, lingered and finally drew apart.

Andrea gave Bonnie a long, slow smile, their hands reached out and, for some time, they lay there. Content to be together. Staring at the hot sky. At a wisp of cloud, which had appeared, it seemed, from nowhere. Andrea watched it move across the broad sweep of blue.

"Bonnie?"

"Uh-huh?"

"Y'know Rick," Andrea felt awkward about bringing Rick into the equation. Especially just after she and Bonnie had made love for the first time. But she had to get it out of her system, once and for all. She moved her head so she could

see Bonnie's face. Bonnie was suddenly quite still. She kept
on staring skyward.

"Well, I didn't *want* him and all that stuff. I want you to
know that, Bonnie. I was testing *myself*. Wondering how it
would be—y'know? Seeing if I could go through with it. I'm
glad he didn't take me up on it now. Because I know it was
you that I really wanted, Bonnie. It was you all the time. Only,
I was too scared to admit it . . ."

"You're a dummy. Y'know that, Andrea Winston?"

"You think so?"

"I sure do. You're such a *girl*; and I love you for it." With
studied nonchalance, Bonnie still gazed skyward. Andrea
grinned, leaned up on an elbow and kissed her full on the
mouth. It felt good. She did it again. They both laughed.
Bonnie rolled over, quickly, grabbed her by the shoulders and
held her down. And kissed her. And for a while they were
lost in each other.

Drawn to the heat, a bunch of mosquitoes danced around
their faces. Bonnie swore, rolled over and swatted them out
of her hair, off her face and arms. Andrea, already sitting up,
slapped busily at her legs. Strange how they hadn't noticed
the little bastards before . . .

They gave up swatting and, laughing at themselves, fell back
onto the soft grass. Their lips still curving with their own
secret smiles, they remained in silence for a while longer.
Neither wanted to break the spell; their amazing, magical
bond that had changed everything for them both.

They grinned and toasted themselves with the last of their
water.

Chinking the sun-warmed bottles together, they drained
the final dregs.

They sat in silence for a while longer. Then Bonnie looked
at her wristwatch. Almost an hour had passed since they'd
made love. She said to Andrea, "You okay to carry on? I vote
we get moving. Been out here in the wilds, livin' next to

nature, for too long. Kinda gets to you after a while!"

Andrea blushed and smiled. "You're the boss," she said.

Feeling hot, happy, and emotionally replete, Bonnie and Andrea both felt a twist of sadness at leaving this, *their* special spot in the wilderness. They fastened up their packs, shrugged into the straps, adjusted themselves and, hand in hand, continued along the trail toward Mulligan Lake.

Chapter Twenty-eight

The car stopped again.

There was a quiet sound of the latch releasing. The trunk lid started to lift open. Gillian, on her back with the belt and rope clamped in her teeth, bolted up. She grabbed the edge of the trunk, flung a leg over it, and rolled. She dropped. She heard the car door shut. Her side rammed the bumper. She heard rushing footfalls as she hit the ground. Flipping over, she thrust herself up and ran.

Holden raced at her from behind. His breath came out in snarls. Gillian hissed in pain as something raked her right calf. She kicked the leg forward as fast as she could and heard the rustly sound of a body smashing onto the pine needles that matted the forest floor. Holden gasped out a quick "Awg!"

A glance back. He was skidding on his belly. He must've made a dive for her.

The thought flashed through Gillian's mind that she should whirl around and try to overpower him while he was down. She tore the belt and rope from her teeth and pictured

299

herself beating him with them, but she kept on running, knowing it would've been foolish to fight him. This way, at least, she was sure to gain the few moments it would take him to get back onto his feet.

She dashed through the pines. Springy limbs smacked her body and bent away. Others scratched. She leaped over rocks, over barriers of fallen trees. Rocks and twigs and pine cones punished her feet. But all the pain seemed to belong to someone else. She was free. Though Holden was pounding through the woods behind her, she still had her lead, she still had her chance.

I'll make it.

He won't get me again!

He'd had her but someone had come along and he'd rushed her into the trunk but with hands still tied to the belt. Untying herself had been easy. She'd been given her chance.

Gillian lunged between two trees The branches tried to hold her back, shoving at her face and chest, but she plowed through. And found herself in a flat, sunlit clearing.

She picked up speed. She tucked her head down and darted her long legs out fast and far. The belt and rope in her right hand flew as she pumped her arms. They lashed her face and shoulder and breast, they whipped her thigh and groin. They scorched her. She wanted to throw them down. But she might need them later. She couldn't waste time balling them up to stop their flailing. So she ran as hard as she could, bearing the pain, hoping the snapping belt and rope would stay away from her eyes.

The sound of Holden's crashing feet went silent. "Stop or I'll shoot!" he shouted.

Gillian sprinted across the clearing. She heard her harsh breathing, the soft crushing noise of her footfalls, the sharp smack of the belt striking her bare skin, the softer *whup* of the rope's lash.

She listened for a gunshot.

She could almost feel a slug crashing into her back. Right between the shoulder blades.

He doesn't want to kill me, she thought. That'd spoil his fun.

He'll try to go for the legs.

The sound of the gun reached her ears, filled her head. It was a quick metallic clack.

Silencer?

She heard the sound again and realized it was the hammer dropping.

The hammer snapped down fast, again and again. Gillian didn't try to count the quick hard clacks, but they went on and on.

She glanced back.

Holden stood in a shooter's stance at the edge of the clearing, far behind her. The front of his pale knit shirt had a dark patch of blood on one side a few inches above his waist. He brought the revolver up close to his face and scowled at it.

That was all Gillian saw before she swung her head forward again.

Empty gun, she thought. *What luck!*

Then she thought, *My good Christ, I'm the one who unloaded it!*

It was the revolver she'd found yesterday in his desk. Had to be. She remembered the cartridges tumbling into her palm, how she had dropped them into her shirt pocket and the heavy feel of them against her breast. Then she had put the revolver back into the drawer where it belonged—where Holden must've grabbed it before driving her from his home.

I saved my life.

The thought astonished her.

Not only had she rendered the revolver harmless, but it had caused Holden to stop while he took aim and snapped the hammer down on all the empty chambers. Now he was far behind her.

You're not out of it yet, she warned herself. Don't let it go to your head. You've had a couple of reprieves, that's all. You're in the middle of nowhere and he's not going to give up.

301

She came to the edge of the clearing, dodged a tree, and dashed into the shadows.

Hide? she wondered.

Not yet. But maybe soon. Duck behind some rocks or something.

He might see you do it. Then he'd have you.

If you're going to do it, you'd better do it now.

Hide. If you get away with it, you can backtrack to the car. Maybe he left the keys.

Fat chance.

Maybe he did.

If the keys are gone, disable the car. Stay on the dirt road; you'll get to a real road. Flag down a car . . .

I'm naked.

Big fucking deal.

Maybe I can find something in his car to put on.

Gillian heard him racing through the woods. A long way off. She looked back and couldn't see him.

Do it! she thought. *Hide!*

Still running as fast as she could, she swung her head from side to side. The tree trunks looked too skinny to hide behind. There were no clumps of bushes in sight. The few rocks jutting out of the forest floor seemed too small.

Climb?

He'll see me.

People don't look up. That'd been a big point in some novel she'd read years ago. The thought had intrigued her at the time, and she'd never forgotten it. People look down and around, but they rarely look up.

Get above Holden, maybe he'll run right by.

Off to the right, not far ahead, stood a pine that was much bigger than most of the others. Its lower branches drooped to within a yard of the ground. Its upper trunk was completely hidden by the surrounding green of its bushy limbs.

Gillian raced toward it. As she ran, she shoved the belt between her teeth. She balled up the rope and pitched it to her right. It uncoiled in midair, sailed down, and dropped over a sapling about twenty feet away. She wished it had gone farther, but that was good enough. It might throw Holden off her trail.

If he sees it.

She dashed the rest of the way to the tree, dropped to her knees and scurried beneath the umbrella of its foliage. She crawled to the trunk. She stood up. The lowest branch was as high as her shoulders. She wrapped herself around the trunk and began to shin up it. The belt was in her way. A few times, it got caught between her chest and the trunk, and tugged at her jaw. But she kept her grip on the belt, freed it when it snagged, and kept on climbing.

She heard the distant crunch of Holden's footfalls.

They were coming closer and closer.

She got a knee onto the lowest branch. Reaching up, she clutched a limb. She carefully straightened herself. She raised her left leg, squirmed against the trunk, found a foothold on the other side of the trunk, and thrust herself higher.

Holden sounded very close now. His shoes were thudding on the forest floor. She heard him gasping for breath.

Peering around the trunk, she saw patches of light through the tree's curtain of foliage. But she couldn't see Holden.

If I can't see him, he can't see me.

She wanted to climb higher.

The branches above her feet looked thick, but not as thick as those she had stepped onto before. If she put her weight on one and it bent even a little bit, a whole section of green on the outside of the tree might shake and give her away.

So she stood motionless, left foot braced on the branch, arms and legs hugging the trunk. Hearing Holden's approach, she pressed herself more tightly against the trunk. She wished she could sink into it and disappear.

The sounds of the rushing footsteps stopped.

Near the place where the rope had landed?

He knows he's lost me, Gillian thought. He doesn't see me anywhere ahead, doesn't hear me running. He's starting to suspect I've tried to hide on him. He's trying to figure out where.

Her heart thudded wildly. Calm down, she told herself. Pretend we're playing hide and seek.

Pretend, hell!

Strange. She'd spoken so fondly of playing hide-and-seek to Jerry. Just yesterday.

And here I am now, playing it for keeps.

She wondered if she had ever tried hiding in trees. And then she remembered that she had—many times. She remembered standing on branches high up, clinging as the tree swayed in the wind, staring down as the kid who was "it" searched the yard and never looked up. The thrill had been like a giggle trapped in her throat.

Had she ever been found when she was hiding in a tree? She didn't think so. They found her when she hid in bushes, under stairs, in window wells, but not when she climbed trees.

Maybe that's the real reason she had decided to climb this one.

The forgotten trick of a kid game.

It worked then, she told herself. It'll work now.

It better.

What's he doing?

For the past minute—maybe longer—Gillian hadn't heard a single footstep. He'd been panting for air when he arrived, but that had stopped very quickly.

If he left, she thought, I would've heard him. He must just be standing there, looking around, listening, waiting. Maybe he thinks I'll decide the coast is clear and come out of hiding.

Maybe he did leave.

That's what he wants me to think.

I'll stay here all day. All night. Whatever it takes.

Footsteps rushed toward her tree.

Gillian's heart lurched. She jerked her face back from the trunk and looked down.

Holden scurried under the hanging limbs, stood and gazed up at her.

Her breath blasted out as if she'd been punched in the stomach.

Holden's knife was lashed to the end of a stick—tied there with the rope she had thrown to lead him astray.

The stick was six feet long.

Before Gillian could move, he jabbed upward with the makeshift spear. Its point sank into her right buttock. Yelping, she reached down for the knife. It pulled out of her and slashed at her hand, but missed.

She tugged the belt from her teeth and twisted herself away from the trunk. She pivoted, her right leg swinging backward through the air, foot kicking at the shaft of Holden's knife-spear, then finding its way onto the same branch as her left foot.

The maneuver had turned Gillian around. She no longer had her back to Holden. She hugged the trunk with her left arm. Her right arm swung, whipping at the knife with the buckle-end of the belt.

The knife circled on the end of its stick. The lashing belt did little to keep it away. It slashed and thrust. Sometimes it got her. It poked the side of a calf. It nicked a hip. It sliced a thigh. It cut a half-inch slit across the top of her pubic mound.

Gillian knew he was toying with her. If he wanted, he could hack her to pieces or bury the blade in her. Instead, he tortured her with shallow stabs and slices.

He stared up at her with wide, eager eyes. His lips were a straight line. His tongue slid out between them as he made a hard sweeping slash at Gillian's belly. The blade missed her by no more than an inch. As it passed, she struck it with her belt. The end of the belt wrapped the wooden shaft and she tugged. Holden tugged at the same instant. The belt jerked from her hand. Holden's lips curled into a smile. He shook his spear. The belt slid down its shaft and dropped to the ground.

Gillian unhooked her arm from the tree trunk. As she side-stepped carefully, Holden jabbed the blade at her face. She flinched and nearly lost her balance. Her right arm waved. Her left hand grabbed an overhead branch. The knife point stung her left armpit, then scraped along the underside of her breast. The blade moved up between her breasts and turned, its edge pressing into her right breast.

She darted her right arm in, grabbed the shaft just below the knife handle, thrust it away from her body and leaped.

Leaped forward, diving, clutching the spear with her other hand as she flew.

Flew over Holden's head.

Insane, she thought. Like diving into an empty pool.

She kept her grip on the spear as she crashed headfirst through a tangle of limbs that beat against her falling body. A branch pounded her hip, throwing her over. Then her back struck the ground.

She raised her head. Her skin was a maze of welts, scratches, and bleeding cuts. They itched and burned. But she couldn't worry about that now.

The dive had carried her through the wall of foliage sur-rounding the pine. The spear was still in her hands. It had snapped in the fall, leaving only a few inches of shaft jutting out below the knife's handle.

But she had the knife!

Gazing between her feet, she saw Holden scuttling through the shadows under the tree.

She gasped, rolled over, pushed herself up and whirled around to face him.

He held the rest of the spear—a long crooked pole. The break had left it with a point. He walked toward Gillian, both hands on the pole, shaking it at her. "Gonna shove it up your ass," he whispered. "Gonna make you a scarecrow."

I've got the knife, she thought. But his words sent ice through her bones. He seemed so sure.

He lunged forward, driving the pole toward her belly. Gil-lian slashed at it. The heavy blade knocked it aside. She threw

306

herself at Holden, swinging the knife in a backhand stroke. He hurled himself out of its path and the blade cut only air. She glimpsed a blur of streaking pole and cried out as a blast of pain shot up her arm. Stunned, she saw the knife fly from her hand.

Holden turned, watching the knife, and started to go after it while it was still falling.

Gillian whirled around and ran.

It's over, she thought.

Christ, I had the knife.

She sprinted.

It's over, but I won't make it easy for him.

Her arm throbbed. Her wounds burned. She felt blood and sweat sliding down her skin. Branches whipped her. Her feet snagged on something and she fell and skidded and scurried up again and kept on running.

In the distance ahead, the forest shadows were broken by brightness.

Another clearing? she wondered.

Maybe a lake!

If it's a lake up there, I'll dive in and swim. Maybe Holden can't swim!

She glanced back.

Holden was racing after her, no more than twenty feet away. He had the pole down at his side, clutched in his left hand. His right hand held the knife.

Gillian dashed out of the trees.

Clear open space ahead.

Rocky ground for a few more yards.

But no lake.

A valley.

Gillian tried to stop.

GOD, NO! was her final thought before she stumbled off the edge.

Chapter Twenty-nine

This is it, Gillian thought as she plummeted.

Her feet hit rock. Her knees shot up, one striking her chin like a pitched hardball.

She was lying on the beach. She could hear the nearby surf. Her skin was sizzling.

I'm going to have a doozy of a sunburn, she thought.

I'd better roll over.

She couldn't move. The sun seemed to be pressing down on her, holding her motionless.

If I don't roll over . . .

A kid ran by, kicking up sand. Grains of it flew into Gillian's open mouth. She started to choke.

Coughing, she raised her head and pushed herself up on her elbows. The sight of her naked, battered body destroyed the dream. She coughed and spat. Blood sprayed her chest. So did bits of something—not sand, though. Chips of broken teeth? Her vision darkened and swam. She twisted quickly onto her side and vomited.

No Sanctuary

When she was done, she squirmed away from the mess. She rolled onto her back and her right leg slipped into emptiness. With a gasp of alarm, she jerked it up and crossed it over her other leg. Her pounding heart sent waves of pain through her head. She patted the ground and felt an edge of rock no more than two inches from her side.

Carefully, she sat up. She looked around, forcing her head to turn on her tight neck.

She was sitting on a shelf of rock that jutted out no more than five or six feet from the sheer face of the mountain. It was less than four feet wide. The center was depressed slightly, and as sandy as a beach.

She started to look down, felt a swell of panic, and scooted cautiously until her back pressed the solid wall of rock. There, she gripped the edge beside her right hip. She took deep breaths. She shut her eyes, but snapped them open, fearful of falling. Too close to the edge. She eased herself closer to the middle.

What am I doing here?

She tried to think back. Her brain pulsed and burned with the headache. Her memory seemed scattered.

She remembered a fall—from a diving board. At Jerry's swimming pool. But that was a long time ago.

At least I remembered it, she thought. A place to start.

The board had torn off her bikini pants. Jerry gave her a robe to wear. She wore it next door, to the place she was staying. That was a house she'd broken into. She must've been on one of her adventures, her intrusions.

She'd gone back to the house. She remembered opening the drier to put the robe in, and . . .

The scrapbook.

Fredrick Holden.

She suddenly remembered. She skipped her mind over the nightmare that started with her capture, touching on bits and pieces of her ordeal, and found the part she needed to remember.

The last seconds.

309

Holden had been chasing her through the woods. She'd rushed right up to the edge of a cliff, tried to stop, teetered for a moment, then fallen. She'd expected her body to be dashed apart on the rocks far below.

By some miracle, she was still alive.

By the miracle of landing on this, she thought, looking at the small shelf surrounding her.

She couldn't remember landing. She must've been knocked senseless by . . .

Holden!

Wincing, she twisted her head and looked up the mountain.

Holden was nowhere in sight.

The wall looming above her was nearly vertical. She couldn't see the top.

From what Gillian could see, however, she guessed that her perch must be well below the edge.

She realized she would have a better view if she crawled out to the end of the shelf and turned her back to the open space.

No way.

Instead, she raised her knees. Her right knee was stiff and swollen, and hurt when she bent it. But she kept it bent along with her left, to hold her feet away from the edge when she scooted forward. With her back a few inches from the wall, she looked over each shoulder and scanned the area above her.

She still couldn't see Holden.

Still couldn't see the top.

But she saw that the rock face was slightly concave. Though the angle was so slight that the mountainside didn't appear to overhang her, there was enough tilt to prevent Holden from climbing down to her.

Unless he had a good long rope.

There was no mountain climbing rope in the trunk of his car, that she knew. And she would bet he didn't have one in the front, either.

Only one way he'll get down here, she thought. The same way I did.

He's a fucking lunatic, but he's not suicidal. *Nobody* would jump off up there on the chance of landing the way I did. Not even me. I would've let him catch me before I would've jumped. Maybe.

If he tries it, he'll miss.

If he lands here, I'll kick him off.

He won't try it. Not a chance. He cares a hell of a lot for his own hide. Here's a bastard who goes *out of state* to do his killings, who drove me hundreds of miles just so my body wouldn't turn up near his neighborhood. He's a bastard who loves himself and wants to live so he can go on torturing and murdering. No way is he going to jump off a goddamn cliff.

But he can't let me live. No way is he going to drive away and leave me breathing.

Gillian slid backward until she was safely against the wall again.

Maybe he thinks I'm dead, she told herself.

He must have gone to the edge of the cliff and looked down. If he did that, he saw me. I was out cold for a while. Was he still looking when I woke up and tossed my cookies?

Maybe, maybe not. Maybe he *does* think I'm dead.

I must've *looked* dead. Gillian straightened out her legs, moaning at the pain in her knee. Yeah, she thought, I look messed up pretty good.

Her skin was shiny with sweat, glowing from the sun, streaked and smeared with blood and dirt, cross-hatched with fresh welts, scratched and scraped, split in six or eight places from knife wounds that looked raw but no longer bled. There were swollen patches of red, a deeper hue than the sun had caused, that would turn into bruises. There were even purple-gray marks left over from the beating at his house like an undercoating of old hurts. Gillian touched her face. She felt dry, puffy lips, a knot on the point of her chin, a left cheek that seemed like twice its normal size. She could actually see slope of cheek below her eye.

311

She ran her tongue gently along the broken edges of her teeth.

And started to weep.

Cut it out, she told herself. I'm alive.

My dentist is gonna love me.

Couple months, I'll look good as new.

If I'm still alive. If I make it out of here.

Holden, he's not gonna leave till he's sure I'm dead.

Maybe he does think I'm dead, she told herself again.

A guy like him, how come he didn't drop some rocks on me? When he saw me down here, he could've bombed me till he crushed my head. How come he didn't?

Maybe he fell.

The thought struck her like a promise of life. She wiped the tears from her eyes.

What if Holden came running out of the trees, full tilt, the same way I did? What if he couldn't stop in time, either, and went right over the edge?

She whispered, "Jesus," through her broken lips.

Then she crawled forward on her hands and knees. When she neared the edge, a falling sensation forced her to lie down flat. She squirmed a few more inches forward, then peered down over the rim.

A short distance below her perch, other rocks protruded from the mountain wall. None were large enough to break a fall. The slope was still nearly vertical for fifty or sixty feet. If Holden went off the cliff, he would've dropped that distance, then crashed onto the boulders that were heaped at the foot of the wall.

Gillian didn't see his body.

Doesn't prove anything, she told herself. The body might've gone down in between the rocks.

Some were the size of refrigerators, others the size of cars. They were all tilted and tipped every which way, with big shadowy gaps between their edges. A body could fall into one of those crevices, Gillian thought, and never be found.

She felt a trickle of joy.

No Sanctuary

But over the years she had lived like a thief in sixty-six houses and she had never been caught until this time. Luck, she knew, had been a factor in that. But the main factor was her mind. She'd gotten away with her intrusions because she was smart. She didn't let herself run on luck, hoping for the best. She studied the possibilities, foresaw the dangers, took precautions, and was always creative and quick enough to keep herself safe.

So now, in spite of her thrill at the thought that Holden lay broken and lifeless among the rocks below, she warned herself not to count on it.

You don't see his goddamn body. Therefore, he isn't dead.

If he isn't dead, what's he doing?

For some dumb *crazy* kind of reason—*why, at a time like this?*—she was back in the white stucco house on Silverston. The deco place. If ever she made it back to LA in one piece, *which, let's face it, doesn't seem too likely*, the memory of the hot tub she'd taken that day would live on in her mind forever.

What happened afterward, though, in number 1309, almost put paid to her illustrious career. Of intrusions, housesittings, that is.

Finito. Full stop.

She wished that it had. Then she wouldn't be here now, halfway up this bastard mountain, bare-ass naked and a murdering psycho after her hide.

Back to the house that time forgot . . .

She'd lain there, soaking up the sheer luxury of that tub, breathing in lilac perfume, like she was in some mystical Garden of Allah.

Then the bathroom door blew ajar. That's right, a puff of wind opened the door.

She remembered thinking, *Holy shit . . .*

And sitting up with a start, arms wrapped around her breasts, shivering in the cold draft. Faint, familiar music wafted through the door. So faint, it was hardly there at all.

313

Then, the weirdest thing. She'd had this powerful urge to get up out of the tub, wrap herself in one of those thick white towels hanging over the towel rail and walk out the door.

Leaving a trail of wet footprints behind her, she padded across the marble landing. No ideas as to where her feet were taking her. In a kind of dream, she let them have their lead. They took her to a white door which had the name A-L-I-C-E printed on it in silver letters. ALICE?

Alice who?

Looking at those letters made her feel like she'd stumbled across somebody's private place. Somebody's *very* private place.

A special place.

The old familiar buzz tugged at the pit of her stomach. It melded into an ache, setting her mons alight with longing.

"Here goes," she breathed. She'd invaded a lot of private space in her time. One more wouldn't hurt.

Her breath came out in huffs, quick and shallow. Not knowing what she would find behind the door, she opened it, slowly, and peeped into a tiny room that was straight from the past.

Chintzy flowered drapes, a doll's cradle, a rocking chair.

And a big, brown teddy bear sitting in the far corner. The bear wore several bald patches and stared across at her with beady eyes. She imagined it saying, *Who are you? You're an intruder. You don't belong here.*

Her eyes turned to the small single bed. Not much more than a cot, really. Floral drapes were drawn around it. Not knowing why, she knew that she *must* open them. It was as if she'd come to this house specifically to discover what lay behind the drapes.

Stepping forward, she did just that. Slowly. Drawing back the fabric with tentative fingers. A gasp broke from her lips. Wide-eyed, she stared at a small wizened figure, prostrate on the bed. It was no more than four feet ten at the most.

Little Bo Peep in a long floral dress, matching poke bonnet and a shepherd's crook by her side. Little Bo Peep with a drunken monkey face and bright rouge spots high on her cheeks. And ludicrously red, cupid bow lips.

The large blue eyes, ringed with thick mascara'd lashes—*false, they had to be, they were so long and curly*—gazed curiously into Gillian's face.

She gasped, clamping a hand over her mouth. She felt the warm towel swish down her legs and fall around her ankles.

My GOD!

This is it. Curtains. I've been caught out. No more intrusions for this baby. Hello, real world—LAPD here I come . . .

"*I'm sorry . . .*" she began. Then clamped her lips together, hard. Something was up. The blue eyes weren't moving.

Slowly, carefully, Gillian reached out and lifted Little Bo Peep's thin, blueveined hand. The bony fingers sparkled with clusters of gold and diamond rings. The hand was ice cold. Stiff. Gillian let it fall back onto the white lace bed sheets.

She exhaled slowly, gratefully. A huge feeling of relief built up inside her. The initial shock over, she looked down at the figure on the bed and felt a brief surge of pity.

No more sheep for this Little Bo Peep, she murmured to herself.

Gillian got out of there. Fast. Checking first, making sure she'd left no trace of her presence behind. Nothing that could involve her with Bo Peep's death. She touched her Minolta, briefly, and grimaced. Yuk. No. No photographs for her files this time.

Anyway. Cases like these, you can't be too sure. Film could get lost, or stolen. Unless the finder was either a weirdo or somebody seriously interested in nursery rhymes, the film could easily end up in the wrong hands.

For a full three months after that, intrusions were out. Gillian had to admit, though, there were days back there when she'd been sorely tempted. She'd resisted, but it hadn't been easy. When she'd felt like giving in, she had only to remember that strange shrunken figure lying dead in its cot.

Yeah. The memory of that house on Silverston still haunted her like some terrible dream.

Would've made a spooky movie, though.

One day, she reckoned, she was gonna meet up with real trouble. Find herself doing time, no sweat. So she quit. No more house-sitting, she promised herself. That last time at Creepy Hollow had scared the shit clean out of her.

Then the old urge, that all-consuming desire, *need*, came flooding back. As inviting, as seductive as ever.

Yeah, Mr. Fat'n'sassy Shrink. I'm hooked on other people's private places. I coulda told you that . . .'n saved myself a whole heap o' money in the process.

If she'd been into visiting shrinks, that is.

Which she wasn't.

She rolled onto her shoulder and looked around. The sheer face of the mountain continued for some distance, maybe a few hundred yards. Then it dissolved like a more gradual slope.

A slope that Holden could descend.

He could go down that way, Gillian thought, approach from below, and get to me by climbing up.

She didn't see him, but the area along the base of the slope was heavily wooded. Holden could be down there, out of sight, making his way through the trees along the edge of the valley.

She spotted a trail among the trees. On the far side of the trail was a stream. It rushed along, shining in the afternoon sunlight. In places, it was white with froth. Gillian could hear the distant sound of it tumbling through the rocks.

She rolled flat again. The trail and stream followed the side of the gulley. Directly below her, the trees opened up. That was good. If Holden descended all the way to the bottom and came through the woods, he'd be in plain sight for a while before reaching the heaped boulders.

Turning her head, Gillian scanned the area to her left. The

trail and stream were visible for only a short distance before
the clearing. They vanished around the foot of a bluff that
was nearly as high as Gillian's perch. She looked back. A
glance at the mountainside was enough to convince her that
Holden wouldn't try to descend on that side. It was steep,
and it stayed steep.

So now we know, she thought, which way he'll come.

If he comes.

If he's not dead in the rocks down there.

I've got two choices, she thought. I can either stay here or
climb down.

I'll have to climb down sooner or later.

But he'd have a hard time getting to me here. He can't
sneak up on me.

Gillian wiped sweat out of her eyes, looked around, and
saw plenty of good-sized rocks within reach.

I can bash his brains in before he ever gets near me.

But he's too smart to make himself a target. As long as I'm
here, I'm trapped and he knows where I am. What if he waits
for night? What if I fall asleep or pass out, and he makes it
up here while I'm zonked?

I can't last forever up here.

She felt the sun beating down on her, broiling her back.
She felt sweat sliding down her skin. Her tongue was a dry
slab.

She hadn't taken a drink since last night. She'd spent hours
sweating inside the trunk of Holden's car.

If I wait too long, she thought, I won't be *able* to climb
down.

She found herself staring at the stream. She listened to it
rushing over the rocks. She could almost taste it.

Through the trees to the left of the clearing, she saw it
cascading, white as snow. Straight in front of her, it formed
a clear, glinting pool. She pictured herself sliding into the
chill water, sucking it into her mouth.

If I start down now, she thought, I'll be there in half an
hour. Maybe less.

If Holden doesn't get me.

If he shows up, I'll stone him. Plenty of ammunition.

Gillian squirmed backward away from the edge, then got to her hands and knees. The movement made her head pound. A wave of dizziness washed by. It left her frightened.

If that happens while I'm trying to climb down . . .

Get going.

She sat down, then scooted herself toward the right-hand side of the shelf. Her feet went out over the edge. Her calves scraped. Then her feet dropped out of sight and the pain reminded her to be careful of her right knee.

What if it's too weak to hold me up?

She kept inching forward. Her legs dangled. She clutched the edge of the shelf with both hands and leaned out.

Her toes were nearly touching the next rock down.

She lay backward and rolled over. Then she squirmed on her belly, easing herself off the ledge until her feet found the rock. Carefully, she pushed herself away from the shelf.

She stood on the foothold, still holding the upper ledge with both hands.

So far, she thought, not bad.

She looked down at her destination. The sparkling pool of the stream.

And she saw Holden pass between two trees as he walked along the trail far below. For moments, he was hidden by the woods. Then he appeared against the edge of the clearing. He still carried the broken stick in one hand, his knife in the other. He turned and gazed up at the slope.

His head suddenly snapped to the side.

He shoved the knife blade down a rear pocket of his pants.

Gillian looked to the left.

"Oh my Christ," she muttered.

Just this side of the place where the trail vanished behind the outcropping were two women with backpacks. The one in the lead raised a hand in greeting. Holden waved to her.

He walked toward the women.

"RUN!" Gillian shouted. "GET OUT OF HERE!"

Neither hiker turned a head.

Gillian yelled and yelled as the gap narrowed between the two women and Holden.

It's the damn stream! she thought.

They were so close to it, the noise of the rushing water was masking her shouts.

She let go of the ledge. Balancing on the rock, she squatted, then she sat down and straddled it. She clawed the slope behind her and pulled loose a chip of stone. She hurled it at the women. It flew out in a high arch, dropped beyond the clustered boulders below, and vanished in undergrowth at the edge of the clearing.

The second hiker glanced toward the place where the stone had landed. But she kept walking. She stopped beside her friend, took off her ballcap, and rubbed a forearm across her brow.

They both faced Holden. He was no more than three feet in front of them. From the gestures, Gillian guessed that they were talking. Holden pointed to the trail behind him. He shrugged. Then his stick whipped through the air. It struck the stout woman across the side of the head. Her straw hat flew off. Her legs folded. Her knees hit the ground and she dropped forward flat on her face.

Gillian heard herself shriek, "NO!"

The other woman spun around and ran up the trail. She flung off her pack. Holden leaped over it. He grabbed the knife out of his rear pocket as he chased her.

She was fast, but Holden gained on her. Reaching out, he grabbed the back of her gray T-shirt. The fabric stretched, tenting out behind her. Then she staggered and danced sideways as if being swung on the end of a rope. Her feet tangled. She went down, tumbling and rolling. Holden pounced on her.

Chapter Thirty

"We could stop anywhere along here," Rick said.

"I'd rather find a place," Bert said, "where the stream isn't so close to the trail. We'd have people hiking right by our camp."

Rick smiled. "Yeah, this trail is Grand Central Station around here."

They hadn't seen anyone except Angus the lunatic since leaving the girls. But Rick agreed with Bert. If they kept going, they might find a good secluded area.

"Why don't we just give it another hour?" Bert suggested. "It'd be nice to get settled while we have some of the afternoon ahead of us."

"How far's Mulligan Lake?"

"More like two hours."

"Andrea and Bonnie'll probably be there," Rick said.

"Well, we won't go that far." She looked at him, a corner of her mouth curling up. "Unless you want to."

"I just want to get someplace where we'll have plenty of privacy."

No Sanctuary

"Me too."

They walked side by side around a bend in the trail that took them past a stone corner. Rick reached below Bert's pack and squeezed her rump. "What have you got in mind?" he asked.

She looked at him and raised an eyebrow. "A little of this, a little of that." Her face turned forward again and she stopped abruptly.

Rick halted beside her.

On the trail at their feet lay a red backpack.

"What the hell?" Rick muttered. "Looks like one of . . ."

She grabbed his arm so hard that pain streaked through it. She was gazing past him, to the right.

Rick turned his head.

He thought, *It's another hallucination, has to be, but how can Bert be seeing it?*

He stared.

The trail where he stood with Bert was slightly higher than the clearing ahead, and gave him a perfect view.

Can't be real. Impossible.

It was worse than his daydreams, his visions, worse than anything he had ever imagined. Julie's death seemed *pristine* compared to this.

One of the bodies was a naked man. He lay on his back near the sprawled remains of a girl. Rick refused to look straight at the girl, to see what had been done to her. He gazed at the man. The man looked as if he were *made* of blood, as if his skin had been peeled off.

Rick let his eyes dart past the third body, a twisted, faceless thing.

Strewn about the bodies was clothing: a pair of cut-off jeans with one leg split open; a yellow blouse; a torn rag of panties; faded blue gym shorts; a gray T-shirt sliced down the front, rumpled in such a way that the letters UC showed. Some of the clothes were sprinkled red as if they had been sprayed from a distance, and Rick realized vaguely that the

321

girls must've already been naked when the blood began to fly.

The girls.

Andrea and Bonnie.

He couldn't look at their bodies, but the clothes were enough.

The other clothes belonged to the man: shoes placed neatly together with socks tucked inside, folded trousers, a knit shirt on the ground near the pants.

Who is he? Rick wondered.

Did *he* do this? Why's he dead?

Bert, standing at Rick's side, bent over and heaved. She had her knife clutched in her right hand. It was pressed to the side of her leg, and the blade jerked as spasms shook her body.

Already has her knife out, Rick thought. Got through the shock and saw the danger. Why didn't I?

If I only had the gun!

Rick drew his own knife from the scabbard on his belt. Then he squirmed out of his shoulder straps. His pack dropped to the trail behind him. He scanned the clearing, the base of the slope a distance to the right, the trees beyond the clearing, the stream to the left and the wooded area on its other side. Saw no one. Imagined Jase and Luke and Wally charging at them from the rear. Whirled around. No one. He raised his eyes. No one scurrying down the rocks.

"RICK!"

He began to turn and everything seemed to be in slow motion. He saw Bert's pack falling toward the trail behind her legs. Her arm began to move upward, pointing with the knife. He finished his turn. The man of blood was sitting up. His eyes were open. He had a red erection.

Rick grabbed Bert's shirt and pulled. She twisted slowly toward him, her shirt coming off her shoulder, her right breast exposed, the knotted fabric across her chest slipping apart. "RUN!" he yelled in her face. His voice seemed far away and echoing. He saw her head shake slowly from side to side, her hair swaying out below the edges of her hat. "GO!" he yelled again, and then he released her shirt and started toward the man.

The man, somehow already up, wasn't coming at them. Instead, he ran away. His back wasn't red. It had a deep tan except for his white, flexing buttocks. He only ran a few steps. His arms reached out. He grabbed a long stick slanting up out of one of the bodies (a broad-boned body . . . Bonnie?). He tugged it out with both hands. It made a sucking sound. He pivoted, swinging it like a baseball bat. Rick, almost upon him, flung up his arms to protect his head. His wrist exploded with pain. But the knife stayed in his numb hand. The man leaped out of his way. Rick couldn't stop. His forward foot came down on a thigh of the corpse. The body turned under his weight. An outstretched arm flopped up as if reaching for him. He tried to miss it as he stumbled, but the toe of his boot smashed the forearm down and he thought, *I'm sorry*, as he staggered past the body, trying to stay up.

Something crashed against the back of his head. He slammed the ground and skidded.

He lifted his face out of the grass.

Was I out? What if it's all over, and Bert . . . ?

He looked over his shoulder.

Bert was on her feet, face to face with the man, trying to wrestle the shaft out of his hands. Her knife was clenched in her teeth. She was being twisted and shaken like a doll, no match for the killer.

Rick started to get up.

The pole was snatched from Bert's grip. She reached for the knife between her teeth. Before she could grab it, the man drove an end of the pole into her belly. Her mouth made a wide O. She stumbled backward, folding, and her rump pounded the ground.

The man left Bert sitting there, turned away, and squatted by the head of the other corpse.

Andrea?

She'd been scalped.

She had a knife in her mouth. But not crossways, pirate fashion, like Bert. The broad handle stuck straight up from her lips. The man clutched it and pulled. Andrea's raw head lifted as the blade slid out.

A huge blade.

The man's eyes, bulging white in his red mask, fixed on Rick.

Rick was almost on him.

The man jerked the knife the rest of the way out, ripping through a cheek. The blade swept past Rick's belly. He felt a hot sting as it nicked his side. As he lunged at the crouching man, he slashed downward. His knife skidded on the man's forehead, sliced the left eyeball, cut through a nostril, tore a diagonal gash through his lips and chin, swept down and split the back of Rick's own left hand.

Even as the knife cut his hand, his charging body smashed the man backward. Onto Andrea's face. Rick, hunched low and off balance, hurled himself over her ravaged body, hit the ground on the other side, and rolled.

He got to his hands and knees. He looked.

The man was scuttling toward him, shrieking, blood spouting from his face. Bert swept by. Flying? She was four feet off the ground, stretched out straight, open shirt flapping behind her like the cape of a super-heroine from a strange, erotic comic book, knife in her right hand. Her bare chest hit the man's back with a slapping sound. He was smashed flat. Bert's arms were out past his side. She threw an elbow high and tried to bring her arm down to stab him, but he thrust himself up, twisting and throwing her off.

He got to his knees, swung around and rammed the knife down. It missed Bert. She was rolling. He went after her on his knees.

Rick scurried toward him and drove his knife down. It sank deep into the man's calf. He yanked it out. His left hand grabbed the man's hip and pulled. His fingers slipped off the slick skin. Snarling, he threw himself forward. His chest pushed against the man's buttocks. He raised the knife high, ready to plunge it into the middle of the back, when an elbow crashed against the side of his head.

The blow dazed him, sent him sprawling.

He lay on his back. The few clouds in the pale blue sky were slowly spinning. His ears rang.

"RICK!" Bert's voice, high and terrified through the ringing.

He lifted his head, turned it.

The ground tilted and tipped, much like the clouds.

Bert was on her back, writhing under the man. He was sitting across her hips, leaning down over her, pinning her wrists to the ground. Blood from his gashed face splashed Bert, rained down on her cheeks and lips, trickled down her chin.

The man's knife stood up straight, its blade embedded in the ground a few inches above her shoulder.

Rick rolled over. As he struggled to raise himself, the man's right hand flew up, releasing Bert's wrist. She wasn't quick enough to block the punch. It crashed against her cheek. Her head snapped to the side. Her body went limp.

The man jerked his knife out of the ground.

He scooted backward, his blood spilling a trail onto her chest and belly and shorts. Then he was sitting on her knees. He slipped the broad blade down the front of her shorts and ripped. The edge came up through her waistband, severed her belt, slit open the tan fabric down her left thigh and parted the small cuff.

Rick forced himself up to his knees while he watched.

What is this man!

Face torn from forehead to chin, eye split open, a bone-deep stab wound in his left calf—and he's *stripping* her!!

He clawed Bert's pants open like a flap, baring her left leg, her groin. He tugged at the other side so hard that her breasts shook. The shorts slid out from under her and down to her knees.

Rick's knife flew end over end.

Jase threw a knife at me last night, he remembered.

325

Hit me handle-first.
This one better do the job.

It flashed past the back of the man's head, missing by more than an inch.

The man didn't even seem to notice.

He was working Bert's pants farther down her legs.

"NO!" Rick yelled.

He turned toward Rick, stared at him with one eye, and spat blood. His red penis was standing rigid and thick.

Rick shoved himself up, took a wobbly step forward, and fell.

The man turned again to Bert. He got his knees between her legs. With the dull edge of his knife, he shoved her left leg aside.

Rick crawled toward him.

He had no weapon and the man had the knife. He didn't care.

"I'LL KILL YOU!" he yelled.

The man ignored him.

Then there was someone else.

For a moment, Rick thought it was one of the girls. It *was* a girl and she was naked and torn and bloody, but not mutilated like Andrea or Bonnie, not a butchered carcass, not dead.

She ducked as she ran, and swept Rick's knife off the ground where it had landed after his throw.

She ran straight toward the man.

His head turned.

She leaped, twisting herself in midair, coming down behind him, between Bert's spread feet. She grabbed the man's hair. Her right knee buckled. She dropped to her rump and threw herself backward, still clutching the man's hair.

He flopped on top of her, head between her breasts.

For an instant, two knives waved above his squirming body.

The knife in the girl's hand flashed down and ripped across his throat.

Blood erupted.

The man flapped his arms, his knife slashing through the red curtain rising from his neck. He kicked his feet high.

Rick thought vaguely that he hoped the bastard wouldn't kick Bert in the face.

The shower of blood diminished, then stopped, as if a faucet had been turned off.

The man lay sprawled motionless on top of Bert and the stranger.

Nobody moved.

Chapter Thirty-one

"Police today received a package containing a scrapbook allegedly belonging to Fredrick James Holden, who was slain Monday during a killing spree that left two hikers dead in the Sierra wilderness.

"The scrapbook, which contained newspaper clippings related to disappearances and killings of an undisclosed number of young women in several different states, was accompanied by an anonymous note which read, 'I found this in Holden's house. He murdered these people.'

"This latest revelation only deepens the puzzle of Fredrick James Holden, the orphan who was taken into the home of his aunt at the age of four and inherited her wealth twelve years later when she was raped and viciously murdered in her bed, along with the celebrated fashion designer Harriet Woodall. In light of the recent developments, authorities now speculate that the double homicide may have been the work of the same man responsible for Monday's killing rampage.

"The scrapbook received today by the police opens the possibility that Fredrick James Holden may have been involved in a nationwide string of sex slayings. But *was* the scrapbook the property of this man? And who mailed it to the authorities? How much might this person know about the trail of killings revealed in the pages of the scrapbook? With more on this story, we take you live to Henry Gonzalez."

"Thank you, Laura. I'm coming to you live from the Encino home of Dr. Richard Wainwright, the prominent ophthalmologist who, along with his fiancée Bert Lindsey, was assaulted by Fredrick James Holden shortly after Monday's double-homicide.

"Dr. Wainwright, is it your opinion that Holden's scrapbook was sent to the police by the woman who called herself Mary Smith?"

"I have no idea. It wouldn't surprise me, though."

"Miss Lindsey?"

"We've talked about it. We both think she may have sent it. She had something to hide, we're sure of that."

"Could you tell us more about her?"

"She was eighteen or twenty, blond, very attractive . . ."

"She was very beaten up. She'd been cut with a knife, and sustained a lot of superficial injuries while she was escaping from the bas—killer."

"We bathed in the stream after . . . after he was dead. All of us were bloody. Then we patched up some of her wounds with my first aid kit."

"She didn't say much."

"None of us did. I think we were all in a state of shock."

"She did tell us that her name was Mary Smith, and she'd been abducted the night before. Holden brought her out to the mountains in the trunk of his car. She said he'd intended to kill her 'like the others.' "

329

"That's one reason we think she might be the one who sent the scrapbook. She seemed to have knowledge of other murders."

"Also the fact that she skipped out on us."

"Wearing my clothes. Not that I resent that. Hell, she saved us. She came out of nowhere like some kind of crazed, avenging angel and slit the throat of that animal."

"But you say, Dr. Wainwright, that she skipped out."

"We took Holden's car. It was on a dirt road about an hour's hike away. She drove until we found my car, which was on a different road about ten miles off. Bert and I took my car, and she followed us. She was supposed to follow us till we found a police or sheriff's station, but she took off."

"She was right behind us one minute. Then she was gone."

"You feel, then, that she had some reason to avoid a confrontation with the authorities?"

"Looks that way."

"But she sent the scrapbook, I'd bet on it."

"Do you have anything you'd like to say to Mary Smith if she should be watching this broadcast?"

"You bet. Mary Smith, whoever you are, we love you."

"We're not interested in revealing your identity to anyone. But we'd like to thank you—in person, if that's possible. I'm in the phone book, Richard Wainwright."

"This is Henry Gonzalez for Eyewitness News. Back to you, Laura."

Gillian pressed the remote button, and the television screen went blank. Leaning back against the bedrest, she sighed.

"They seem like nice people," Jerry said.

"They are."

He took hold of her hand. "There's that old Chinese proverb . . . I think it's supposed to be Chinese."

"That you're responsible for people after you save their lives?"

"That's it."

"That's bullshit."

Jerry laughed softly.

"She said they love me."

"Yeah."

"That's really nice."

"I don't think there's any reason to worry that they'll tell on you."

"No."

"Even if they did, it's not that big a deal. There'd be publicity, though. And the cops would want to talk to you."

The hell they would. Like, how's that again? How many times did you say, Miss O'Neill—er, Miss Smith? You broke into sixty-six homes?

"But you'd be a hero. You already are. Mary Smith is."

Fuck Mary Smith. And Gillian O'Neill. Time I got myself a new alibi. How about Trisha Scott? Mmmm . . . Okay. Try this for size:

Following the outstanding success of "Gone Midnight," a sequel to this record-breaking blockbuster movie, is now in the pipeline. As we speak, award-winning screenwriter, Trisha Scott, is completing yet another great script.

Our mole at Sierra Studios tells us filming is due to start early next year . . .

"Sure. A hero. And I'd probably get prosecuted for violating Holden's civil rights."

"Maybe you'd better stay anonymous. But like I said, they won't tell. How about having them over?"

"Like a dinner party?"

"A swim and a barbecue."

"That might be nice. But let's wait a while till it all calms down. And I'd like a chance to heal before anyone sees me in a bikini."

"Yeah," Jerry said. "Don't want to put them off their food."

Gillian slapped his thigh.

"You look fine," he told her.

"Sure. Like I went through a garbage disposal."

And she suddenly pictured the carcasses of the two young women, the way they had looked when she stood above them

331

after crawling out from under Holden. Then she was on her mountainside perch, staring down, and they were still alive and she heard their screams over the rush of the stream as Holden worked on them.

Gillian felt herself shrivel inside, tight and cold. Goosebumps rose on her skin.

"Jerry?"

"Uh-huh?"

"Jerry. D'you love me?"

"Do bees like honey? Does night follow day? Did Rhett love Scarlett?"

"Funneee. I mean it, pal. I need to know if you *really* love me. Y'know? *Really* care."

"As in, follow you to the ends of the earth?"

"You got it."

"Where's this leading, Gill? And why so serious, at this hour?"

"Because, dummy, I am about to spill a whole mess o' beans. Like tell you a story, the like of which you've probably never heard before. And all of it is true. It's about me. So. I need to trust you. I need to know that you love me enough to say, hey, what the heck. It's you I love, not your goddamn life history."

Jerry leaned up on an elbow and looked at her. Tears were coursing down her cut and bruised cheeks.

"My God, Gillian. What's wrong?"

Okay. She'd had a rough time. A terrible time, what with Fredrick Holden an' all; and he her uncle, too. But he had an overwhelming feeling that there was something else. That something much bigger was on her mind.

"If you love me and we stay together, I want you to *know* me. The *real* Gillian O'Neill. No matter how many alibis I have, what I do for a living, what position I sleep in at nights, what brand of coffee I drink . . . I just need to come clean, Jerry. And after you've heard what I have to say, I want you to be honest. Tell me you love me and that my secrets'll be safe with you. Or, tell me you don't want to know, and I'll just clam up and go to sleep."

She looked so miserable that he took her in his arms and shushed her, just like a baby. Love, compassion and concern for her welled up inside him. He'd never felt like this about anyone before, in all of his life.

"There, now, my love. No need to worry about a thing. I do love you—believe me, I do. Just the way you are. No frills. No hidden agendas. Just you. If you're about to tell me that you're an award-winning scriptwriter, don't bother. I already know. Anything else, I don't need to be told."

Turning to him, she whispered, "Hold me some more."

He did.

They lay on their sides, wrapped in each other's arms. Jerry held her gently.

"How come you know I write screenplays?"

"You told me. You said you 'scribbled.' Remember? Well, I watched this film a while back. About this diehard female mercenary caught up in some kind of Greek political plot. Good swimmer, too. Swam in mountain lakes, hid out in caves and all that stuff. Come to think of it, just the damn fool sort of thing you'd probably get up to. Caught the name of the screenwriter, too. Matched yours."

"A regular Perry Mason. You shoulda told me." She smiled and gave a small yelp.

"What is it . . . ?"

"My cut lip just opened up again."

Jerry held her closer and she snuggled into the curve of his body. He felt warm and smooth. Soon, the gripping chill inside her melted and a wonderful relief flooded her being.

One day, she promised herself, one day, I guess I'll tell him the full story. Not yet, though: Not tonight.

Gillian tightened her arms around him. She pressed herself hard against him, and the feel of his body on her bruised and wounded skin was as soothing as a kiss.

Master of terror

RICHARD LAYMON

has one word of advice for you:

BEWARE

Elsie knew something weird was happening in her small supermarket when she saw the meat cleaver fly through the air all by itself. Everyone else realized it when they found Elsie on the butcher's slab the next morning—neatly jointed and wrapped. An unseen horror has come to town, and its victims are about to learn a terrifying lesson: what you can't see can very definitely hurt you.

ISBN 13: 978-0-8439-6137-9

RICHARD LAYMON

They call it Beast House. Tourists flock to see it, lured by its history of butchery and sadistic sexual enslavement. They enter, armed with cameras and camcorders, but many never return. The men are slaughtered quickly. The women have a far worse fate in store. But the worst part of the house is what lies beneath it. Behind the cellar door, down the creaky steps, waits a creature of pure evil. At night, when the house is dark and all is quiet…the beast comes out.

THE

CELLAR

ISBN 13: 978-0-8439-5748-8

RICHARD LAYMON

For years morbid tourists have flocked to the Beast House, eager to see the infamous site of so many unspeakable atrocities, to hear tales of the beast said to prowl the hallways. They can listen to the audio tour on their headphones as they stroll from room to room, looking at the realistic recreations of the blood-drenched corpses....

But the audio tour only gives the sanitized version of the horrors of the Beast House. If you want the full story, you have to take the Midnight Tour, a very special event strictly limited to thirteen brave visitors. It begins at the stroke of midnight. You may not live to see it end.

THE MIDNIGHT TOUR

ISBN 13: 978-0-8439-5753-2

RICHARD LAYMON

The Beast House has become a museum of the most macabre kind. On display inside are wax figures of its victims, their bod-ies mangled and chewed, mutilated beyond recognition. The tourists who come to Beast House can only wonder what sort of terrifying creature could be responsible for such atrocities.

But some people are convinced Beast House is a hoax. Nora and her friends are determined to learn the truth for themselves. They will dare to enter the house at night. When the tourists have gone. When the beast is rumored to come out. They will learn, all right.

THE BEAST HOUSE

ISBN 13: 978-0-8439-5749-5

"If you've missed Laymon, you've missed a treat!"
—Stephen King

RICHARD LAYMON

Many people have a hobby that verges on obsession. Albert Prince's obsession happens to be cutting people, especially pretty girls. There's nothing he loves more than breaking into a stranger's house and letting his imagination—and his knife—run wild. Albert's on the run now, heading cross-country, but he's not about to stop having fun....

A pregnant young woman, a teacher, a librarian, an aging Southern belle, a famous writer and a budding actress. All of them have troubles and all of them are looking for something in their lives. Unfortunately, what they'll find isn't necessarily what they wanted. What many of them will find instead is Albert and his very sharp knives.

ISBN 13: 978-0-8439-5752-5

To order a book or to request a catalog call:
1-800-481-9191
This book is also available at your local bookstore, or you can check out our Web site **www.dorchesterpub.com** where you can look up your favorite authors, read excerpts, or glance at our discussion forum to see what people have to say about your favorite books.

RICHARD LAYMON

SAVAGE

Whitechapel, November 1888: Jack the Ripper is hard at work. He's safe behind locked doors in a one-room hovel with his unfortunate victim, Mary Kelly. With no need to hurry for once, he takes his time gleefully eviscerating the young woman. He doesn't know that a fifteen-year-old boy is cowering under Mary's bed....

Trevor Bentley's life would never be the same after that night. What he saw and heard would have driven many men mad. But for Trevor it was the beginning of a quest, an obsession to stop the most notorious murderer in history. The killer's trail of blood will lead Trevor from the fog-shrouded alleys of London to the streets of New York and beyond. But Trevor will not stop until he comes face to face with the ultimate horror.

ISBN 10: 0-8439-5751-4
ISBN 13: 978-0-8439-5751-8

COVENANT

WINNER OF THE BRAM STOKER AWARD!

The cliffs of Terrel's Peak are a deadly place, an evil place where terrible things happen. Like a series of mysterious teen suicides over the years, all on the same date. Or other deaths, usually reported as accidents. Could it be a coincidence? Or is there more to it?

Reporter Joe Kieran is determined to find the truth.

Kieran will uncover rumors and whispered legends—including the legend of the evil entity that lives and waits in the caves below Terrel's Peak....

JOHN EVERSON

ISBN 13: 978-0-8439-6018-1

GRAHAM MASTERTON

A new and powerful crime alliance holds Los Angeles in a grip of terror. Anyone who opposes them suffers a horrible fate…but not by human hands. Bizarre accidents, sudden illnesses, inexplicable and gruesome deaths, all eliminate the alliance's enemies and render the crime bosses unstoppable. Every deadly step of the way, their constant companions are four mysterious women, four shadowy figures who wield more power than the crime bosses could ever dream of. But at the heart of the nightmare lies the final puzzle, the secret of…

THE
5TH WITCH

ISBN 13: 978-0-8439-5790-7

DEMON EYES

L. H. MAYNARD
&
M. P. N. SIMS

Emma had just started her new job as personal assistant to Alex Keltner, the charismatic and powerful head of Keltner Industries. So when he asked her to attend a party he was throwing that weekend at his secluded estate, she knew better than to refuse. It would be her first party amid the extremely wealthy and powerful elite....

It will be a party she'll never forget...if she survives. At first it will be simply odd. Mysterious warnings. Strange, seductive guests. An atmosphere of lust and sexuality. Video cameras in the rooms. But as the weekend progresses, Emma will slowly learn the true nature of the guests and her mysterious host—and the real, grotesque purpose of the party.

ISBN 13: 978-0-8439-5972-7

JOHN SKIPP
AND CODY
GOODFELLOW

Pastor Jake promised his followers everlasting life…he just didn't say what kind. So when the small-town televangelist and con man climbs out of his coffin at his own wake, it becomes Judgment Day for everyone gathered to mourn— or celebrate—his death. Jake is back, in the rotting flesh, filled with anger and vengeance. And accompanied by de-mons even more frightening than himself. What follows is a long night of endless terror, a blood-drenched rampage by the man not even death could stop.

JAKE'S WAKE

ISBN 13: 978-0-8439-6076-1

☐ **YES!**

Sign me up for the Leisure Horror Book Club and send my FREE BOOKS! If I choose to stay in the club, I will pay only $8.50* each month, a savings of $7.48!

NAME: _____

ADDRESS: _____

TELEPHONE: _____

EMAIL: _____

☐ I want to pay by credit card.

☐ VISA   ☐ MasterCard.   ☐ DISCOVER

ACCOUNT #: _____

EXPIRATION DATE: _____

SIGNATURE: _____

Mail this page along with $2.00 shipping and handling to:
Leisure Horror Book Club
PO Box 6640
Wayne, PA 19087
Or fax (must include credit card information) to:
610-995-9274
You can also sign up online at **www.dorchesterpub.com**.
*Plus $2.00 for shipping. Offer open to residents of the U.S. and Canada only.
Canadian residents please call 1-800-481-9191 for pricing information.
If under 18, a parent or guardian must sign. Terms, prices and conditions subject to
change. Subscription subject to acceptance. Dorchester Publishing reserves the right
to reject any order or cancel any subscription.